JUST PLAIN OLD JEREMY

by Doug McKim

SAME OLD STORY PRODUCTIONS

VICTOR FERUS, President and CEO

Just Plain Old Jeremy *Second Edition 2018*

Same Old Story Publishing 2012, 2018
1607 Sixth Street # 1
La Grande, OR 97850

1027 Posey Hill Rd.
Mt. Juliet, TN 37122

www.SameOldStoryPublishing.com

10 9 8 7 6 5 4 3 2

This book is a work of fiction. Names, characters, places and incidents are products of the author's imagination. Any resemblance to actual events, locales, or persons, living or dead, is purely incidental.

ISBN: 978-1-945450-09-9

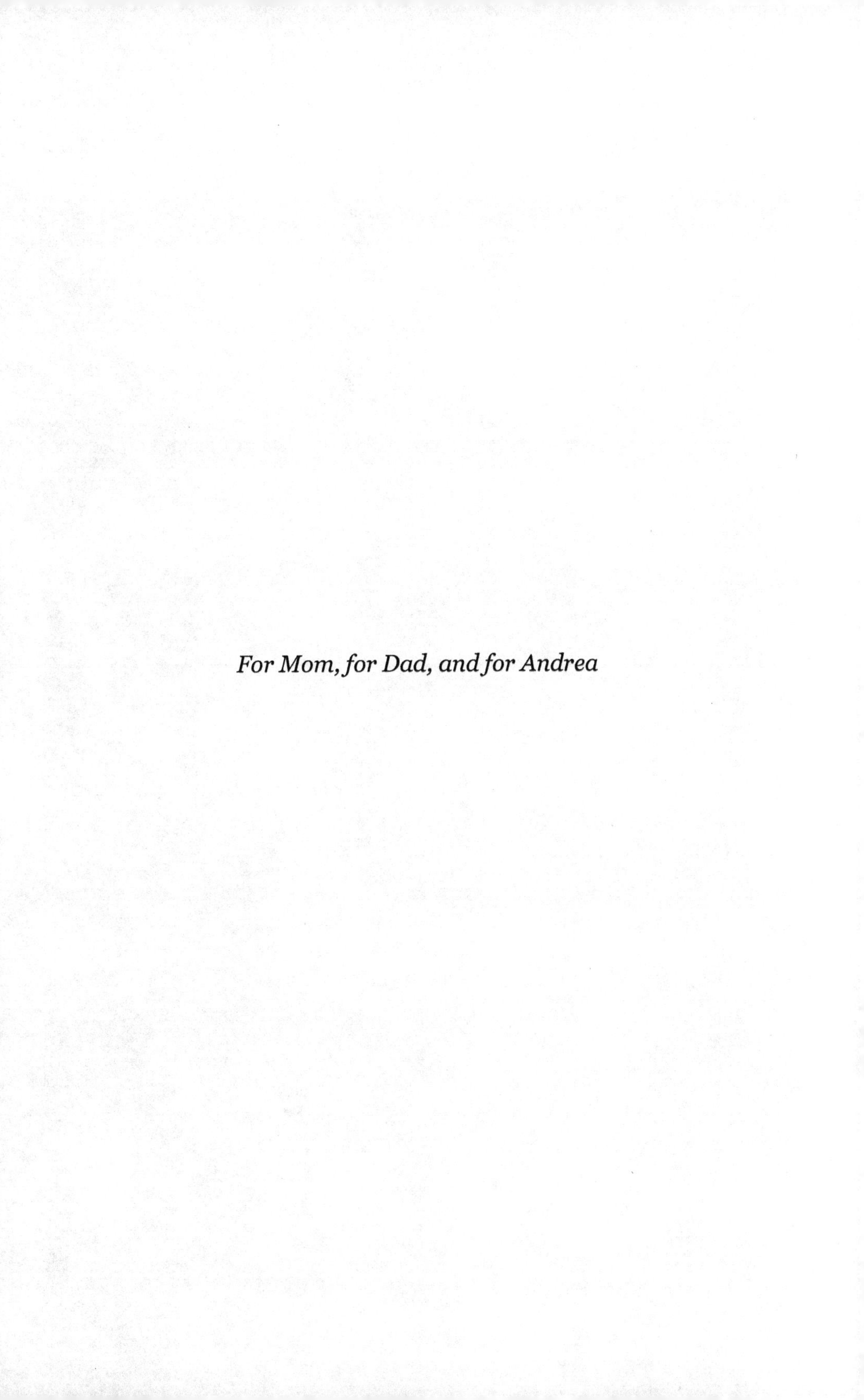

For Mom, for Dad, and for Andrea

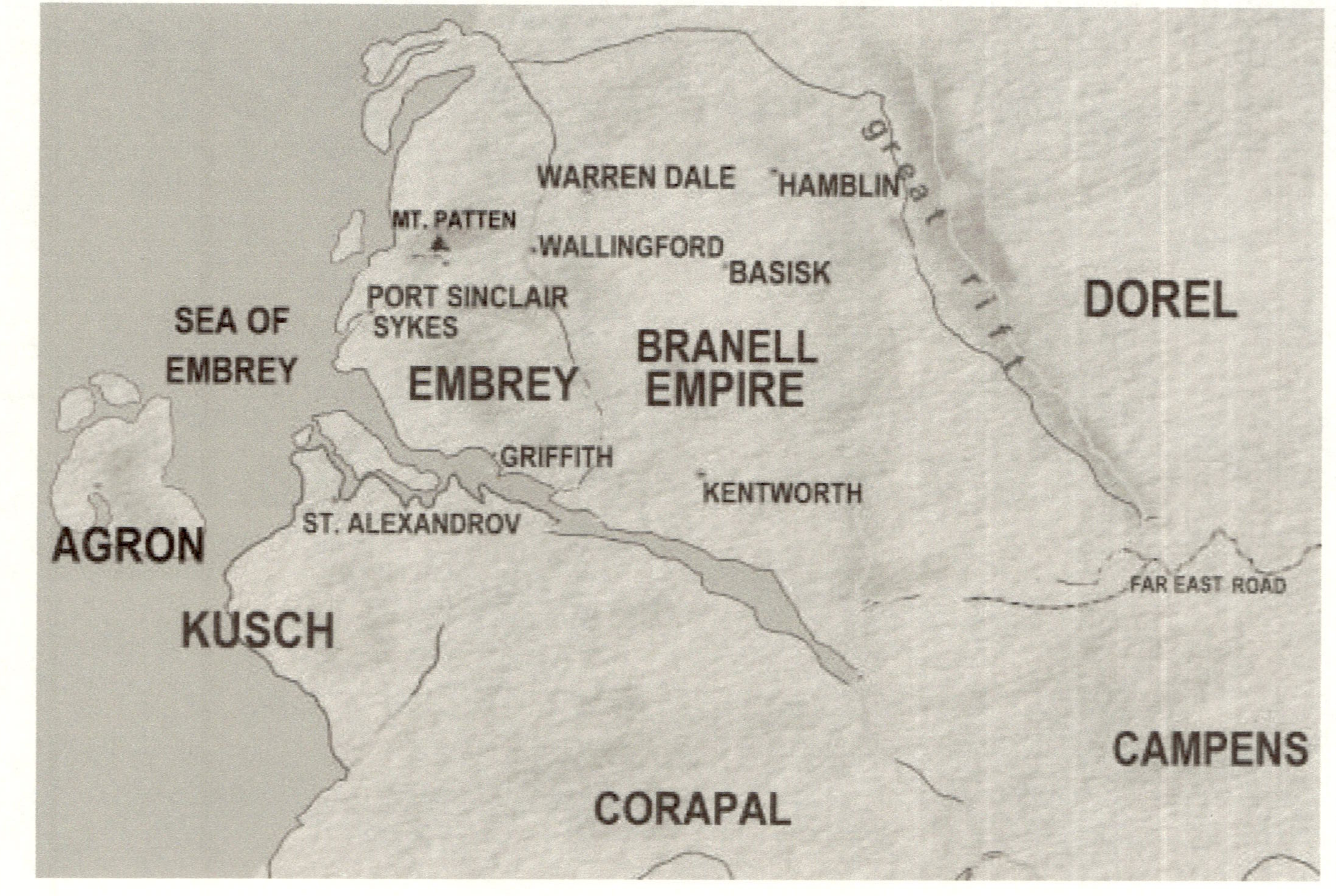
WARREN DALE
HAMBLIN
great rift
MT. PATTEN
WALLINGFORD
BASISK
DOREL
SEA OF
EMBREY
PORT SINCLAIR
SYKES
BRANELL
EMPIRE
EMBREY
GRIFFITH
KENTWORTH
AGRON
ST. ALEXANDROV
FAR EAST ROAD
KUSCH
CAMPENS
CORAPAL

PREFACE

This book is a prequel, of sorts, to another novel titled ARE YOU MAN ENOUGH? (ISBN – 978-1-945450-00-6). It takes place about twenty years prior to the earlier story.

Like many tales of imaginative fiction, ARE YOU MAN ENOUGH? introduced readers to unique terms, ideas, and vocabulary. Many of these concepts have also found themselves in JUST PLAIN OLD JEREMY.

I'm aware that readers of JUST PLAIN OLD JEREMY may not yet know about ARE YOU MAN ENOUGH? Therefore, I have compiled a list detailing background information, pertaining to both novels.

I hope no one gets bored with this long-winded spiel, so please bear with me . . .

Branell, aka the Branellian Empire

A nation of high altitude deserts, rolling green foothills, and spectacular, granite mountain ranges. Branell has been in a seemingly endless Border War with its western neighbor, Embrey. Branell and Embrey were once part of the same nation, and their citizens speak the same language.

Once Branell and Embrey became separate, independent countries, they've been in a constant state of war.

I introduced a young Branellian boy named Garry in ARE YOU MAN ENOUGH? I hoped to give Garry traits which distinguished him from his Embrian counterparts. I have a nephew who, in his youth, occasionally wore kilts. One day in 2006, my nephew dropped by for a visit wearing such a garment and, well, there was the inspiration for Garry.

With that in mind, some of Branell's menfolk wear kilts.

Leaders and the Brotherhood of Faith Church

The Brotherhood of Faith is a religion, similar to Christianity in its theories, beliefs, and practices. Leaders are men who, usually in their late teens, enter the Leadership. Leaders are men sworn to vows of celibacy, while also living lives of poverty and . . . you get the idea.

Male students of parochial schools owned and operated by the Brotherhood of Faith wear uniforms consisting of skullcaps, sandals, and long-sleeved tunics which hang slightly above the knees, with no pants or tights to conceal the legs.

Kusch and the Kuschan Religion

Kusch is a nation south of Embrey and Branell. Its citizens usually have

Scandinavian or Russian names. This is not to suggest that Kuschans are Scandinavians or Russians, but to merely point out that they have Scandinavian or Russian names.

St. Alexandrov is Kusch's capital city.

Many Kuschans believe in a celestial being known as the Kuen. All "good Kuschans" believe that fighting and possibly dying for the benefit of all mankind is pleasing to the Kuen.

The Kuen randomly selects a mortal man to become the Kued. The Kued is thereby expected to surrender his own self-interests and desires. He pledges to protect humanity, an obligation which he gives his life for.

The Kuen then chooses someone new to assume the position of the Kued.

Soraq is a winged demon, and a source of misery, evil, and unhappiness in the Universe.

In the past, Embrey and Kusch were at war. One of their final skirmishes took place in a small, remote Kuschan village known as Anumun.

Embrian forces spent several months occupying Anumun. During this time, Embrian officers and soldiers treated the Kuschans deplorably, and conducted themselves in a heinous, savage manner.

Kuschan brigands and warriors finally removed the Embrians from Anumun. Only one member of the Embrian Army survived their ill-fated retreat. This account is detailed further in ARE YOU MAN ENOUGH?

Kokashima *is a Far-Eastern, Oriental nation which recently normalized relations with nations Embrey and Agron.*

Last but not least . . .

Campens Rose'
Campens is a fertile, wine-growing country. One of its most sought-after and illegal products is a beverage known as Campens Rose'. I have no clue what this stuff tastes like, so I leave it up to your imagination. It must be really good, because several characters in both books have paid extremely high-prices for it!

I must give thanks to writers of the past, most notably Mark Twain, James Fenimore Cooper, and Edgar Rice Burroughs. I see Jeremy Kentworth as a combination of Huckleberry Finn, "Hawkeye" from "The Last of the Mohi-

cans" and, most especially, "Tarzan of the Apes." It'd be vulgar, indeed criminal, not to mention the influences which have played such an important, integral part of the following narrative.

So, there you have it. I hope this information clarifies everything for you, my faithful, undaunted reader. I'm deeply honored for you taking the time to enjoy this humble tale.

For your efforts, I am extremely grateful . . .

Doug McKim

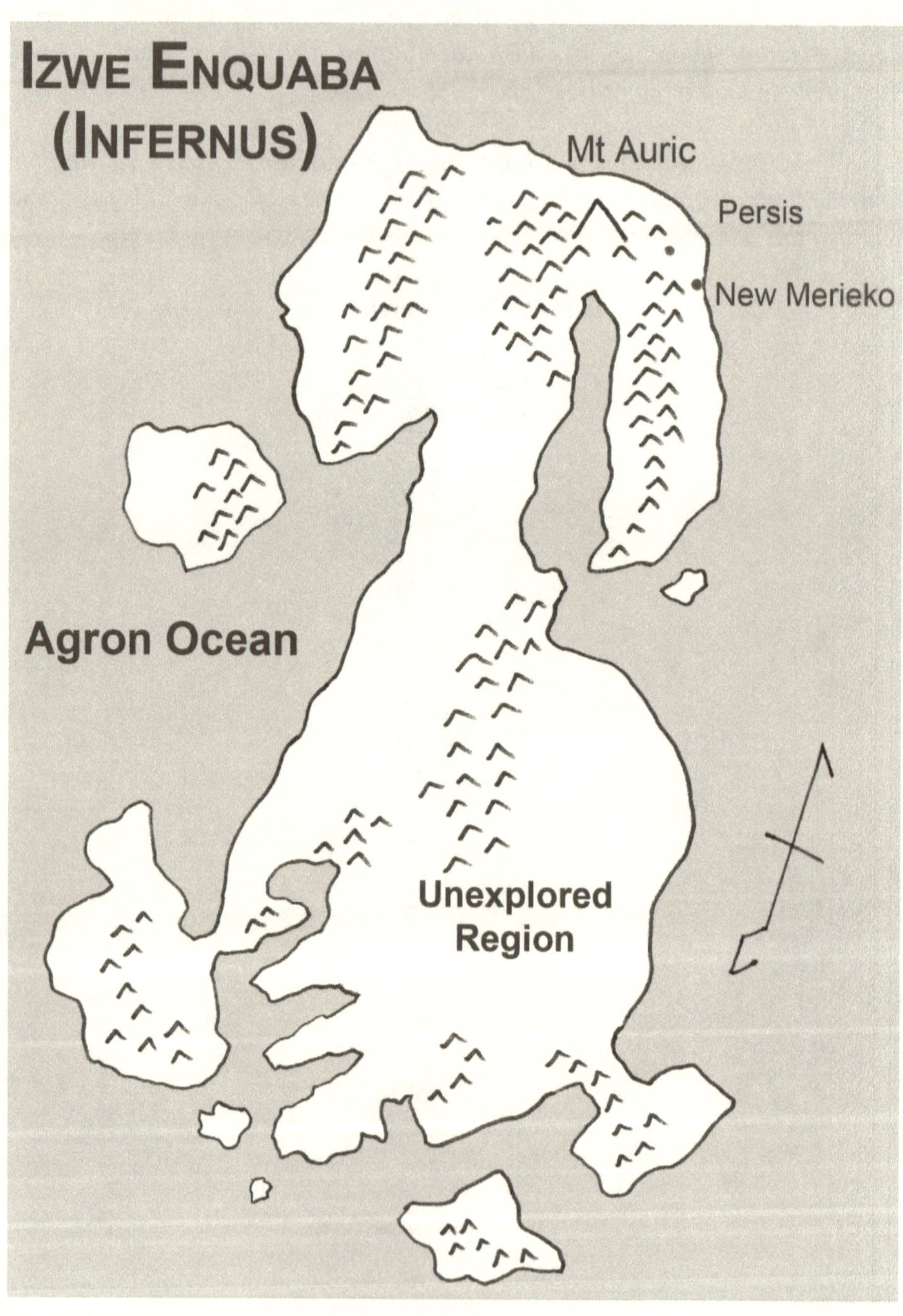
Izwe Enquaba
(Infernus)
Mt Auric
Persis
New Merieko
Agron Ocean
Unexplored
Region

JUST PLAIN OLD JEREMY

As he went to his father's funeral, Cody Kentworth stopped at the crumbling, decaying steps of Lord Bernard's Cathedral, for a moment of rest and reflection.

Cody's father, JT, was not a healthy man. He had a severe limp which made life difficult and painful. His once trim, muscular frame grew flabby, as a voracious appetite for food and liquor put further strain on an overtaxed heart. The burdens of owning and operating KENTWORTH'S, a small business selling beverages, dried goods, and tobacco in downtown Merieko (merry-echo), placed further tolls on him.

Some wondered how JT ever got to the age of thirty-seven. He made good money as a merchant in western Agron, yet was plagued by extreme melancholy. The premature death of his wife, years ago, left him an empty, bitter, and resentful man.

Only when JT received visits from his stepfather Rey, a Leader in the Brotherhood of Faith Church, did he ever smile.

During Rey's latest stay in Merieko, JT dropped dead behind KENTWORTH'S counter. This happened minutes before closing time at six p.m. He had just sold a pint of Campens Rose' to a customer, when his complexion turned ashen and pale. He complained of severe chest pains, while his breathing grew short and shallow.

He then collapsed to the hard-wood floor . . . and left his son Cody an orphan at sixteen.

Cody and Rey were in KENTWORTH'S second-story apartment preparing supper. Neither imagined their lives were about to change, forever. Once the customer screamed out, Cody and Rey raced downstairs. There, they *found JT twisted in an odd, distorted manner, upon the floor. His lifeless eyes stared blankly at one wall.*

Cody, Rey, and the customer carried JT through a narrow stairwell into the apartment, then placed him onto a bench. Rey left KENTWORTH'S to inform friends and family of this passing. Meanwhile, Cody held a vigil over his father.

An unnerving silence haunted the cramped apartment, as Cody suffered unbearable loneliness and loss. He was never very close to JT, yet depended on him for financial and emotional stability.

Cody faced the reality that he had only himself to depend on, now. During Rey's absence, he coped with the shedding of countless tears, the anger of life's cruelty, and hopes that maybe, just maybe, JT was reunited with his wife in Heaven above.

Cody stared at the thin sheet covering his father, pondering a question he could not ignore, or run away from:

What about me?

Cody stood five-four, with long, dishwater blond hair reaching to his scrawny shoulders. He had fair skin, which rarely tanned but easily burned. Like his father, he was born in the faraway nation of Branell. Similar to those of his native homeland, Cody often wore a thick, turtleneck sweater, white knee socks, shiny black brogans, and a kilt. He had small, squinty eyes, high cheekbones, and a slightly pugged nose.

The confines of the tiny apartment were torturous. The only sounds came from the crackle and pop of wood burning in a stove, the traffic of pedestrians and horse carts traveling the cobblestone streets outside, and the pouring of rain against the windows and shingled roof of KENTWORTH'S. Cody threw sticks of firewood into the stove, to hold back autumn's chill.

An inability to stay busy was Cody's worst enemy, now. He could do little to pass the time until Rey returned, other than to remain with his father. A meal of cornbread and a pot of beans on the kitchen table was left uneaten.

Rey returned to the apartment, minutes before midnight. There was no point in sleeping. Funeral arrangements had to be made. Cody and Rey sat at the kitchen table, planning a celebration of JT's life. Both spoke openly of their shock and grief. Cody often nestled in Rey's arms, where he felt safe and comfortable. Rey was never as much of a stranger, as JT seemed to be. He went out of his way to befriend Cody, while JT remained guarded and reserved. Rarely did JT grant Cody companionship and affection, especially after his wife died. Nor did he speak of his childhood. As the two resided under the same roof, few words were exchanged.

JT and Cody may have loved each other. There were doubts as to whether they actually liked each other.

Leader Rey was a thin, tall gentleman whose height exceeded six feet. Nearing the age of sixty, he had a full head of coal-black hair. A gray beard concealed his ruddy, pockmarked cheeks and chin. His large, calloused hands spoke of hard work, sweat, and toil. His role as a spiritual advisor and mentor never excluded him from tough, physical labor. His deep, baritone voice revealed love, compassion, and care for his fellow man.

Rey and Cody spent the long, sleepless evening in the apartment overtop KENTWORTH'S. Morning couldn't come, soon enough! By dawn, the rain had finally stopped. Blasts of a cold wind from the Agron Ocean swept over Merieko, leaving blankets of frost and ice. Cody and Rey took turns chucking sticks of wood into the warm fire, and somehow kept their spirits up.

The two men had a long day ahead of them. They ate a breakfast of beans and cornbread. There was no point to let the food go to waste. By seven in the morning, a half-dozen friends and neighbors arrived. These were business associates, drinking buddies, and loyal customers. After granting words of support and comfort, they carried JT to a horse-drawn hearse. A graveside service was scheduled at noon.

Cody dressed in a formal jacket, white silk shirt, and an emerald green kilt. Rey would officiate the service. An hour before noon, Rey and Cody locked the doors of KENTWORTH'S behind them, then began their long walk to the cemetery.

Within two city blocks, Cody wished to go on his own, by taking an alternative route.

"Cody," said Rey, in concern. "The funeral's in just a few minutes . . ."

"I know," sighed Cody, leaning against the cast iron pole of a corner street lantern. "I just wanna be alone . . . I got to be alone . . . for a while . . ."

"But you will be there?" inquired Rey.

Cody nodded, 'yes.'

"Promise?" begged Rey.

"I'll be there," said Cody, with a crooked smile. "I promise."

Rey placed his hand upon Cody's shoulder, then reluctantly left him on the cold, damp street.

Once Rey was out of sight, Cody concealed his face under one hand and allowed the tears to fall freely. His insides battled between needs to express the sadness engulfing him, and the requirements of getting tough about it. He de-

bated on even attending the service.

No getting out of it . . . he had to be there! JT was the only dad he'd ever have! Even then, Cody remained indecisive. Should he stroll aimlessly through the city of Merieko, return to the lonely apartment above KENTWORTH'S, or simply give up and throw himself into a river?

Cody vowed to push forward, despite overwhelming pains of loss. He'd be at the funeral, all right, but not because Rey or anyone else wanted him there. He wished to attend on his own terms, and nothing more.

Cody wandered through the back alleys and boulevards of Merieko. He soon stopped at the decaying, crumbling steps of Lord Bernard's Cathedral, for a moment of rest and reflection.

Years before, the Brotherhood of Faith Church attempted to bring the Word of God to the rough, rowdy, and raunchy world of Merieko. It was a disaster. Where the structure was erected with pride and dedication, it had eroded to wreck, ruin, and neglect. Its tall steeple, pointing more than fifty feet above the ground, thick marble walls, and stone angels were pathetic reminders that God avoided a community dominated by rogue figures, soldiers, sailors, smugglers, derelicts, and cutthroats. Most of Lord Bernard's windows were shattered, as an open front door swung back and forth in the breeze. Rusty hinges creaked in harsh winds. The cathedral was now a shelter for the homeless, or a hideaway for those escaping the law.

Merieko was a port city of nearly a hundred-thousand people. It was a shipping and trading town, where bootleg items were sold, bartered, and distributed to nations such as Embrey, Branell, Kusch, Campens, and Corapal. There were very few schools, churches, or civic centers in Agron. Most residents were Farlanders, those who located to Agron to make their fortunes.

And many fortunes were made in Merieko. Several residents had obtained wealth, just to lose it in card games, the arms of loose women, or bad dealings. Commerce usually centered around the buying, selling, and trading of liquor, gambling, and sex. It wasn't unusual to find bodies floating in ditches or rivers, victims of poor decisions or moral digressions.

A few legitimate businesses did flourish in Merieko. Occasionally, they still handled illegal goods and cargo. KENTWORTH'S was one such establishment. JT and Cody had adopted their surnames after the Branellian capital, a common practice for men of respect and prestige. In Agron, it was typical for individuals to label themselves after their birthplace or occupation, with names as Sykes, Marks, Alexandrov, Hamblin, Basisk, or Baker, Taylor, Smith, and Cook.

Cloudy skies above threatened more showers. It was late-October, as trees slowly shed their orange, red, and brown leaves. Autumn would eventually surrender to the blustery cold of winter.

Cody sat at the chipped, cracked, eroding steps of Lord Bernard's Cathedral. He was a toddler when his mother succumbed to pneumonia. JT and Cody then left Branell and moved to Agron, where they opened KENTWORTH'S.

Well, the shop was JT's idea. Cody questioned if he wanted to spend his life indoors, selling booze, dried goods, and smoking weed to ruffians and low-lifes. Should he stay in Merieko and continue running the store, or return to the rugged, high mountains and lush, green valleys of Northern Branell?

Cody was alone in his confusion, and largely ignored by those strolling past the ruins of Lord Bernard's Cathedral. By now, the wind had messed up his hair, swept under his kilt, and chilled his pale, hairless legs.

Cody lacked sleep, and his eyes were red and moist from sorrow. A few people smiled as they passed by, and wished him a good morning. None of these folks knew JT Kentworth. Nor did they care that he now belonged only in memories.

Nor did anyone care about a sixteen-year-old orphan.

Folks die everyday . . . Does that truly matter, now?

Never had Cody felt this lonely or alone . . . until that very moment.

Overcome by sadness, Cody answered with uncontrolled sobs. Fear entered the picture, as he doubted his abilities to survive on his own. He felt sorry for JT, yet also resented the man for dying. JT was a good provider, but hardly a warm man. Cody sought the same relationship that other boys had with their dads. JT made promises to take Cody hunting and fishing, but never carried through on any of them. The store was always a priority. By the end of the day, JT was exhausted, and often fell asleep in his favorite chair, minutes after supper.

KENTWORTH'S was a profitable enterprise, and regular customers would likely grant Cody the same respect and courtesy given to JT. Still, did Cody have the courage to carry on, without his father there to support him?

Cody got to the cemetery, minutes before the funeral started. Nearly a hundred people were there to pay their final respects. Most everyone gave Cody a warm smile and greeting. Rey sighed in relief, knowing that the boy had finally arrived.

Cody squeezed through rows of well-wishers and supporters. He was met with kind words, pats on the back, embraces, and even a smooch on the lips from a lady of the night. Cody managed a nervous smile. People did care about him, after all!

Yet, there was no escaping the painful, inevitable reality of why everyone was at the cemetery. This was not a pleasant outing, filled with revelry and good cheer. JT Kentworth was dead, and this truth revealed itself in the fancy pine casket, the presence of a grim-faced undertaker, and a deep hole in the ground. In less than an hour, JT would to be lowered into the cold earth, where he'd remain from now until the end of time.

Cody approached the casket, failing to control his frail emotions. He tried to accept JT's death . . . but was mired in useless denial. As Cody gazed upon the casket, cruel honesty and hopelessness slammed into him like tidewater sweeping over sand. Panic mixed with the worst pain imaginable. Cody's eyes met Leader Rey's, as his vision blurred with tears. His knees nearly buckled, as he leaned against the casket to avoid collapsing. Rey and a middle-aged cousin named Hilary prevented his fall. Hilary was a short, heavyset woman who wore her graying hair in a bun.

As Rey held Cody up, Hilary cupped her soft, warm hands into his. Both led Cody to a row of chairs next to the grave, as onlookers again wished him well.

Cody and Hilary sat together, as Rey whispered words of love and encouragement. Hilary kissed Cody's cheek, leaving smudges of thick, sloppy lipstick. Rey took his place at the podium, as Hilary patted Cody's knee, and wrapped one arm around his shoulders.

Cody was lost in his own thoughts, and had scant memory of the next few minutes.

Cody struggled to maintain a brave face. Hilary pressed her body to his, and voiced sentiments of compassion. Cody leaned against Hilary and wept, touched by the levels of attention afforded him.

Thunder rumbled overhead. Rey promised to keep his words to a minimum, so everyone could get out of the weather. Two gravediggers stood at one side, sharing a pint of ale and dreading thoughts of filling in the grave. For them, the funeral was business as usual. They were eager to complete their work, then spend the rest of their day at a local pub. Out of respect, they kept such thoughts to themselves. After all, JT often sold them rum and tobacco at a discount.

Cody recalled very little of Rey's spiel concerning the life of JT Kentworth. Such words gave him no reprieve from the hell he went through. They only made things worse! Rey never held back his feelings for JT. The two men knew each other, long before Cody was even born. Long distances and the difficulties of travel failed to break the bonds between Rey and JT.

A few raindrops sprinkled onto the gravesite. True to his word, Rey cut his speech short, and soon everyone returned to their own lives and responsibilities. As all men are reserved to living one life, they're also given only one funeral. For good or for ill, JT's memorial had drawn to a close. The gravediggers hastily went to work. Rey let out a sigh, exchanged glances with Hilary, and prayed that his humble service was accurate and adequate.

In less than ten minutes, the only ones left in the cemetery were Rey, Cody, Hilary, and the gravediggers. Breaking away from his role as a minister, Rey pitched in and helped cover the casket with sod and clay. This gave Cody and Hilary an opportunity to chat alone. Hilary held her darling little Cody tightly in her arms, granting him a faint sense of security and safety. She vowed to give Cody a home and shelter, should things not pan out at the store. Cody considered this generous offer. Yet, he doubted whether he was able to live with Franklin, Hilary's spouse. Franklin held little regard for JT and Cody, since they made a living selling demon rum and tobacco. He even refused to attend JT's funeral, and probably found humor in this tragedy. Why would a man like Franklin show Cody any kindness, now?

Rey spoke of his long-standing relationship with JT, with hopes of a reunion on Judgment Day. Not only were Rey and JT extremely close, they were like father and son.

In time, Hilary left Cody in his misery. Well, the funeral was over now, and life had to go on . . . but not as normal. Already, Cody missed JT terribly, and why wouldn't he? Still, Cody was troubled with realizations that JT had been a mystery and an enigma to him. As several people shared comical stories about JT, Cody felt increasingly isolated. It agonized Cody that he knew very little about his dad, and feared that he'd never learn anything more about him, now that the man was gone.

* * * * *

Time passed. The nights grew longer, the days shorter. Occasionally, a downpour of rain drenched the port city of Merieko. Cold winds swept through the narrow streets and corridors, as everyone prepared for another dismal winter.

Despite a period of mourning and grief, Cody and Leader Rey opened KENTWORTH'S each and every day. Cody knew the routine like the back of his hand, and stayed busy by serving customers. On Wednesdays, whiskey drummers and teamsters delivered freight. With the oncoming holidays, the shelves were stocked full with liquor, tobacco, and gifts.

Cody cried himself to sleep, every night for a week. After long, vivid dreams, he'd wake up, more exhausted and weary than when he went to bed. In the mornings, he fought hard to get through the workday. Constantly, he had to convince himself to fill the wood box, ignite the heating stove, light the candle lanterns, and open KENTWORTH'S. He endured ten long hours of work. He pasted a smile on his face, and made the patrons feel appreciated. Often, customers arrived to pay their condolences for JT. Cody graciously accepted such kindness, though hated being reminded of that which he couldn't escape.

Rey gave Cody frequent breaks to grab a bite to eat and catch his breath. Within time, the boy grew accustomed to this new schedule, although it was temporary and short-lived. Rey planned to visit other friends and acquaintances throughout Agron, before eventually leaving the island nation.

Cody never knew where home was for Rey. Anytime the question got raised, the only answer Rey gave was "the west."

"The west?"

There was nothing in the west until one got to the faraway nation of Ko-

kashima. *Cody never appreciated Rey's vague answer. He knew better than to press it. Rey may have been a kindred spirit. He also had a fiery temper, which Cody learned to avoid.*

Cody dreaded the day a stagecoach took Rey away. Both men woke early that morning, so Rey made sure he had everything for his trip. The Leader felt guilty for abandoning Cody. But life went on, and so did business. Cody claimed he'd be fine on his own. His dour expressions said otherwise. No sooner did the stage arrive, and Rey stepped outside to board it when Cody broke down and wept. After a short cry, he accepted his lot, built a warm fire downstairs, and got ready for another day at KENTWORTH'S.

Cody kept busy at night by performing an inventory of JT's personal items. Anything was preferable to boredom, thinking, and painful solitude. The boy resented slow, tedious evenings. Sleep wasn't so much a respite from the rigors of the day, so much as a reminder of what he had lost. Nearly every dream was haunted by the presence of his parents. Each morning, Cody woke to the reality that he'd never again enjoy their company and companionship.

Scrounging through JT's things, Cody decided to give away particular heirlooms to those who'd better appreciate them. Activity was the best cure for the blues! Occasionally, Cody found certain trinkets and other silly little keepsakes which reminded him of his dad. Once more, he'd struggle not to weep.

There was a closet in JT's bedroom that Cody never once entered. It remained locked up and sealed, since recollection. Rarely did Cody question the off-limit status of that which lay behind the closet door. He still had yearnings to explore it. Whenever JT visited local pubs, billiard parlors, or sporting ladies, Cody knew of a key to that place of mystery. However, he debated the wisdom of going in there. JT never spoke of its contents, hidden safely away from view.

But JT was dead and buried, and left Cody as the sole proprietor of KENTWORTH'S. Cody had a responsibility and obligation to check out everything under his roof.

Everything under his roof.

Cody spent several days mustering his courage to enter the forbidden closet. Finally, temptation proved too great. After an hour of pushing himself to do so, Cody approached the closet door, key in hand.

Cody's heart beat rapidly, as the rusty door creaked open. His breathing grew swift and shallow. He wondered if he had violated the sanctity of his father's spirit. Yet, the mystery was resolved! With no one monitoring him, Cody bravely stepped inside.

The closet's odor was uninviting, but not overpowering or offensive.

Initially, Cody was disappointed at what he found, by faded candle light in the dark, dank closet. Little was in there, other than aging weapons such as a bow and arrows, a rusty old knife, a set of darts, and a blowgun.

A blowgun?

The blowgun was made from thin wood, and nearly three feet long. Carefully, Cody blew out the years of dust and dirt which had accumulated in the device. He examined it with curiosity and awe, before leaning it in one corner.

Hanging from a back wall was a long-sleeved, leather shirt, dried and stiff from age and lack of wear, moccasin shoes made from animal hides, and a loincloth.

A loincloth?

Cody spotted a filthy crate with home-made brew, and pouches of tobacco. JT often bought such things from a tattooed man, or a grouchy old coot with long, white whiskers and cold, menacing eyes. Both men were originally from Agron, and spoke in hushed tones of their home, far to the west.

The west?

Were those two also from the exact area as Rey, a land hidden somewhere between Agron and Kokashima?

Cody knew there were unchartered islands scattered throughout the Agron Ocean. He never gave them much thought . . . until now.

Cody scoured through the crate and found a bundle of thin, yellow paper. It was a handwritten manuscript, which immediately grabbed his attention.

Cody brushed off the dust and musty cobwebs from the manuscript, then took it to the kitchen table. He poured himself a glass of his favorite cider, then fetched a buttered pastry from the pantry. He was briefly distracted by sounds of a fist fight, across the street in one of the rowdier taverns.

After filling the stove with firewood, Cody sat down, relaxed, and began reading the aging manuscript . . .

* * * * *

Insula Infernus ain't a very big island, and is somewhere in the north Agron Ocean. It looks kind of big when you're on it, but it ain't big if you look for it on most maps, if you can find it on most maps. You can't find it on most maps, which is probably a good thing.

Infernus is a good place to live, for anyone willing to abide its unpredictable, dangerous nature. It's a world of evergreen forests, with lots of other plants and animals. Very few Farlanders know about it, and fewer have gone there. Even fewer stay. This is probably a good thing, because too many Farlanders have a bad habit of getting lost, then getting ate by critters.

In the past hundred years or so, lots of explorers have traveled to Infernus, to poke around for valuable minerals and agricultural goods. Pirates, mercenaries, and adventurers traipse into Infernus for booty, while trying to get the better of the island's strange civilizations. Farlander kings have commissioned daring, foolhardy, and stupid men to set-up colonies, while setting up diplomatic ties to Infernus. This is done secretly. Hardly no one knows about the different critters living on Infernus, which is probably a good thing.

Some Farlanders have done real good, if they know how to live within Infernus' harsh, uncompromising nature. Successful colonists learn how to grow crops, and which kinds of farms animals to take with them to this new land. Unsuccessful colonists usually leave, after too many of their friends and neighbors get ate by critters.

If old timers tell you never to set foot into wicked territories, it's best to do what they say. Curiosity or just plain stupidity gets people ate.

Infernus' tallest mountain is Mount Auric, in the northeast part of the island, just north of a peninsula. Mount Auric was named after an Embrian king who was one of the first Farlanders to visit Infernus. It's right around ten-thousand feet high, and has a thin layer of snow on it most all the time.

A major waterway is the Persis River, named after Auric's mistress Persis, who went with him to Infernus. It's a fast-moving river with lots of rocks and rapids. The Persis River drops from a huge waterfall, about two-hundred feet overlooking the town of Persis, which was also named after Persis. Most people live in Persis, where they get by from working real hard, along with having a cooperative spirit of their friends and neighbors, persons and winged men alike.

Cody lifted his head from the manuscript.
Winged men?

When Farlanders first met up with winged men, it brought on fascination, fear, curiosity, and real bad feelings. While most of his men stayed shy of the winged men, King Auric decided to meet up with these strange critters. It was a question of survival, pure and simple. Winter was coming, and Auric needed the winged men's help and knowledge. He didn't know what he was doing, and his men was dying off, real quick like. Auric took twelve of his best men and met up with a tribe of nice winged men, who lived in a narrow draw where the town of

Persis is now. Auric and his men was armed to the teeth. They also brought lots of gifts, to keep from starting a fight against them critters. Mistrust, suspicion, fear, and revulsion separated the two sides, since this was the first meeting up with critters that neither side met up with before. Talking consisted of hand gestures, and the trading of food and supplies.

Auric persisted in opening a dialog with the winged men. He learned it don't pay to trade liquor with the winged men, since there ain't nothing worse than a drunken winged man. He also learned the winged man words for water, grass, trees, shelter, sky, run, run fast, and go away. One of the nicer winged men, a guy whose name Auric never learned how to say because it was too hard to say, helped Auric and his men out a bunch.

Throughout the years, most Farlanders and winged men got along with each other, and sometimes lived in the same houses. Embrian soon became Infernus' main language, which is probably a good thing. Winged man words are too hard to say.

There are two types of winged men. The Green Winged Men get to be around five feet fall when they grow up. They got long pointed ears, olive-shaped eyes, and flat, pugged-noses. Their arms and legs are slender and wiry. Their hands got sharp claws. Their skin is reptilian and scaly, like a fish or a lizard or something. Patches of fir surround the face, run along the backbone, and on their wings. Their knees are double-jointed and knobby. The Greens like dark places and night. They don't care much for warmth or sunlight. They're downright ugly.

The Brown Winged Men have small, leaf-shaped ears, long snouts, and teeny little eyes. They are covered with short, brown and white hair, except on the belly, under their wings, and around their privates. Their hands and feet look more like a person's, than a critters. The Browns are taller than the Greens, and got much bigger wings. They ain't near as ugly as the Greens.

The Browns usually befriend Farlanders, to their own detriment. Not all Farlanders bring warm hearts, kind spirits, and big smiles. Some bring knives, swords, bows, arrows, and big clubs used to kill winged men and other critters. Some colonists treat winged men poorly, because they think the winged men are in cahoots with this stupid Kuschan god of evil named Soraq. The Kuschan religion don't say nothing about being nice to winged men, or any other critter. Some Farlanders don't like winged men just because they don't.

The Greens don't like Farlanders, colonists, or hardly nobody much. They are real clannish, and live in caves, marshes, and other dark places in the northeastern peninsula. Most Greens don't learn to talk Embrian, and ain't got no use for people, for this one exception.

Along with fruits, vegetables, bugs, and tree bark, the Greens got a hankering to eat human flesh.

Cody laughed so hard he nearly dropped the manuscript. Whoever wrote it must have been quite the storyteller!
Then again, who did write the manuscript?

John Mucker was an odd, lonely sort of man, even by them who knew and liked him. He wasn't an easy man to know, nor to like. He never made it easy to know him, nor to like him.

Mucker was around the age of thirty-five, and a sort of angry fellow who never said much, except when he got all riled up. Then mainly he scowled and growled a lot. He had a small hump on his back, and a bad limp, from an accident onboard an Agronian schooner which ran aground the shores of Infernus, some fifteen-years back. He suffered from lots of pain, but never harped about it. He had bits of gray hair in his long, black beard, and gray hair at the temple. His voice was grouchy and gruff. His eyes was deep-set, his nose long, broken, and crooked, his jaw square, firm, and hard. He was a scary man, and never invited much conversation, other than when he was drunk. He was filled with painful memories and feelings, which he never revealed except around them he trusted.

Mucker never trusted too many folks. Trust was stupid. Stupid, dumb, and deadly. Trust gets folks killed. Also gets them ate.

Mucker never learned how to read nor to write. Didn't mean he was stupid. He never saw no need to read nor to write. He did have a real bad temper though, and it was never smart to tangle with him. Them who did usually ended up dead, or wishing they was dead.

Who knew what Mucker thought about when he took long walks alone, along the coast of Infernus, not far from Persis? Reckon he thought of his old stomping grounds near the fishing ports, bars, and bawdy houses of Merieko. He once had himself a woman, which he vowed to marry after getting home from a trip to Kokashima.

It was on that same trip when Mucker ended up on Infernus, during one of the worst storms in the Agron Ocean. Rumor had it that an illegitimate kid awaited him, which he never got to know. Probably for the best.

Mucker never let others join him on these long walks along the beach. Probably for the best, since he never wanted no one bothering him. Anyone stupid enough in wanting to join him either got hollered at, or a fist sandwich for being so stupid.

While working for a real mean farmer in Agron, Mucker joined up with a small group of freebooters. One had to be tough, fierce, and mean to join up with that lot. Mucker was likely the meanest of them all. Whether he liked killing or not, he got real good at it. When his ship got lost at sea, his rivals hoped he was swallowed up by the deep, blue sea. They learned otherwise, when Mucker went to the Farlands to sell or trade Infernus' best booze and smokes.

Mucker sat on a rotting log a spell, to stare across the Agron Ocean. He was worried, but never fretted much in the open until he got drunk. Then mostly he just griped.

Mucker wasn't born on Infernus. Though he lived there, some of the natives still called him an outsider, a foreigner, a Farlander. Never to his face, though. Mucker figured he belonged on Infernus, and it belonged to him. He set his mind to defending the island, along with them who lived there, from harm. Harm from the outside world. From outsiders, from foreigners, from Farlanders.

Mucker would've done anything to defend the Brown Winged Men, some who come to accept him as one of their own.

Mucker made a steady pace back toward his teeny little shack on the outskirts of Persis. Sweat rolled from his creased face. The heat was bad enough to whip them not used to the harsh climates. The heat and humidity got so bad, as to make folks hanker for sundown, when a person could go tell lies outside, even with thick bunches of skeeters biting them.

Mucker just left the beach and headed toward a narrow trail leading into Persis. He heard a familiar, high-pitched squawk, from up above. It was a couple of Brown Winged Men flying overhead. Only Brown Winged Men can make that kind of weird, high-pitched squawk.

Mucker looked up and saw Malachi and Nikolai coming his way. Both was sons of the Brown Winged Man head honcho, Chief Lorenzo. Mucker had no idea how old Malachi and Nikolai was. In person terms, they was like people in their late-teens or early-twenties.

Malachi was next in line to rule over the Browns. He was a rare breed in their tribe, because he had no brown fir on him. Only white. Pure white. His brother Nikolai was learning to be the Brown's medicine man. Both was respected by the tribe, and thought of as handsome young bachelors. Don't know if they was all that handsome. In people terms, they looked sort of freakish. But the Brown Winged Women sure thought they was handsome, because they chased after them two all the time.

Nikolai aimed to live under the Browns' old ways and traditions, by upholding their pagan religion. Meanwhile, Malachi joined up with the Brotherhood of Faith Church, and got into real bad arguments with his kin over it. He never liked arguing religion with his kin, which is probably a good thing.

Unfortunately, Lorenzo and Nikolai made it a habit to argue religion with Malachi, since he was going to be chief one day. Lorenzo and Nikolai was scared that when Malachi got to be chief, he'd favor his religion over theirs. They was scared of their religion dying out, because more and more Brown Winged Men joined up with the Brotherhood Church. Them two didn't like that.

Mucker never believed in no kind of religion. He believed in getting drunk and fighting them he didn't like nor agree with. This wasn't always a good thing.

Malachi and Nikolai landed next to Mucker, all worked up and anxious to fetch him.

"What's stickin' in yer craw?" asked Mucker, in his typical grumpy voice. "Well? Speak up! Think I got all day?"

"Pirates from the Roderick Dundee have kidnapped some of the children from New Merieko!" said Malachi, knowing this news would aggravate Mucker, which it did. Bad. Real bad.

The Roderick Dundee was a pirate ship that stole food, gold, and people from Infernus. They stole women and kids to use for slaves for sex and stuff.

This news got Mucker all riled up. He wasn't all that riled up about kids getting kidnapped from New Merieko. New Merieko was a newer colony a few miles up the coast. Mucker figured there was already too many colonies and colonists who did nothing but push politics and religion on everyone else, while getting ate by critters. What got Mucker all riled up is that he never liked nobody stealing nothing from Infernus, without his permission. Nor did he like the Roderick Dundee. It was a pirate ship owned by an ornery Agronian pirate named Stossee. The last thing Mucker wanted was pirates poking around Infernus, without his permission.

Mucker was always in a bad mood. Just hearing the name Roderick Dundee made him that much worse.

Sick and tired of having the pirate ship off the coast of Infernus, he figured to put a stop to it, right there and then.

* * * * *

Not too far from where Mucker ran into Malachi and Nikolai, about a half-dozen smugglers and pirates took about a dozen or so little kid hostages to a couple of launches, not too far from where the Roderick Dundee was moored off of Infernus.

The Roderick Dundee was a real big ship, with four masts and a crew of more than eighty men, toughened up by years of barbarism. Its sails was painted red, blood red, to scare those unlucky enough to meet up with it on the open seas.

Just the size of the Roderick Dundee was enough to scare most folks off. It was more than a hundred feet long. It was led by a guy named Captain Slane. He was one of the smarter guys under Stossee's command. Stupid or careless captains usually got their heads cut off, either by Stossee himself for this mean son of his named Strunk.

Them pirates treated their hostages shamefully. The hostages was mostly little kids. One of them was a brown-haired, sad-eyed boy of around nine, whose whole body was covered up by tattoos. That was Paransky, an orphan who stowawayed onboard a ship heading to Infernus.

Paransky survived mostly on other folks' generosity. Some folks wasn't so generous toward him. Some was downright mean to him, mainly because Paransky was an orphan, was all covered up by tattoos, and therefore a heathen.

Fernandez was another kid hostage. He was a dark-skinned boy, around fifteen. He was real skinny, and never got too far away from his mom and dad. He was a real bad sissy who whined a lot, wrung his hands a lot more, and never was no good about sticking up for himself. He dressed up in the uniform of a Brotherhood of Faith Church school, which had a tan skullcap, sandals, a long-sleeved tunic hanging a wee bit above the knees, and nothing to cover up his scrawny, bare legs.

Fernandez was a scaredy-cat, and the worst sissy of them kid hostages. He cried his eyes out, even after them pirates told him to shut up. The more he cried, the more they told him to shut up. Fernandez was taught by some preachy types that deep, dark woods is places of mystery and evil. Since most of Infernus' woods is deep and dark, Fernandez was scared most all the time.

The only grown-up hostage of the bunch was Weston. He was an Embrian diplomat sent by his King Marco to try and talk the Brown Winged Men into a trade agreement. Weston was in his thirties. He was taller than most people, with a dark red beard, bright blue eyes, and a real nice smile, whenever he had reasons to smile. He was a cousin to King Marco, which helped him get a diplomat job. He just got into Infernus the night before, and was staying in New Merieko when pirates snatched him and all them kid hostages up. Them pirates aimed on sending a ransom note to King Marco, to get some gold for Weston's return, preferably with his head and other body parts intact.

The pirates was headed by a short, skinny man with greasy hair parted down the middle, and an even greasier, pencil-thin mustache. This was McCoy, a nasty little cutthroat who won Stossee's favor by knowing how to cut throats.

He'd of just as soon killed Weston, if there weren't no profit in keeping him alive. That never stopped McCoy and them other pirates from bully-ragging the kid hostages, for no other reason other than because they enjoyed it.

"Get your lazy backsides into the launches!" barked McCoy, about to slap the kid hostages across their noggins. "Get into those launches, or I'll slit your throats!"

Fernandez turned and gave McCoy a weird look.

McCoy never liked the weird look Fernandez gave him, because he sent the back of his hand into the scaredy-cat's face. Fernandez lost his balance and landed in the sand, next to them launches. He covered his face up with both hands and whimpered.

"Get up!" yelled McCoy, whipping out a knife hanging from his belt. "Get up! Get up, by god, or I'll stick you!"

As them other pirates laughed, them other kid hostages got into the launches that much faster.

"Why did you have to hit me?" bawled Fernandez. "Why?"

McCoy booted Fernandez in the gut.

"Don't kick him!" yelled Weston, stepping in front of McCoy to keep him from tromping Fernandez some more.

"I'll kick him if I please!" hollered McCoy, waving his knife in Weston's face.

This amused them other pirates no end, while scaring them kid hostages even more. Them pirates almost hoped McCoy did slice Weston because they liked seeing people die. It never made no difference if it was an Embrian diplomat getting sliced, and worth more to keep alive. Some of the kid hostages screeched and hollered because they didn't want to see no one get killed, especially not a nice guy like Weston. A girl kid hostage turned her head away, too scared to see McCoy carve Weston up.

The only sounds came from the wind, the tidewater sweeping onto the beach, and the howls of some poor critter getting ate by another critter, in the woods.

Weston stood his ground and shielded Fernandez, so McCoy couldn't kick him no more. Even though Weston was scared of getting his throat cut, he never said so.

McCoy wasn't that big a guy, and had to look up to Weston and reach even higher to wave the knife in his face. Weston had been all over the world, and had been in worse scrapes than the one he was in now. Still, he didn't want to get killed, especially not by a sawed-off, greasy-haired type like McCoy. He also didn't want to see McCoy stomp all over a sissy like Fernandez.

Truth was, McCoy was more scared of Weston, than Weston was of him. McCoy was probably a bigger scaredy-cat than Fernandez, but got by from talking loud and fierce to impress them other pirates. He wasn't above cutting people's throats in their sleep, where they couldn't fight back. That sort of throat-cutting suited cowards like McCoy. Normal people don't cut throats in the first place. Normal people don't like killing, period. McCoy liked it too much. Then again, he wasn't normal.

As well, McCoy never liked nobody standing up against him, because it made him look bad in front of them other pirates. To show he wasn't scared, he looked straight into Weston's eyes and said, "Out of my way, Embrian dog, or I'll cut your eyes out and feed them to . . ."

"Y'aint cutting nobody's eyes out and feeding 'em to no one!" a loud, gruff voice called from the woods.

Mucker stepped out into the open with a knife, a sword, a bow, and a bunch of arrows.

McCoy and them other pirates never met Mucker before. They already heard of him.

As most of them other pirates talked in nervous, hushed tones, McCoy smiled. He was more scared of Mucker, than he was of Weston. His one comfort come in knowing there was more pirates, than there was Mucker. If they could kill a guy like Mucker, they'd leave Infernus with scarier reputations to reckon with.

Mucker stopped within fifteen feet of the pirates and hostages. "Let them kids go," he said, in a low voice. "Then I'll let you leave, with yer hides and yer heads."

"And if we don't?" asked McCoy, smiling even when that little voice in the back of his head told him to skedaddle.

"Prepare to die," said Mucker, flatly.

Some of the pirates laughed, thinking they had nothing to worry about from Mucker. This one scaredy-cat pirate was all too eager to do what Mucker said.

McCoy took a couple of steps toward Mucker. "We mean these children no harm," he said, playing dumb to finagle himself out of a scrape. "We're simply taking them home, to their loving parents in Agron . . ."

"Ain't what I heard," said Mucker. "Heard tell you kidnapped them kids from New Merieko. Well, I'm here to kidnap them back."

"Who told you that lie?" argued McCoy, his temper getting the best of him. He'd never get shy of Mucker, without killing him first.

Mucker pointed up at the sky toward Malachi and Nikolai, flying overhead.

As he waved them down, the two winged men landed next to him on the beach.

The sight of them two winged men scared the daylights out of the kid hostages, and never did Weston no good, neither. None of them hostages never saw a winged men, before. Some of the kid hostages thought that Mucker was a demon, and the winged men his devil-angels.

Weston had read dispatches written by Farlanders living on Infernus, telling of winged men and other critters. He never believed a word of it, but sure did now.

The sight of them winged men, along with the pirates and Mucker and everything else, told Weston to keep his mouth shut. He wasn't as scared as Fernandez, but no one was ever that scared. For the sake of the kid hostages, Weston tried to be brave. He was failing, bad.

Weston was a diplomat, and had to act all brave even when he wasn't. He wanted to talk on behalf of them kid hostages, but didn't know what to say to Mucker or the winged men.

Before Weston got the chance to say anything, Fernandez and this little Kuschan boy up and ran off, screeching like stuck cats.

Weston tackled Fernandez and somehow held him to the ground. The little Kuschan boy ran into the nearby trees, screaming and hollering and carrying on about that stupid Kuschan god of evil named Soraq.

A few seconds later, the little Kuschan screamed as he got ate by something.

Them other kid hostages also screamed.

Them pirates thought the whole thing was funny, for no reason other than they was mean. The two winged men was upset, most especially Malachi because he hated seeing anyone get ate by critters.

Mucker got as mad as all get-up. He looked down at Fernandez, who was held to the ground by Weston. He wanted to pop the scaredy-cat's head off. First, he had to save them hostages, then pop the scaredy-cat's head off. "You let them kids go," he told McCoy, in that scary way he talked before killing someone. "You let them kids go, an' I'll let you go."

"And if not?" taunted McCoy, figuring Mucker and the two winged men was no match for him and them other pirates. "Do you truly believe you're going to give us a fair contest, just you and those filthy animals beside you?"

Mucker didn't say nothing. He didn't have to. His squinty eyes and angry look said plenty. That was enough to motivate the more cowardly pirates to think twice. It was also enough to motivate the dumber ones to challenge Mucker.

This one big brute standing behind McCoy did just that, by whipping his sword out and attacking Mucker.

Next thing anyone knew, Mucker whipped out his own blade and impaled the big brute through the guts.

The big brute dropped to his knees, giving McCoy a look of shock, surprise, and disbelief. He opened his mouth to back-talk Mucker, but instead collapsed, and couldn't say nothing more. He was too dead to say much of anything.

Them other pirates didn't say much neither. The big brute was their best fighter, and who among them was dumb enough to make that same mistake?

Mucker pointed his sword at the Roderick Dundee. "Go," he repeated, sick and tired of saying it again.

"You think that's going to stop us?" shouted McCoy, acting as if the big brute's death didn't bother him. "You truly expect us to simply hop into those launches, tell Captain Slane to turn tail and run, and that's the end of it? You've got a lot of nerve, mister! You truly believe we're merely going to depart, without a fight?"

Mucker got all fed-up. And disgusted.

"Well, you've got another thing coming, sir!" hollered McCoy. He was fit to be tied, not only for being scared, but because he hated it when others knew he was fit to be tied. "We'll be back, you can count on it! And when we do, I'll render payback on you, and on those mangy freaks with you!"

While Nikolai thought that McCoy's comments was funny, Malachi got upset over them.

"Freaks?" asked Nikolai, attempting to imitate McCoy. "And who exactly are you addressing, sir? Yourself?"

"You!" shouted McCoy, mad because a winged man had the gall to talk down to him. "The whole bloody lot of you! You, and every other wretched creature on this island! It'll give me great pleasure to slaughter you stinking winged men!"

"Go," repeated Mucker, tired of McCoy's threats and posturing.

"On whose authority?" asked McCoy. "Yours, and the two toadies with you? What makes you lord and master over Infernus? You've got a lesson coming! And it'll give me great joy to teach you that lesson!"

Mucker grinned. "You giving me a lesson?"

McCoy latched onto Fernandez' hair, then yanked him out from under

Weston. Next thing anyone knew, he stuck his pig-sticking knife against Fernandez' gullet. "First I'll rid myself of this miserable wretch!" he said, as Fernandez whined and moped and carried on. "Right here, right now!"

"If it's blood you want, why not mine?" asked Weston, getting to his feet. "Let the boy go. My cousin is King Marco of Embrey. The boy means nothing to you. Take me, and . . ."

"You're next on the list, Embrian," snickered McCoy. "I'll settle with you, after I slit this wretch's scrawny throat . . ."

A single arrow then flew out of the nearby woods and hit one of them pirates in the chest. The pirate let out a squall like he was being killed, which he was.

"Hit the dirt!" called Weston, tackling a girl kid hostage standing next to him.

Another pirate drew his sword, ready for a brawl, when a second arrow pierced his throat. The pirate flew backwards, as his head-mashed into one of the launches.

Before anyone else knew it, a third arrow struck a third pirate in the eye.

That left only McCoy and this one scaredy-cat pirate, who took it upon himself to skedaddle. As the scaredy-cat pirate hopped into the closest launch, he got shot in the back by a poison dart.

Squalling like a near-dead pig, the scaredy-cat pirate fell as a burning sensation crawled all through him. This was followed by numbness, paralysis, hallucinations, mumbling, blubbering, frothing at the mouth, then death.

"Muck told you to go!" a loud voice hollered from the trees. "Get to it, while the goin's good!"

McCoy let go of Fernandez, once he learned he was as good as whipped.

Fernandez run as hard as he could toward the trees. He was neared scared to death by Mucker, the two winged men, the pirates, and everything else. He was too scared to even think about the critters that ate the Kuschan boy.

Malachi flew after Fernandez to fetch him back. But Fernandez was way too fast, as he ran into the woods.

A few seconds later, everyone heard a loud thumping sound, as Fernandez ran into a fist sandwich.

A few seconds later, Fernandez was dragged back by the scruff of the neck by Vic McClusky, and a bunch of Green Winged Men.

This arrival caused quite a stir amongst Weston and the kid hostages. If everyone thought the Brown Winged Men was scary, it was nothing compared to the Greens, who was the ugliest, scariest critters on Infernus.

McClusky was a big, tall guy, even taller than Weston, and had muscles stacked on top of muscles. He was younger than Mucker, by a year or so. His hair had already turned totally gray. His face resembled a granite mountain, all chiseled, hard, and rugged. Hanging from his mouth was a cigar.

Walking next to McClusky was two Green Winged Men named Ricardo and Ugo. That wasn't their real names. Their real names was something people can't pronounce, so McClusky gave them names anyone can pronounce. All Green Winged Men was ugly, but Ricardo and Ugo was the ugliest. They liked to fight and had the scars to show it.

In the past, the Greens and Browns was at war. There was now a truce between the two tribes, though there was still airborne skirmishes between them. Both Malachi and Nikolai had gotten into a scrape or two with Ricardo and Ugo. When the two Browns saw the two Greens, they didn't say nothing but gave each other real mean looks.

Mucker and McClusky was still friends, sort of. McClusky first got to Infernus the same time Mucker did, when they got shipwrecked together. Mucker made friends with the Brown Winged Men, as McClusky sided with the Greens.

Why a man was so stupid to side with the Greens, no one knew. But that's exactly what McClusky did. Maybe the only reason the Greens never ate McClusky was because he was too nice to them, to eat. He was nicer to the Greens, than he was to people, which made no sense at all.

"What took you so long, Clusk?" asked Mucker, in his usually grumpy voice.

"Wanted to see how you'd handle the situation before I stepped in to take charge," said McClusky, in his usual cocky voice.

McCoy swallowed nervously, figuring something bad was going to happen to him.

"What're you hanging around here, for?" McClusky asked McCoy. "Mucker told you to go, didn't he?"

McCoy nodded, but never said nothing.

"Then go!" hollered McClusky. "Or I indulge my boys' appetite for people meat, and serve you up for their next meal."

"What? . . . What about my partners?" asked McCoy, staring at the dead pirates around him.

"A'ready on the menu!" laughed McClusky. Meanwhile, some of the Green Winged Men picked the dead pirates up with their taloned feet, and hauled them off to their caves in the peninsula.

"You'd be advised to get on one of them launches, then head back to the

Roderick Dundee," Mucker said to McCoy. "Go tell Captain Slane to high-tail it outa here."

"I've got my orders to stay put," said McCoy. He acted all brave and strong, though he was all weak and chicken-hearted.

"And I'm givin' you orders to take a hike," said McClusky. "You and everyone else onboard the Roderick Dundee. My boys get real hungry. They might just invite you and your associates to their cook-out, tonight."

"An' leave them kids here," added Mucker. "Y'aint got no business takin' 'em. We'll keep the Embrian diplomat, too. Might need him for a laugh or two."

With his tail between his legs, McCoy got into one of them launches and slowly paddled back to the Roderick Dundee.

Malachi watched as the Green Winged Men flew off, packing the dead pirates away to eat. Brown Winged Men ate no kind of meat, especially not people meat. Yet, the Greens' eagerness to eat people meat gave all winged men a bad name. Malachi was a member of the Brotherhood Church, and wondered if he really was one of God's creatures, or if any of the Browns was children of God.

Or was they the children of that stupid Kuschan god of evil, Soraq?

"Don't get too friendly with them green-hided buggers," Mucker warned McClusky. "They're right kindly, now. What happens if they get their fill of ya, an' throw you on the grill?"

"I ain't got nothing to worry about," said McClusky. "Neither do you, Muck. Neither do the Browns. They only want what you want. What we all want. Peace."

"What about them Kuschan sailors yer getting all buddy-buddy with?" asked Mucker. "Don't go turnin' yer back on them, neither."

"Those Kuschan sailors on the Matyushenko mean business," said McClusky. "So do I. More and more Farlanders are headin' this way. We're needing trading partners, as well as a strong military presence, to keep that which is rightfully ours."

"You know as well as I do them Kuschans ain't gonna get friendly to no winged men! Kuschans a'ready got their minds made up about fellas like Nik and Malachi, here. That includes yer boys too, Clusk. The Browns and the Greens ain't no tradin' partners to the Kuschans, but demon spawn that, accordin' to their way o' thinkin', needs killin'."

"Would you settle on the Branellians?" argued McClusky, giving Weston the stink eye. "Or Embrians? We'll have to settle on one group of Farlanders or t'other, sooner or later. Why not Kuschans?"

"I'd rather settle on no more Farlanders pokin' around here!" hollered

Mucker. "What makes you so sure them Kuschans'll stop at bein' tradin' partners, and start causin' trouble? Just you watch, Clusk. They'll try takin' over! They'll kill us both, just 'cause we're friends to them they think is the worst evil ever. Then nothin' on Infernus is safe!"

"And I say we'd best side ourselves with another country, before we got everyone and their dogs swarming over here, then get into a land grab. Gonna happen, unless we do somethin' now to stop it. I've already talked to the officers on the Matyushenko, Vaslov and Antonov. They ain't gonna try to colonize Infernus."

"That little boy who just died was a Kuschan," said Weston. "Kuschans are already colonizing here."

"So are Embrians!" yelled McClusky, getting real mad at Weston.

"We were kidnapped at New Merieko," said Weston, watching what he said around McClusky and Mucker. "Most of the colonists are Agronians, but there's a few Kuschans there too, including a holy man named Yevgeny."

"I'm fixin' to set up our own navy, along with a fleet of trade ships," said Mucker. "I'm talkin' to Chief Lorenzo about it, one o' these days. We don't need no Kuschans here, or anyone else. We don't need their military, their ugly faces, or their religion! Keep 'em all out, and we'll keep our own government, our own thinkin', and our own way of life."

Mucker and McClusky gave each other the eye, like they was about to fight. The four winged men also got into the act too, by chattering back and forth in their weird winged man talk. Mostly, they was arguing about who really was in charge of 'Izwe Enquba,' which is what the winged men call Infernus.

Why bother calling the place 'Izwe Enquaba'? Easier just to call it 'Infernus.'

McClusky, Ricardo, and Ugo finally got mad and stomped away.

After a couple of seconds or so, Mucker turned to Weston. "What business does a cousin to King Marco got here?" he asked. "Well? Speak up! Say yer piece, 'fore I get the mind to feed you to them green-hided buggers."

Weston smiled, nervously. "My cousin, King Marco, wants to develop diplomatic ties to Infernus."

"Ain't interested," said Mucker.

"Please, sir, you don't understand!" stammered Weston. "Trust me, we're not looking for more territories, or to set-up a military post here. Trade, you understand . . . Free and legal trade, between you and the Sovereign State of Embrey!"

"I haul goods into Sykes 'bout four times a year," said Mucker. "Five, if the winds and enemy navies don't stop me. I'll getcha back to Embrey, in exchange for your hard work and sweat on one o' my boats."

"Aren't you at least willing to open up a dialog between Embrey and Infernus?" gulped Weston.

"No," said Mucker. He eyeballed the little tattooed boy, with them other kid hostages. "How'd he get all them scribbles on 'em?"

"I don't know," said Weston. "He's an orphan, and a stowaway. He scrounges for food in New Merieko."

Mucker never said so, but he felt kind of sorry for the little tattooed boy. Part of him even wanted to care for him, with his sad, sensitive eyes and awkward nature. "Looks feeble enough," said Mucker, acting tough to hide his true feelings. "Can't he talk?"

"I've never once heard him speak," said Weston.

"Well?" growled Mucker, to the tattooed boy. "Talk! You gotta mouth, ain'tcha? A name? By-god, boy! Talk!"

The tattooed answered by booting Mucker's shin.

Mucker answered by lifting the tattooed boy up by his gullet. "I'll carve this rascal a mouth, right across the windpipe! Think he can get away with kicking me, an' ..."

"Paransky!" the tattooed boy said, not so much afraid of Mucker as he was defiant. "The name's Paransky, sport!"

"Paransky?" mumbled Mucker, not sure whether to slap the tattooed boy's face off, or laugh at his own expense. "Kinda name is that?"

"Mine!" said Paransky, daring Mucker to whomp on him.

"Well, if you decide not to kick me nomore, I'll fix you a plate o' grub, soon as we get into town," said Mucker. "Might even roll you a smoke. Savvy?"

Paransky smiled real big.

"I'm also here on a more ... personal business," said Weston, hesitantly. "King Marco had a brother living in Branell. The two haven't spoken in years, due to the Border War."

"So?" questioned Mucker.

"Years ago, during a failed peace talk between Embrey and Branell, Marco's brother Prince Terence defected, relocated to northern Branell, and assumed the role of a Branellian lord."

"What's that gotta do with me?" asked Mucker, impatiently.

"With you, nothing."

"Then get to the point!"

"Terence died about a year ago, last September if I recall," said Weston.

"Terence and his first wife, named Shelley, separated some time ago, but not before she gave birth to a son."

"And?" asked Malachi, more interested in this tale than Mucker or Nikolai.

"Shelley and her son went on a long sea voyage," said Weston. "Our spy network states that they came here, to Infernus."

"Yer point?" asked Mucker, tiredly.

"Shelley passed away, a few weeks after she got here," said Weston. "The boy was adopted by a Leader of the Brotherhood of Faith Church. A man by the name of . . . Rey, I believe."

Mucker never said nothing, but just kind of gawked at Weston.

"The boy is to inherit a large parcel of land, and a considerable fortune, in northern Branell," continued Weston. "I'm here to take him to the continent with me. Although a state of war exists between Embrey and Branell, King Marco has assured the boy's safe passage to the border."

"What's the boy's name?" asked Mucker, already sensing the answer.

Weston smiled real big and excited. "The person I'm looking for is named Kentworth . . . Jeremiah Kentworth."

"Jeremy Kentworth?" gasped Mucker, as Malachi and Nikolai looked on in shock and disbelief. "You sure? Jeremy? Our Jeremy?"

Cody was jolted from his chair. First from the mention of Leader Rey, then by the name Kentworth in the manuscript.

There was also a loud, chaotic racket from outside. A woman's screams, along with profanity, shattered the stillness of the night. Wild-eyed, Cody jumped up and glanced through the window, where drops of rain splattered against the pane of glass.

Shrieks drowned out the vulgar rants of a low, husky voice. Disruptions were common in Merieko. The nearby streets were lined with taverns, billiard parlors, and brothels.

Nearly a minute after this ruckus started, it escalated as a female's cries grew more erratic, and an angry voice echoed throughout the cramped, cluttered boulevards of Merieko.

Cody dashed downstairs, sprinted through the store with its variety of merchandise lining the walls, and cautiously went outdoors.

Across the street from KENTWORTH'S was the worst fight Cody had ever saw.

At the entrance of an adjacent alley, a man crumbled to the ground, grasping his belly which had been punctured by a knife. Blood mixed with rainwater, streaming through the gutters. Meanwhile, a half-dozen men beat and kicked another guy in the wet cobblestone street. A lewd woman stared at the injured man, who rolled himself into a ball. The woman knelt to examine the injured man, as his assailant was throttled within an inch of his life.

A witness from across the street caught sight of Cody, standing at KENTWORTH'S doorway. Briefly, Cody and the witness traded glances.

Due to the rain and darkness of night, Cody found it difficult to make *out the witness's scraggly features, scarred face, and crooked nose.*

The witness stepped toward Cody. "Whadda ya think yer starin' at?" he growled, waving a blackjack at Cody.

Cody backed into the store, slammed the door, and hastily locked it.

The noise and insanity of the commotion rattled his nerves. Bloodshed was routine in Merieko, and Cody thought best not to get involved in it.

Cody leaned against the door, took a deep breath, and gradually calmed down. Rarely did he feel safe in Merieko to begin with! Now that he was alone, he felt even more endangered and vulnerable. He wondered if it wouldn't be better to leave the store, and find another place to live. He had friends and relatives . . . many friends and relatives in Merieko. He knew that his cousin Hilary wanted to take him in, yet dreaded thoughts of dealing with her husband, Franklin.

Merieko was home, all right. It was also a city of vice, crime, and corruption.

Cody cursed Leader Rey for leaving him. He cursed his father for dying. He cursed himself for staying in a neighborhood with random acts of brutality.

The sounds of the commotion from outside frightened Cody. He wanted to get shy of Merieko altogether . . . that very night, if possible! But that wasn't possible, and Cody knew it. As long as no one broke into the store and assaulted him, he'd be fine. It was best to keep to himself from now on, and not poke his nose into trouble.

Present in Cody's mind, away from the mayhem found in the muddy streets of Merieko, was the manuscript . . .

The mention of Leader Rey, a tattooed boy named Paransky, and the name 'Kentworth' had aroused Cody's attention. Still, he couldn't help but to doubt the story's truth and validity.

C'mon, Cody! . . . .

Winged men?

As peace officers arrived to break up the fight, Cody went upstairs, poured himself another glass of cider, sat down, and returned to his reading.

* * * * *

On a bald ridge above the village of Persis, a young abarbeaus ate a ground squirrel. He then lazed in the early-morning sun, relaxing a spell to digest his meal.

Little did the abarbeaus know that the squirrel was his last meal. Little did he know that it was just a few seconds from getting dead.

Abarbeauses was probably the meanest, nastiest critters on Infernus. Grown-up ones stood around four to five feet tall, from the snout to the tip of its tails. They was a bright red color, with a furry mane around its neck, face, and spine. They was like a cross between an ape, and a breed of ornery wild cat. They ran around the more uncivilized parts of the island. While they ate berries and other bushes, they ate meat more than anything. They didn't care where the meat come from, whether it come from a squirrel, a deer, a bird, a winged man, or people.

Because people was one of the abarbeaus' favorite foods, people had to be real careful in the backwoods. The whole island swarmed with the mangy, flea-bitten critters, and nothing was safe from them. They was known to traipse into colonies and snatch up little kids, old folks, little winged kids and old winged folks. It was smart never to traipse around after dark, when the abarbeaus was their thickest and meanest. Bad enough if you got one abarbeaus after you. You get a whole horde of them after you, might as well write yourself off as ate. Abarbeaus was pack hunters, meaner and nastier in groups, when no one or nothing stood a chance against them.

Cody chuckled at the last few paragraphs. He was now convinced that the manuscript was nothing more than a tall tale.

The young abarbeaus got done eating the ground squirrel, and sat in the warm morning sun feeling all happy. The critter licked its paws and lips, sitting around like it didn't have a problem in the world, not knowing it was about to get killed by a girl named Ericha, and her best friend ever, Jeremy Kentworth.

Ericha was something of a princess, in the people world of Infernus, on account that she was related to King Auric IV. She never acted like no princess. She never wanted to. She wore moccasin shoes, buckskin shirts, and loincloths, just like Jeremy.

Buckskin shirts and loincloths?

Jeremy and Ericha bathed naked together in the lakes, rivers, and streams of Infernus. They never thought nothing of it. Everyone else thought too much of it. Most folks never liked it, because they figured that Jeremy and Ericha was either doing nasty stuff, or thinking awful strong about it. Ericha was fifteen, and a real pretty redhead with long hair hanging below her shoulders. Her legs was long and tanned, a bit sinewy but still fitting her girly frame.

Jeremy Kentworth might have been a Branellian, but never figured himself as such. He never had notions of heading east to the Farlands, and called Infernus home. He was a little bit older than Ericha, though she was just a little taller. He was kind of a tough little cuss, not too tall nor muscled up, but no one folks cared to tangle with. He wore long-sleeved shirts that he made himself from critter hides, and loincloths. He hated wearing people clothes because they was too hot and scratchy, and made him sweat on hot days. He was kind of good looking, but rough around the edges. His brown hair covered up his ears. He had fair but tanned skin, from being outside most of the time. He got taught by Rey how to read and write. He knew how to do both kind of good, but just never liked either all that much.

Jeremy cut and tanned his own clothes from the critters he killed. By what he learned from the smarter Brown Winged Men, they used the brains from dead critters to keep the hides from going bad, then made shirts, shoes, and loin-cloths out of them.

According to old laws and customs of the Brown Winged Men, the tribal medicine man Nikolai blessed Jeremy and Ericha's shirts, in the thought that they'd protect wearers from any and all danger, be it from weapons or from critters.

Jeremy and Ericha went out hunting for deer, birds, or squirrels who lived below the timberline of Mount Auric. They killed critters to help feed the people of Persis. On that day, they went after an abarbeaus.

Nobody ate abarbeaus much, because their meat was too tough, greasy, and stinky. People killed abarbeaus mainly for bragging rights. Them who killed an abarbeaus was held in high regard. Jeremy had already killed a bunch of them, to fix more clothes that he wore for pride and protection. He also made a wee bit of spending money from Farlanders who was too lazy or scared to kill abarbeauses themselves.

Jeremy and Ericha come across the young abarbeaus who had just ate the squirrel. Jeremy wanted to kill the abarbeaus, but Ericha never killed one yet, and had a hankering to. They snuck up on the young abarbeaus and hid behind a log, in a shaded spot under some trees. They never made a sound as they smiled in anticipation of killing the abarbeaus, who just ate the squirrel.

Ericha took careful aim with a long bow and, at almost thirty yards away, fired an arrow at the young abarbeaus. The arrow hit the abarbeaus under the right shoulder.

Squalling like it was getting killed, which it was, the young abarbeaus up and tried crawling off. Instead, it crawled around helplessly in the clearing, making a high-pitched racket spooky enough to make a man's skin crawl.

"Shoot it again, Ericha!" laughed Jeremy, all excited and happy. "Shoot it, before it gets away!"

Ericha took a second shot, and this time nailed the abarbeaus' chest.

As the abarbeaus went into a real bad case of the death-flops, Jeremy and Ericha run up to slit its throat with the knives hanging from leather belts, cinched above their loincloths. Blood spilled from the abarbeaus' neck as its eyes glazed over, glassy, still, and dead.

Jeremy slapped Ericha's back and congratulated her.

Ericha slugged Jeremy's shoulder, mighty pleased that she finally killed her first abarbeaus.

Jeremy gave Ericha the eye, because she whomped him. "Whatcha do that, for?" he asked.

"Because I killed it, and you didn't!" laughed Ericha, like a mean little school girl.

"You killed it," hollered Jeremy, "'cause I letcha!"

"And now you're jealous!" cheered Ericha, gawking at the dead abarbeaus. She was surprised that she actually killed one! Carefully, she ran her hands over its still-warm body. "Aren't we supposed to chant some kind of heathen prayer over it?"

"Yeah," said Jeremy. "But I forgot the words and besides, it's mainly in winged man gibberish, and I can't talk it. Let's just be glad that you killed it, before it killed you. Okay?" He gave Ericha an ornery grin. "Whoever kills one has to cut the heart out and take a bite."

Ericha gave Jeremy an ornery look back, though she sure wasn't grinning. "That . . . that's what I'm supposed to do, ain't it?" she groaned.

The whole idea of chomping into critter hearts was more of a Green Winged Man tradition. Ericha didn't want to give Jeremy the satisfaction of refusing to perform this ritual. On the other hand, she didn't care to get sick over it, neither. "You're just jealous because you didn't kill it!" she claimed.

"Reckon yer gonna rub that one in my face, ain'tcha?" groaned Jeremy.

"No," laughed Ericha. "I'll take a bite, then rub it in your face!"

"So? You gonna do it, or not?"

Ericha looked at the dead abarbeaus, as it slowly bled out. She reluctantly cut into the ribcage, then split it open. A foul odor and steam crept out of the chest cavity. Ericha turned away to keep from barfing, as Jeremy looked on in awe and anticipation. It never bothered him to skin out or gut critters in the field. It got to be second nature, to him. Though Ericha had done her share of skinning and gutting, she was a newcomer to it, compared to Jeremy.

Ericha held her breath as she reached in to cut out the heart, which until a few minutes ago had pumped blood through the critter's body.

The warm, stinky heart completely filled Ericha's right hand. Blood dripped through her fingers, where it spilled onto her shirt, loincloth, and bare legs. Jeremy smiled, not only proud of Ericha, but also envious of her. Ericha finally killed her first abarbeaus, something most people never dreamed of! Still, Ericha had to bite into the heart, an obligation Jeremy wouldn't let her live down. "Well?" he asked. "You gonna do it, or not?"

Ericha eyeballed the heart with disgust and disdain, disguised as celebration. She knew what she had to do! The idea was both appealing and appalling. Ericha wanted to wipe the grin from Jeremy's face. She even regretted killing the poor critter.

Slowly, Ericha lifted the heart up to her mouth to take a bite when, in the corner of her eye, she spotted a big bad male abarbeaus walking toward her.

And then another . . .

And then another . . .

Jeremy and Ericha heard a fierce racket from behind. They turned to see a fourth abarbeaus, and then a fifth, coming toward them. In no time, they was surrounded.

Ericha was scared, but not Jeremy. For some weird reason, he thought the whole thing was funny.

Them five abarbeaus didn't like what happened to the younger one. They looked Jeremy and Ericha over, up one way and down the other, growling and snarling as they circled in.

It weren't no secret how Ericha felt, right about now. She wanted to forget all about what she done to the young abarbeaus, and high-tail it out of there. People run fast, if they got to. Abarbeaus run faster, when they get real hungry and know they'll catch what they're after.

The average person would've just figured himself as good as dead now, before whining, crying, and pleading for his life. Abarbeaus can't talk people talk and don't care what sorts of dirty names comes out of someone's mouth. Whining, crying, and pleading don't do no good. Neither does cussing. When abarbeaus get after someone, that someone takes off a running. Running only prolongs the misery of it all. Chances are they'll still get ate.

Jeremy knew he was in a fix. Still, he couldn't help but to laugh. Getting ate by them critters wasn't no laughing matter, but Jeremy never figured he'd get ate. He always figured he'd get out of scrapes and was more worried about Ericha than about himself.

One of the abarbeaus stepped forward to pounce on Jeremy.

"Jeremy!" squalled Ericha, throwing the young abarbeaus' heart at the one fixing to pounce on her best friend.

The heart splattered all over the abarbeaus' face. Not only did this divert the critter, it also provoked it.

The abarbeaus leaped into the air, as mad as a wet hornet. Jeremy was ready with a fancy Embrian sword, which hung from a sheath on his leather belt.

The attacking abarbeaus got impaled on the sword. The force of this attack sent Jeremy flying.

Jeremy landed next to Ericha's feet, giggling like the numskull that he was. Ericha got up, ready to take a stand against them other four critters.

The abarbeaus flip-flopped on the ground, with Jeremy's sword still in it. Jeremy hopped to his feet, wanting to fetch the sword from the neared-dead abarbeaus.

Ericha waved her knife at the other critters, baring her teeth to scare them off. It didn't help none, as Jeremy stood next to her, giggling like an idiot.

"You moron!" screeched Ericha. "Don't just stand there! Do something!"

Ericha's loud talk only made Jeremy laugh that much louder.

"It ain't funny!" screamed Ericha. "Do something!"

Before Jeremy could do anything, one of them other abarbeauses jumped at him.

Jeremy ducked, as the abarbeaus leaped over him and accidentally landed smack-dab into the middle of another one. That only made the two abarbeauses mad at each other. The next thing you knew they got into a wild, hair-raising fight. Grass, gravel, loose dirt, and fir flew everywhere.

In a crazy, blurry haze, the fighting abarbeauses stirred up a mess, and at one point landed in the middle of the young abarbeaus which Ericha just killed. A third one got all riled up over this commotion and jumped in the middle of the other two's fight. This gave Jeremy and Ericha time to skedaddle on out of there. It didn't keep that last one from chasing after them.

Jeremy and Ericha ran through the deep, dark woods, as one of the critters chased after them.

As them other three got done with their stupid fight, two joined in the chase, leaving one too hurt to do much of anything.

Jeremy and Ericha could run real fast. Problem was, the abarbeaus could run faster. And were.

Things only got worse when Jeremy and Ericha reached the banks of the Persis River.

At first, Jeremy and Ericha thought about fording the river. Abarbeaus can't swim and hate water. But the river was too swift and too deep. Any thoughts of crossing might lead to drowning, and if a person drowns they're just as dead as if they got ate.

With that in mind, Jeremy whipped out his bow and arrows to do battle with the critters.

With their backs to the rushing currents and rapids of the Persis River, Jeremy and Ericha knelt down to take aim into the deep, dark woods, waiting for them critters to jump out and pounce at them. Jeremy stopped laughing. He was more scared of getting hurt, than getting ate. He plain refused to get ate by something that mean and mangy. He was still more scared of something bad happening to Ericha, because she was a girl and prone to getting ate by mean, mangy things.

A few seconds later, one of the abarbeaus ran toward Jeremy and Ericha. He didn't count on Jeremy shooting him with an arrow to the throat. That stopped the first abarbeaus, who spent the last few seconds of life flip-flopping real bad, until he flip-flopped into the river and floated off someplace.

Then a second abarbeaus pounced out of the woods and went after Ericha. She shot that one in the leg with an arrow, but didn't kill it. She finished it off by whipping out her knife and sticking it, over and over and over, in the guts. It went into a bad case of the flip-flops, and died on the riverbank but not in the river.

Just when Ericha got done killing the second abarbeaus, the third one attacked her. Jeremy saw what was going to happen, and jumped in front of Ericha to save her. It didn't work none though, because that third abarbeaus pounced on both Jeremy and Ericha.

Jeremy, Ericha, and the third abarbeaus flew into the deep water of the Persis River.

The abarbeaus tried eating Ericha. Jeremy kept sticking his knife into the abarbeaus, to keep it from killing her. As the abarbeaus tried biting Ericha's neck, she also tried to keep her head above water. The abarbeaus made it difficult. Even as Jeremy was killing it, the abarbeaus kept biting at Ericha's neck. This whole time, Jeremy, Ericha, and one abarbeaus got swept down the currents, banging into rocks and going through some of the swiftest, deepest, fastest waters of the Persis River. If the abarbeaus didn't get Jeremy and Ericha, then the river just might.

The third abarbeaus was as good as dead. It forgot about trying to kill Ericha, and tried killing Jeremy instead. It threw its last ounce of strength into its extended claws, reached out, and tore a big hole into Jeremy's shirt. Never broke no skin, though.

Jeremy sank his knife into the critter's throat. The river turned a bright red as blood spilled out of the critter's neck.

The critter took its last breath, then either drowned or bled to death. It didn't matter. Dead was dead, as the critter floated off, never to try and eat Jeremy and Ericha no more.

Jeremy and Ericha weren't dead yet. They risked drowning, if they didn't mash their heads against the big rocks they banged into. Jeremy grabbed onto Ericha's waist, and kept her head above water, while doing the same for his.

Jeremy and Ericha went over a small, bumpy waterfall, where the river flowed into a shallow lake.

Jeremy threw Ericha into his arms and packed her to a stony bank. They dried off and did an inventory of what was left of their weapons. One of their bows ended up missing, as did all of their arrows. Jeremy's sword was still stuck in one of the dead abarbeauses, way upon the hill.

Jeremy and Ericha killed a horde of the fierce critters but had nothing to show for it. The buckskin shirts they wore, made to protect them from all harm, was torn up. They still had their knives, which was something. More important, they had their lives, which was even better.

The biggest problem come from Ericha's loincloth, or a lack of it. Her loincloth got swept off someplace, either from the swift currents and rapids of the Persis River, or during her fight with the abarbeaus.

The missing loincloth wasn't that big a deal with Jeremy. He'd seen Ericha in the raw before, during them times they swam and bathed naked together in lakes, rivers, and streams around Persis. No matter. Ericha spent much of the time covering her crotch with both hands.

"What'cha getting so worked up about?" snickered Jeremy, a twinkle in his eyes.

"How am I supposed to get home?" whined Ericha. "If my father or little brother catches me like this . . ."

"Wrap that around your legs and privates," said Jeremy, giving his damp shirt to Ericha.

"I suppose you're getting a thrill, looking at me," moped Ericha.

"Aw, I dunno," said Jeremy, kind of blushing. "I'd rather fetch me a drink and a smoke from Mucker and Seely."

"That stuff's going to kill you."

"Booze and smokes? If anything kills me, it's not having 'em! Gonna bum me a smoke off of Mucker, soon as we get to town. A shot of whiskey might even do the trick!"

"Leader Rey says he's going to murder you if you don't stop smoking and drinking!" warned Ericha. "He hates it when you sneak it into the church!"

Jeremy didn't say nothing. He just stood there with a silly grin. Deep down inside, he wondered if Leader Rey wasn't right . . . about a lot of things.

Jeremy saw himself as the son of two fathers, Rey and Mucker. He looked up to Mucker for his survival skills and Devil-May-Care attitude. He respected Rey's unselfishness and devotion to the Almighty Big Man, living way up there in the sky.

"Admit it, Jeremy," flirted Ericha, smiling as she rubbed her warm hand over his bare chest. "You like me . . . Don't you?"

"Well, yeah," he said, all nervous-like. There weren't no arguing Ericha's beauty, and Jeremy wondered what it'd be like, with her. He never done it before, and had conflicting feelings for Ericha. On one hand, she was a buddy, and kind of like a sister. Who'd ever dream of doing it with a buddy, or a sister?

On the other hand, Ericha wasn't his sister . . .

"Kinda . . . I mean, you know . . . as a friend," stuttered Jeremy. His face got real red, from embarrassment. "C'mon . . . You know what I mean! What's the big deal?"

"You want me!" laughed Ericha, as a joke and as a taunt. "Don't you?"

"Ericha . . ."

"You want me, Jeremy!" giggled Ericha, slapping him on the butt. "Admit it! You want me . . . Don't you?"

Jeremy's throat tightened. He was at a loss of words and couldn't come up with anything smart-alecky to say. He wasn't ready, willing, nor able to speak his mind on that particular subject. When they was little kids, the last thing Jeremy wanted to do was to do it with anybody, and surely not with Ericha!

But now things had changed, and somehow he just wasn't able to look at her quite the same way, as he did when they was youngsters.

In the back of his mind, Jeremy wondered if maybe, just maybe, he did want to do it with Ericha . . .

* * * * *

As Nikolai and Malachi flew off to New Merieko, Mucker took Weston and the kid hostages to Persis.

It was a real slow walk, where Mucker kept telling everybody not to get too close to the trees. Abarbeaus and other critters could attack at any moment.

They was especially prone to attack when little kids was around. Mucker and Weston knew they wasn't enough to save everyone, if critters got the hankering to make off with any or even all of them kid hostages. Mucker told everybody to keep their mouths shut, and don't make no sounds, or do nothing to attract critters.

Not wanting to get killed and ate like the little Kuschan kid, everyone did what Mucker told them. The exception was Fernandez, who whined and carried on like he was being killed, which he wasn't.

Weston and the kid hostages entered the city of Persis. They was amazed to see people working, playing, and talking with Brown Winged Men. The two groups somehow managed to form a society, and got along real good.

Persis was made up of shacks and old bamboo huts, lining a narrow draw where the Persis River ran through. The streets and walkways was put together, with no plan in mind. Everything just kind of zig-zagged along houses and buildings, with hardly no straight lines.

Mucker, Weston, and the kid hostages got to town to see people and winged men fish, harvest their gardens, and chat amongst themselves. In the skies above, winged boys and winged girls played a game kind of like rugby using a ball made out of an abarbeaus' gut.

Near the northern end of town a big waterfall loomed over the city, where it drained into the river.

Being a diplomat, Weston laid eyes on lots of places and things. What he saw in Persis was beyond belief. Some of the kid hostages was fascinated by nice winged men and women, who came to greet them like friends and neighbors. Fernandez was scared by all them nice critters, and had to be dragged along by Weston.

Mucker got fed-up with Fernandez. Kid hostage or not, he thought awful strong about feeding him to the critters.

Paransky, the little tattooed boy, clung onto Mucker's hand. Already, he took a liking to the old pirate, the way a youngster hangs onto his mommy and daddy. That was all right. Mucker had already taken a liking to Paransky.

The farther Fernandez got into town, the worse scared he got. His hands clutched tight to Weston's arm, where he nearly cut off the circulation. The scaredy-cat figured he had entered the depths of Hell, where there weren't no return. "I don't like it here!" he squalled, his eyes darting everywhere. The more scared he got, the more his eyes darted around, horrified at them things he figured was monsters. But they wasn't monsters. They was just Brown Winged Men, being nice to Weston and them kid hostages. That's what Brown Winged Men do.

Be nice to people who ain't always nice to them.

By now most of the kid hostages was taken in by the Brown's grace and charm. A few of the Browns was taking Weston and the kid hostages to the Brotherhood of Faith Church, which sat next to a bald field overlooking Persis, under the waterfall at the northern part of town.

Like all kids, the Brown Winged Kids meeted and greeted the kid hostages. Pretty quick it seemed like everyone was the best of friends. Weston was amazed to see how well the kid hostages adapted to this new place. It was like he had stepped into a dreamland, a place where fantasy was real, and the real world got left behind. Weston was reluctant to get all friendly with the winged men. He never saw nothing like them before, and his grown-up mind collided with what he was seeing with his own eyes. Infernus wasn't like no place that could come out of a jaded, cynical world.

Weston wondered if maybe he had stepped into a fairy tale. Was he a little scared? Who wouldn't be, after first running into critters like that! He wasn't near as scared as Fernandez. Nothing could be that scared, except that poor little Kuschan boy who was so scared that he run off into the woods and got ate.

Fernandez was so scared, so much so that Weston wouldn't dare to be. Them kid hostages looked up to Weston, so he had to be brave, even when he wasn't. Weston had to make it look like he wasn't at all scared. He tried to show Fernandez that it didn't make no sense to be scared. He tried to show Fernandez that the Brown Winged Men wasn't monsters at all, or if they was, they was nice monsters and not interested in eating people, like what the Green Winged Men did.

Somewhere in the middle of town, Fernandez dropped to the ground, rolled himself in a ball, then screeched like a little bitty baby. He was so scared that Weston thought he'd go plum off his head.

While this shameful display was kind of amusing to a few onlookers, it upset others so much that Weston had to kneel down and try to calm Fernandez.

"Get up!" urged Weston, all embarrassed because of the show that Fernandez put on in front of everybody. "Come on, get up! You're making a fool of yourself!"

"They're going to kill us!" cried Fernandez. "I want to go home, to my mom and dad . . ."

"Fernandez," whispered Weston. "Don't you think if they were going to kill us, they would've done it by now?"

"I want to go home!" bawled Fernandez, as a bunch of people and even a few winged men giggled at him.

"Get a hold of yourself!" shouted Weston, as he shook Fernandez. "We're safe here! . . . Can't you see? These . . . things aren't going to hurt us . . ."

There was no convincing Fernandez of nothing. He figured he already set foot in the infernal regions, where there wasn't no escaping. He wanted to run on home to his mommy and daddy, in New Merieko. By now, he figured the whole island was Hell, including where his folks was. All of Infernus was Hell on Earth, and he was as good as dead.

Fernandez threw himself into a panic and made a run for it. He tore loose from Weston and sprinted like a wild man toward the woods.

Weston might have been all patient and understanding with Fernandez, but not Mucker.

Before Fernandez got a few steps away from them other kid hostages, Mucker applied five hard knuckles to his face.

Fernandez' eyes fluttered a time or two before he dropped to the ground, knocked out cold.

Mucker was right pleased with himself, for what he done to Fernandez. Most everyone approved with cheers, uproarious laughter, and applause.

Weston knelt to check on Fernandez, making sure Mucker never killed him. Luckily, Fernandez wasn't killed, though he might have felt like it when he'd come to. Weston gave Mucker an angry look, but never said nothing. He didn't want Mucker giving him that same treatment he gave Fernandez.

Leader Rey showed up to check on the situation. He was real tall and handsome, with a black beard and hair. He was an ordained minister in the Brotherhood Church, and cared about everybody on Infernus, people and winged men both. The church had no real stronghold on Infernus before Rey got there. He built a good, solid church building near the bottom of the waterfall. The church had a regular attendance of people and winged men. Even them who wasn't church members got helped out by Rey.

Years before, Rey was on a ship heading toward Kokashima, but ended up on Infernus instead.

Some didn't like the Brotherhood Church. They included Mucker, who hated all religions. He liked being a good heathen. Nikolai and the Browns' head honcho, Chief Lorenzo, didn't like it neither. They thought that Rey was an okay guy who did a lot of good things. What they didn't like that Malachi, who was destined to be head winged man honcho, was a member of Rey's church.

The first thing Leader Rey done was to check on Fernandez. While he didn't care much for what Mucker had done, at least now the scaredy-cat couldn't run off.

Before Weston even got to know Rey, he felt safe and secure with him. Rey was one of the nicest men on Infernus, and had an odd way of making people feel real safe, even when they wasn't. Somehow, Weston just knew that he and them kid hostages was in good hands with Rey. It wasn't just the Brotherhood robe that Rey had on, but the way he carried himself. Weston figured he'd grow to like Rey, and that they'd become the best of friends.

"I'm Weston," he said, shaking Rey's hands. "I was sent by King Marco of Embrey to develop diplomatic ties with the island of Infernus."

"I'm Leader Rey," the other guy said, looking at Fernandez with a bit of curiosity and concern. Rey knew that Fernandez was a church member, by the school clothes the kid had on. "What happened?" he asked, examining the big black bump on Fernandez' noggin.

Weston pointed at Mucker, who smiled real big for whomping Fernandez over the head.

"Why?" asked Rey, none-too-happy with Mucker.

Mucker just snickered. It was this kind of snickering which made Rey real mad.

"This boy is afraid of . . . them," said Weston, motioning at a few winged men, women, and kids. "He was making good an escape, when . . ." Once again, Weston pointed at Mucker.

Rey thought better than to get into it with Mucker. First of all, Mucker didn't like getting told off by no one in the church, nor did he care about what Rey had to say about anything. Rey never killed no one. Mucker had, lots of times. The last person Rey wanted to fight was Mucker. Chances were, Mucker probably never killed no Leaders in the Brotherhood of Faith Church. Chances were, he thought about it a time or two.

Rey placed Fernandez in his arms and lifted him off the ground. "Follow me to the fellowship hall," he said. "Our volunteers will prepare meals for you. Has anyone notified these childrens' family that they're here?"

"Two . . . winged men flew to New Merieko," said Weston, slowly getting used to the idea of being in a place populated by men with wings.

"Winged men?" asked Rey.

"Nik and Malachi," said Mucker, all-too-happy to be rid of Weston and them kid hostages. Without saying another word, he began taking Paransky to his shack, on the outskirts of town.

"Where are you leading him?"asked Rey, perplexed by the little boy with them tattoos all over him.

"He's stayin' with me an' Seely," grunted Mucker, riled up because Rey had the gall to question him about it.

"But we've got food and medicine set up for everyone!" explained Rey, scared of the example Mucker and Seely might set for Paransky.

"He's comin' with me," growled Mucker. He gave Rey the eye, the same eye he gave people before killing them.

"But why?" asked Rey, wanting to help out Paransky as much as he did them other kid hostages.

"You wanna know what's gonna happen, soon as them nosey church women git a look at this kid?" asked Mucker. "Tell ya what's gonna happen. All them old busy-bodies are gonna look at them markings scrawled over his body. They ain't gonna see what's underneath all them tattoos, just the tattoos!"

"No they won't!" argued Rey.

"Sure about that?" hollered Mucker. "I know how church women are! How all you church people are! Yer gonna up an' start frettin' about them. Yer gonna decide he's just some pitiful soul, destined and doomed to the bad place when he croaks. So then you'll have to bend over backwards to save 'em, whether he needs savin' or not! The boy's better off with me, me an' Seely. We ain't gonna judge him none."

"So he'll end up like you and Seely?" scolded Rey. "He'll stay with you, and then what? He'll be hooked on booze and tobacco, that's what! Then he may be condemned, but not by me, or by all those other 'church people', but by a higher authority!"

"What?" barked Mucker.

"What will his parents have to say about him staying with you?" asked Rey.

"Sir," Weston cut in, watching his words real careful around Mucker. "The boy's an orphan."

"That's another reason he should come live with me at the church," said Rey, looking Paransky up one side, and down the other.

"And I say he's stayin' with me!" yelled Mucker. "Better to die a good heathen, than to live a high an' mighty, holier'n thou, pious hypocrite!"

Rey sighed. It didn't do no good to haggle with the likes of Mucker. Once Mucker got his mind all made up, it was done made up, and that was the end of it. All haggling did was to either make people mad, or make them dead.

"Suit yourself," whispered Rey, still searching for a means to fetch Paransky away from Mucker. "One more thing, though, before you leave."

Mucker snarled at Rey, but didn't say nothing.

"I'll be over to check up on the child, from time to time," said Rey, not in a mean sort of way, but to show that he cared.

Mucker and Rey glared at each other. Weston and the kid hostages was scared that them two men might fight. To them who knew Rey and Mucker, this was just their way of agreeing to disagreeing. In an odd sort of way, they had a lot of respect for each other, but never said so. Both men loved Infernus and the Brown Winged Men in their own way, and served the island the best way they knew how. Both men needed to be on Infernus, to keep the place going and making it a fine place to live.

Mucker made a low, grunting noise, turned around, and walked off with Paransky.

Weston sighed. He was glad that Mucker helped him and the kid hostages out. He wasn't sad to see the old coot leave.

"Come with me," Rey said to Weston and the kid hostages. "We've got meals prepared at the fellowship hall. If anyone needs medical attention, I'm also a physician." Rey smiled. "Mostly, I doctor pigs and horses. I can also mend broken arms and wings, if need be."

"Leader Rey," said Weston, strolling through the narrow, winding lanes of Persis. "We lost one of the children on the beach . . . A small Kuschan youngster. He got frightened when he saw the winged men with that Mucker character. Before anyone stopped him, he sprinted away, and . . ."

"And that's the last you saw of him," said Rey.

"But not the last we heard of him. A few seconds later, he heard a blood-curdling scream and then . . . nothing."

"Sorry to hear about it," said Rey, twisting his face up the way he did when he got worked up about something. He made that face a lot, more than he wanted to. "I'd better arrange to speak with the child's parents."

Weston took a good look around. He figured that Persis was probably the strangest, prettiest place he'd ever seen in his whole entire life. He'd been everywhere in the world, but nowhere quite like this!

Persis was surrounded by an evergreen forest, with more trees than you can shake a stick at, and lots of plants everywhere. The rolling foothills was covered by thick, green grass and shrubs. Narrow bridges spanning the river linked the small village. Most everybody smiled as they met the kid hostages. The villagers, both people and winged men, was curious of the newcomers, but not cold, mean, or judgmental. The only mean ones in Persis were a few pirates and ruffians who hung around the taverns and houses of ill-repute, on the southern part of town.

Weston couldn't help but to marvel at the sight of Brown Winged Men flying overhead. Nor could he ignore the big waterfall overlooking the church, or the snow-covered peak of Mount Auric, way up in the distance. Weston sucked in mouthfuls of air, his thoughts trapped in a state of disbelief, intimidation, and awe.

"You're a diplomat from . . . where?" asked Rey.

"Embrey," said Weston. "I was sent by my cousin, King Marco, to establish diplomacy and trade with Infernus."

"I'm sure that pleases Mucker," said Rey, sarcastically.

Weston laughed. "I'd rather not go there. I was afraid he might kill me, if for no other reason than because he doesn't like my looks."

"His bark is worse than his bite. I try not to get on his bad side. I usually fail."

"I noticed," said Weston, and he and Rey had a good laugh.

"So, you're King Marco's cousin?" asked Rey, stepping past a Brown Winged Woman cradling a newborn baby in her arms.

"Yes, sir."

"I was born in Embrey," said Rey. "I haven't been back in a while. So, tell me . . . what sort of man is King Marco?"

"A tough customer, not one to bicker with or to challenge in a duel. But I know few men who love Embrey as much as he does."

"And how are things with the Border War?"

"The same," said Weston. "Men die, nothing is resolved. We still hate the Branellians, and they still hate us. Little has changed for the better."

"I see . . ."

"I also have a cousin here on Infernus." Weston cleared his throat. "I have yet to meet him."

"Oh?"

"A young man of about . . . . I'm guessing fifteen or sixteen. Maybe you know him. His name's Jeremiah Kentworth."

One could hear a pin drop, as Rey almost dropped Fernandez onto the cold, hard ground. His face got all serious and pale-looking.

"Did I? . . . Did I say something wrong?" asked Weston, nervously.

"It depends," said Rey. His voice lacked emotion, though his eyes practically drilled holes through Weston. "Exactly . . . what business do you have with my son Jeremy? . . ."

Seely used to be a good-looking guy, when he hung out in the pubs and bawdy houses near the docks of Merieko, on the Agronian coast. He was around six feet tall, and a lanky fellow with a slightly hooked nose, chiseled jaw, and bright blue eyes. He had long red hair which won the attention of innocent young damsels and sporting ladies.

Even with the toil and sweat of earning a meager wage in the shipyards, Seely never lost his taste for booze or women.

Almost every night, Seely went to bed with some gal, which he spoiled in drinks and gifts. Almost every morning, he woke up broke, so broke he struggled to pay the rent in the flea-bitten flats and shanties he called home.

Seely had hardly nothing bad to say about no one, and smiled most all of the time. He was real close friends with McClusky and Mucker, and soon joined their band of ruffians and buccaneers.

That was a long time ago.

Seely was younger than both McClusky and Mucker. Sure didn't look like it now. Once them three guys got shipwrecked on Infernus, Seely's thirst for hooch got the better of him. His young appearance and optimistic outlook gave way to that of the scraggly-faced, yellow-hided, bloodshot eyes of a drunk. His red hair turned white, his skin wrinkled, eyes and chin sagged, and mouth drooled. He carried hardly no weight over his body because he didn't eat nothing. Just drank. Drank from morning till night. He never worked, but relied on them who, for whatever stupid reason, felt sorry for him. He never changed his clothes, and stunk real bad. He never harmed a fly and was mostly nice to people kids and Brown Winged Kids, simply because it was in his nature to be that way.

Them few times he was sober enough to think such thoughts, Seely wondered why Mucker put up with him.

McClusky refused to have any more dealings with Seely, after he turned into a filthy, stinking drunk. McClusky never drank hardly nothing, never enough to get falling down drunk. He never liked Seely much in the first place. McClusky figured that Seely was too nice to join the pirate trade. After one particular nasty brawl, Seely flat refused to carve up a little cabin boy on an enemy ship, and instead tried to spare his life. The boozing got real bad, after another pirate cut out the cabin boy's heart, right smack in front of Seely.

Seely never got over that, and every night went to bed haunted by memories of watching the cabin boy die.

It come as no surprise how Seely reacted when Mucker showed up with a strange-looking little kid with tattoos scrawled all over his body.

"Boy!" cheered Seely, taking Paransky by the hand and setting him at the rickedy little table, in the middle of the rickedy little shack. "Come on, boy, make yerself at home!" he laughed, happy to have a guest in his house. He was probably too drunk to notice all them tattoos. He almost slapped Paransky's back hard enough to knock all them tattoos off. "What do they call ya, boy? Do ya got a name?"

"Paransky!" the boy shouted, giving Seely the eye.

Seely gave Paransky a strange look, though it didn't wipe the happy smile off his face. "Paransky?" he asked, wondering if he heard the name right.

"Yeah, Paransky!" the boy hollered again. "You got a problem with that, sport?"

"I ain't got a problem with it, iffen you ain't got a problem with it!" laughed Seely. He put a shot glass in front of Paransky, then filled it with cheap brandy.

When Paransky saw what Seely had done, he smiled real happy-like.

"Where ya been hiding yerself, Muck?" asked Seely, filling his old buddy's glass with the same elixir he gave Paransky.

"Aw, off savin' a mess o' Farlander runts from themselves," groaned Mucker, sitting down at the table next to Paransky. "Only one worth savin' was this one here. Worse one was this cowardly Agronian in a Brotherhood school get-up, and some blasted Embrian diplomat pokin' his nose around here. Oughta kill 'em all, that's what I oughta do. Kill 'em all! Kill the Agronian coward and the Embrian diplomat and be done with it!"

Seely just smiled, too drunk to understand what Mucker said.

"Bad enough with the Roderick Dundee pokin' around here," griped Mucker. He downed his brandy in one swallow, then refilled his glass. "Now we gotta deal with more stupid colonists in New Merieko, McClusky tryna make deals with them Kuschan dogs onboard the Matyushenko, and now a stinkin' Embrian diplomat! Tell ya what, Seely, we oughta form a small army, and kill 'em all!" Mucker gawked at Paransky. "All except this one. Only good one in the whole rotten lot!"

Seely laughed, and blew hot, stinking air in Paransky's face. "Well, if he's the only good one in the whole lot, I'd hate to see what them others look like!"

"What do you know about it?" hollered Mucker, almost knocking the table over. He though strongly about wrapping his hands around Seely's throat. "You wasn't there when I saved this boy and them other ones from that loud-mouth McCoy and them other scallywags, so shut up about it!"

Seely kept one eye on Mucker. Mucker never took a swing on Seely, though he threatened to on more than ten occasions. For the time being, Seely also kept his mouth shut, though he kept right on smiling. It was both funny and scary to get ol' Mucker all riled up.

"Don't go listenin' to that mouthy old soak," said Mucker. He rolled out a smoke and give it to Paransky. He couldn't help but to take a liking to the little tattooed boy. Mucker knew nothing of where Paransky come from, who his folks were, how he got all them tattoos all over him, or how he ever ended up on Infernus. All Mucker knew is that Paransky needed a good roof over his head, good grub in his stomach, and a good bed at night. All Paransky was liable to get at the church was a mess of hooey and sermonizing. Hellfire, brimstone, and endless lectures on the evils of drinking, smoking, and loose women.

To hell with that! There weren't that many pleasures in life to begin with. Life consisted of hard work for very little reward, constant worries and fears of tomorrow, lack of appreciation from them who don't know nothing, broken bones, broken teeth, gray hairs, toothaches, and death. Maybe booze, smokes, and loose women was the only pleasures a man could expect in a cruel world, and in a short, cruel life. Who was Rey or anybody else to deny a poor little tattooed boy a little happiness and enjoyment in this pathetic existence?

Mucker fetched a small stick lying next to a potbellied stove, ignited with a few burning coals, and lit Paransky's smoke. Paransky smiled real big as he took a drag. Already, Paransky was real happy in Mucker's company, the sort of happiness he'd never get with them churchy old hypocrites up at the church.

"How do ya like it?" asked Mucker, putting his hand on Paransky's shoulder.

"Like it? I love it!" cheered Paransky. He took a drink from his brandy, then coughed and gagged from its burning, overpowering effects.

Judging by the boy's eyes, the sandy color of his hair, and the shape of his face, Mucker wondered what Paransky would've looked like, without all them tattoos. Chances were, Paransky would've probably been kind of good-looking, but a bit twerpy.

Well, a lot of little kids are twerps! It's only about the time they get to be eleven or twelve when they're suddenly endowed with the ability to know everything!

Mucker was struck with a sense of loss and melancholy. The same ship that brung Paransky also brung more Farlanders, with their idiotic Farlander attitudes and ways. Mucker felt crushed by forces he couldn't control or even fight off, either with his wits or bare fists.

The village of Persis had a good thing going. There wasn't too many lazy folks there. Them who was lazy either got over it, or they starved. People and winged men worked for themselves, and they worked for each other. Folks planted their own gardens, cut firewood, hunted, and fished. Some folks planted one kind of fruits and vegetables, others grew others. People got by through barter. If one fellow had too much corn and wanted watermelons instead, he'd make an honest, fair trade. Or maybe he worked for it. If a guy killed a buck and figured he couldn't preserve all of it for his own use, he'd share it with another guy who helped drag it out of the mountains, skinned it, then gutted it. Fair trade.

Some of them Farlanders was lazy. They left their homelands because they didn't like what was going on back there. And what did they bring with them to Infernus? The same troubles they swore to leave behind! Infernus didn't need their politics, didn't need their religions, and sure didn't need new people with new ideas on how other folks should live! Them Farlanders come here to start over. Mucker had to change his way of living, and adapted to Infernus' hard, rugged lifestyle. Them new colonists in New Merieko had to do the same, or they'd starve to death, or get ate. Get ate by abarbeaus or some other critter, or get ate by the Green Winged Men.

If them new colonists wanted to make it, they had to tighten their belts, man-up, and get tough in a tough land! And if they couldn't hack it, then by-god they'd best get their butts back to the Farlands, and leave the people and winged men here alone!

To make things worse, McClusky and Lorenzo wanted to make trade deals with them filthy, vodka-drinking Kuschans!

And to make things worse, some Embrian diplomat wanted the same thing for his country, along with looking to fetch Jeremy Kentworth up and haul him off to the Farlands!

Never seemed that long ago when Jeremy first showed up at Infernus, still a little bitty baby, sucking on his mama's tit. Well, Jeremy's ma died, and pretty soon just about everyone in town took turns taking care of him . . . be it Leader Rey, or the church's Brown Winged cook and wash-woman Evelyn. Sometimes Jeremy's caretaker was the so-called King of Infernus, a descendant of King Auric named Errol who was also Ericha's daddy. Even Mucker had a hand in looking after Jeremy.

Together, the villagers of Persis turned Jeremy into a fairly reliable, self-sufficient character, who wasn't scared of hard work, or getting blood or dirt on his clothes and hands. There wasn't much of nothing that Jeremy was scared of, sometimes at his own peril. Jeremy didn't have enough sense to be scared, a matter which scared them who loved and cared about him.

And now some nosey Embrian wanted to fetch Jeremy back to the Farlands, and make a swell out of him!

"What's the matter with you, Seely?" growled Mucker. "Paransky's hungry, and here you up and let the fire almost go out. That tater soup we had last night's cold!"

"Too hot to go building too much of a fire, this early in the day," snickered Seely.

"If you git any lazier, yer gonna forget how to breath," said Mucker, running outside to grab sticks of wood from the wood pile. "A lazier man I'll never know than you!"

Seely just smiled real big but didn't say nothing.

"And I a'ready know yer too lazy to sift the dead flies outa the grub," mumbled Mucker, chucking a few sticks of wood into the stove. With an old rusty ladle, he stirred last night's tater soup to fix for himself, Seely, and Paransky.

Mucker was always in a bad mood. Having to go save Weston and them kid hostages never helped none. Well, them kid hostages was one thing. They was kids, and couldn't help but be dragged the thousands of miles from the Farlands to Infernus by their idiot parents, who didn't know what they got themselves into.

Mucker should've just killed Weston, first for being an Embrian diplomat, then for thinking he was going to fetch up Jeremy and haul him off to the Farlands and make a swell out of him.

Times change. Mucker never aimed to.

Times usually change for the worst. They bring in new people with their new ideas, new ways of doing things, and new plans for the people and winged men of Infernus. Mucker figured he never had to put up with it, and neither did nobody else!

Times change, usually for the worst. Mucker never did like it, never would like it, and saw no call to put up with it!

Infernus had its own way of doing things. It was a good way, for them willing to abide by it. Mucker saw no good in the Roderick Dundee poking around, and never saw no good in them vodka-drinkers onboard the Matyushenko.

And now there was some Embrian diplomat, trying to set up a trade and diplomacy with the island of Infernus, along with fetch someone up that Mucker knew and loved like a son.

There was some things worth fighting for, and Infernus was one of them! So was Jeremy Kentworth. And, by-god, if the situation called for fighting, then by-god Mucker was going to fight for what he knew was right!

* * * * *

Fernandez woke up in a nice, warm bed in a backroom of the Brotherhood Church in Persis. At first he didn't know where he was.

The scaredy-cat thought maybe he was back home in Agron, in the safe, secure confines of his old house, someplace in Merieko. Somehow, though, the room just never looked like his old bedroom. The sights, sounds, and smells around him weren't quite right, neither.

At that point, Fernandez didn't know where he was at. All he knew is that he was all alone in a back bedroom in the Brotherhood Church, wearing his stupid Brotherhood school uniform.

Fernandez tried to get up, but the pain of this big black bump on his noggin kept him from it. That blow Mucker gave him still hurt like sin. It was kind of a hot day in Persis, and Fernandez felt all sticky and sweaty. He wanted his overprotective mommy to fix him a bath. He looked all around, and couldn't recognize nothing in that back bedroom, or even the bed he was in.

Fernandez slowly sat up. His scrawny legs was weak and wobbly. He was too disoriented and confused to be scared. All he knew is that he didn't know where he was, as his mind thought back to them moments before Mucker whomped him with five hard knuckles.

It seemed more like a foggy nightmare, than reality. Fernandez couldn't make no sense out of a dream involving pirates, winged men, or little Kuschan boys running off and getting ate. Who in their right mind could believe such stories? None of it could be real!

Could it?

One thing for certain was that Fernandez missed his mommy and daddy and had no idea where he was. As usual, fear started to get the best of him. When in doubt, he called on his mommy for answers, as well as assurances and loving arms. "Mom," he whimpered, his eyes getting all big and anxious and scared. "Mom? . . . Dad? . . . Mom? . . ."

It wasn't his mom who walked in there, but an old winged woman who worked at the church, named Evelyn.

Evelyn was a Brown Winged Woman who was kind of pretty, if you could call winged women pretty. She was one of the nicer winged people, and never had nothing bad to say about no one. She was real close friends with Leader Rey, and one of the first winged converts to the Brotherhood Church soon after he got to Infernus. She always had a real big smile on her face, and did when she walked into Fernandez's bedroom with a plateful of grub she fixed in the fellowship hall.

When Fernandez saw Evelyn, he realized the business with the pirates and the winged men and the ate-up Kuschan boy wasn't no nightmare, but the truth. He commenced to yelling, hollering, and screeching like he was being killed, which he wasn't. He wasn't in his old bedroom in Merieko, his mommy and daddy wasn't nowhere to be seen, and all of a sudden this nice monster up and went into the room, with a plateful of grub.

"Get away from me!" screamed Fernandez. He hopped to the corner of the bed and threw his arms out to save himself from a nice monster named Evelyn. "Go away!"

When Evelyn saw Fernandez get scared, she didn't know what to say or do. She was told by Rey to fetch Fernandez some grub, which she did in her usual way, all kindly and warm-hearted and smiling all the time. She never expected Fernandez to let out with a howl loud enough to wake the dead.

Once Fernandez laid eyes on Evelyn, he figured he was as good as killed, and there wasn't anything left to do but to scream, like the end had come.

Evelyn sat the plate of grub on a table and tried to calm Fernandez down by giving him a hug, which only made things worse.

Fernandez figured that Evelyn wasn't trying to comfort him, but instead trying to eat him, and he carried on as such. By now, he screamed like he never screamed before, and caught the attention and ire of everybody in Persis.

Evelyn backed off in confusion. She was only trying to be nice, and not hurt Fernandez. Pretty soon, Fernandez rolled himself in a ball and cried like a little bitty baby.

"What's going on in here?" hollered Rey, dashing into the bedroom like all Hell had broke loose. "What's all the commotion?"

"I only did what you told me," said Evelyn, not knowing why Fernandez was so scared. "I filled his dish, came in here, and he . . ."

"It's my fault," sighed Rey. "Let me take care of this, Evelyn."

"But, sir . . ."

"Let me take care of this," repeated Rey. "Go to the fellowship hall, and I'll see what I can do."

Evelyn felt real bad because she scared Fernandez and didn't mean to.

"Son," said Rey, taking Fernandez's hand. "Nothing's going to hurt you."

Fernandez peeked through his fingers to see Rey sitting next to him on the bed.

"Listen to me," said Rey. "Nothing's going to hurt you."

"Who are? . . ." stuttered Fernandez. "Who are? . . . Who are? . . ."

"My name's Rey. I'm a Leader in the Brotherhood of Faith."

Fernandez didn't say nothing, though he wasn't screaming no more.

"What school did you attend in Agron?" asked Rey.

"What?" asked Fernandez, wanting to trust Rey but still too scared to calm all the way down.

"I notice that you're a student in one of our schools," said Rey, still thinking the scaredy-cat might weird out and try running off. "Was it in Merieko?"

Fernandez still didn't say nothing, but just kind of nodded YES.

"Lord Daniel's Academy?" asked Rey.

Fernandez nodded YES.

"Speak up," urged Rey.

"Yes, sir," whispered Fernandez.

"Pardon me, I didn't hear. Say again?"

"Yes, sir."

"I see," said Rey. "Is Anthony still Head Leader there?"

Fernandez never said nothing.

"Listen to me," repeated Rey, tiredly. "Is Anthony still Head Leader at? . . ."

"He . . . he died . . ."

"Died?" gasped Rey.

"A . . . a few years ago," mumbled Fernandez.

"I'm so sorry to hear it. So, who's Head Leader now?"

"Leader . . . Leader Thor."

"Thor?" groaned Rey. "Why him?"

Fernandez shrugged.

"What's your name?" asked Rey.

"Huh?"

"Your name, son? What's your name?"

"Fer . . . Fernandez," he said, ashamed because he was scared of nice winged monsters who somehow talked good Embrian. "My folks call me 'Nandy'."

"'Nandy'?"

"Yes, sir."

"Think I'll just stick with 'Fernandez'." Rey smiled. "So, do you live in New Merieko now?"

"Yes . . . Yes, sir."

"Malachi was sent to New Merieko to bring your parents here. They should be arriving any moment."

"What was that thing who came in here?" asked Fernandez, nervously.

"'Thing'? What 'thing'?"

"That devil who tried to eat me!"

"That was no devil!" explained Rey. "It was my housekeeper Evelyn!"

"Housekeeper?"

"Yes, my houskeeper. She came to bring you a bite of lunch."

"That thing's your housekeeper?" gasped Fernandez.

"Evelyn's my housekeeper," sighed Rey. "She's also my friend."

Fernandez bugged his eyes out.

"Evelyn's a Brown Winged Woman, not a 'thing'," said Rey. "There's no need for you to be afraid of them, Fernandez. Not at all."

"They're monsters!" squalled Fernandez, believing Rey was also some kind of monster, conjured up as a person.

"They're not monsters!" shouted Rey.

"What? . . . What do you call them?" screamed Fernandez.

"They're only monsters if your narrow mind and weak heart tells you so!" yelled Rey, wanting to slap some sense into Fernandez. "Infernus is home to them, the same as it's my home! Your home, too!"

Fernandez figured he had no choice but to make a run for it. He would have too, had Rey not grabbed hold of him, and threw him back onto the bed.

Fernandez was determined to get past the monster conjured like a Brotherhood Leader, past all them monsters outside, and even past all the people who wasn't monsters, but still in cahoots with them. He was determined to run off into the woods where he'd get ate.

But first he had to get past the monster conjured like a Brotherhood Leader . . .

Rey had his fill of Fernandez, and whomped the scaredy-cat as hard as he could with the back of his hand.

Fernandez flew back, where he hit his head against the log wall of the bedroom. Knocked a little silly, he had no choice but to sit still as Rey set him straight.

"The Brown Winged Men, or for that matter the Green Winged Men, have lived on this island far longer than humans," said Rey. He looked straight into Fernandez' eyes, wanting to get through to the scaredy-cat before whomping him again. "Infernus is their home, they were born here. You and I are visitors to the island, not them. I often wonder if we're the 'monsters' here, not the winged men."

"But they're not people!" hollered Fernandez. "They don't look anything like us!"

"Yes, but most are my friends."

"Friends? How can you be friends with them?"

"Why shouldn't I be friends with them?" asked Rey.

"They're animals! They're not people. They're nothing like us!"

"They probably feel the same way about you." Rey took a real deep breath. "Honestly, I find them more friendlier than people, and certainly more friendlier than most Farlanders."

"Yevgrav is dead because of your friends!"

"Yevgrav?" Rey stopped for a second or two. "Was he the Kuschan boy who? . . ."

"He tried running away from your 'friends' . . . and so did I!"

"Yes, and he's dead! You'd be dead too, had you followed him!"

"Those things killed him!"

"It wasn't 'those things' who killed him!" hollered Rey. "It was his fear! Just like your fear's killing you! I'm very sorry about Yevgrav, but you must believe me when I say that you're safe here. You and the other children who were rescued from the pirates."

Fernandez didn't say nothing, though he didn't feel at all safe.

"I've lived here on Infernus for many years," said Rey, hoping Fernandez calmed down so neither he nor Mucker would whomp on him some more. "Trust me, I feel much safer here than I did in Sykes, or even on Agron." Rey smiled. "Now, do us a big favor by eating the food Evelyn brought you."

"I don't want to," moped Fernandez, rubbing the big black bump Mucker give him.

"Why not?"

Fernandez never said nothing.

"Why not?" repeated Rey, getting madder by the minute.

"It might be . . . poisoned," said Fernandez.

"It's not poisoned!"

"How do I know that?" whimpered Fernandez.

Rey dipped the spoon into the beet soup the church ladies fixed up in cafeteria and took a bite. "It's not poisoned," he said, his impatience with the scaredy-cat at the breaking point. "Now, are you going to eat this wonderful food we prepared for you, or must I shove it down your throat? Or must I get a couple of pug-uglies in here, to tie you up in chains until we can find a way to get you off this island?"

Fernandez covered up his face under both hands and cried like a little bitty baby.

Rey threw his arms up in the air, about to give up on Fernandez and keep him under lock and key until someone returned him to Agron. Fernandez never had no business at all on Infernus. It was a mistake for him and his folks to move there in the first place.

What frightened Rey was what Fernandez might say about Infernus, when and if he ever got back home to Agron. Few people knew about Infernus, and even fewer still knew anything about the winged men. Most everybody on Infernus wished to keep it that way. This is where Rey and Mucker was in total agreement. If somebody like Fernandez started blabbing about the critters he saw on Infernus, pray nobody believed him!

Rey gritted his teeth. "Are you going to be a good boy, or do we lock you in here, and prevent you from hurting yourself and others?"

"I can't help it!" bawled Fernandez. "I've never been this scared in my life!"

"Why?" pressed Rey. "Why?"

"I'm afraid of the winged men!" sobbed Fernandez, scared and ashamed of being scared.

"What for? I lived here since about the time you were born, and believe me when I say that neither of us have anything to be afraid of."

"But they scare me!"

"Why?"

"They . . . they . . . . They don't look like something God created!"

Rey rolled his eyes back and sighed. "So who did create them?"

"The Devil!" hollered Fernandez. "This place is Hell, and the winged men are of the Devil!"

Malachi stood outside of the bedroom. He overheard Fernandez' spiel about the Devil, and got real reluctant to go inside. When he finally did, Fernandez threw a mighty big fit. "Get him out of here!" he screeched, bugging his eyes out.

Fernandez' mommy and daddy also went into the bedroom. His daddy, Paolo, was a former indentured servant from Agron who went to Infernus to seek his fortune and start over. He was a short, little fat guy with a bald head, a bushy mustache, and a nervous twitch. Frida, the scaredy-cat's mommy, was a short fat lady with gray hair.

When Paolo and Frida saw their 'little Nandy' on the bed, they sighed in relief.

Fernandez forgot all about the monsters and ran up to give his folks a big hug. Once the family hugged and kissed and did what families do when they reunite, Rey and Malachi went outside.

The warm temperatures and sunlight was exactly what Rey and Malachi needed. Outside, a few people and winged men wondered about all the hollering and screaming going on. Rey didn't say nothing, and only hoped the scaredy-cat figured things out on his own.

As Rey enjoyed the sights and sounds of Persis in early-autumn, Malachi was awful quiet. He was never one to say much of anything anyway, but now he wasn't saying much of nothing. Rey couldn't help but to take notice. He also couldn't help but to ask about it.

Malachi didn't say much at first.

Rey wanted to know what was eating at Malachi, and wanted to know now.

"I believe in God," said Malachi. "I believe in the same God as you, Leader Rey, and want so badly to live by His principles."

"I know that, Malachi," said Rey. "I wish that everyone in the congregation was as loyal to the faith as you."

Malachi looked off in the distance, staring at nothing in particular.

"You overheard what that idiot kid was carrying on about," figured Rey.

Malachi got real worked up about Fernandez' screaming and squalling about winged men being of the Devil, and other stupid stuff. Finally, he come right out and said so. "Are the winged men the children of God, or children to that winged demon Soraq?"

"I've known you since you were a child," said Rey. "You might be many things, Malachi. Trust me, you're no demon."

"But if God created men in His own image, then who created the winged men? I mean . . ." Malachi stopped for a second. "Can God ever accept us into His kingdom? Or are we doomed because we aren't people, but something truly demonic?"

Rey and Malachi crossed a small footbridge over the Persis River, where a couple of people kids and winged kids was fishing. Both smiled and greeted the kids, as they went on their way. In no time, they found themselves in the low foothills overlooking the village, where they was free to speak their minds.

"Are all humans evil?" Rey asked Malachi.

"Of course not," answered Malachi.

"So, if all humans are not evil, then how can anyone claim that all winged men are evil?"

Malachi got all teary-eyed, like he was about to break down and cry.

"You and I even know a few Green Winged Men who love their families," said Rey. "They work hard to protect their children, and do what they can to keep themselves, and Infernus, out of danger."

Malachi frowned. He agreed with much of what Rey said. On the other hand, he never did like the Green Winged Men, and never saw no call to trust or respect them. His father, Lorenzo, urged a ceasefire between the two tribes. Malachi wanted to keep the Greens in their place, as far away from the people and Brown Winged Men of Persis. The Greens' hunger for people meat gave all winged men a bad reputation. A lot of Farlanders figured that all winged men ate people meat, and wouldn't believe nothing else.

"Some day soon, Malachi, you'll take a leadership role over the Brown Winged Men," said Rey. "But it's not just the Browns who will come to you for help and advice. You'll also have to keep the peace between the Browns, the Greens, the human population, and those Farlanders who come to the island. As we both know, some Farlanders come here with less than honorable intentions."

"Yes sir, I know," said Malachi, sick with fears that he may not always do the right thing. He kind of blamed himself, not only for what happened to that little Kuschan boy who got ate, but Fernandez' hatred of winged men. He had a tough job ahead of him, and prayed he was up to it.

Did God answer the prayers of the winged men, the same as for the prayers of people?

"Some of the people in our church oppose the winged men," said Malachi, his voice all high-pitched and sad. "I do believe in God, and do that which pleases Him! I hope you understand that, Leader Rey!"

"I do," said Rey. "You let me worry about those in the congregation who oppose your involvement in the church. They're my responsibility. As long as I live and breath, you and your winged men Brothers are wanted and welcome to Sunday meetings."

* * * * *

Cody lifted his head from the manuscript, and noted a chilly dampness in the apartment. It had stopped raining outside, yet there was a chance for the season's first frost by morning.

Cody stretched his back, placed the manuscript onto the chair, and tossed a couple of sticks into the wood stove. He returned to the table and, to his dismay, found a dead fly in his apple cider.

Cody cussed under his breath, opened the nearest window, and dumped his apple cider to the filthy alley, below. A cool, wet breeze entered the room. Cody closed the window, then filled his glass with fresh cider.

Cody sat at the table, yawned, and looked up at a cuckoo clock. It was midnight, and exhaustion had gotten the best of him. He wished to stay with the manuscript. Regrettably, he had to open KENTWORTH'S at eight in the morning.

Cody had known Leader Rey since he was a toddler. Rey made annual trips to Merieko to visit JT, and often stayed for several days before returning home . . .

Wherever home was for him . . .

In the discussions Cody sat in on between JT and Rey, there was never any mention of winged men. NEVER! Chances were, the manuscript was a tall tale, featuring actual people alongside fictional ones, in an imaginary setting.

So, just who did write the manuscript?

And why?

Cody yawned as he peeked outside to a full moon. Most of the clouds had disappeared. It'd be cold by morning. Cody dreaded winter. Merieko received little snow, yet the north winds and rain dampened the spirits of those living in that wild, reckless city.

Cody went to a window and looked down into the street. The fight which took place earlier had long ended. There were no signs or evidence of violence, whatsoever. A few men stood outside of a tavern, chatting quietly, as a prostitute stood on a street corner, soliciting for johns.

Despite the moment's tranquility, the image of one man dying in the street, while another one threatened him, would haunt Cody for days and weeks to come.

More than anything, Cody wished that Rey would come back to stay!

Cody fetched a quilt, sat in an easy chair next to an oil lamp, and resumed his interest in the manuscript. He was tired and weak, and his eyelids

*grew heavy. Still, he was enthralled and entertained by the story found in an
old, fragile document . . .*

* * * * *

Weston sat at a table in the church dining room, eating potatoes, carrots,
smoked meat, and a side dish he couldn't recognize. Despite the scary events of
the day, him and all them kid hostages was real hungry. Weston sat in one corner
of the open-air facility, which lacked walls on all sides. A number of poles held up
a thatch roof. A breeze blew cool damp air from the waterfall. The dining room
was packed. People, winged men, and volunteers showed up to meet and greet
Weston and them kid hostages.

By now, the kid hostages' folks showed up to come get them. The one exception was the folks of the poor little Kuschan boy who run off and got ate. They
met up with Leader Rey and a Kuschan pastor named Yevgeny, to make funeral
arrangements and pray the Kuschan boy into Heaven, Paradise, or some other
wonderful place dead people head off to when they die.

Fernandez and his folks sat at the next table to Weston, and had lunch.
Although he was real glad to be with his mommy and daddy, the scaredy-cat was
still scared. This, even as the critter/monsters went out of their way to be nice to
him.

Paolo, the scaredy-cat's daddy, acted real nice to the winged men and
people of Persis. Frida, his wife, wasn't nice at all. Although she wasn't that
scared of the winged men, she thought she was better than they was.

Weston quietly watched Paolo trying to get his family to be nice to their
hosts. Frida never went out of her way to be kind nor friendly to critters that,
in her mind, were just animals who could talk real good Embrian. Fernandez
weirded out whenever a winged man, winged woman, or winged kid got within
ten feet of him.

Weston was agreeable to the winged men. He was, after all, a representa-
tive of Embrey and smiled a lot, even when he had no reason to. Mucker's rude
behavior, along with the Green Winged Men and a big brute named McClusky,
told him to walk softly and watch what he said. Embrey had recently signed a
peace agreement with Kusch, soon after a military blunder in a Kuschan stink-
hole known as Anumun. The last thing Weston wanted was to start another war
with the Kuschans on Infernus. The Kuschan warship Matyushenko off the coast
told Weston never to cause no trouble.

Weston wondered if Mucker was right about some things. Certain Farlanders got no business being on Infernus. A few colonists had done real good on

the island. As well, some people was born on Infernus, and never once set foot in the Farlands.

Could be they was better off not heading to the Farlands? . . .

Could be that Infernus was better off without a lot of the Farlanders . . . including Weston?

It never took no genius to see that some Farlanders never took kindly to winged men, including Frida and her scaredy-cat son, Fernandez.

And what about the Kuschans, who's religion said that a Devil named Soraq come in the form of a winged demon?

Weston sort of calmed down, after a long, hard day. He still felt awful sorry for that little Kuschan boy who run off and got ate. It was a misunderstanding that caused a bad tragedy.

How many more misunderstandings could Weston expect?

Some redheaded, freckle-faced kid of twelve walked into the dining room. The kid was slightly taller than normal boys his age. He was dressed in a faded green, fluffy-looking shirt, tights, and well-polished, shiny boots. He carried himself like a regular swell, and wore a cocky grin like he owned the joint. The kid had a high-opinion of himself, which was totally undeserved.

Weston threw a wool napkin on his dish, stood up, and introduced himself to the swell.

"I'm Prince Ari," the swell said, shaking Weston's hand in a tight, firm grip.

"Prince Ari?" asked Weston, making sure he heard the swell right.

"My father is King Errol," said Ari. "King Errol of Infernus."

"Forgive me, Prince Ari," snickered Weston. "I was under the impression that the top dog here, if I may use the expression, is Chief Lorenzo."

"Well, there . . . there's two kings of Infernus!" claimed Ari, getting all offended. "Lorenzo and my father. They both hold reign over Infernus."

"I see," said Weston, chuckling to himself for offending the swell.

"My ancestor is King Auric IV," said Ari. "He came here a long time ago, and civilized Infernus."

"I see," repeated Weston.

"My real name's Auric, after my esteemed ancestor, but . . ." Ari stopped. "Are you the Embrian diplomat?"

"Well, I am an Embrian. I was sent by my emperor, and my cousin, King Marco, to make agreements with Infernus, based upon mutual respect, trust, and cooperation. I'd like to speak with your father, King Errol of Infernus."

"I'd take you to him, but he's cutting firewood."

"Cutting firewood?" smirked Weston. "That doesn't sound like a kingly occupation to me."

Ari just shrugged.

"I'd also like to speak to Lorenzo," said Weston. "As well as a young man staying here. Maybe you know him. His name's Jeremiah Kentworth."

"Jeremy Kentworth?" groaned Ari.

"Well, if that's what you call him."

"That's his name . . . Jeremy Kentworth." Ari shook his head in dismay. "What can you possibly want with him?"

"My business with Jeremiah Kentworth is confidential. I take it, Prince Ari, that you don't like him."

Ari frowned.

"And where may I find Jeremiah Kentworth?" asked Weston.

"Where you'll find my pea-witted sister, Ericha."

Weston laughed. "And where may I find Princess Ericha, the Pea-Witted?"

Ari gave Weston the stink eye.

"Forgive me." Weston cleared his throat. "Where may I find Ericha?"

"Who knows? Her and Jeremy run around the island, dressed like a couple of bloody savages, like they haven't got any brains in their heads. Ericha is a princess, at least she's supposed to be. And here she goes prancing around the forest with Jeremy, wearing animal skins and these skimpy underpants things."

"Jeremiah, too?" snickered Weston.

"He started it, Mr. Weston!"

"I'm here to speak with the leadership of Infernus," said Weston, scratching his head. "That includes your father, Prince Ari . . . naturally. While I'm here, I must also see my cousin, Jeremiah Kentworth."

"He's your cousin?"

"Yes, though I have yet to be introduce myself to him. When may I expect him back?"

"Who cares?" groaned Ari. "He lives here in the church with Evelyn and Leader Rey. He's likely to be found with an old scallywag named John Mucker, and a drunken ne'er-do-well, Seely."

"I've already met John Mucker. I need to meet with your father, King Errol . . . and Chief Lorenzo, too! Can you give them that message, Prince Ari?"

"As you wish," said Ari, smiling real big as he bowed, then rushed outside.

"Errol's no more a king than I am," whispered Evelyn, serving grub to the kid hostages and their folks.

"Oh?" asked Weston.

"It's true that Errol and his children are descendants of King Auric," said Evelyn. "The title's ceremonial now, nothing more. It means very little, and amounts to even less. By the time Ari takes the throne, it'll mean nothing."

"I see."

"I wish Ari could see. As far as I can tell, he's just another kid. He sure thinks he's something."

"That he does," agreed Weston. "What are your thoughts about Jeremiah Kentworth?"

"Jeremy?" Evelyn smiled. "He's an odd sort, but very likable. Not an ornery bone in his body, our Jeremy. He takes risks most of us wouldn't dream of!"

"Really? In what way?"

"By hunting the most dangerous animals on the island. Leader Rey fears it'll be Jeremy's undoing. So do I."

"I see," said Weston, rubbing his chin.

"What business do you have with Jeremy, Mr. Weston?"

"I'm not at liberty to say. No offense, I hope."

"None taken," laughed Evelyn.

"If you don't mind, I'd like to take a walk around Persis, and gain my bearings."

"Did you enjoy the meal?"

"Yes, very much so," said Weston. "Thank you for your hospitality. Thank you very much."

"Anything more I can do for you, Mr. Weston?"

"No, thank you," said Weston, eager to get going. "I'll be back for supper. For now, I must chat alone with my cousin . . ." Weston grinned. "Jeremy Kentworth."

* * * * *

Cody placed the manuscript on his lap, then closed his eyes for a breather.

When he reopened them, the bright morning sunlight peeked through a window. Sounds of frantic pecking on KENTWORTH'S door shook him from a peaceful slumber. Confusion ruled over Cody, until he realized that he had dozed off.

Cody dropped the manuscript to the floor, as pages scattered in all directions. The chill of early daytime crept into the room, as a once-roaring fire in the stove had died out.

Cody glanced at the cuckoo clock. It was ten past eight. The store should've opened by now!

The knocking at the door grew increasingly louder.

Cody tossed the quilt to one side. He ran downstairs, then passed the shelves filled with liquor, tobacco, and dried goods. An icy chill in the store room reminded Cody that he failed his duties to the business.

The first customers of the day were usually homeless vagrants, wishing to exchange splitting firewood for a cheap bottle of port. Not today. Now, it was Cody's cousin Hilary, delivering a tray filled with warm pastries.

Cody smiled graciously and let Hilary in.

Sitting outside on a wagon was Franklin, Hilary's husband. The man disapproved of the vice bought, bartered, and sold at KENTWORTH'S. Even then, Cody invited Franklin inside, out of the cold. Franklin preferred to wait on the wagon. He resented having to hitch up two horses, travel across town, and "subsidize a misguided lad, who lacked all hopes of salvation."

Since JT's death, Hilary begged Cody to close the store and come live with her and Franklin. Cody was tempted by the offer. Regrettably, Franklin's constant badgering and hostile behavior would undermine such an arrangement.

Hilary placed the pastries on the counter, as Cody hurried to light the room and build a fire. While Hilary fretted and moped over Cody, Franklin remained perched on the wagon, waiting impatiently for his wife to come along. A few drunks arrived to earn their daily bottle, by performing meager chores for Cody.

Hilary kissed her 'Darling Little Cody' on the cheek, got in the wagon, and suffered Franklin's harassment.

Cody ate some of the pastries Hilary made for him, then resigned himself to ten hours of work. The routine involved long periods of boredom, with spurts when business picked up. He pasted a grin on his face, dealt with the occasional rude customer, and somehow got through it.

By six in the evening, he locked the door, blew out the lanterns, and retreated upstairs to his sanctuary. He finished the pastries, then chugged them down with a glass of apple cider.

Regularly, Cody had spells of melancholy and sadness. He had no choice but to suffer the humiliation of uncontrolled tears and sobbing. This was followed by grudging acceptance of JT's passing. It was a pain best handled by time, while sucking it in and taking it like a man.

Cody took a deep breath, uttered a prayer, and gained the courage to push onward.

Cody stoked up the fire, then filled his glass with more cider. He sat at his favorite chair, and resumed the strange adventure scrolled in the aging manuscript . . .

Weston circled the village of Persis, and thought it was real pretty. The draw where the town sat was filled with tall, evergreen trees. Brush, bushes, and weeds kept their lush beauty, even in early autumn. The citizens of Persis, people and winged men alike, seemed real nice and cordial. Very few treated Weston as a stranger. The whole place was otherworldly, out of place, and out of reach for a man of experience, wisdom, and plain old common sense. Yet, there it was! The same Earth which held grand cities as Sykes, St. Alexandrov, Basisk, and Merieko also gave life to Persis.

As Weston headed toward the Brotherhood Church, he saw Leader Rey chatting privately with a young Kuschan couple. Weston frowned. The couple with Rey was the folks of the little Kuschan boy who got ate. As far as anyone could tell, the little Kuschan boy's body was never found. Figuring it was probably a barbeaus who got him, there wouldn't be nothing left.

Sitting with Rey and the Kuschan couple, at an outside table and bench, was a Kuschan pastor. Weston recognized him as Yevgeny, who traveled with him on the same boat to Infernus.

Weston didn't know whether to head toward the bench and table, where the two holy men talked words of comfort and joy to the Kuschan couple. There ain't much comfort and joy when a little kid gets ate, but that's exactly what Rey and Yevgeny was talking. As Rey was talking the comfort and joy, Yevgeny repeated it in Kuschan.

Yevgeny was twenty-five, and recently ordained in that silly Kuschan religion. He was a little guy, barely standing more than five feet tall. His eyes was kind of eagle-like, in their fierceness and determination. He had short black hair, an olive complexion, and a square, manly jaw. From a distance, he kind of looked more like a teenager, than a grown-up. Yevgeny talked real good Embrian, and had a high-pitched, pretty-sounding voice. He talked better Embrians than most Embrians! Weston learned that Yevgeny was educated in Sykes, not long after the war between Embrey ended. Yevgeny lived in the Kuschan village of Anumun when the Embrians invaded it. He still held a grudge over that whole mess.

Once in a while, Weston talked with Yevgeny during their trip to Infernus. Yevgeny was real high and mighty in the Kuschan religion. Maybe too high and mighty.

Weston kind of liked Yevgeny, but never quite trusted him.

Weston backed off and started to turn around when Rey motioned him to the bench. Weston hesitantly walked toward the bench, but kept his distance.

Rey, Yevgeny, and the Kuschan couple held hands to pray. Afterwards, the Kuschan couple walked off someplace, to cry their eyes out.

"Pleased to see you again," Yevgeny told Weston.

"The pleasure's all mine," said Weston, smiling as he sat down.

"I assume you two have met," said Rey.

"On our voyage here," said Weston. "I'm impressed with your mastery of Embrian, Pastor Yevgeny."

"I traveled to southern Embrey when I was fifteen," said Yevgeny. "I studied there at Lord Werner's Academy in Griffith, before attending the University of Sykes."

"Tell me, Pastor Yevgeny," said Rey. "What are your thoughts of our beloved Sykes?"

"It isn't St. Alexandrov," said Yevgeny, in a snooty sounding voice which didn't go unnoticed by Rey and Weston.

"So . . . what brings you to Infernus?" asked Rey, getting kind of mad but not saying so.

"There are Kuschans wishing to make their homes here," said Yevgeny. "It's my duty to accompany them, as their spiritual guide."

"What brings you personally to the island?" asked Weston.

Yevgeny didn't say nothing right at first. He just smiled in this weird, creepy-crawly sort of way, and made Rey and Weston nervous.

After almost a quarter of a minute, Yevgeny finally said, "The Kuschan child would still be alive, had that vile Mucker fellow not confronted the smugglers, without stupidly bringing those things with him."

"Are you referring to Malachi, and his brother Nikolai?" asked Rey, talking real carefully though he was getting real mad.

"It was the presence of those things," said Yevgeny, "which motivated

Yevgrav to run for his life . . . and regrettably to his death."

"Who told you that?" asked Weston, also getting mad.

"That Agronian boy, Fernandez," said Yevgeny. "I believe he's a member of the Brotherhood of Faith, Leader Rey."

"Pastor Yevgeny," said Rey, controlling his temper. "I can assure you that neither Malachi nor Nikolai acted maliciously, in their assistance of 'that vile Mucker fellow'."

"I'm partly to blame," said Weston. "I tried to stop Yevgrav. I was only able to stop Fernandez. It's me you should blame, not the winged men . . ."

"They're not human," said Yevgeny, "and shouldn't be afforded the same rights, respect, or considerations."

"It's simply my opinion, Pastor Yevgeny," said Rey. "If that's the way you feel, then why are you here?"

"Haven't I the right to express myself, openly, here in the wilderness?" asked Yevgeny, with a snotty grin.

"The 'wilderness'?" snapped Rey.

"That's what I said," spoke Yevgeny. "The wilderness."

"I admit that most of the island is unsettled, and uninhabited," said Rey. "The southern part of Infernus is unsuitable to be inhabited, as far as we humans are concerned. As for your arguments that wing men aren't 'human,' I won't dispute that. But some are my friends, and several attend my church, Pastor Yevgeny."

"But what about those things living in the . . . .darker regions of the peninsula?" asked Yevgeny.

"Are you referring to the Greens?" asked Rey.

Yevgeny nodded YES.

"I wouldn't go there," said Rey. "And I don't go there. I have spoken to a few Greens, those who speak Embrian. I've never set foot in their homes. I know better not to. They don't bother me, so I don't bother them."

"Forgive me if I've offended you," said Yevgeny. "I here am new, and I must assimilate myself . . . much the same way the small boy struggled to assimilate himself, before he entered Paradise."

"I've taken courses in world religions before entering the diplomatic corps," said Weston. "Your first impressions of the winged men are that of your god of evil. From what I've seen, the winged men are nothing like . . . well, nothing like Soraq."

"You're right, Mr. Weston," said Yevgeny. "My first thoughts of the winged men are that of Soraq."

"I'm sorry that the small boy came to that same conclusion," said Weston. "But, as far as I can tell, there's nothing evil or demonic about the Brown Winged Men. I don't think they're capable of hurting anyone."

"Truly?" asked Yevgeny, like he wanted to start a fight. "Just after a few hours upon meeting them? Are you sure we can trust them, Mr. Weston?"

"I can vouch for their character," said Rey, getting madder and madder at Yevgeny. "Why did you come to Infernus, if your opinion of the winged men is hostile?"

Yevgeny snickered.

"The winged men were on this island, long before I got here," said Rey, tiredly. He made this same spiel to the scaredy-cat Fernandez, and would say it to Yevgeny. "They've got more to fear from us as we do of them. The winged men are indigenous to Infernus. It's their land we tread upon, and I'm not about to step out of line and ruffle their feathers . . . if you get my drift."

"I'm a diplomat," said Weston. "While living and working in another country, I've learned to adapt to their culture, and way of life."

"Are you suggesting that we must abandon our own beliefs and lifestyles, anytime we venture away from home?" asked Yevgeny. "The Kuen would never tolerate that from me, and I cannot tolerate it from myself."

Rey sighed. "That's not what I'm saying."

"Leader Rey," said Yevgeny, still wanting to argue. "Isn't it true that, according to your faith, evil often introduces itself in the form of purity and innocence?"

Rey was sick and tired of being sick and tired. "Take my word," he said. "I've lived on Infernus for many years, and you've got absolutely nothing to fear from the winged men. That's all I've got to say about it, and that's all you're going to say about it."

Yevgeny just bowed, but never said nothing.

"Are you planning a memorial for the child?" asked Rey. "I'd like to attend."

"As would I," said Weston.

"It's up to the parents to decide," said Yevgeny. "It's getting late, and I must return to New Merieko."

"I'll arrange for stewards to safely accompany you to the colony," said Rey. He felt glad that Yevgeny was leaving, but was too nice to say so. "We may agree to disagree. In time, I'm sure we'll become the best of friends."

"Once I get settled in," Weston said to Yevgeny, "I hope you will accept a dinner invitation."

Yevgeny grinned, but didn't say nothing as he walked off.

Rey and Weston looked at each other, nervously. It was best to keep their eyes on Yevgeny. If somebody mucked up the uneasy calm and stability of life on Infernus, it might just be somebody like him.

* * * * *

Jeremy and Ericha headed back into Persis right around sunset. A cool breeze blew through the narrow draw, which brought welcome relief to them folks sitting around outside, telling lies and gossiping.

Jeremy and Ericha took a quick, refreshing bath in the river, and their hair was still wet. Jeremy was dressed only in his moccasins and loincloth. Ericha wore both her shirt and Jeremy's, to replace the loincloth lost during her fight with the abarbeaus.

The two teens also lost most of their weapons, while fighting critters. Jeremy wanted to fetch back the sword, which was still stuck in a dead abarbeaus. He hoped another critter didn't haul the dead abarbeaus off someplace. He held a lot of value in the sword, even if he got it at no cost. He wondered if he could get a second sword the same way he got the first one, which come from a dead pirate stupid enough to challenge Mucker to a fight.

Grub sounded better than a sword. Jeremy wanted to fetch a little dried meat to fill his stomach, then borrow a smoke and a chew from Mucker and Seely. He was dying for a cold one!

Jeremy and Ericha saw Rey talking to a newcomer. Ericha made sure Jeremy's shirt was wrapped around her legs and hips real good, so it didn't reveal nothing bad.

Rey was never happy about Jeremy and Ericha roaming around the woods like barbarians. He also disliked them skinny-dipping together. It was one thing, when they was youngsters. Rey now worried how long it'd be before Jeremy and Ericha got all hot and bothered, and couldn't help but to mess around out in the weeds someplace.

If they ain't already done it.

Jeremy and Ericha was too young to have kids of their own. If Jeremy ever got Ericha knocked up, he'd never live long enough to raise kids, once Errol got a hold of him. Rey was Jeremy's step-daddy, and he feared losing face if the kid got too friendly with Ericha.

Jeremy and Ericha smiled real big at Rey and the newcomer.

It was their smiling which got Rey that much more worked up. It only got worse when he noticed that Ericha had Jeremy's shirt wrapped around her legs and hips.

Was she missing her loincloth? If so, how?

Ericha's hasty little "hello" as she rushed off did nothing to calm Rey down.

"I'm gonna go in, fetch me a shirt, then head over to Mucker's for a drink and a smoke," said Jeremy, with that silly little grin of his.

"Put another shirt on," ordered Rey, more pushy than normal. "Then come right back."

"You don't understand!" yelled Jeremy. "I gotta get me a smoke! Bad!"

"You don't understand!" Rey yelled back. "You don't need a smoke, at least not yet." Rey motioned at Weston. "This gentleman wants to speak to you, on a very urgent manner."

"But . . ."

"Don't argue with me," said Rey, tiredly. "Get a shirt on, then come right back."

Jeremy and Weston gawked at each other for a spell. Without saying nothing, Jeremy run off to his bedroom, in the back of the church.

"Is that Jeremiah?" asked Weston, smiling real big.

"That's Jeremy," said Rey.

About a minute later, Jeremy headed back to the table and bench, chewing on a piece of jerky. He didn't know what Rey wanted, but figured it was just to nag about something. Rey nagged about everything, and Jeremy wasn't in no mood for it. He'd rather head off to Mucker's shack, where a smoke, a chew, and a shot of home brew awaited him.

Jeremy had on a long-sleeved shirt, made from an abarbeaus hide. It had some embroidery of a dove in flight at the heart, a swell stitch job Evelyn done for him. Jeremy hoped his business with Rey and the newcomer was short. He wanted to kick back and tell lies with Mucker and Seely.

"Nice to meet you at last, cousin," said Weston, smiling as he offered his hand to Jeremy.

"'Cousin'?" asked Jeremy.

"This is your cousin Weston, from Sykes," said Rey. "He's also cousin to King Marco of Embrey. King Marco is also your uncle, Jeremy."

Jeremy knew he was kin to Embrian royalty. He was no more impressed by that, than Ericha was by her ancestor, King Auric IV. His first thoughts of Weston were kind of 'so-what?'. He gave no thought to kin in the Farlands. They was as distant to him as the moon and the stars.

"How are you, Jeremiah?" asked Weston. "You are Jeremiah, aren't you?

Jeremiah Kentworth?"

"I'm Jeremy," he said, shaking Weston's hand with an awkward smile. He was more interested in a drink and a smoke than he was jawing with a diplomat.

"'Jeremiah' or 'Jeremy'?" asked Weston.

"'Jeremy'," the kid snickered. "I don't like being called 'Jeremiah'. I'm just Jeremy. Just plain old Jeremy."

"Just plain old Jeremy?" snickered Weston.

"That's right . . . Just plain old Jeremy."

"Well, this may come as a surprise to you, Jeremiah . . . Jeremy," said Weston. "But you're about to get rich . . . or, should I say, you are rich."

"Rich?" asked Jeremy.

Weston cleared his throat. "Your father died not too long ago, and . . ."

"My father ain't dead!" laughed Jeremy, throwing his arm around Rey's shoulder. "Why, he's sitting right here!"

"Your biological father," said Rey. He regarded Jeremy as flesh-and-blood, and was touched that the kid referred to him as his father, even if he rarely showed it.

"That's right," said Weston. "Your real father, in Branell."

Jeremy had few memories of Branell, and even fewer memories of his real pa. He had vague recollections of a few men in his life, while in the north of Branell. There was this real tall man with bushy eyebrows and a thick mustache and mutton chop sideburns. There was a fat, loudmouthed storekeeper who cussed all the time. There was a mousy, timid little rum-drummer who constantly wrung his hands.

Was any of these guys his real dad . . . or none of them?

Jeremy sometimes had the hankering to meet up with Terence Kentworth. Still, he was kind of relieved to hear about Terence's death. In the end, he'd just carry on as before, with his friends and 'family' on Infernus.

"So Jeremy, it's like this," said Weston. "Once my business here is completed, I'm to take you to Embrey. Once we get to Sykes, my government will provide you with an escort to Branell, where you're to inherit an estate, along with the wealth and title which comes with it."

Jeremy stared at Weston for the longest time. He couldn't believe a word of what was just told him. After about a minute or so, he asked, "Where's the punchline?"

"There is no punchline," said Weston, startled that Jeremy didn't jump for joy. "You're to come with me to Embrey, where . . ."

"I ain't going," said Jeremy, real anxious-like. "I can't go with you to Embrey, Mr. Weston . . . I can't . . . and I won't!"

"Why not?" asked Weston, his face turning kind of pale. "I thought you'd be excited . . ."

"The Farlands ain't home!" hollered Jeremy, loudly.

"They soon will be!" said Weston.

"Not for me they won't!" cried Jeremy. "I'm home, a'ready! Home, on Infernus!"

"Jeremy," said Rey. "Aren't you the least bit curious about? . . ."

"Well yeah, sorta," said Jeremy, not knowing what to do next. He suddenly felt all alone, abandoned, with nobody to fall back on or turn to. He looked over at Rey. His throat tightened, as his heart almost beat clean out of his own chest. "I still don't think I'm wanting to leave. I want to spend the rest of my life here, with you, Rey."

"And I thought you'd be thrilled with this news, Jeremiah . . . Jeremy!" said Weston.

Jeremy nearly fainted as he got to his feet. "I gotta go," he mumbled. "Gotta fetch me a shot of home brew, a chew, and a smoke . . ."

"Jeremy," said Rey, easing the kid back onto the bench. "You're not going to Mucker and Seely's for anything . . ."

"But I gotta!" cried Jeremy.

"Sit down," ordered Rey.

"But I can't sit down!" hollered Jeremy.

"Sit down!" hollered Rey. "Sit down, calm down, and let's talk this over . . ."

Jeremy did what he was told.

"Mr. Weston," said Rey. "Does my son have to lay claim to the estate right away? I mean, can't he wait until he's at least eighteen?"

"Branellian law states that if Jeremiah . . . pardon me, Jeremy," said Weston. "If Jeremy doesn't claim that which is rightfully his in a year or two, the estate will be awarded to the King."

"How much property are we talking about?" asked Rey.

"From what I've heard, we're talking fifty, sixty-thousand acres, at the very least," explained Weston.

Jeremy and Rey's eyes bugged out.

"With cash amounts exceeding one-million Branellian shillings," added Weston. "So, you see, it's in Jeremiah . . . Jeremy's best interests to claim that estate. As soon as possible, I'd say."

"And I feel it's in my best interests to fetch me a drink and a smoke," said Jeremy, hopping to his feet. "As soon as possible, I'd say!"

"You're not going anywhere!" yelled Rey.

"I ain't going to Branell," said Jeremy. "That's for damned sure!"

"Why not?" asked Weston. "I thought you'd be happy!"

"Branell ain't home!" screamed Jeremy. "Not for me, it ain't!"

"It soon will be," said Rey. "Look, son, I agree with Mr. Weston. It just may be in your best interests to stake out that estate, settle down, and find yourself a wife. Sounds like a good place to raise children, as you raise a worthwhile crop."

"But why?" asked Jeremy, thinking Rey had stabbed him in the back. Rey was a man that Jeremy placed above all other men. And now that same man wanted Jeremy to pack up and leave a place he loved, for a land he had no interest in! "I thought you cared about me, Rey!"

"I do," said Rey. "But . . ."

"But, what?" yelled Jeremy, sadly. "Why do you want me to go? You think there's something in it, for you? You and that stupid church of yours?"

"That's enough!" hollered Rey, wanting to slap Jeremy's face off. "I only want what's best for you!"

"But I don't wanna go to Branell!" screeched Jeremy. "I wanna stay here! I wanna stay with you, Rey. You, Mucker, Evelyn, Malachi, Nik, Ericha . . ."

"I don't want you to leave," explained Rey. "You know how I feel about you, son."

"Then why should I go?"

"Long-term, there's nothing for you here," said Rey. "You'll have a good life in Branell, on your own land. The same land you'll work with your two, strong hands. It'll be a fine place to raise a family, watch your children grow, and something to leave them once you're dead and gone."

"But what if I don't want it?" asked Jeremy. "If I gotta leave what I a'ready got, here? Move way the hell and gone? . . ." Jeremy stopped, knowing his bad language bothered Rey. "Move clear over to Branell? I ain't so sure I'm wanting it."

"What do you have here that's so special, Jeremy?" asked Rey. "You've got nothing here. You own no property . . ."

"What about my friends?" argued Jeremy. "People I think of as my family? You and Evelyn? . . ."

"Mr. Weston, will you please excuse us?" asked Rey, acting all nicey-nice. "I'd like to have a word with my son, Jeremy."

Weston had a rough day, already. The smugglers, the Kuschan boy getting ate, his discovery of a "new species" on Infernus, and his chat with Pastor Yevgeny left him wiped out and exhausted. "I'll retire to my quarters," he said, pointing at a small bedroom Rey offered him during his stay. "See you both for dinner, tonight."

"I look forward to it," said Rey.

"Jeremiah," said Weston. "Forgive me . . . Jeremy?"

"Sir?" said Jeremy, nervously.

"Perhaps you don't understand this," said Weston. "But it means a great deal to finally meet you in person. I've known about you for years . . . ever since you were born, actually. I'm so glad to make your acquaintance . . . Jeremy Kentworth."

Jeremy shook Weston's hand. After a moment or two, he mumbled, "Glad to meet you too, Mr. Weston."

"I'm not Mister Weston. Just Weston."

Jeremy smiled. "A'right, Just Weston."

"I didn't tell you about this inheritance to upset you," said Weston. "I thought you'd be ecstatic! Honestly, kiddo, I wish I was in your shoes! I've only been to Branell once, on a bungled peace mission. I'm not sure I liked it that much, either. Still, we're talking about a financial arrangement which, frankly, you'd be a fool to pass up. Why give the Branellian King something he doesn't deserve? It's your land, Jeremy! Take it!"

"But with me in Branell, and you in Embrey, won't that make us enemies, Weston?" asked Jeremy, sadly.

Rey and Weston didn't say nothing.

"I ain't really that keen on the idea of leaving Infernus," added Jeremy. "I don't wanna leave Infernus, not for all the money or land in the world! This is where I'm at, and where I'm wanting to stay."

"I . . . I'll see you both for dinner, tonight," stuttered Weston, then headed to the church.

Jeremy looked at Rey, knowing he'd get told off for one thing or another. Rey made it a habit to tell him off at least once a day, whether he needed it or not. "Boy, I'm sure dying for a shot of home brew, a chew of tobacco, and a damn fine smoke!" he joked.

"Jeremy," said Rey. "I've got a question for you, and I expect a straight answer. What happened to Ericha's loincloth?"

Jeremy's giggling only made things worse.

"Is there something for me to worry about?" asked Rey, impatiently.

"Whadda you mean?" asked Jeremy, with a dumb, innocent look.

"You know what I'm talking about! Have you and Ericha? . . ." Rey's wild imagination had got the best of him, as he had thoughts of Jeremy and Ericha romping around naked in the bushes, someplace. "Is there something going on between you and Ericha that we need to talk about? Man-to-man?"

"Like what?"

"Jeremy . . ."

"Ericha lost her loincloth when we got into a fight with an abarbeaus," laughed Jeremy. "It got swept right off her somewhere in the river."

"The river?"

Jeremy shared his version of the little misadventure with critters up in the mountains.

"Very well," said Rey, wanting to whomp Jeremy's head, just because. "Is there anything going on between you and Ericha, that we should talk about?"

Jeremy blushed, and turned his head away.

Rey knew that Jeremy was almost grown-up, with grown-up thoughts, and needing a grown-up's privacy. "Don't worry," he said. "I won't judge you harshly for it. I can only counsel you . . ."

"You ain't got nothing to worry about," said Jeremy, nervously. "Honestly, there ain't nothing going on between me and Ericha, and there ain't nothing gonna happen!"

"But do you want something to happen between you and Ericha? And do you suppose that's what she wants?"

Jeremy shrugged. He didn't want to do 'it' with Ericha . . . did he? The way Ericha carried on at the riverbank, she probably gave it a thought or two!

"Jeremy," said Rey. "That business of you and Ericha bathing nude together . . . It has to stop."

"But why? Ain't nothing gonna happen, if that's what you think!"

"But what if something does happen?"

"I a'ready told you!" hollered Jeremy. "Ain't nothing gonna happen! Nothing happened, and nothing's gonna happen! Why can't you trust me?"

There was silence as the only sounds come from the waterfall, as a flock of geese squawked overhead.

"Ericha's beautiful," said Rey, after a while. "Isn't she?"

Jeremy blushed as he grinned real big.

"And you're getting where you . . . kind of like her," said Rey. "Right, son?"

"Kinda," whispered Jeremy, embarrassed.

"And I'll wager that she kinda likes you, too."

"Yeah, Rey . . . she kinda does."

"And that's why you two must stop bathing together," said Rey. "And while you're at it, isn't it time for you to ditch the loincloth and wear some decent clothes?"

"I wear pants for Sunday service! I mean . . . when I show up for Sunday services. Anyway, I hate pants!"

"So, tell me this . . . What future is there in you and Ericha traipsing through the forest, dressed as savages?"

"That's my business," argued Jeremy.

"Jeremy," sighed Rey. "I want you to strongly consider on claiming your inheritance in Branell."

"But why? Didn't I just get done saying that I don't want it?"

"What about your future? With that amount of money, you'll have a good future! A safe future! Not just for yourself, but for the woman you choose to marry, and for the children you'll raise together."

Jeremy got all teary-eyed. Everybody and everything he knew and loved was on Infernus. He wondered if Rey was trying to get rid of him.

"What do you expect to have, if you stay here?" asked Rey. "Running around, dressed in rags with Ericha? Or constantly running over to get drunk and Mucker and Seely?"

"It's my life, ain't I?"

"Not much of a life, if you ask me," said Rey.

Sure beats being dead." Jeremy spit. "What about you, Rey? Why do you want me to leave? This is your home, ain't it? It's my home, too! I don't see you wanting to head to Branell with me. Mucker and Seely ain't about to, let alone Nik or Malachi!"

"What about Ericha?"

"What? . . . What about her?"

"Will you at least consider the inheritance, if Ericha tagged along?" asked Rey.

"Errol won't let her."

"Not yet, maybe. But she's almost a grown woman."

"What about you, Rey?" asked Jeremy. "Are you going to move to Branell with me?"

"Me?"

"You . . . You're like a dad to me, and have been ever since I can remember. More of a dad to me than Terence Kentworth!"

"You haven't always treated me as such, Jeremy."

"I'm sorry," said Jeremy, though he didn't sound that honest or sincere.

"I do have an obligation to accompany you as far as Embrey. I might even go as far as the border. You were born in Branell, I wasn't. The Branellian authorities may not allow me passage. Don't worry, you'll still have Weston with you most of the way." Rey put his hand on Jeremy's shoulder. "That is, if you decide to go."

"Do you want me to go?"

"I'll miss you more than anything," said Rey. "No, I don't want you to go. But you have to do that which is in your best interests. Accept your inheritance! You'll be a man of wealth and importance. With such a title comes tremendous responsibility. I hope you realize that."

Jeremy laughed. "I know you don't like hearing me say it, but I gotta fetch me a shot of home brew and a smoke!"

"I'm performing a baptism tonight. A winged man and woman want to convert their child into the Brotherhood of Faith. You're right, Jeremy. I don't like seeing you smoke and drink. But when my back's turned, you'll go right on ahead and do it, anyway."

Jeremy smiled.

"Mucker has a small boy with him," said Rey. "An odd-looking youngster named . . . Paransky, I think. Do me a favor and keep an eye on Paransky. Make sure Mucker and Seely don't corrupt him too badly. And don't corrupt yourself anymore than you've got to. All right?"

"Okay," agreed Jeremy. "Why do you say he's odd-looking? Is he butt-ugly, or what?"

"His entire body's covered with tattoos. A shameful sight." Rey cleared his throat. "One more thing, Jeremy."

"Yes, sir?"

"If you do accept your inheritance, make no mistake about it. I'll miss you so much, it'll be the death of me! I'll pray daily for those few occasions you'll make it back home to visit me!"

Jeremy tried but failed to get kind of weepy. He threw his arms around Rey and gave him a great big hug. "I'll miss you, too!"

* * * * *

Cody's thoughts were jumbled. He had several questions bouncing through his head, and very few answers.

Cody's legs shook as a few pages slipped from his tired grasp. He fetched a candle then entered the damp, chilly closet. There, he examined a dusty bottle of home-brewed liquor, along with the shirt hanging in one corner.

The shirt had an embroidered sketch of a dove in flight, near the left shoulder.

Cody took the shirt to the kitchen table. He sat down to run his fingers along the rough, fragile hide. It had stiffened from age and lack of wear. Cody felt an odd, unexplained connection to the garment, and wondered who it belonged to. He placed the shirt against his chest, seeing how he'd look with it on.

JT Kentworth walked with a limp, which got worse over time. Cody couldn't imagine his father being an athletic, outdoorsy type.

He'd be the last person to wear a loincloth!

So, who was Jeremy Kentworth? Or did he even exist?

Was he an uncle, a cousin . . .

. . . or merely fictional?

It was frustrating! Cody had really gotten into the manuscript! He still refused to buy the premise, despite the presence of living, breathing individuals . . . be they Leader Rey, John Mucker, and a tattooed guy named Paransky.

So, who was Jeremy Kentworth?

JT? . . .

JT Kentworth? . . .

Jeremy Kentworth? . . .

Cody never knew what the initials "JT" stood for. His father never told him. He remained a closed, elusive man, and rarely discussed his past or childhood.

Was JT in fact Jeremy Kentworth? Couldn't be! JT resembled little of the young man in the manuscript . . . for the exception of owning land in northern Branell. Still, JT occasionally revealed streaks of a wild, unpredictable nature. He also showed painful longings of distant memories, dreams and goals he once had, which eluded him.

One thing was certain; Cody's mother wasn't named Ericha! Nor was she a redhead, or prone to being outside. She was a homebody whose fair skin easily burned in harsh heat and sunlight. She was no hunter, let alone one to eat the heart of an animal . . .

Such as an abarbeaus . . .

If those animals truly existed!

And Cody knew better than to accept anything as strange as "winged men."

So, just who was Jeremy Kentworth?

Was he an uncle, a cousin . . . or just some kid with the same last name as Cody?

Well, whoever he was, Jeremy Kentworth wore a shirt with an embroidery of a dove in flight, near the left shoulder . . .

. . . Perhaps the exact shirt Cody sat on the table.

But, no matter what, Cody would not, could not believe everything in the manuscript.

He almost wanted to . . .

Cody stoked up the fire in the wood stove and poured another glass of apple cider. He lit another candle, sat in his favorite chair, and resumed his attention to the yellowed, warped manuscript before him.

Jeremy strolled through the village of Persis in the early-evening. The skeeters were out in force now, and had a fine time chomping them who sat outside enjoying the cool air.

Even with them pesky critters buzzing around, Jeremy felt safe, secure, and in touch with his surroundings. Walking through the narrow, zig-zagging, crooked streets of town was like staring into the face of a friend. Jeremy knew the place like the back of his hand, and knew most everybody there. There weren't no strangers in Persis. If there was, they didn't stay strangers for long. It never paid to be shy or standoffish. The people and Brown Winged Men went out of their way to make anybody feel right at home. Thanks to guys like Mucker and McClusky, them of hostile intent was dealt with quickly and harshly. The boneyard was filled with ruffians and varmints who brung any trouble to Infernus.

Jeremy didn't want to leave Infernus! No way did he want to leave! He was happy on the island, and couldn't imagine living anyplace else. The even thought of moving away was downright awful, maybe even scary!

It was true that Jeremy was born in Branell. He didn't see himself as a Branellian. In his heart and mind, he was from Infernus, pure and simple. Jeremy was a teensy little boy when he left Branell, and had few memories of it. He barely recalled the long voyage to Infernus. He felt no ties nor connection to Branell, whatsoever.

Based on Mucker's attitude about the Brindai Continent, the place was no-account, stupid, and vile. The only reason Mucker went east was for trade, barter, and cold-hard cash. He hauled tobacco, fruits, vegetables, and booze to Agron, Embrey, and Kusch, in exchange for their stuff.

Due to Mucker's efforts, Infernus sort of had ties to the Farlands, which was done secretly. If Mucker ever got caught by rival pirates or some country's navy, it spelled curtains for him, and all them involved. If he wasn't strung up from the yard arm, he'd die at the end of a sword. No way could he be taken alive!

Little by little, Jeremy had a bit of curiosity about that which laid beyond the shores of Infernus. He didn't know how long it'd take to reach Embrey or Agron, and from there to his land in the Northern Branellian Mountains. He was torn between simply staying put, or heading out across the ocean, to give his inheritance a look-see.

He was too scared to go it alone.

Jeremy turned to see the rugged, snow-covered peak of Mount Auric in the moonlight. Below that was the waterfall, with an endless stream sweeping out of the high country. Jeremy's heart sank. The sight of Mount Auric and the waterfall was reminders of the harsh, exciting life for them who called Infernus home. In the skies above, a few winged boys and girls played, well into the night. Pretty soon they'd come in, have their suppers and, after their good-night kisses, fall fast asleep.

Jeremy's heart told him to stay put, and forget all about his big money and even bigger land in Branell. He still felt pressured by Weston, who went all that way to tell him about his wealth and property. Even Rey pushed Jeremy to go check it out.

Jeremy was heart-broken, and even kind of mad. He couldn't understand why Rey was so hot-fire and eager to get rid of him. A sense of betrayal told Jeremy to go and have it out with both Rey and Weston. Fear told him not to fly off the handle, or rock the boat. Love struggled to figure out why Rey wanted Jeremy to take the inheritance, and move far, far away.

Mainly, Jeremy wanted to do nothing more but to hunt, fish, cuss, smoke, chew, and drink. Rey always said that hunting, fishing, cussing, smoking, chewing and drinking wasn't much of a life. How would he know? Rey was a Brotherhood Leader, and ignorant of such things as hunting, fishing, cussing, smoking, chewing, and drinking.

Anyways, maybe Jeremy really didn't have much of a life on Infernus.

But it was his life . . . wasn't it?

Jeremy headed to a small shack at the edge of town, where he'd fetch a shot of whiskey, a chew of tobacco, and a smoke. He peeked inside and saw Mucker and Seely sitting at the rickety old table, both drunk as lords. The room was filled with smoke, along with other bad stinks. The only light came from a rusty lantern, hanging from a rafter.

Saliva drooled down Seely's unshaven chin. His eyes was red and droopy.

He never did much but just stared off into space with a crooked half-grin, like he never had no worries in the world.

Mucker was bad drunk, and cussed up a storm about anything and everything he had the mind to cuss about. He was always in a rotten mood about something, be it McClusky and the Green Winged Men, the Roderick Dundee, or the Kuschan warship Matyushenko.

Seemed like that, more and more, there was something that put Mucker in a rotten mood, which only got worse and worse. The only thing that made him smile at all was when Jeremy come around. "Sit down before ya fall down!" he laughed, pulling up a stool for Jeremy to plop down and relax his lazy bones.

Jeremy smiled. Life had few pleasures as it was. Much of it involved traipsing around in the woods with his bow and arrows, or off fishing somewhere in the mountains. One of the best pleasures of all meant kicking back with a smoke, a chew, and a drink. Jeremy always looked forward to smoking, chewing, and drinking, which took his mind off the big bucks and the big land awaiting him in Branell.

Mucker poured Jeremy a shot of Agronian rotgut into a dusty old glass.

Jeremy straight-shot it, then let Mucker pour him another. He rolled himself a smoke, and lit it in the lantern hanging above his head from the rafter.

Seely sat in one corner, mumbling to himself. The little tattooed boy, Paransky, sat between Mucker and Seely, coughing and gagging from the thick smoke, and even worse stinks coming from the two men. He never minded puffing from the crooked roll-your-own hanging out of his mouth, or sipping the rotgut Seely give him earlier. He looked real happy and content to be around two old boys who never judged nor bully-ragged him for being a little tattooed boy. Mucker and Seely treated him like he was nothing better nor nothing worse than just a fella.

Jeremy nibbled at his second shot, wondering what he was going to say, or how he was even going to say it, around the likes of Mucker. He got scared of how Mucker and Seely would take the news of his big money and big land in Branell. He already guessed what Seely was going to say and do. Seely was liable to get all melancholy and sad, then force a stupid-looking grin through the dripping of snot and tears.

Jeremy also already knew what Mucker would say and do. For the moment, Mucker was too busy badmouthing the Roderick Dundee and Matyushenko, and threatened to blow them both out of the water when he got the chance. He badmouthed McClusky and the Green Winged Men, for making deals with a mess of heathen vodka-drinkers. He badmouthed Weston for being a good-for-nothing Embrian, poking his nose where it didn't belong.

Finally, he badmouthed the pious Brotherhood hypocrites who wanted nothing to do with little tattooed boys, other than to pray them into Heaven, while at the same time condemning them to Hell.

Mucker held off from badmouthing Rey too much, as to not rile Jeremy. Mucker and Rey hardly saw eye-to-eye on anything, but still wanted what they thought was best for the people and winged men of Persis. They also wanted what they thought was best for Jeremy, although they'd end up arguing and haggling about that before long.

Jeremy figured it was best not to say nothing about the big money and the big land in Branell, at least not for the moment.

Mucker got louder and louder, and drunker and drunker. Seely also got drunker and drunker, but never said much the whole time Jeremy was around. He just sat in the corner, slobbering all over himself. He finally got tired and put his head on the rickety old table, then fell asleep. Saliva drooled out of his mouth, or come out as bubbles while he snored bad enough to wake the dead.

Most of it ended up on the table, or on the floor. Some of it ended up on Paransky.

Mucker hated watching Seely drool all over everything. He always got disgusted with him, but for some strange reason still stood up for the old soak. As Seely drooled everywhere, the only thing spilling from Mucker's mouth was cuss words, which got worse throughout the night.

Jeremy owed Mucker an awful lot. It was Mucker who taught him how to hunt, fish, cheat at cards, fight, and do all kinds of bad stuff without getting caught. Even then, Jeremy got real tired of Mucker cussing, ranting and raving about everything. None of it made him feel better about the mess he found himself in. It only made him feel more sadder and confused.

Between Mucker's hollering and Seely's slobbering, Paransky didn't do or say much of anything. He only got kind of interested in Jeremy's shirt and loincloth. It wasn't so much what he said, but the way he eyeballed Jeremy's clothes, with a happy grin on his face. He even took a liking to Evelyn's embroidery job.

Mostly, Paransky looked up to Jeremy with some sort of hero worship and awe. Finally, he got up the guts to ask, "Can you can me some of them clothes like what you got on, sport?"

"It might take a while," told Jeremy, feeling right proud at the way Paransky was eyeballing him. "I got me a set of clothes like these that I wore, when I was about your size. They might fit you. Wanna try 'em on, one of these days?"

Paransky got all wild-eyed and excited. He showed his approval by nodding YES over and over and over again, wearing a big toothy grin through them ugly tattoos all over his face.

Not long after he got there, Jeremy got tired and left, feeling more at odds over his big land and all his big money he had coming to him. As the night went on, the more the issue ate at him, until he darn-neared went off his head over it.

* * * * *

Ever since he found out about his big money and even bigger land in Branell, Jeremy Kentworth got awful quiet. He was usually a loud, rambunctious, happy-go-lucky fellow. But all of a sudden, he got hit with something he never expected.

After him and Ericha fought with them abarbeaus, Jeremy figured he'd get to town, change his shirt, then fetch a "who-gives-a-damn?" smoke, chew, and drink from Mucker and Seely. He didn't figure on running into some weird little kid with tattoos all over him. And the last thing he expected was to run into a distant cousin, from way down east in Embrey.

And to find out that he was supposedly the richest person on the whole island!

Well, if Jeremy stood to gain a huge fortune in the Farlands, what harm was there in checking it out? Was he willing to give up the easy-living and comfort of family and friends, for the wealth and prestige he'd get in the vast countryside of Branell? There was considerable favor in the idea of making good with the inheritance. Even then, the thought seemed scary.

Well, hell! Anybody could use that kind of money! Jeremy didn't want it all for himself. He imagined building a bigger, fancier church for Rey, to fit the larger numbers of winged men and people joining up. He thought of buying a bigger, faster freighter for Mucker. He even figured on giving Weston a cut, just for being kin.

Jeremy could never play the role of a hoity-toity, country gent. He was afraid of turning into a well-to-do, fancy-dressing, wine-swilling, nose-stuck-in-the-air snob, beating his horses in wild fox-chases across rugged lowlands, while treating his servants and groundsmen in the same rotten way. He'd marry some snooty society dame who'd want a mansion in the country, and another in the city. He'll play a lousy game of one-upmanship, throwing lavish shindigs and social gatherings to impress the neighbors. As his wealth grew, so would his fat belly. The meaner he got to his workers, and to his critters, the meaner he'd get to them of meager status and standing.

What kind of a life was that? Who says it was better than smoking, drinking, chewing, and cussing with Mucker and Seely?

The more Jeremy imagined himself in such a lifestyle, the less he wanted it. Might be best to sell the land, take his money, and head on home to Infernus. Once he got back, he never be somebody or something other than what he already was. Not a man of high expectations, and surely not Mister Jeremiah Kentworth, or for that matter not even Jeremy Kentworth.

Just plain old Jeremy . . .

Just plain old Jeremy, living happily in the faraway island of Infernus.

Day had given way to night. A cool breeze swept through the narrow draw. Folks lit their homes with candles and lanterns, and were sitting down with their suppers, a cold drink after a long hard day, or relaxing with a pipe. Jeremy overheard a guy reading a verse or two from the good book to his kids, while in the next hut a newly-married couple ruffled the sheets of their featherbed, making a baby. An old boy sat on his stoop, laughing heartily from the intoxicating effects of gin. Dew from the waterfall dampened the night air. Silhouettes of trees covered the hillsides, and highlighted the starlit horizon. The moon was full, and guided Jeremy through the winding walkways of town. The sounds of crickets chirping was like music to the ears of them who savored the rough, rustic, simple life afforded the people and winged men of Persis.

A loud, high-pitched shriek told of some poor critter getting ate in the forest. Only idiots, morons, and newcomers rambled into the woods after dark. The abarbeaus owned the woods, now.

Jeremy walked softly, as he pondered thoughts of leaving Infernus. The more he thought about it, the more he realized that just about everybody in town was like family to him. Jeremy grinned and said 'howdy' to most everyone he met. They came back with kind words and warm smiles. They was nothing less or nothing more than just plain folks.

Nothing less or nothing more than just plain old Jeremy.

What if he woke up one day, to find out that he was no longer just plain old Jeremy?

What if he left Infernus, come back a few years later, and found out that he was now a stranger?

Jeremy felt alone, isolated, confused, and at-odds with the comfortable and the familiar. He couldn't see himself living nowhere else but Infernus! Behind his dumb grin was sadness, doubts, and a loss of who he truly was. He didn't know who to turn to, or even to go to for answers.

In the distance, he saw the rear living quarters of the church. Rey and Evelyn prepared supper for some visitors. He saw Weston take his place at the table, by faded candlelight, along with other folks. A couple of familiar redheads made themselves right at home.

It was "King" Errol, his bratty son Prince Ari . . .

And Ericha.

Ericha.

Ericha, his best friend in the whole wide world, and the prettiest girl in the whole wide world. Someone Jeremy saw not only as a chum, but maybe even as a wife.

Was Ericha aware of the mess Jeremy was in . . . and how did she feel about it?

"Jer?" a familiar voice said in the stark loneliness of night. "What's wrong?"

Jeremy turned to see two of his best guy friends on the island. Randen was a handsome young winged boy, if one could call a winged boy handsome. Well, all of the winged girls thought Randen was handsome, so maybe he was. Randen's age was similar to that of a person around sixteen or seventeen.

Like Malachi, Randen was almost a pure white color, a rare breed in the Brown tribe. He was a devout member of the Brotherhood Church, and one of Leader Rey's favorites in the congregation. If Rey told Randen to jump, then Randen would ask "how high?" and then double the order. Randen worshiped the ground Rey walked on, even more than Jeremy did. He was probably a lot nicer to Rey than what Jeremy ever hoped to be. Some figured that Jeremy took Rey for granted too much, where Randen wouldn't and couldn't.

Some of the winged men figured that Randen was like Malachi, too eager to sell out their traditions. A few of the more hardcore Browns viewed him as a traitor. This was a split among winged men that wouldn't be resolved anytime soon, but still threatened the unity of the Brown tribe.

Jung-su was seventeen, and come from a Far-Eastern country called Kokashima. He first got to Infernus around the same time as Jeremy. He was also an orphan. In Jung-su's case, his explorer parents made the dumb mistake of traipsing off into Infernus' southern regions, where smart people never traipse off into.

Jung-su lived with Jeremy for a spell, under Leader Rey's roof at the church. He had a hankering to be free and independent. When he was thirteen, Jung-su moved out of the church, and tried making it on his own by squatting in some of the abandoned huts throughout Persis. When this didn't pan out, he ended up sharing a room with Prince Ari under Errol's roof. There, Jung-su done all the stinky rotten chores around the house, that neither Ericha nor Ari had a mind to do. He washed the dishes, done all the laundry, and kept the house tidy. He chopped the firewood, raised the garden, and did all the things nobody else saw fit to do, even Errol.

That worked out for a while, until Errol's small cottage got even smaller, while the kids got even bigger.

After a few years, Jung-su got tired of doing these folks' dirty work, then turned his attention to doing other folks' dirty work. He went from Ari's cramped bedroom to a cramped shed, behind one of the seedier saloons in the seedier part of town, a dump called The Black Eye. There, he done all the cleaning and cruddy jobs for the joint, and always got cussed out for it. He made a modest wage, and lived in the shack for free, by putting up with the customers' foul mouths and insults.

Jung-su was a good member of the Brotherhood Church. Him and Randen volunteered as youth leaders for people kids and winged kids of the congregation. Rey depended upon Jung-su and Randen to keep its youngest disciples in their place, and not get too noisy or rowdy during service.

Jung-su wasn't a very big kid, and had to look up to most people and winged men. He had long dark hair hanging to his shoulders, and a round face. He was one of the few Orientals on Infernus which, depending on the company, either gave him favor or bully-ragged him over it.

"Why the long face?" Randen asked Jeremy, his soft, melodic voice breaking the lonely silence of the night.

"Aw, nothing," said Jeremy, turning away from Jung-su and Randen. "Nothing . . . really . . ."

"Congratulations," said Jung-su, offering Jeremy a handshake.

Jeremy looked Jung-su in the eye. "What do you mean?" he asked, nervously.

"I heard about your inheritance," said Jung-su, his bright smile shining through the hazy darkness. There was a hint of envy in his tone. "Congratulations, Jer. I'm . . . very happy for you."

"How'd you find out?" snapped Jeremy, going from sadness and confusion to getting real mad and nasty.

Randen and Jung-su wondered why Jeremy got so riled up.

"Who told you?" demanded Jeremy, like he was stabbed in the back.

"Leader . . . Leader Rey told us at Youth Group, tonight," stuttered Randen.

"Reckon he's jumping for joy to see me go!" hollered Jeremy. He was fixing to have it out with Rey for blabbing, then jump Weston for putting him in that sort of predicament in the first place.

"Well . . . not really," said Jung-su. "He seemed more . . . worried, it looked to me . . . Why, we thought you'd be excited!"

"Not hardly," sighed Jeremy, feeling bad for hollering at Randen and Jung-su.

Nobody said nothing for a spell. The only sounds came from a bawling baby, along with the constant roar of the waterfall. A blind man could see that Jeremy was all worked up. Nobody knew quite why, including Jeremy.

"What's wrong?" asked Randen. "We thought you'd be happy!"

"You thought wrong," whispered Jeremy. "Maybe I dunno how I'm supposed to feel, or even what I'm supposed to do."

"Don't you want that inheritance?" asked Jung-su, in disbelief.

"Sorta . . . kinda . . ." Jeremy leaned against the corner post of a nearby barn. "Maybe . . . Maybe not . . ."

"You're not making sense, Jer!" laughed Jung-su.

"Some people say I never have!" sighed Jeremy. "If you listen to Rey, I don't make a lotta sense about a lotta things!"

"What's wrong, Jeremy?" asked Randen, not as a question but as a demand. "What's ailing you?"

"Look, I don't mind the idea of a whole bunch of money coming my way," said Jeremy. "It's just that . . . I dunno . . . Guess I just don't wanna pack up and move away . . ."

Like all young critters on Infernus, people and winged boys alike, Randen was curious of the outside world. Unlike Jeremy and Jung-su, he'd never been off the island. Because he was a winged man and not a person, Randen already knew that his kind wasn't welcomed nor wanted anyplace, but on Infernus.

Because of the growing numbers of Farlanders heading to Infernus, he worried just how much longer it'd be before he wasn't no longer wanted there.

Jung-su was born in Kokashima and, like Jeremy, knew little of his birthplace. It wasn't Kokashima that he hoped to eventually call home. He had no intentions of spending his whole life on Infernus, and saw greener pastures far away from the island. In time, he aimed to settle down and make his fortune in Agron or Embrey.

Jung-su hardly spent a shilling of the hard-earned he made at The Black Eye. Mostly, he hated every minute working in that dump, and hated the way them lowlifes treated him. He knew it wasn't his fate nor his destiny to die an old man at a job that never appreciated him in the first place. Jung-su wanted to head off someplace different where he'd make a go of it in business or, like Rey, become a Leader in the Brotherhood Church. He was torn between a devotion to God, or becoming a merchant in Sykes or Merieko. He felt real confined and limited on Infernus, and never saw no kind of a future there. He couldn't never understand why Jeremy was dead-set on traipsing around the island in critter skins and rags. Still, he never made it a habit of getting into it with Jeremy over it.

On the other hand, Jung-su never held back in saying, "I don't know about you, Jer, but I'd be thrilled about your inheritance!"

"You, maybe," mumbled Jeremy, feeling worse than before. "Not me."

"Why not?" asked Jung-su, smiling as he looked at the waterfall, in the bright moonlight. "I'd be leaving first thing in the morning! Forget that . . . I'd be leaving now! I can't wait to get off this rock!"

Jeremy frowned at Jung-su. His mean eyes said a lot more than words ever could.

"It's a mighty big world out there, Jer," added Jung-su, not scared of Jeremy's mean eyes. "Please try to understand. I'm glad that Rey and Errol took me in. I can never pay them back for the kindness they showed me, which is a lot more than what I'll ever get at The Black Eye. I just don't think there's anything tying me down here."

"What about your friends?" questioned Randen, feeling bad because Jung-su was so happy about leaving.

"You'll get more friends," said Jung-su, patting Randen's wings. "Anyway, life goes on, and you'll soon forget about me . . ."

Jeremy got to feeling worse, as the night went on. His stomach rumbled, and he needed grub. He hated thoughts of breaking bread with the likes of Prince Ari, but relished thoughts of being with Ericha. It seemed that, more and more, she was in his thoughts, to the point where it made him happy, but also scared.

"'No-Teeth' Murnau is taking a few colonists from New Merieko to Agron," said Jung-su, in anticipation. "I've already talked to him about it, and if I can raise the fare he'll let me go with him."

"What?" both Jeremy and Randen hollered at the same time. "'No-Teeth' Murnau?"

"Yeah," said Jung-su, shocked at the other guys' reaction. "What . . . what's wrong with 'No-Teeth'?"

"What's not wrong with 'No-Teeth'?" argued Jeremy.

'No-Teeth' Murnau was the captain of a trashy little schooner called the Edith-Marie. For a hefty price, 'No-Teeth' would haul freight and people to and from Infernus.

'No-Teeth' was a well-known and familiar figure around the filthier parts of Persis. A boat ride anywhere on the Edith-Marie was usually a memorable experience, which most folks never cared to repeat. Them who was her passengers also acted as crew, and had to work and sweat their way across the Agron Ocean. 'No-Teeth's grub was known for its crass horribleness, too.

Them who started out liking 'No-Teeth' usually ended up hating his guts by the time they got where they was going. It was figured that only criminals, deviants, and morons caught rides with 'No-Teeth'. A lot of them also ended up drowning, either because of lousy weather or because they made another person mad at them and got tossed overboard.

'No-Teeth' was called 'No-Teeth' because he had no teeth. He also spoke the worst and weirdest Embrian that everyone ever saw, because he had no teeth. He was also from some far-off country where folks couldn't keep their Js straight from their Ys. This was a real bad annoyance to Jeremy, who hated being called Year-mee by 'No-Teeth.'

Jeremy took pity upon Jung-su, first for being dumb enough to hitch a ride on the Edith-Marie, and then having to spend all that time answering to the name Yung-zu . . .

"I know you was never keen about living here," said Jeremy, sadly. "But I never dreamed you were so stupid as to throw in with 'No-Teeth'."

"Come with me!" urged Jung-su. "We'll catch a ride with him to the Farlands. I'll even tag along when you check out your property in Branell! Come on! Please? What do you say, Jer?"

Jeremy didn't mind ideas of having Jung-su tag along. He hated thoughts of heading east on a floating junk heap like the Edith-Marie. He valued his life more than his big money and big land in Branell! "I ain't about to set foot on any boat with the likes of 'No-Teeth'!" he hollered, worked up because Jung-su didn't know no better.

Life on Infernus would never be the same without Jung-su! It was horrible whenever anybody Jeremy knew either croaked or moved away. As he got older, it seemed that more and more people he knew either croaked, or moved away.

More than anything, he hated thinking of the day where he either croaked, or moved away.

If Jung-su hopped aboard the Edith-Marie, it was a cinch that he'd either croak and move away! Thoughts of seeing Jung-su leave tore at Jeremy's heart. How could anybody in their right mind let Jung-su head out with 'No-Teeth'?

As if Jeremy needed something else to fret about!

Jeremy hoped that Jung-su's talk of leaving on the Edith-Marie was just that, talk. However, Jung-su was something of a do-er, and more of a do-er than most folks. Jeremy was a do-er when it come to killing critters. Jung-su was a do-er when it come to crappy, menial work. At any rate, Jung-su was always doing a lot of talking about leaving Infernus, especially after he went to work at The Black Eye.

Jeremy couldn't hardly blame Jung-su for wanting to get out of The Black Eye. Them people down there wasn't nice at all, and was really mean to Jung-su. Pirates, cutthroats, and whores took great pleasure in taunting and belittling him.

A lot of people, Rey, Ericha, and Jeremy both, tried getting Jung-su never to go to work at that dive. Some figured that he should've stayed working and living with Errol and his bunch. At least Errol and Ericha treated him like a white man, except for that Little Oinker, Prince Ari, who never treated nobody no good.

Jeremy sighed. Them two shots of rotgut he drunk at Mucker and Seely's started to wear off, and Jeremy knew he had to get on home, fetch a bit of grub, and head off to bed. He kind of looked forward to having a bite together with Ericha, maybe even kind of/sort of/maybe with Errol. Ari was another story. The only thing Jeremy wanted to do with Ari was avoid him.

"Come to the Farlands with me," begged Jung-su. "Leader Rey is writing a letter to enroll me into Lord William's Academy, in Sykes. It'll give us a chance to hang out together, before we go our separate ways. Please, Jer? What do you say?"

Parting ways with Jung-su broke Jeremy's heart. Jeremy knew Jung-su almost his whole life, and thoughts of no longer having him at hollering distance or arms-length hurt more than he could stand.

"Be seeing you fellas," said Jeremy, figuring that, once more, he was losing. He shook Randen and Jung-su's hand, hoping they couldn't see a teardrop or two in his eyes.

"What do you say, Jer?" pressed Jung-su. "No-Teeth's planning another trip in just a few days, and . . ."

"If I'm heading to the Farlands, it sure ain't gonna be with 'No-Teeth'!" snapped Jeremy.

Neither Randen nor Jung-su said nothing, just looked at Jeremy like he was fixing to bite their heads off.

Finally, Randen mumbled, "See ya, Jeremy," and he and Jung-su turned around, headed off, and disappeared into the night.

Jeremy took a deep breath, let it out slowly, then meandered back up toward the church, for what he hoped was a quiet supper.

* * * * *

Jeremy went through a back doorway of the church, then headed to the living quarter's kitchen, where Rey, Evelyn, and their guests waited on him. Evelyn had fixed a real nice supper of game birds, corn, and a frosted cake. Only the best wine was served, in real fancy glasses. A single candle, in the middle of the table, lit a small, cramped space.

Jeremy got to the dining room, as just about everybody greeted him. Everybody but Prince Ari, who had nothing good to say about Jeremy or nobody else.

Jeremy responded with a sarcastic, snotty grin. Figured he had nothing to smile about, anyway.

King Errol was right around Jeremy's height. He was a stout, barrel-chested, muscled-up man with thinning red hair combed in the middle. His face looked like it had been chiseled from granite. He had a wrinkled forehead, and small, piercing eyes. He was fifty, and a widower struggling to raise two kids on his own. He wore the same clothes he had on to cut firewood, and was covered in dirt, sawdust, and sweat.

Prince Ari was dressed in his nicest duds, a frizzly, violet shirt and black tights, like he was all high-and-mighty, which he wasn't.

Ericha was dressed up real nice, too, in a long white gown with no sleeves. She couldn't stand dressing up that good, but Errol made her wear something other than a loincloth.

Weston looked right handsome in a formal, black jacket, flashy neck tie, white silk shirt, tight pants, and spit-shine boots. This was the same sort of get-up he wore for important diplomatic dinners, to impress heads of state who wasn't so easily impressed.

Jeremy knew that his breath stunk of tobacco and booze. Still recovering from the rotgut, he accidentally bumped into the table. Grudgingly, he sat next to Prince Ari. He wanted to sit next to Ericha, but Rey and Weston messed that up, by sitting next to her instead.

"Jeremy," said Rey, sternly. "Get into your 'Sundays,' then return to the table. Please?"

"Why?" groaned Jeremy, annoyed with the presence of guests, except for Ericha. "I never get dressed in my 'Sundays' when it's just you, me, and Evelyn. Why's tonight any different?"

Rey smiled nervously, but wanted to strangle Jeremy. "It's not appropriate to wear that . . . attire when there's company. Put something on a bit less . . . savage, then join us for . . ."

"Is it appropriate for you to blab to Randen and Jung-su about my big money and my big land in Branell?" barked Jeremy.

While Rey and Weston got shameful, guilty looks on their faces, Errol, Ericha, and Prince Ari got real bewildered and confused.

"According to Mister Weston," said Jeremy, angrily. "I'm a rich man! I got money now, lots of it! Y'all wanna kiss my fat ass over it?"

"What did you say?" growled Errol, like he was about to bust Jeremy's face. "That the way you always talk around the dinner table?"

"Jeremy," whispered Rey, with a fiery blush and clenched teeth.

"It also means I'm a proper Branellian gent," said Jeremy, the rotgut getting the best of him. "That means I oughta be able to dress any way I damn well please! Hell, if I come traipsing in here, bare-naked, seems I got a right to do that too, as a proper Branellian swell!"

"What are you talking about?" asked Ericha, nervous and anxious and scared. "Please, Jeremy? What are you talking about?"

"I'm sorry I said anything to Randen and Jung-su," apologized Rey. "But I'm worried about you, and I just thought . . ."

"The problem is that you didn't think!" hollered Jeremy. "Look, I don't know why I'm still hanging around here. This church ain't even home to me no more, let alone Persis, or this whole rotten, stinking island. According to Mister Cousin Weston here, I oughta just pack my bags, right here, right now, and catch the first tub going east. Even if it's with 'No-Teeth' on the Edith-Flipping-Marie!"

"Jeremy," warned Rey.

"That's not what I meant, kiddo," said Weston.

"Then what do you mean?" demanded Jeremy, in betrayal.

"I was only doing what I felt was right, by informing you of your inheritance," said Weston. "You act like it's my fault that you've got a fortune coming your way, and that I'm murdering you by letting you in on it."

"What?" gasped Ericha. "What inheritance?"

"Ain'tcha heard?" cried Jeremy, high-pitched and screechy. "I'm a rich boy, boys and girls! Helluva rich boy!"

Errol, Ericha, and Prince Ari stared at Jeremy.

"I got me an inheritance in Branell!" said Jeremy, smiling despite the pain it brung him. "Sit around in my big house up on the hill, wear my best 'Sundays' even on my worst Tuesdays, drink expensive hooch by the gallons, hire toadies to smooch my fat ass before kicking their sorry ones, just 'cause I'm rich enough to do anything I damn well please!"

"What are you talking about?" asked Errol, fed-up with Jeremy's foul language and carrying on.

"Jeremiah . . . Pardon me . . . Jeremy's father passed away not long ago," said Weston. "And left him with a considerable estate and fortune in northern Branell. Not to mention cash amounts of . . ." Weston cleared his throat. "More than a million shillings."

The room fell silent. Errol and Ari smiled real big, while Ericha got all upset and anxious. Rey didn't say nothing, though he felt conflicted over everything. He still figured it was in Jeremy's best interests to accept the big money and the big land, yet knew it'd change everything, and hopefully not for the worst.

"Well, I'll be," said Errol. He knew that Jeremy was of royalty, though the kid never acted like it.

Of all the people to be blessed with such fortune . . .

Why Jeremy?

Jeremy and Ericha stared at each other. Their eyes welled in tears. The two had been the best of friends since recollection. Thoughts of them two parting ways seemed wrong and unimaginable.

"Yup," said Jeremy, his voice cracking. "I'll be heading over to Branell and claim my inheritance. I'm gonna be a swell, dress like a swell, eat and drink like a swell, and strut through the whole joint like I own it, which I will. By the time I find my way back here, if I find my way back here, I'll be a stranger. None of you will even know nor remember me. Nor will you give a hang. Them who do will be too ashamed to say so. By that time, I won't be a part of Infernus nomore. I'll be a lousy, good-for-nothing Farlander!"

"Bon voyage, jungle boy!" cheered Prince Ari. "Then why don't you swell up like a good little swell, and float away?"

"Ari!" scolded Ericha. "Tell Jeremy you're sorry, or I'll never speak to you again!"

"You shut up, Ericha!" laughed Ari. "Nobody said I liked you, neither!"

Jeremy dipped his hand into Prince Ari's grub, then rubbed a huge glob of it into the brat's face. As most everybody reacted in surprise and horror, Ericha let out with a silly giggle.

"Hell yeah, I'm leaving a'right," said Jeremy. "Soon as I tie Ari's feet to an anchor, then throw 'em over the side!"

Errol hopped to his feet, wanting to stomp a mud hole into Jeremy's guts.

"Mind your manners, Your Majesty!" hollered Jeremy. "Sit down and shut up, or I'll get Nikolai to cast a spell on you, by turning you into a frog or a toadstool or a shithouse!"

"That's enough, Jeremy!" shouted Rey. "Either you act like a man around our guests, the kind of man I've always wanted you to be, or go straight to bed!"

"I'll do one better!" Jeremy yelled back. "I'll go straight outside. And when I get back . . . if I get back, I'll be wearing jewelry around every part of my body, even them places where the sun don't shine!"

With that, Jeremy stomped outdoors, and slammed the door behind him.

Jeremy took a deep breath of cool, dewy air. He counted to ten once or twice, then slowly got a hold of himself. He peeked through a window to see Rey apologizing to everybody.

Jeremy knew he done wrong by acting so badly. He didn't care. He felt his whole world being pulled out from under him. What good was it in being civil, subtle, or nice?

Jeremy stormed to the empty field, between the church and the waterfall. He sat down at the riverbank, and looked up at the countless stars, seemingly no more distant to him than where he was liable to be going. To an unknown ground, in an unknown region of an unknown country, someplace in the Farlands.

Crickets chirped, a critter howled in the woods, and the waterfall dampened the night air. Jeremy never felt so scared, isolated, or alone in his whole life.

Then Ericha appeared to him from out of the darkness. She had stripped out of that annoying gown she had on for supper, and now wore a sleeveless, leather shirt and a loincloth. The silhouette of her thin, feminine frame and long, tanned legs gave Jeremy reasons to smile. Although Ericha never said nothing right at first, the look on her face asked ARE YOU ALL RIGHT?

"I'm a'right," said Jeremy, though he sure didn't sound like it.

Ericha sat next to Jeremy, and put her arm around him. The warmth of her body against his was like sunshine at the end of a rainy day. She finally got up the nerve to ask, "Are you? . . . Are you going to Branell?"

"I dunno," sighed Jeremy. "Maybe I oughta. We can sure use the money."

"'We'?"

"I mean all of us. You, me, Rey, your old man, Mucker. All of us. What else can I do with all that money? Look, I really don't wanna go to Branell, but . . . I just don't know what else to do, or even what I'm supposed to do!"

For almost a half a minute or more, neither Jeremy nor Ericha said nothing.

"If you do go . . ." asked Ericha, real nervous and scared, "how long before you . . . come back?"

"I dunno," mumbled Jeremy. "If I come back . . ."

"'If?'" whispered Ericha, like she would cry her eyes out.

"If I head off to Branell, I sure don't wanna go it alone," hinted Jeremy, staring straight into Ericha's eyes. Did he want her throwing in as a friend, a buddy, or just somebody to share the adventure with?

Or was it something more intimate and meaningful that Jeremy needed from Ericha? He never felt this close to Ericha, or this attracted to her, since they first met as teensy little kids.

Ericha would be a lot more fun than Jung-su.

What Jeremy hoped to do with Ericha, he'd never care to try with Jung-su!

Without giving it a second thought, Jeremy took Ericha's hand into his. The sight of a teardrop seeping from Ericha's eye was as clear to him, as the love and devotion he felt for her.

Jeremy threw his arms around Ericha, as they fell to the grassy turf of the field. A steady breeze blew a mist from the waterfall. As Ericha embraced Jeremy, they pressed together under the starry, moonlit skies of Infernus.

They held each other tightly, not quite yet as lovers, but only as the dearest of friends. This wasn't based on notions of fooling around somewhere in the bushes, but something way more spiritual. Jeremy and Ericha always gave each other squeezes, like they was brother and sister, or the best of best buddies. They had been through life and death over the years and would forever be comrades and chums.

Jeremy gave Ericha an innocent little kiss on the cheek. He wondered what it'd be like to do it with her, while wondering if she had the same thoughts about him.

Ericha put her lips to Jeremy's ear and whispered, "Promise you'll never leave me . . ."

"I promise, Ericha," sobbed Jeremy. "I promise . . . I promise to promise! I promise!"

"Promise me we'll always stay together," added Ericha, tears spilling from her eyes. "Promise me that, Jeremy Terence Kentworth!"

* * * * *

Cody gasped. His heart raced, both hands shook and sweat. Panic swept over him like the tide. Disbelief collided with written evidence of thoughts that he had already considered, yet refused to accept.

Jeremy Kentworth . . .

Jeremy Terence Kentworth . . .

JT Kentworth?

What if JT was the loin clothed boy in the manuscript?

Cody struggled to regain his composure and common sense. He feared losing his mind. His first impulse was to leave the apartment, go for a long walk, and come to terms with what he had just read.

Merieko was no place to roam around after dark. There were too many creeps and crazies out there! A few weeks before, a local boy was found dead in the river, nude from the waist down. He'd been sexually assaulted, before getting his throat cut. This incident was a reminder of the unpredictable, often violent nature of Agron's largest city.

Cody laughed so hard that he cried. Then, for several minutes, he was overwhelmed with sadness. He wondered if he finally had clues into JT's past . . . a past never once revealed to him.

Cody chuckled at the secrets of a man he only thought he knew.

And then, once more, he wept in realizations that JT was, and always would be, a mystery to him.

Was there any truth to the manuscript?

Or was it merely a reflection of the fantasy life of a tired, frustrated, crippled Merieko merchant?

No matter what, Cody refused to believe in winged men. He couldn't buy the possibility of such creatures living in a distant, unknown land, far to the west.

What if there was no truth to the story at all?

Cody needed answers. Were any of his kin, living nearby, willing to disclose JT's past? What about Leader Rey, who was expected to return after visiting friends and followers throughout Agron?

Cody threw more firewood into the stove, poured himself a glass of apple cider, then stared blankly through a window into the empty, unnerving darkness of night.

He wasn't sure what to believe, anymore . . .

Cody shed tears for JT. There was love between father and son. Love. Love, but never a strong, solid bond. Walls always separated Cody and JT, walls the boy wanted to tear down and tear away. JT was closer to Rey than he ever was with Cody. Cody loved JT, but he also resented him for the lack of quality time the two spent together.

Too late . . .

Too late, now . . .

Cody cried like a baby as he cursed JT, a man he loved more than anyone, but never really knew.

Cody began to think that it might be best to move across town, then live with warm, kindly cousin Hilary, and cold, unfriendly Franklin. What good was that? As much as Cody resented JT, he despised Franklin that much more! At least Hilary had the decency to check on Cody, bake him pastries, give him hugs and kisses . . .

. . . And love.

Cody wiped tears from his face and eyes. He debated on going to bed or continue reading the manuscript. Sleep would only evade him, now. His mind was too clouded and cluttered by troubling, confused thoughts, at odds with themselves.

The chill of night seeped through a crack in the door, separating the apartment from the store. Cody stoked up the fire, then returned to the easy chair and resumed his interest in the story.

What more would he now learn about Jeremy? . . .

Jeremy Terence? . . .

JT?

* * * * *

Jeremy never knew how much he really loved Infernus, until he was afraid of leaving it forever.

Jeremy and Ericha slept together, in the empty field between the church and the waterfall. They slept. Messing around never entered the picture, even when Jeremy thought about messing around. He stayed clean, honorable, and a virgin. Ericha was still a buddy, a chum, and his best friend. Sure, the two could've messed around! In the past, their folks trusted them not to mess around. Now, Rey and Errol was afraid of Jeremy and Ericha messing around, maybe even making a baby.

Jeremy never slept good. He spent too much of the night worrying where his life was heading. Through the long, lonely hours of darkness, he stayed next to Ericha. Familiar sights and sounds surrounded him. These was sights and sounds he grew accustomed to.

Sunlight finally peeked over the horizon. Jeremy couldn't stand lying around, thinking. The longer he lied around, the more he thought. The more he thought, he more he worried. The worse he worried, the worse trapped he felt. Trapped by fears that his life had spiraled out of control.

Jeremy sat up and accidentally woke Ericha. He didn't want to bother her, and hoped she'd go back to sleep.

"You okay, Jeremy?" asked Ericha.

"Yeah," groaned Jeremy, tiredly.

"It isn't yet morning! Where are you going?"

Jeremy shrugged. "I dunno. For a walk."

"Want me to come with you?" asked Ericha, hoping Jeremy said YES.

Jeremy usually enjoyed Ericha's company. There weren't no problems that one of them faced, that the other couldn't solve. The truth was, Jeremy kind of wanted Ericha with him. Problem was, it might have made things worse.

Jeremy had to go it alone, and figure things out on his own. He smiled real big, pretending that everything was okay. "Go back to sleep," he whispered, kissing Ericha's cheek. "I won't be gone long, I promise."

Ericha was kind of hurt. "But . . ."

"It's nothing," said Jeremy. "Just a stretch of the legs."

Even the sound of Ericha's voice was painful. It was like the constant roar of the waterfall, the chirping of crickets, or the songs of birds.

Jeremy rubbed Ericha's shoulder. Her image in the faded light of dawn made him wonder what it'd be like to wake up with her every morning, for the rest of his life. "Go to sleep, Ericha," said Jeremy. "I'll be back before ya know it. . ."

"But I feel so warm next to you," said Ericha.

Jeremy gave Ericha another kiss on the check, then slowly headed out on an early-morning jaunt, into the hills above Persis.

Jeremy wandered into a narrow draw beyond the waterfall. The sun had risen, and formed long, hazy shadows across the landscape. Jeremy was armed only with a knife hanging from a belt around his waist. He hoped to find the sword left sticking into one of the abarbeaus him and Ericha killed the day before. If nothing more, this stroll took his mind off of the big land and even bigger money.

A mile or so north of Persis, the dewy chill of dawn gave way to the warmth of daylight. Jeremy got winded after walking uphill along a stony path, and stopped for a breather. He sipped cool water from a spring, sat down at a clearing, and looked out across the bright, blue Agron Ocean. It was the same Agron Ocean he'd cross if he went to check out the inheritance. Jeremy squinted at that huge body of water, as blinding rays beamed across the waves.

Just how far off was the Farlands? Jeremy didn't know. He was just a little kid when he got to Infernus. He had only foggy recollections of the long sea voyage from Embrey, a short stop at Merieko, then a long stretch to Infernus. Now he pondered a similar trip eastward, thousands of miles across the sea.

Jeremy was a Branellian, so why wouldn't he want to head back to his birthplace? 'Cause he didn't belong there, that's why! He belonged in Infernus, 'cause it belonged to him!

Infernus seemed either like the whole wide world, or nothing but a tiny dot on a really big world. Once in a while, Jeremy hiked above the timberline to the summit of Mount Auric, Infernus' tallest peak. From clear up there, a person could almost see the whole island. He'd been told never to head beyond unmarked borders, where no smart person dared to tread.

Jeremy never went into the eastern peninsula, where the Green Winged Men lived. His opinion of the Greens was like Malachi and Mucker's. He never bothered the Greens, and they never bothered him. When he was little, Jeremy was scared of them, kind of like how he used to be scared of ugly bugs and critters. Now, he had no reason to get scared of them, at all.

Jeremy sat on a steep hillside, where he had a clear view of Persis. He could hear the rumbling of the waterfall. People and winged men had already started their day, way down below.

Jeremy took off his shirt. The warm sun felt real good against his bare skin. He took a deep breath, then let it out in a sigh. Jeremy loved Infernus, more than he could tell! He didn't want to leave it, not for a single, solitary minute! Infernus wasn't the whole wide world. It probably never amounted to nothing. But Infernus was home. And it's where Jeremy wanted to stay.

Ericha wasn't in the Farlands. She was on Infernus.

Jeremy wrapped his shirt around his waist, and headed deeper into the woods. He stopped occasionally to drink from creeks and streams. He kept a close watch for critters. He wished he would've taken some bows and arrows, and a canteen with him. He planned to spend most of the day on this hike.

The woods had a strange, magnetic effect on Jeremy. He dreamed of building a cabin up there, someplace. He thought of setting up a still to make his own home brew, to put Mucker's all to shame! He'd plant a garden next to a river or a creek and spend his life in the outdoors. Better to live a life in nature than to get fat and lazy as a fat, lazy swell in Branell!

Jeremy smiled. He wasn't about to accept that big money or that big land, no matter how big it was! Branell wasn't home. It wasn't never going to be home, and wouldn't never be home!

Now that Jeremy had it all figured out, it was time for him to see if Ericha has as much of a spark for him, as he had for her!

Jeremy got to the clearing, where him and Ericha fought all them abarbeaus the day before. He fetched a handful of rocks, to protect himself from getting ate. He hoped to find the sword, which was a prized possession.

"This sure is pretty country," someone said from the deep, dark woods. "No wonder you like it . . ."

Jeremy nearly jumped right out of his skin. His first thought was to high-tail it back to Persis. His eyes got big and wild, and heart beat real fast. He looked all around, wondering who he heard talking a moment ago.

It was Weston, who stumbled through the woods with a big, dumb grin on his face.

"It's only you!" hollered Jeremy.

"Yeah," said Weston, sarcastically. "It's only me."

"That's right," sighed Jeremy, tiredly. "Only you."

Weston grinned. "You know what, Jeremiah . . . Jeremy! I just saw the darnedest thing a moment ago."

"What, Mister Weston? . . . Weston, I meant! What's the darnedest thing you ever saw?"

"There's a dead animal not far from here, with an expensive sword impaling it."

Jeremy laughed. "That's my sword."

"Your sword?"

"Yeah, mine. Yesterday, me and Ericha killed that critter, and some of his buddies. Later on, their buddies tried killing us."

Weston scratched his head. "Huh?"

"They didn't get the job done," snickered Jeremy. "We killed them, instead."

"That sword belongs to you?"

"Yeah," said Jeremy, wandering into the clearing to fetch the sword left in the dead abarbeaus.

The dead abarbeaus and them other dead critters swarmed with flies, and stunk to high Heaven. Where Weston got sick at the sight and smell of the dead critters, Jeremy paid them no mind. There was lots of dead critters all over Infernus, and he got used to smelling them.

Jeremy placed one foot against the dead abarbeaus, gave the sword a good yank, and pulled it loose. "I stuck this one here good enough to kill it," he boasted, giving the sword a looking over. "But I didn't kill it good enough, because it went into a bad case of the flip-flops. Anyway, me and Ericha was too busy killing his buddies, or running off, to worry about it."

"A lucky find. I'm glad I was of service to you, Jeremy." Weston laughed. "See, I got it right this time . . . Jeremy."

"I'm glad you found this sword for me," said Jeremy. "But you ought not be out here by yourself, not with all the critters we got roaming about. Figure yourself lucky one of them didn't pounce on you. They're as thick as fleas in this patch. We better get shy of this place, before they decide to get revenge on their dead buddies me and Ericha killed, yesterday."

"I never got to sleep last night," explained Weston, apologetically. "So, at first light I got out of bed and couldn't resist the urge to go exploring, you might say."

"I wouldn't go traipsing out in these woods alone, and for sure not in the dark."

"You were alone."

"That's different. I know these woods like the back of my hand. Just like I know the attitudes of the critters we got around here. It ain't smart for Farlanders to traipse out here alone, especially if you don't know your way around."

"You don't like Farlanders," assumed Weston.

"How did you know?"

"By the way you say the word 'Farlander'. I heard if from John Mucker, and now I'm hearing it from you. You don't like Farlanders, and you resent me for being one."

Jeremy frowned. "Guess that's because I seen or heard of too many Farlanders traipsing around out here, just to get ate. It's horrible packing out what's left of Farlanders, after the abarbeaus had their fill of them."

"That's probably what happened to that poor Kuschan boy yesterday," mumbled Weston.

"Probably."

"Well then, perhaps I should refrain from the habit of exploring. It's what I've always done, since I became a diplomat. I get a lay of the land, by stepping out of my comfort zone to go . . . exploring." Weston chuckled. "Now, if you don't mind my asking, why is it permissible for a half-naked boy to 'go traipsing around out here, alone'?"

Jeremy gave Weston the eye. "What do you mean, 'half-naked'?"

"Well, just look at yourself! The only thing keeping your backside and pee-pee from sunburning is that flimsy piece of cloth tied around your privates."

"That's my business, Mister Weston."

Weston shook his head. "I'm not starting out too well with you. Am I, Jeremy?"

"Look, I don't mean to get on my hind legs with you," sighed Jeremy. "But take my word for it. It ain't smart to go traipsing around these woods, especially if you don't know your way around. It just ain't that safe. As far as me being 'half-naked', that's the way most winged men dress. Reckon if it's good enough for them, reckon it's good enough for me."

"You've gone native."

"If you wanna call it that," said Jeremy, defensively.

"Yes, but it's not . . . civilized. Certainly not for a gentleman as yourself, who stands to gain a sizable fortune, along with the privilege which comes with it."

Jeremy frowned as he sat on a decaying log, at the edge of the clearing. He looked up at the granite mountains, shining in the morning sun. Chilled by a cool wind sweeping in from Mount Auric, he slipped his shirt back on.

"I do declare," said Weston. "I'm really not starting out too well with you."

Jeremy shrugged. "Reckon not."

Weston sat next to Jeremy on the log. "You don't want it," he said, quietly. "The money, the land, the title . . . You're not wanting it. Right?"

Jeremy shook his head, NO. "What I could really use right now, is a smoke, a drink, and a chew."

"Sorry," said Weston. "I left mine at home."

Jeremy and Weston laughed. Weston was a cousin, and tried acting like one. He was trying to make a strong connection to Jeremy, and the least Jeremy could do was to meet him half-way.

Weston reached into his vest pocket for a small, steel flask. "I'm not supposed to give alcohol to minors," he whispered. "This is our little secret . . . between family, of course."

Jeremy's eyes got all big and bright as he took a swig. What he tasted was one of the best whiskeys from the Farlands! Once the hooch hit his tongue, his mood got a bit more upbeat and jovial. He even felt a wee bit better.

"Meaning, we say nothing to Rey about this," added Weston. "I've got the highest respect for your stepfather, and I hope it's mutual. Still, I wish to stay on his good graces. The same goes for you, Jeremy."

"Don't worry," cheered Jeremy, happily taking another sip. "You're safe with me now, Weston!"

Rey never slept all that good the night before. He tossed and turned, embarrassed and hurt by the "show" Jeremy put on for his guests.

Rey's opinions of Ari was like most folks. Yet, he thought highly of Errol, who worked real hard to support his two kids. Errol knew that his role as 'king" never amounted to much.

Ericha was a good member of the Brotherhood Church, and Jeremy's best bud. Rey knew there was more to Ericha and Jeremy's relationship than all that. If them two kids was happy together, not only as buddies but eventually as man and wife, then Rey was fine with it. He just hoped they didn't rush into something, if they ain't already done that particular something by now.

Ericha left the dinner table right after Jeremy pulled his stupid shenanigans, and neither went home afterwards. Throughout the long night, Rey peeked outside to see Jeremy and Ericha sleeping together in the field between the waterfall and church. Not once could he hear them moaning, groaning, or making the bushes shake. It didn't matter. Rey was scared of them two already messing around. He wanted to trust Jeremy and Ericha, and prayed they wasn't up to no good. He also wanted to respect their privacy, while thinking that messing around was nothing but a natural part of life. Rey had went into a house of ill-repute the night before going into the Leadership, not only to get it out of his system, but to learn more about living, along with the fun of messing around.

Rey wasn't sure if it was messing around, or what might lead to messing around, that made him fret. He loved Jeremy and Ericha and wanted them to make the right decisions. He knew of too many young people and winged men raising babies before they was already fully grown up. Such things never come to no good, as the boy would run off somewhere in the Farlands, and leave the girl raising the baby on her own. The last thing Rey wanted to see was Jeremy and Ericha get mixed up in all that.

Rey was up at five to do a little work in his office. It was fall, and the morning chill urged him to build a small fire in the stove. He ate a meager breakfast of jerky fried up on the wood stove. At sunrise, he went for a walk, and smiling warm and pleasantly as he said HELLO to everyone he run into. It was a put-up smile, as he was too worked up and anxious to smile for real.

During his walk, Rey ran into Ericha, who convinced him that nothing bad went on between her and Jeremy, other than talking and sleeping. She also said that Jeremy went on a hike up in the mountains, to figure out what he was going to do about the big money and the big land he had coming to him in Branell.

Rey thanked Ericha, wished her a good morning, and prayed that Errol never tanned her hide for sleeping outside with Jeremy. He wasn't in no mood for family drama, and knew it was best never to get tangled up in it.

By the time Rey got back to his office, the small fire almost made it too hot in there. He opened a window to air everything out, then did some paperwork. He wasn't worried about Jeremy getting into trouble with Ericha. Instead, he was worried about Jeremy getting stupid or careless up in the mountains. He imagined seeing Jeremy thinking he had to kill a critter, if for no good reason than to kill a critter, and end up getting killed instead.

Mostly, Rey worried about Jeremy, if for no good reason than to worry about Jeremy. He wondered what life would be like if Jeremy up and moved off to Branell. On one hand, he'd be real happy for Jeremy. At the same time, he'd miss his stepson badly, and never get over it.

An hour or so after sunrise, Rey heard a knock on the door, and asked the person to come in.

It was Jung-su.

Rey smiled. He liked Jung-su an awful lot, not only for being a pretty good kid, but for being a good youth leader in the church. He also liked Jung-su for trying to become a responsible, independent grown-up, even when he was still a boy. In some ways, he respected Jung-su more than he did Jeremy. Jung-su was already more of a grown-up than Jeremy would ever be.

Rey greeted most boys in the church with a handshake or a pat on the back. It was different with Jung-su. Jung-su was a hugger. He hugged Rey every time he saw him, even if he had already saw him a little bit ago. With that in mind, Rey got up and met Jung-su half-way across the room, in anticipation of a hug.

Jung-su grinned his big toothy grin as he gave Leader Rey a hug. When

Jung-su lived with him and Jeremy, Rey thought of him as a son, and something of a big brother to Jeremy. Rey loved Jung-su like kin. He'd always love Jung-su, the way he'd always love Jeremy.

Rey would always love Jeremy, even if he didn't always like him.

"Ericha said you wanted to see me," said Jung-su, as he and Rey sat at the desk. The heat from the wood stove still lingered on, and already Jung-su had sweat pouring off of him. "What can I do for you today, sir?"

"I'd like you and Randen to make a trip into New Merieko," said Rey.

"What's in New Merieko?"

"An Agronian boy, just a little younger than you and Jeremy, by the name of Fernandez."

"Is he the one who pitched the fit when he got into town yesterday with Mucker and that diplomat?" asked Jung-su.

"Fernandez hasn't stopped pitching a fit since he was born. Now he's pitching a fit because he thinks that Infernus is Hell, and he's trapped right smack-dab in the middle of it."

"Why's he here, then?"

"His father wants to make a go of it, on Infernus," said Rey. "He spent much of his life as an indentured servant, paying off his own father's bad loans after the old boy hanged himself in an outdoor privy. Well, the debts have finally been paid in full and Paolo, Fernandez's dad, wants to start over."

Jung-su looked at Rey, curious.

"Paolo wants to stay," said Rey, "But his wife Frida, and Fernandez are talking about leaving Infernus the next time 'No-Teeth' Murnau schedules a voyage to the Farlands."

"What's that got to do with me and Randen?" asked Jung-su.

"I'd like you boys to pay Fernandez a visit."

Jung-su rolled his eyes back, in dread.

"It may not be as bad as all that," said Rey. "I want you and Randen to introduce yourselves to Fernandez and his folks, spend part of the day with them. Kind of a 'welcome to Infernus' sort of thing, you might say. I want you to convince Fernandez that he's perfectly safe here, while Randen convinces him that he's got nothing to fear from the Brown Winged Men."

"Good luck with that," sighed Jung-su. "I heard that Fernandez had to be dragged into town yesterday by Mucker and that diplomat! That is, until Mucker had his fill of the sissy, and corrected the problem by belting him over the forehead!"

"I won't argue with that," agreed Rey, tiredly.

"It'd be just our luck that Fernandez will get one look at Randen and me and have a heart attack! He's probably never laid eyes on an Oriental before, and . . ."

"Jung-su . . ."

"From what I heard, that sissy's afraid of his own shadow!"

"Probably," said Rey. "But you will do this for me . . . won't you, Jung-su?"

"Do I have to?"

"Do I have to write a letter on your behalf to the staff of Lord William's Academy, once you get there?"

Jung-su smiled, knowing he was being set-up by Rey.

"Don't worry," said Rey. "I'll still write that letter for you. I'm sure you'll do well for yourself when you get enrolled into Lord William's . . . if you still plan on attending, that is."

"Yes, sir."

"I'll make that letter extra-special flowery," said Rey, cleverly. "All I want is for you and Randen to try and make friends with Fernandez. I'm aware that it may not work. For all we know, Fernandez is the world's worst momma's boy . . . But, for whatever stupid reason, I've got a soft spot in my heart for that particular momma's boy. I also have a soft spot for Paolo. I think he's a good man who wants to do right by moving his family here. And if you and Randen's efforts pan out, not only will you be helping that family, but me as well."

"Yes, sir," said Jung-su, wondering what he was getting himself into. "I'll do my best. You can count on that."

"I knew you wouldn't let me down."

"And I do appreciate the letter you're writing for me."

"Speaking of the Farlands," said Rey, nervously. "I heard that you're planning on making that trip on the Edith-Marie . . . with 'No-Teeth' . . ."

Jung-su never said nothing, but figured he was in trouble.

"Going to the Farlands is one thing," said Rey. "It doesn't take into account how I feel about you. I'll miss you more than anything, though I know you'll be safe once you reach Embrey."

"Yes, sir."

"It's the voyage that worries me."

"Why?" asked Jung-su, getting kind of mad.

"I've talked to too many survivors of the Edith-Marie. 'No-Teeth' has a bad reputation for recklessness on the open seas. And that food . . ."

"I'll be fine! You don't need to worry about me. I can take care of myself!"

"It's a long way from here to Agron," said Rey. "Are you sure you can take care of yourself, if that leaky old crate sinks, capsizes, or meets up with pirates?"

"That can happen to anyone!"

"I know you'll be all right," said Rey, in a condescending tone. "I haven't got a right to worry, you being an adult and everything . . ."

"I am an adult, Leader Rey!" hollered Jung-su. "I've been on my own since I moved out of Errol and Ericha's and went to work at The Black Eye. And I'll be perfectly safe with 'No-Teeth'! I'll get there on the Edith-Marie, just you see! Just what have you and Jer got against 'No-Teeth', anyway?"

"He charges way too much for fare. His crew, what he has of a crew, are some of the foulest characters to see the inside of a bar or a bordello. And . . . that food . . ."

"I'll be fine!"

"Why are you so fired-up on leaving us, that you're willing to risk life and limb with a man like 'No-Teeth'?" asked Rey.

Jung-su frowned. "I don't want to spend the rest of my life on this island, and I can't stand much more of The Black Eye! No disrespect, sir, but I really do want off this rock. I want to see the world, while I'm still young enough and not burdened by a wife or other responsibilities!"

"Do you want off this rock badly enough to die alongside 'No-Teeth'?"

"Enough to live somewhere else, instead of being trapped on Infernus!" said Jung-su, sick and tired of being sick and tired.

"I can understand why you don't want to work at The Black Eye. Honestly, I don't know why you're compelled to stay there, considering how badly they treat you."

"Money," said Jung-su, flatly. "Just money . . ."

"Look. Forget about The Black Eye. If it's money you want, I'll find youn-some work here. And I'm sure Errol can still use a hand . . ."

"Sir . . ."

"And, if I were you, I'd be looking for a way out of that filthy little shed you're living in!" added Rey. "So you're tired of The Black Eye? Fine! I'm glad to hear it, Jung-su! I've been worried sick since you went to work for them. Come back to work for me. If you're looking for another place to live before you leave for the Farlands, I see no problem in letting you stay here with me and Jeremy . . ."

Jung-su sighed. Thoughts of moving back in with Rey and Jeremy was a defeat, a way of giving up his independence, along with the right of calling himself a grown-up. He had his mind set. He wanted to move away from Infernus, as soon as possible, and wouldn't be stopped from it! He looked Rey straight in the eye and crossed his arms. He was done fighting, and wouldn't have nothing more to say about it.

"I'm sorry," breathed Rey, kind of teary-eyed. He wasn't going to win this one, unless Jung-su had a change of heart. "Seems I'll be losing Jeremy one of these days. The thought of seeing you go, too . . . well . . ."

"No disrespect, sir," interrupted Jung-su, "But I just can't help that. I'm sorry, but I've just got to paddle my own canoe. Let Jer do the same."

Rey nodded YES. "I want you and Randen to please be careful going to New Merieko. Rest assured, I do appreciate your efforts . . ."

Jung-su smiled as he and Rey went to the door. He reached out and gave Rey another hug. "Don't worry, sir," he said. "I'll be back before sundown."

"I know that," said Rey. "I hope you and I can have dinner together some evening, before you leave and . . . get on with your life. Your adult life."

"That I will!" said Jung-su. "You can count on it!"

"I know, Jung-su," whispered Rey, as the emotions got the better of him. He couldn't keep from giving Jung-su a fatherly kiss on the cheek. "I know . . ."

* * * * *

Jung-su and Randen got to the small, growing community of New Merieko at mid-morning.

Months before, there wasn't nothing there but a long, narrow stretch of beach, nestled against a thick growth of brush and trees. Who imagined putting a town in that place? The ground was hard, uneven, and rocky. Trees, plants, and weeds grew together in a mangled up, tangled up mess. A creek ran through the joint, as crooked as a dog's hind-leg, and often flowed over its own banks. Abarbeaus and other critters roamed everywhere, making this area difficult, dangerous, and mighty darn scary.

Why build a colony there?

In less than a year, a few brave, brazen, and foolhardy men went in and carved the landscape into a town. Workers cut down a bunch of trees through a long, narrow gap measuring a hundred yards wide, and almost two-hundred yards long. Them of dumb minds and stout hearts flattened and leveled the ground, while diverting the creek for irrigation and drinking water. Stumps was the only evidence that huge trees once covered the joint. Them same trees was cut into lumber, to build the huts and homes which made up New Merieko.

Jung-su and Randen carefully trekked along a trail from Persis to New

Merieko. They heard plenty of critters howling at their arrival. All stayed hidden in the dense, evergreen forest. The two boys talked quietly, as to not attract man-eating and winged man-eating critters. Randen wanted to fly to New Merieko, and offered to give Jung-su a 'piggy-back ride.' Jung-su would have none of it. He might not have been too scared to move away from Infernus, but was sure afraid of heights!

Jung-su wore a school uniform he got from Leader Rey, for when he greeted newcomers to the island. It consisted of a brown skullcap and long-sleeved tunic which hung down almost to the knees, sandals, and nothing to cover his skinny legs. It was kind of like the school outfit Fernandez had on, but a bit older and worn out. On warm days Jung-su didn't mind them clothes so much. On cold days, he hated them. The worst thing was the skeeters, which took pleasure biting his bare shins, knees, and thighs!

It took Jung-su and Randen about an hour to walk the meandering trip to New Merieko. Neither had been to the colony much, unless Rey or somebody else sent them on a lousy errant. More and more houses and buildings had went up since Jung-su's last visit to the village. The first time he went there, it was populated only by big, brawny, hard-living, hard-drinking men sleeping in bunk-houses. In truth they probably slept very little, and spent their nights killing the critters who tried to eat them. Now, there was almost as many women and kids roaming around New Merieko and there was carpenters and others forging a city out of the wilderness.

Jung-su was amazed by the number of people living there. It resembled a civilization, no longer a lumber camp. As kids and their moms loitered on the beach, or cooked meals, the men sawed boards and logs, and built newer structures.

Jung-su almost thought twice about leaving Infernus, as he saw opportunity in New Merieko. As Randen went out of his way to be nice to the colonists, he was afraid they wouldn't be nice back. While a few folks was fascinated and intrigued by the sight of a critter they never once seen before, others regarded winged men as demon spawn and monsters.

Jung-su smiled when he saw what appeared as a Brotherhood Church going up in New Merieko. Leader Rey was performing double-duty as a preacher. He first held Sunday services in Persis, then headed to New Merieko and had church outside. Little-by-little, a small church made head-way, along a narrow, winding lane which was New Merieko's main thoroughfare.

Jung-su didn't quite know what he wanted to do when he got older. He haggled over plans of becoming a merchant, businessman, or Leader. The formation of a church steeple towering over New Merieko made him contemplate on gaining his Leadership status in Embrey, then returning to head this new branch of the church.

Where Jung-su got all happy when he entered New Merieko, Randen got real scared. He hated going places where he felt outnumbered. He wasn't outnumbered in Persis, or even on the whole entire island of Infernus. That day, he was the only winged man in New Merieko. The mean, dirty looks some of them people in New Merieko gave Randen made him want to turn tail and run, or better yet fly away.

New Merieko was a busy place when Jung-su and Randen got there. As Jung-su smiled at the construction taking place all around him, Randen couldn't find any reason to smile at all, based on the hatred and suspicion he got from them folks.

As people smiled and greeted Jung-su, they mumbled to themselves about Randen. Before he even got half-way through town, Randen figured he had every reason to forget all about helping Fernandez, and head back to Persis, where he wasn't an outsider or a spectacle.

A brawny man with red hair and a touch of gray at the temples and sideburns stepped off a ladder, a hammer in one hand. He headed toward Randen and Jung-su, wiping sweat from his wrinkled, sunburned forehead. He acted like he owned the joint, not just the building he worked on, but the whole entire town of New Merieko. He tucked the hammer under one arm and offered Jung-su a handshake. "Can I do for you boys?" he asked, in a low, booming voice.

Jung-su gave the man a hearty handshake and asked, "Where may I find an Agronian family, by the names of? . . ." He had to stop and think. "Forgive me, sir. I forgot the couple's name, but they've got a son named Fernandez."

The man had to think a spell before he asked, "That Frida and Paolo you're talking about?"

"Yes, those are the names," said Jung-su. "Paolo and Frida. Where may we find them?"

"Who are you, and who sent you?" the man asked, in a not unfriendly but not-so-friendly tone.

"I'm Jung-su, and this is my friend Randen. We were sent by Leader Rey of the Persis Brotherhood of Faith, to check on Paolo and Frida . . . Oh, and on Fernandez, too!" Jung-su cleared his throat. "And who are you, sir, if you don't mind my asking?"

"Greenleaf," the man said, boastfully. "Originally from northern Embrey."

"Glad to make your acquaintance," said Jung-Su.

Randen was far from glad to make Greenleaf's acquaintance. The longer he hung around there, the worse he felt. In the corner of one eye, he saw a couple of small boys pointing at him, then whispering to themselves. He didn't like the looks of that at all, and wondered if it wasn't best for Jung-su to handle Fernandez by himself. Randen wanted to fly back to Persis, as fast as he could.

"Well, I can direct you to Paolo's," said Greenleaf, not sounding too keen on the idea. "Don't know how they might act toward visitors."

Neither Jung-su nor Randen said nothing, but looked at Greenleaf as if to ask WHY?

"Paolo's been having a terrible time with his wife and son," said Greenleaf. "All Frida and Nandy talk about is returning to Agron. I can direct you to Paolo's, all right, but if they're not up to visitors . . ."

Greenleaf pointed to a hut sitting at the left of what one might consider the end of New Merieko's main street. After that was nothing but thick weeds and forest. "There's Paolo's place," he said. "You can pop in there if you want, but if they're not up to visitors . . ."

"Don't worry," said Jung-su, his big smile not near as big as it was when he first arrived. "We'll just introduce ourselves as youth leaders for the Brotherhood of Faith, let them know if they need any help to just call on us, then we'll be on our way."

Greenleaf looked at Jung-su and Randen, kind of strangely. He never said nothing, but acted like them two boys was from some other world or something.

"Have a nice day," said Jung-su, trying to act all nice and friendly, even though Greenleaf never returned the gesture. "We'll just wander to Paolo and Frida's, then be on our way . . ."

Jung-su and Randen headed toward the last house on the left, both feeling kind of unwanted. What good thoughts Jung-su might have had about New Merieko, he no longer had them. More and more, he wanted off of Infernus, altogether! He didn't care whether Leader Rey liked it or not, he was going to leave when 'No-Teeth' made his next trip to the Farlands. He'd take Rey's letter on his behalf, then enroll himself into Lord William's Academy in Sykes.

Then it'd be a cold day in Hades before he set foot on the island, ever again!

"I'd better go," said Randen, nervously. "I don't think they like us here."

"What's wrong?" asked Jung-su, trying to be funny though he saw nothing funny about the mess they was in. "You think these people are afraid of Orientals?"

By now, it was hot outside, and Jung-su and Randen was dying for a drink. There was plenty of creeks and streams between Persis and New Merieko that had good water, assuming there wasn't something rancid or dead in it. Some of the huts and houses in New Merieko had their own wells, but who among these folks would offer a cold drink to an Oriental kid or kid winged man?

Jung-su and Randen approached Paolo's house, a modest little place barely able to hold the three people living in it. Fernandez shared the same bedroom as his mommy and daddy, because he was too scared to sleep in a room by himself. Paolo aimed to get started on adding an extra bedroom, but was slow at it.

Like many homes in the island, there weren't no real door on Paolo's, just a blanket or sheet hanging over the entrance for privacy. Newcomers figured it was too hot for doors or glass windows on Infernus. They'd get over such notions, on a bad night whenever a critter snuck in to eat their pets or children. After getting such terrible surprises, most people would install doors and windows!

Jung-su shot a funny, nervous glance at Randen, as he pecked on the side of the hut, as there weren't no door to peck on.

"Yes," a tired, weary voice said from inside. A woman peeked through a window, not far from where the door should've been.

"We're from the Brotherhood of Faith Church," said Jung-su. He figured this visit was a dumb idea, and the best thing would be to skedaddle on out of there. "Leader Rey sent us to . . . check up on you, and make sure everything's okay . . ."

Frida opened up the thin sheet they used as a door. She was shocked at the sight of Jung-su and Randen standing there. No words was exchanged, as Frida got into something of a staring contest with the two boys.

"My name's Jung-su, this is my friend Randen," he said, forcing a smile. "We were sent by Leader Rey and . . . y' know . . . the Brotherhood of Faith Church over in Persis . . ."

"Who?" whined Frida, bothered by what she viewed as an intrusion, and not as a nice little visit.

"Leader Rey at . . ." Jung-su motioned to the west. "Y' know . . . at the church . . . Well, he sent us over to . . ."

"Oh?" asked Frida. "Leader Rey?"

"Yes, ma'am," said Jung-su, not sure whether to laugh or slap Frida's face off, for the nasty look she gave him. "You see . . . our Leader, Leader Rey, wanted to make sure you were all right . . ."

Paolo then stuck his head outside. He'd been sleeping and what little hair he had was all messed up, and both eyes drooped worse than normal. "Good morning," he said, surprised to see Jung-su and Randen. At least he acted nicer than Greenleaf or Frida. "May I help you?"

After Jung-su introduced himself and Randen (again!) while stating what their business was (again!), he politely asked, "Is your son here?"

"Nandy?" asked Frida, like Jung-su and Randen had something bad in mind, when it came to her kid. "What do you want with? . . ."

"Leader Rey wanted to make sure he . . . all of you, were all right . . . y' know, after yesterday," said Jung-su, trying not to smirk.

"Yesterday?" whined Frida, all wild-eyed and anxious.

"I heard that Fernandez had quite a scare yesterday," explained Jung-su. "Y' know, with the pirates and all . . ."

"They sent you?" asked Paolo.

Jung-su almost laughed, not because this was funny, but because it was so frustrating! "We're youth leaders from the church, me and Randen," he said. "Leader Rey thought it would be a good idea for those in Fernandez's age group to . . . y' know . . . spend a little time with him . . . help him to make an adjustment to life on Infernus . . . y' know . . ."

Paolo seemed real pleased with Jung-su and Randen. Frida was another story, as she figured that the boys' visit would lead to her little Nandy's demise.

"Come in, come in," greeted Paolo, opening the sheet enough to let Jung-su and Randen inside. "Fernandez, these young men wish to see you . . ."

The cooler temperatures of the hut was inviting to Jung-su and Randen. Paolo seemed nice enough to the visitors, but not Frida, who ran the house with an iron fist and a mean voice, to keep her whimpy husband and son in their place.

Jung-su and Randen found Fernandez sitting at a tiny dining room table, working on some schoolwork that Frida tutored him in.

Fernandez looked up from his pen and paper. He smiled when he saw another kid, dressed in the same kind of school clothes he had on.

This was short-lived, as Fernandez looked over at Randen, which he regarded as a demon, there to eat him or convert him to the Devil.

"Get him outa here!" shrieked Fernandez, hopping from the table to cower in one corner of the dinky hut. He covered his face up under both hands, then carried on like a little bitty baby. "Get him outa here!"

Frida threw her arm around Fernandez, to assure him that he wasn't going to get ate.

Randen decided he'd had enough of this. He sprinted outside, as Jung-su hastily followed him.

"Come back!" hollered Jung-su, thinking Fernandez's reaction to Randen was both comical and disgusting. "Please, come back! He'll be fine once he realizes how nice you are . . ."

"No, he won't!" Randen hollered back. "We'll never realize 'how nice I am,' because he'll never give me that chance!"

"Randen," sighed Jung-su. "Look, I don't want to be here either, but . . ."

"That coward doesn't want me around!" yelled Randen, loud enough for them in the hut to hear. "Forget it, Jung-su. There's no point in me staying. Maybe you can convince Nandy that he's safe on the island, but I can't."

"Randen . . . please?"

"I'll let Rey know how well this went," said Randen, sarcastically. "Go back inside, and enjoy your visit . . ."

"Wait just a minute, Randen . . ."

"What?"

Jung-su gave Randen a real big hug.

Randen was kind of embarrassed by Jung-su's gesture, but what else could he expect from a hugger?

As the two boys broke free, Randen said, "See you when you get home . . ."

"Not if I see you first," snickered Jung-su, as Randen turned and walked away.

Randen sighed. He was sick and tired of Farlanders. Some went out of their way to be nice to winged men and live according to the unwritten rules of Infernus. It seemed that more and more of them wanted to change things, to suit them and only them. And part of that change meant treating winged men as inferior, second-class critters . . .

Randen walked through New Merieko, wishing the place burned to the ground, and all of them Farlanders would go back to where they come from.

"You!" a Kuschan-sounding voice called out. "You there, winged man . . . You!"

Randen stopped, turned, and saw a young guy standing at the doorway of a hut. The guy was short, even shorter than Jung-su. He looked and sounded kind of like a kid, based on his appearance and the occasional high-pitched ring in his voice. Yet, his piercing eyes told of experience well-beyond his years, which sent a chill down Randen's spine.

"Come here," the guy said, beckoning Randen to get closer.

"Yes?" asked Randen, slowly approaching the guy.

"Are you knowledgeable of this part of the island?" the guy asked, his tone cold and indifferent.

"Sort of . . ." Randen shrugged. "Why?"

"There's an odd-looking animal which keeps trying to get in my house through a back window. I thought you'd know what it was."

"It's probably an abarbeaus," said Randen, nervously. "Stay clear of them! Better yet, arm yourself, so if it comes back . . ."

"It wasn't an abarbeaus!" the guy yelled, glaring at Randen with two scary eyes.

"What then?"

"Why, I've never saw anything like it! It looked like a cross between a large predatory bird and an elephant! Rather huge it was, and . . ."

"What's an elephant?" asked Randen.

"You don't know what an elephant is?" the guy questioned, as if Randen was stupid. "Where have you been your entire life?"

"No place," said Randen, with a nervous grin. "Just Infernus . . ."

"Oh, well then . . . My apologies . . ."

"So, what's an elephant?"

"Come with me," the guy whispered. "It may still be there . . . behind my hut . . ."

"Okay," said Randen, eager to see this critter the guy was talking about.

When the guy and Randen got behind the hut, there wasn't nothing back there but a small clearing, along with thick brush and trees. Other than the sounds of boards getting sawed, hammered, and nailed, it was deathly quiet. No one was in sight, except for the guy and Randen.

The guy pointed at a narrow trail, heading who-knows-where into the woods. "There!" he shouted. "It lives out there . . . somewhere! Every night, it comes toward the house from that very spot! If we go there, we may get a better look!"

"I . . . I don't know what you're talking about." Randen gulped. "I've never seen or heard of anything like that . . ."

"There!" the guy hollered, pointing toward a dark, murky area of the forest. "Did you see it?"

"See what?"

"Walk in front of me," the guy said, "and we'll see if it's still there . . ."

Randen hesitantly tip-toed to the edge of the woods. The guy took the rear, smiling in anticipation of catching a glimpse of that weird, elephant critter thing. Randen couldn't see or hear nothing, other than the chattering of birds, and the high-pitched shriek of something getting ate. Such rackets was typical on Infernus, so typical they hardly caused a fuss.

There wasn't nothing strange out there, not enough to go out of the way to look for.

Randen took a deep breath. He figured the guy was seeing things, by thinking he saw an elephant thing that supposedly snuck up on his hut at night. The guy was just a typical Farlander, which amounted to a know-it-all who didn't know nothing about Infernus!

Already fed-up by the way Fernandez had acted toward him earlier, Randen turned around . . .

. . . Just as the guy drove a long-bladed knife into his chest . . .

* * * * *

"You say that I'm safe with you," said Weston, as Jeremy handed him the flask. "Does that take into account my wishes for you to accept your inheritance?"

Jeremy's mood got gloomy.

"Well, here I go again," mumbled Weston. "Guess I'm really not starting out too well with you."

"Aw, hell . . ." groaned Jeremy. "You're okay."

"Sure, I'm okay, assuming I drop ideas of you going to Branell."

"Infernus is home, Weston."

"I know what you're getting at," said Weston. "Believe me, I sympathize."

"Then why do you keep insisting on me going someplace where I'll be a stranger?"

"But you won't be a stranger! Not for long. You seem the amiable type. Trust me, you'll make friends easily."

"Yeah. As soon as them friends find out about all that loot and land, they'll get a lot friendlier!" Jeremy shook his head. "With friends like that . . . I ain't wanting it."

"So, you're just going to allow the Branellian king to take that which isn't rightfully his? Without even putting up a fight?"

"What if it ain't worth fighting for?"

"Will you feel that same way when you're thirty?" asked Weston. "What about forty? You won't stay young forever. And, if you don't mind my saying, you won't always look so vibrant and healthy in a loincloth."

Jeremy grinned. "You been talking to Rey."

"We share the same concerns. The older a man gets, the more wrinkled and flabby he looks."

"I won't!"

"That's what I thought when I was your age!" laughed Weston. "You won't stay young forever, no matter how many wild animals you kill in these woods, or how . . . savage and primitive you look doing it."

"It's my business, ain't it?"

"I guess," breathed Weston. "Just like it was my business to come all this way and give you some news which I thought you'd be happy about! Just like it was my business to come here and finally meet my cousin Jeremiah Kentworth, in person." Weston got to his feet. "Guess I was wrong. Just like it was wrong for this Farlander to think he'd be welcome here, or that I'd have success developing diplomatic ties! Maybe the best thing for me to do is swim back to Embrey . . . this very day!"

"Then why don'tcha, Mister Weston?"

"But, before I go," added Weston. "Won't you at least consider on going to the Farlands with me, and look that property over?"

"Why should I?"

"I'm trying to do you a favor. Why do King Josiah a favor by giving him your inheritance? He doesn't need it, he's rich enough as it is! You may have need for such wealth! The older you get, the more you'll want and need it. Aren't you going to at least take the time to see what you stand to lose? Or do you stay here and be nothing but just plain old Jeremy?"

"Isn't that enough, just to be me? Just plain old Jeremy?"

"What will change your mind?" asked Weston. "Help me help you. Tell me, kiddo . . . What will change your mind?"

Jeremy stared off in the distance, as a breeze swept through his hair.

"What if we talk someone into throwing in with you?" asked Weston.

Jeremy laughed. "We already know it won't be Mucker!"

"I wasn't even going to ask that . . . gentleman."

Who, then? Rey?"

Weston grinned. "I was thinking more in line of that lovely young redhead you're so fond of."

"Ericha?"

"Who else? Surely not Prince Ari!"

"Errol won't let her go with me," moped Jeremy.

"Ericha can't stay young forever, either. Whether Errol likes it or not, he can't keep her under his thumb for the rest of her life."

Jeremy frowned. "Whatever makes you think I want her with me?"

"Did you two not spend the whole night together under the stars?" snickered Weston. "I see that twinkle in your eye, whenever you two are together. Just like I noticed that admiring look on her face, when you rubbed mashed potatoes and gravy in Ari's face."

Jeremy blushed.

"Ericha's of an age where she has to start making up her own mind about things," said Weston. "And, if you don't mind my saying, she also has to dress more appropriately."

"What do you mean?"

"I'm a man, the same as you are. Whenever I see Ericha running around in a loincloth, I worry that my manly thoughts will get me into trouble. I'm sure you feel the same way . . . . Eh, kiddo?"

Jeremy's blush got a lot redder.

"Considering how close you two are to each other," said Weston, "I'm sure she's had womanly thoughts about you."

"What? . . . What are you getting at, Mister Weston?" stuttered Jeremy.

"You know what I'm getting at, Jeremiah. Rey has confided in me. He's afraid that your manly thoughts and her womanly thoughts will get you both into trouble."

"I'm telling you what I told Rey!" hollered Jeremy. "Nothing like that happened, and nothing's ever gonna happen! Why does everyone think that me and Ericha's been? . . ."

"Why did she spend the night with you, after you decorated her brother with last night's dinner? Speaking of which, I'd avoid Errol for a while, if I were you."

"What? . . . What for?"

"If you have to ask that question, you're not as smart as I thought," said Weston. "Ericha never went home last night. She was with you the whole time. Fathers have a bad tendency to let their imaginations run wild."

Jeremy sighed.

"If we can talk Ericha into going with you to the Farlands, will you consider claiming your inheritance?" asked Weston.

"What about Errol? Do you think he'll let her go, after what I done to the Little Oinker?"

"Well, you know women. If Ericha pesters Errol bad enough, he might be happy to get rid of her. As for Prince Ari, he won't mind seeing her leave. I get the feeling Ericha and Ari don't like each other very well."

"Ari won't mind seeing me leave, that's for sure," mumbled Jeremy. "Do you think Ericha can pester her old man bad enough to leave the island with me? Ericha was born here. So was Ari. After Errol's wife croaked, he's gotten awfully protective of them. The next time Errol sees me, he's liable to have an axe in one hand, and a shovel in the other."

"Issuing an insincere, heartfelt apology to Errol can't hurt," said Weston, sarcastically. "If worse comes to worse, you might even have to bend down to kiss his fat, cantankerous . . ."

Before Weston finished talking, there was a loud rustling sound coming from the trees and brush.

Jeremy figured that him and Weston was getting attacked by a mess of critters. He hopped to his feet and kept a close watch, his sword at the ready.

"What? . . ." mumbled Weston. "What is it? . . ."

"Shh!" whispered Jeremy, both excited and scared at thoughts of fighting more critters. "Might be an abarbeaus . . ."

"Abarbeaus?"

"Keep still," warned Jeremy, "and maybe they won't . . ."

Randen staggered out of the trees, toward Jeremy and Weston. He was exhausted from flying. He was bleeding from gashes in his chest, gut, and wings. He was bad scared of something, yet relieved to see the two men.

"Randen?" gasped Jeremy, unnerved by the winged kid's condition.

"Am I glad to see you!" laughed Randen. He took a couple of clumsy, feeble steps into the clearing, then collapsed to his knees.

Jeremy dashed to Randen. "You okay?" he asked, high-pitched and raspy.

"I was in New Merieko with Jung-su," explained Randen. He was breathing heavily, and had trouble staying conscious. "When this angry Kuschan . . ."

Before Randen could say anything more, a couple of abarbeaus pounced on him from a tree. His words were now replaced by a shrill scream, which echoed all through the woods.

Weston dragged Jeremy away from Randen. Both men looked on helplessly, as Randen was torn limb-from-limb by the two abarbeaus. A third one joined in on the kill, as Randen got ate alive.

In response, Jeremy swung his sword and decapitated one of the abarbeaus.

The area got even bloodier, as the headless abarbeaus went into a bad case of the flip-flops. Jeremy tried to save Randen, by attacking the last two abarbeauses.

He never expected one of the abarbeaus to leap at him.

The abarbeaus' mouth gaped wide open, as it flew right into the middle of Jeremy. With one swipe of its claws, it ripped holes through Jeremy's buckskin shirt.

Jeremy fell back into the clearing, as the sword flew from his hand. He let out a defiant scream, blocking the beast's advances with his arms, legs, and feet.

The abarbeaus circled around Jeremy, saliva drooling from its mouth. Jeremy assumed a defensive position on his knees. He fetched the knife hanging from his hip and shoved it at the beast. The beast jumped away from Jeremy.

The last thing the beast expected was to have Weston kick it in the face.

This only aggravated the beast. It forgot all about Jeremy and went after Weston.

Weston tripped over one of the dead abarbeaus which was killed the day before. Swarms of flies and a foul stink went everywhere. Weston slammed into the ground, with the wind knocked out of him.

The beast let out an ear-shattering roar, as Weston let out an ear-splitting scream.

Weston tried crawling away backwards, thinking he was as good as ate. In a last-ditch attempt to save his life, he latched onto Jeremy sword, as the abarbeaus pounced at him.

Weston swung the sword at the lunging abarbeaus and slashed it across the chest. Blood spurted from the chest, as the abarbeaus landed upon Weston. The abarbeaus was the same as killed, but tried to even the score by snapping its teeth at Weston's throat.

Weston desperately pushed the critter away from him. He got to his feet and ran the sword into the critter's guts, over and over and over again, until it was nothing but a mutilated mess.

That left only one last abarbeaus, who was in the process of eating Randen. Blinded by rage, Jeremy knifed the last abarbeaus a bunch of times, until its lifeless remains splattered all over Randen's corpse.

Jeremy couldn't do nothing to help Randen, but had the satisfaction that them critters wasn't going to eat anymore of the poor, dead kid winged man. Jeremy and Randen had grown up together, and this loss was a painful blow. Jeremy's eyes welled up in tears. He wanted to get tough about it, and not show how upset he was.

"You okay?" asked Weston, putting one arm around Jeremy's shoulder.

"What's it look like?" groaned Jeremy. Unable to hold it back any further, he put his face against Weston's chest and wept.

Weston gave Jeremy a hug. There weren't no point in words. Words would never describe what had just happened. It was just enough that Weston was there when Jeremy needed him the most.

One thought held tight in Weston's mind. Somehow he couldn't shake it, no matter how hard he tried.

What exactly did Randen mean by "angry Kuschan?"

* * * * *

Two small Agronian boys sprinted past the open door of Pastor Yevgeny's hut, as he stood there, toying with the blade of his sharpened dagger.

It was getting real hot and humid in New Merieko, even in early-autumn. Construction got under way for more houses. There was the constant racket of sawing, pounding, and hammering. Housewives worked to make their new dwellings suitable for their kids to live in. When they wasn't busy, they gossiped with the neighbor ladies. Mostly, they adapted themselves to the climate and geography of Infernus. Hardly none of them was used to the long, warm days, the horrible insects, or the strange plant-life of the island.

The colonists of New Merieko left their native homelands to start over. Even then, they basically brought over variations of their values, customs, and lifestyles which was left behind. Agronians hung out with Agronians, Embrians hung around other Embrians, and Kuschans hung out with their own kind.

Yevgeny stood at his doorway, toying with the blade of his dagger. He inspected the weapon as if it was an extension of his own body and spirit.

Yevgeny took possession of the dagger, since he first found it lying in a mud hole on the outskirts of Anumun, in northern Kusch. He was an orphan, thanks to the invading Embrian army, back when Embrey and Kusch was at war with each other. Yevgeny had to fend for himself after his whole entire family had been massacred. He was only twelve-years-old. He lived in any kind of shelter imaginable, and survived on any grub he could find, usually that which got thrown out by the invading Embrians. He witnessed the savage and perverse brutality of the Embrian officers and enlisted men, who concealed their crimes against Kuschans behind the pretense of civility and honor.

Yevgeny's cousin Lina was taken in by an Embrian captain who violated her as a cheap little concubine, while claiming she was his fiancée'. Only after his intentions were revealed did the captain remove them, by slitting Lina's throat. Yevgeny answered this atrocity by castrating the Embrian captain . . . then slitting his stinking throat.

This was the first time Yevgeny used the dagger to kill another man. It wouldn't be the last. After Yevgeny got over the shock and horror of killing, he enjoyed butchering the Embrian soldiers entering his country.

Yevgeny's actions against the enemy soon became the stuff of legend. His bloodshed was feared, revered, and unsuspected, especially from one so childlike and "innocent."

Yevgeny snickered. None of the Embrians who ravaged Kusch knew that the killer was a small, squeaky-voiced kid who tended to the enemies' horses, mules, and livestock. He performed these chores, not for the animals' sake, but to access more victims.

After a year or so, there was so many victims that even Yevgeny lost count.

Yevgeny's dagger came in real handy against Embrians, just like it'd come in real handy against other critters. Critters so hideous, disgusting, and vulgar, they'd make Embrians look human in comparison.

Yevgeny had just used the dagger on one such critter, before it flew off into the hills overlooking New Merieko. He did severe damage to the critter's wings, guts, and chest, before it flew off someplace.

Yevgeny laughed. Winged men sure was stupid! They made Embrians look smart! As the critter visited New Merieko with a slanty-eyed gook, he was called over to Yevgeny's hut, not knowing he'd soon meet the steel of a dagger. The dumb critter had no idea of the surprise awaiting him.

That was, until Yevgeny pierced its wings, chest, and guts!

Yevgeny hoped the critter wouldn't get far. The wretch bled quite profusely from its wounds. With luck, it wouldn't reach Persis to report what Yevgeny done to it. With luck, the critter would have to stop in the hills separating Persis from New Merieko.

With luck, it'd die the same way as that poor Kuschan boy.

Who'd dare accuse a Kuschan pastor of the crime? That same Kuschan pastor who, years before, tended to the Embrian Army's horses and mules, studied at the University of Sykes, and now spread the word of the Kuen to the wilderness of Infernus.

But was killing one of them winged critters a crime? Surely not in the mind and heart of the Kuen!

Yevgeny returned the dagger to its sheath, placed it in the top drawer of a bureau, then went outside to a hot, humid autumn day. It wasn't noon yet, and already newer houses and structures were erected. At Leader Rey's urging, a fellowship hall for the Brotherhood Church was underway. Yevgeny had used his own hut as a meeting place for Kuschan believers. Once the number of his countrymen had increased on the island, a suitable church would go up.

But before more Kuschans arrived, Yevgeny sought to get rid of each and every foul, disgusting, wretched critter on the island. Them same critters who bore more than just a passing resemblance to the Kuschan god of evil, Soraq.

Yevgeny spotted young Fernandez in the shade of a lone tree, with Paolo and Frida. The gook who accompanied the winged demon into New Merieko was looking over the construction of a new Brotherhood Church. Yevgeny frowned. Rarely did Nandy leave his folks' sight. Small wonder them pirates was able to snatch up them other kids, including the poor Kuschan boy who'd never again see his parents.

Not in this world, anyway.

Fernandez was a dutiful boy. He wasn't one to stir up trouble. But he was a sissy and a momma's boy, dressed in a pathetic school uniform which showed off two scrawny legs.

Fernandez was scared bad of winged men. And why not? Winged men was not of this world. They was an abomination, freaks of nature which could never, should never be viewed as moral, conscious beings! Leader Rey was a decent man, but foolish for thinking he'd convert winged men to a monolithic god. Them critters was primitive, uncivilized, and unworthy of life.

Yevgeny suffered no shame or guilt for knifing that dumb winged man, anymore than he felt bad for the Embrian invaders he butchered, years ago. He sought now to cleanse Infernus of the winged demons in the same manner he cleansed Kusch of the Embrians. He needed help. If only he'd get Fernandez away from his folks, long enough to make a strong, persuasive argument. Then maybe he'd persuade the Agronian sissy to persuade other colonists to fight the winged demons.

Until all winged demons was forever swept away from the surface of the Earth.

* * * * *

Chief Lorenzo's hut sat kind of smack-dab in the middle of Persis. It wasn't a very big building, but kind of small for one of such importance in Infernus politics and royalty. The hut was big enough for meetings and counseling sessions. Its seating resembled a town hall or a church, and was shaped for both people and winged men. Living quarters was in the back.

The hut sure wasn't splendid nor lavish. It was practical, not showy or pretentious. Lorenzo was one of many Brown chiefs to live in the hut. Though he was one of the biggest of the island's big-wigs, he lived like most people and winged men in Persis. Lorenzo was in charge of making real tough decisions, which affected the whole entire island. His rulings wasn't always popular, and on more than a few occasions there was calls to replace him.

Lorenzo knew he wasn't going to please everybody. He only hoped that his plans never brung any harm to them around him. He cared deeply about each and everybody in town, people and winged men alike.

In people terms, Lorenzo was almost sixty, and one of the oldest winged men on Infernus. He married late in life, and was reluctant to give up being chief of the Brown Winged Men. He figured that his eldest son and heir apparent, Malachi, was too young to assume power. There was always strong differences of opinion between father and son, mostly involving religion.

Like Lorenzo, Nikolai held onto traditional gods, values, and customs. Malachi's spiritual conversion to the Brotherhood Church, along with his friendship to Rey and Mucker, conflicted with Lorenzo. Quietly, Lorenzo considered on by-passing Malachi's rise to the throne, in favor of Nikolai. Neither son knew any of this. Lorenzo hoped and prayed that he'd never have to make such a thankless decision.

When Lorenzo opened diplomatic and trade ties to Kusch, this was met with head-scratching confusion, or all-out anger and hostility. Most folks didn't even know what a Kuschan was, other than they come from the Farlands, and talked in a tongue far different than that of Embrians, Agronians, and Branellians.

That morning, Lorenzo and his two sons was to meet with two Kuschan naval officers, Admiral Vaslov and Commander Antonov, from the warship Matyushenko. Based on Vic McClusky's urging, the Green Winged Men had already joined up with the Kuschans. Now, Lorenzo was to talk with them. He hoped that such a move might bridge Infernus with the Farlands, and help sustain peace between the Brown and Green Winged Men.

Like Mucker, Malachi was opposed to meeting with the Kuschans. Out of love and respect to Lorenzo, he hated to disagree with his dad. He was even kind of scared of Lorenzo, not from the risks of physical pain, but rather emotional. Lately, Malachi and Lorenzo argued more than they ever got along. The two winged men couldn't be in the same room nomore, without it turning into a hollering match. It was that much more difficult, since they still lived under the same roof.

At first, they simply agreed to disagree. More and more, they hardly talked at all.

"Father," said Malachi, trying to be careful with not only what he said, but how he said it. "The Kuschans believe in a winged god known as Soraq."

"And?" questioned Lorenzo, holding back his anger before the inevitable hollering and insults.

"Soraq is a winged deity, with the mind and the body of a man . . ." Malachi cleared his throat. "Soraq . . . Soraq is evil. Soraq is the source of all misery and grief in the Universe . . ."

"What does that have to do with us?" interrupted Lorenzo, impatiently.

"Some of the colonists in New Merieko think we look like Soraq," explained Malachi. "Some of them even think we are Soraq."

"Who?" asked Nikolai, more curious than concerned.

"Fernandez . . ." Malachi stopped. "The Agronian boy who threw himself into a panic yesterday . . ."

"So, because of the stupidity of a fifteen-year-old human, we're not supposed to sign treaties with the Kuschans?" argued Lorenzo. "Is that it? Is that what you're getting at? . . ."

"It's not just that Agronian boy!" shouted Malachi. "It's a lot of the colonists in New Merieko . . . especially the Kuschans . . ."

"So, what do you expect us to do about it?" questioned Lorenzo. "Run the Kuschans off, or try changing their opinions of us? Or should we just fly over there and kill them?"

Malachi knew where this was going. Where all of his conversations with Lorenzo had gone! There wasn't no real point in Malachi and Lorenzo talking anymore. They wasn't conversations, just hollering contests where neither side won.

Even then, Malachi strongly opposed dealing with the Kuschans, and couldn't budge in this matter. "I know that more Farlanders are coming here," he said, trying to stay calm though his voice revealed bitterness and regret. "There's nothing we can do to stop them. However, if they wish to move here, shouldn't they live by our laws and rules? This was our land before it was theirs. So, if they are to come here, shouldn't they respect our way of life, and? . . ."

"Our religion?" said Lorenzo. "Shouldn't they also respect our religion? You may be a Brown Winged Man, Malachi, but you sure don't think like one."

"I am a Brown Winged Man!" cried Malachi, gritting his teeth.

"Is that why you're a member of the Brotherhood of Faith?" challenged Lorenzo. "You say that the Farlanders should live by our laws and rules? Very well, son, I agree. But, please tell me why you're a devout member of a Farlander faith? Well? Can you explain this to me? Are you even going to try?"

"What point is there in trying?" asked Malachi. "You won't listen. You never listen."

"Father does have a point," said Nikolai. He loved his big brother but took Lorenzo's side on everything.

"I'm afraid of Farlanders gradually outnumbering us," said Malachi. "I understand why you want to meet with them, and trade with them. But why not secretly, like what we've been doing already, with Mucker in charge?"

"I agree that Mucker has been good in forging illegal trade between us and the Farlands," said Lorenzo, grudgingly. "Our tobacco and liquor have found great favor among those in the Brindai Continent."

Nikolai let out a clever laugh.

"Let us not forget that Mucker is a brute, a hate monger, a fear monger, a whore monger," said Lorenzo. "He is of a crude, nefarious character, never to be trusted nor respected."

"I trust and respect him," said Malachi.

"I know you do," said Lorenzo, sarcastically. "Just like you respect and trust Leader Rey, along with that dim-witted stepson of his, Jeremy Kentworth."

"What about Mucker's actions in saving those children from New Merieko yesterday?" asked Malachi. "Or Leader Rey housing and feeding them, until their parents got here?"

"With the loss of one Kuschan boy," added Nikolai.

Malachi didn't say nothing. The Kuschan boy was already scared, the same with Fernandez. Malachi and Nikolai's arrival sent them both over the edge, leading to the Kuschan boy running into the woods, and . . .

This was to haunt Malachi, clear to his grave. Such events made him wonder if the winged men were indeed children and disciples of Soraq.

"It worries me what you'll do when you become chief, Malachi," said Lorenzo.

"What do you mean, Father?" asked Malachi.

"You're a member of the Brotherhood of Faith," said Nikolai.

"So?" asked Malachi, in a snotty tone.

"So?" snapped Lorenzo. "So? You claim to mistrust Farlanders, yet you've been converted to a Farlander faith! Why is that, Malachi? Can you please explain it to us?"

Malachi only shook his head.

"If I didn't know better, I'd think you were a Farlander," mumbled Lorenzo. "If I didn't know any better, I'd think you've gone 'human' on us. Why, most of your friends are Farlanders . . . Leader Rey, John Mucker, Jeremy. It's like you're ashamed to be around winged men. For all I know, you're ashamed to be a winged man . . ."

"But I am a winged man!" screamed Malachi.

"Then act like one!" said Lorenzo.

Malachi sighed. His friendship with Rey meant a lot to him. He treasured the Brotherhood's message of love and peace, while rejecting the winged mens' pagan gods, representing different elements, climates, thoughts, and emotions. Still, he wondered if there was a place in the one true God's heart for the winged men . . . the same God who created humans in His own image.

This idea never troubled Malachi as much as the Kuschans' idea of evil personified by a winged demon, which lead him to ask . . .

Are the winged men of Infernus the sons of God? . . .

. . . Or the children of Soraq?

* * * * *

Admiral Vaslov had been a member of the Kuschan Royal Navy since he first entered a midshipmans' berth at the age of twelve. That was more than forty years ago.

Vaslov was a proud career officer, with citations and awards covering his chest. He was a distinguished-looking man with a well-trimmed, gray beard. He stood ramrod straight in his bright blue uniform, and constantly thrust his chest out like a rooster. His shiny awards glistened in the sunlight, nearly blinding mere civilians he happened to meet.

Commander Antonov was a much younger fellow, not yet thirty. He wasn't from an illustrious military family, nor did he have strong connections to royal or military big-wigs. He was drafted into the navy, while still a lad. After a final battle between Embrey and Kusch, he was awarded his country's highest honor, the Kuschan Star, for saving several men from a burning, sinking ship. He was also presented with an officer's commission. He was a handsome man, and revealed a warm smile behind a thick, black mustache.

Antonov saw no glory, heroism, or valor in war. Instead, he wished to be an emissary for peace. He never cared for the Kuschan faith, with its stories and fables of the Kuen, the Kued, or the Soraq. However, he had heard about the winged men of Infernus, and wanted to have a look for himself.

Vaslov was raised within the stupid Kuschan religion. He never viewed winged men as evil, but rather as primitives who had to be treated subserviently. This was his second trip to the island, and quietly he deplored the winged men.

Like Antonov, Vaslov worked as a diplomat for King Leonid of Kusch. He didn't like it. In his mind, winged men were "lower than niggers and Orientals, maybe even worse than Embrians." Winged men was animals, nothing more. Treating Lorenzo as anything special was an insult. Still, Vaslov had to play the part. He had his orders. He'd carry them out.

He also wanted more medals on his chest, along with a seat on the Kuschan Parliament.

Vaslov and Antonov was joined by Vic McClusky and two Green Winged men, Ricardo and Ugo. As they got into Persis, Antonov's shock, surprise, and amazement at his first glimpse of the village was like Weston's. As he meandered to Lorenzo's hut, Vaslov didn't wish to make a spectacle of himself.

It was clear that a few people and winged men had never seen a Kuschan naval uniform before, which was quite eye-catching and beautiful (at least Vaslov thought so!). At the same time, a few folks knew that Vaslov and Antonov was Kuschan naval officers, and they never much liked seeing Kuschan sailors poking around Infernus. Their angry stares and bad mumbling told Antonov to walk the straight and narrow and cause no trouble while he was on Infernus.

There was more than a few Brown Winged Men who took offense to seeing Ricardo and Ugo with McClusky and the Kuschan sailors. It never made no difference if there was a ceasefire between the two tribes. Anger and hostilities still run deep. As the Browns gave Ricardo and Ugo ugly stares, the two Greens returned the gesture, and made it twice as ugly.

"May we come in?" greeted McClusky, peeking through an open door of Lorenzo's home and meeting hall.

Even after fighting with Malachi, Lorenzo smiled as he met his guests. Nikolai followed Lorenzo to greet the Kuschan officers. Malachi plum refused to support this arrangement, which granted Kusch exclusive trading and diplomatic rights to Infernus.

"Please come in," said Lorenzo, welcoming his guests into the hut. He didn't like seeing Ricardo and Ugo with McClusky, but wouldn't get into it with them. Nikolai also thought less of the two Greens, but kept his mouth shut to appease Lorenzo.

"Chief Lorenzo," addressed McClusky, grinning. "Like you to meet Admiral Vaslov and Commander Antonov, of the Matyushenko."

Antonov was equally fascinated and frightened by the winged men. He pasted on a strained smile, reached out his right hand, and introduced himself.

"I'm Chief Lorenzo of the Brown Winged Men," said Persis' top-dog. "This is my son, Nikolai."

"Pleased to meet you," said Nikolai, taking Antonov's hand.

Malachi frowned as Ricardo and Ugo entered his father's home. He once got into a form of aerial combat with the two Green Winged Men and had the scars to prove it. For nearly a minute, he traded mean-eyed glances at Ricardo and Ugo.

"Son . . . Malachi," said Lorenzo, pleading to his oldest child. "Malachi . . . come introduce yourself to these gentlemen . . ."

With his heart breaking, and without saying another word, Malachi brushed past his father's guests and left the hut.

Malachi stepped outside, not knowing what to do next, or even what he could do next. He was split between spending time with Rey, or reporting the Kuschans' arrival to Mucker.

Malachi's insides was all tied up in knots. In time, he was expected to take his place as chief of the Brown Winged Men. Was he up to it? He had to be up to it! Nikolai wasn't interested in being chief. He wanted to be the tribal medicine man. Therefore, Malachi's path was set. Soon, he'd be chief. He wished to stay true to his faith in God, while respecting them who remained with the traditional winged man religion.

A chill ran down Malachi's spine. What if times changed, and attitudes changed, to make the role of chief obsolete? Errol had taken on the responsibility of "ruling" over the people population of town, though it was ceremonial. With that in mind, what if Malachi never held onto the reign of power?

Due to the growing numbers of Farlanders heading to Infernus, what if the days of the winged men was over?

Malachi approached the church. He found Rey chatting with a young people couple, who wanted to get married. In times of doubt and confusion, Malachi flew to the summit of Mount Auric, hoping the peace and solitude helped him solve problems. However, a cold wind swept across the western parts of the island, making the mountains kind of cold and frigid.

Mucker wished to talk to Lorenzo about building a small fleet of trade ships, along with a standing army and navy to protect Infernus. The pirate had to know about Lorenzo's meeting with the Kuschans. Malachi gulped. Mucker would get real mad with this news. Malachi dreaded being the one to give it to him. What choice did he have?

Cautiously, Malachi entered the opened door of Mucker and Seely's shack, where he found the outcome of last night's drunk-fest. Mucker sat at the rickety old table, dealing with his typical morning hangover. He sipped from a shot of home brew and sliced off hunks of jerky for breakfast. Seely was asleep at the table, his head next to a rusty candle holder. He snored loudly, as saliva dripped over the table. The little tattooed boy Paransky was rolled under a black blanket in one corner of the shack, sleeping away.

His mouth filled with grub, Mucker told Malachi to pull up a chair.

Malachi sat quietly, looking for a nice way to tell Mucker of the Kuschans.

"Got something in yer craw?" grunted Mucker, tiredly. "Spit it out."

Malachi frowned. "My father ...." he said, hesitantly. "My father . . ."

"What is it?" growled Mucker.

"My father is involved in a trade deal with two members of the Kuschan Navy . . ."

Mucker slammed his fist against the table, and nearly collapsed it. Seely's head bounced up and down into the table, but didn't wake him up. He continued snoring away, a river of saliva drooling across his chin onto the rickety old table.

Mucker stomped outside and headed toward Lorenzo's hut. Malachi followed Mucker, trying to calm him down. It didn't do no good. Mucker hated Kuschans, he hated Green Winged Men, and he was fed-up with McClusky and Lorenzo trusting them. At first, he wanted to give everybody words. If words didn't cut it, then it'd be time to get mean and nasty.

Real mean and nasty.

Without permission or an invite, Mucker barged into Lorenzo's hut. Malachi was right behind him. Mucker didn't care if he was welcomed to this meeting or not. He hoped this entrance (or was it an intrusion?) ruffled a few feathers. He didn't care if his actions further strained Malachi's relationship with Lorenzo or Nikolai. He was mad, spitting mad, at Lorenzo's decision to meet with a couple of lousy Kuschans and McClusky, and wouldn't keep quiet over it. The future of Infernus and the Brown Winged Men was at stake. Someone had to screw up this arrangement between Lorenzo and them two Kuschan dogs . . . and that someone was John Mucker!

Mucker went into the hut just as Lorenzo and Nikolai sat down with McClusky, Vaslov, and Antonov. "You want yer grandkids growin' up speakin' Kuschan?" he roared, loudly.

Lorenzo lifted his head up from a scroll written by the Kuschan King Leonid. He saw Mucker and Malachi heading toward him. This wasn't no social call. Lorenzo's thoughts ranged from animosity, to fear, to contempt. It upset to see Malachi standing next to . . . and alongside . . . a ruffian like Mucker.

Vaslov and Antonov reacted with surprise. McClusky just grinned. Whether Mucker liked it or not, Infernus would have a trade deal with Kusch. Old Muck had to go along . . . or get left out and left behind.

"It's a done deal," said McClusky. "Or soon will be, soon as we go over a few facts and figures . . ."

"There ain't no done deal!" hollered Mucker. "Not with me, there ain't! Only facts and figgers I'm lookin' at is the mess yer getting us into!"

McClusky shook his head. "Now wait just a minute, Muck . . ."

"We ain't got no minute!" said Mucker. "Ain't no minute to spare! We're liable to have lots to lose, if you sign somethin' with them damn vodka-drinkers!"

"I'm the one signing this agreement, Mucker," said Lorenzo. "Not Vic McClusky. I do this for the benefit of everyone on Infernus, not for self-serving buccaneers . . . like you."

"It ain't gonna help no one but Kuschans!" said Mucker, glaring at Vaslov and Antonov.

The Kuschans traded glances. Neither had met Mucker, but knew of his name and fiery reputation.

"You think them Kuschans'll give us a fair shake?" asked Mucker. "Only ones they're lookin' out for is themselves, and their heathen king!"

"I invited these men here," said Lorenzo, motioning at the two sailors. "I never invited you."

"I invited myself," said Mucker, grinning. "That's the only invitin' I know."

Antonov stood and approached Mucker. "Perhaps we should introduce ourselves . . . I'm Antonov, Commander in the Kuschan Royal Navy . . ."

"Don't bother introducin' yerself," said Mucker. "I a'ready saw yer ship moored off our shores. Y'all ain't gonna be around long enough to make my acquaintance. I know why yer here, and it ain't to help Infernus."

"Hold on, Mister," said Antonov, standing his ground. "You're not giving us our due . . ."

"You don't deserve no due!" growled Mucker. "The only due yer givin' is to yerselves! You don't give a hang about me, the Brown Winged Men, or them ugly Green buggers Clusk brung in here!"

Ricardo and Ugo scowled.

"That's enough!" shouted Lorenzo.

"Will be enough if you let them Kuschans get their paws on this island," said Mucker. "Will be enough for all of us once Kusch has had enough of us. They'll kill ever'body and ever'thing around here, an' get us outa our miseries. They ain't got no use for winged men. You ain't no where bein' equals in their eyes!"

Vaslov's complexion got real pale.

"For all they care, you ain't nothin' but a mess o' Soraqs here," said

Mucker. "That means you, Lorenzo. You, yer boys, them two mangy Greens Clusk brung in here. You ain't got no idea what Kuschans think of the likes of you, with that silly superstition of theirs. Well, you'll get an education, soon enough . . ."

"He's right, Father," said Malachi, looking away from Lorenzo's angry gaze. He found himself isolated from his own kind. The chances of him becoming chief was slowly, gradually, painfully slipping away. Occasionally, he even fantasized of becoming a person, even if it meant losing an ability to fly. His love for his people friends, with their one God in Heaven, clashed with being a winged man.

And though Malachi never feared the people of Infernus, he feared Farlanders, with their lands far to the east, lands he'd never set foot upon.

Lorenzo also felt the sting of being at odds with Malachi. Years before, he loved no one more than his oldest son. That love was mutual. Lorenzo took great pride teaching Malachi how to fly, while exploring the various regions of the island. At first Lorenzo took it easy, so Malachi could keep up. It wasn't long before Lorenzo fought to keep up with Malachi! He soon gave up trying! Malachi was easily the fastest winged man on Infernus!

That love between father and son was fading, now. Memories couldn't heal the growing tension and words caused by a Brotherhood minister named Rey, and his strange ideas which stole a son away.

Memories. Memories of love, of admiration and respect of needing a father, that same father who taught his oldest son how to fly! That same loving father who taught his son so many things! That same loving father whose heart was now breaking!

Malachi wanted to reach out and embrace Lorenzo, then seek forgiveness. Father and son could agree to disagree, but could it bring them back together? Or was their disagreements enough to forever break the bonds which once united them?

It agonized Lorenzo to know that McClusky and the two Kuschans played witness to an argument between father and son, which threatened an important trade agreement.

Malachi turned around, stormed from the hut, and flew away.

Nikolai ran outside to stop Malachi, but it didn't do no good. Malachi flew toward the snow-covered peak of Mount Auric. No way could Nikolai catch up with him. Instead, he looked skyward, as he watched Malachi glide against a clear blue sky, until he faded to a tiny white dot, far in the distance.

Nikolai wandered back inside, his tense expression dampening an already stressful morning. Quietly, he sat next to Lorenzo and Admiral Vaslov.

"See what you done?" grunted Mucker.

"What I done?" argued Lorenzo.

"That's right . . . what you done!" said Mucker. "We had a good thing going until he . . ." Mucker pointed at McClusky ". . . Called them filthy Kuschans in here, not to mention that Green riff-raff he hangs around with!"

McClusky hopped to his feet. Him and Mucker had been friends for a long time. McClusky saw a bright future for Infernus, by forging a trade agreement with Kusch, and figured Mucker stood to gain from it too.

"It's like what I keep tellin' ya," sighed McClusky, needing to talk some sense into Mucker. "There ain't no stoppin' Farlanders into comin' here. The way I see it, we'd best side ourselves with Kusch. Won't get no better deal than that. Lot better deal than what we're liable to get from Weston or any other Embrian trash."

"And I say we're better off without any Farlander trash," said Mucker, leading McClusky outside. "You think we'll get a fair shake from Kusch? What do they get, in return? How long you figger before the whole island's swarmin' with that cur? I can't trust 'em, as far as I can throw 'em! We don't stand a chance, not with them! Why, that superstition'll stir up shit 'round here. Ain't none of us gonna be safe, it Kusch gets a foothold!"

"Look, we're gonna have to side with Farlanders, soon or later," said McClusky. "Vaslov and Antonov . . . they ain't bad fellas! All they want is a trade of goods, between us and them. No colonization or emigration in the works. Just an exchange of goods and resources. We scratch their backs, they scratch ours. A trade agreement, nothin' more. Just fair trade."

"Fair trade?" asked Mucker, walking away. "Once them Kuschans get what they want, there ain't gonna be nothin' left for us, if we're even still alive. You call that 'fair'?"

After a half-hour or so of solitude on the summit of Mount Auric, Malachi began flying home to Persis. Despite his fights with his father and brother, he knew he had to weather their criticisms. He was still unhappy about the trade agreement with Kusch.

When he was younger, Malachi read a few chapters of the Kuschan book of faith, and it scared him. Some of them Kuschans got so worked up with the "winged demon" bit they went out and killed every bird and bat in sight. That might have been a good deal for bugs, rodents and worms, but not for birds and bats.

Malachi met very few Kuschans that he really liked. He especially disliked their idea of Soraq. He feared that Kuschan immigrants might use it as a reason to kill winged men.

Malachi spotted Weston and Jeremy building something that looked like a huge bonfire with tree limbs and decaying logs, in a clearing down below. The bodies of a few stinking abarbeauses covered the pile . . . along with the remains of something with wings.

Malachi circled the clearing a couple of times, landed, then asked Jeremy and Weston what they was up to.

Jeremy and Weston traded glances.

"What's going on?" pressed Malachi, nervously. "What . . . Who's that on your pile of? . . ."

"Randen," whispered Jeremy, tossing a heavy branch onto the pile.

"Randen?" cried Malachi. "Randen? What? . . . What happened?"

Jeremy pointed at one of the dead critters on the brush pile, which by now stunk awful bad.

"They killed him?" asked Malachi, fighting back tears.

"They helped," answered Jeremy, in anger and disgust.

"Randen showed up here a while ago," whispered Weston, motioning Malachi to one side. "He was . . ." Weston took a deep breath. "He was injured when he got here. He wasn't flying. He couldn't, even if he wanted to."

"How?" cried Malachi. "Why? . . ."

"I think . . ." Weston paused. "Well, I think someone tried to murder him."

"Randen?" screamed Malachi. "Why would someone murder him?"

"Get to the point a'ready, Weston!" hollered Jeremy. "Randen got knife-stuck a buncha times!"

Malachi shook his head in denial, then turned away from Weston and Jeremy. "Randen?" he wailed. "Who'd do such a thing to him? Why?"

Malachi was at odds with himself. His youth moved him to cry like a little kid. Yet, as heir-apparent of ruling over the Brown Winged Men, he had to take charge . . . or at least act like it. He had to stand up to Lorenzo and Nikolai! If he wasn't able to stop a pitiful trade agreement, what'd happen when an even worse mess come up?

"I was talking to Jeremiah . . . Jeremy," said Weston. "We were just sitting around here, talking, when . . . Randen stepped out of the trees. He was bleeding, and . . ."

"And then a bunch of damn critters pounced and started eating him," interrupted Jeremy, angrily. "Wasn't nothing we could do to stop them."

"Did Randen say anything before he? . . ." Malachi swallowed. "Before he died?"

Jeremy and Weston stared at each other.

"Well?" asked Malachi, impatiently. "Did he say anything? . . ."

"He . . . he made mention of an 'angry Kuschan'," said Weston, hesitantly, "before the abarbeauses attacked him . . ."

That done it. All Malachi had to hear was 'angry Kuschan'. He took flight and headed straight to Persis.

"I don't know what he's thinking, but I don't like it," said Weston.

"He don't like Kuschans," said Jeremy. "Neither do I. Neither does Mucker . . . or for that matter you, Mister Weston."

"Should we go back, then? The look on Malachi's face when . . ."

"Shouldn't we stay here and tend to Randen?" asked Jeremy, mockingly. "It ain't getting no cooler, and I had too much respect for Randen to just let him rot out here!"

"Malachi opposes Lorenzo's talk with the Kuschans. Now he has the means to stop it! I want to be there to help plead his case, when he explains what happened to . . ."

"You want to die the way Randen did?" asked Jeremy.

"Who says I will?"

"You're a Farlander, and I've had to scrape up what was left of Farlanders, after they stood too close to the trees!"

"Fine, so I'm a Farlander!" snapped Weston. "But . . ."

"Stay here and help me give Randen a decent cremation," urged Jeremy. "I don't like the idea of staying here alone to tend to the fire, and you're liable to get ate worse than Randen did. Stay here and help tend the fire with me. Please, Weston? Then we'll return to Persis, together."

"But I want to help Malachi!"

"Don't worry about that." Jeremy forced a grin. "Soon as Mucker finds out what happened up here, Malachi won't need our help. If you're looking for a way to halt Lorenzo's stupidity, then Mucker's the only way you'll ever need . . ."

* * * * *

Among the last to hear of Randen's death was Lorenzo and Nikolai, who was meeting with McClusky and the two Kuschan naval officers. By now, the two winged men had concluded their meeting with Vaslov and Antonov. Agreements were made, contracts signed, as a king's seal stamped by Admiral Vaslov had closed the deal.

Vaslov and Antonov smiled cordially as they shook hands with their winged counterparts. Antonov performed this gesture with honest affection. He was fascinated by Lorenzo and Nikolai's kindness and hospitality. His first encounter with this unique species turned out real good.

Antonov was a veteran of a brutal and vicious war with Embrey, and witnessed countless atrocities. For him, Persis equated to peace, comfort, and safety, something he experienced little of in the past. Like many Kuschans in the military, he returned to his old hometown to find it in ruins, its citizens left to freeze or starve during the long, cold winter. Antonov felt an odd sense of security with Lorenzo and Nikolai. For the first time in years, he gave himself the chance to take a breath, ease his mind, and relax.

For Vaslov, shaking hands with a new trading partner was a "show" he put on, usually with them he never liked all that much. The sooner he got shy of "inferiors," the better. Vaslov was on edge, not only because of the two Green

Winged Men Ricardo and Ugo, but because of Mucker. He never felt welcome or wanted on Infernus. He was glad for what he done for king and country. Mostly, he looked forward to setting sail for Kusch, as soon as possible!

McClusky stood to one side, with a self-satisfactory grin. This was a personal victory for him, as he saw a way for the island to link up with the Farlands, while upholding the seclusion it had since time began.

No one expected Mucker to storm back into the hut and holler, "Told ya what was gonna happen if you got mixed up with Kuschans! Well, by-god, it just happened!"

A chill ran down Vaslov's back as he turned to see Mucker.

"What are you talking about?" demanded Lorenzo, more frustrated than anything.

"Someone up and killed Randen!" told Mucker, mad as a hornet.

"Randen?" gasped Lorenzo. "Murdered?"

"From what I hear tell, a Kuschan done it!" hollered Mucker, giving Vaslov and Antonov the stink eye.

"We know nothing of this!" claimed Vaslov, in fear and defiance. Instinctively, he placed one hand on his sword. "There are no Kuschans I know who'd do such a thing, and surely no one from the Matyushenko!"

"Oh, yeah?" grunted Mucker. "From what I heard, some damned Kuschan knifed Randen a mess o' times. As he tried getting away, he got attacked by an abarbeaus!"

McClusky laughed. "Then why don'tcha just up and kill a mess o' abarbeaus, and call it even?"

"You shut the hell up," Mucker ordered McClusky.

McClusky was taken aback by Mucker's harsh command. "You can't tell me what to do, Muck!"

"I just did," said Mucker. "Told ya to shut up. I said it, I meant it, so shut the hell up."

"Randen's dead?" questioned Nikolai, in horror and disbelief.

"So said Jeremy," explained Mucker.

"And who told Jeremy?" sighed Lorenzo. He kind of liked Jeremy, though his opinion of the kid was the same as Prince Ari's.

"He was there when Randen got killed and ate by them hairy buggers," said Mucker.

"I won't take this man's word for it," balked Vaslov, keeping an eye on Mucker. "He wants you to back out of our agreement, Chief Lorenzo." He said the word 'chief' in a slightly sarcastic tone.

"You callin' me a liar?" growled Mucker.

"Yes sir, I am!" shouted Vaslov. "You and this . . . Jeremy fellow. How do we know it wasn't you and Jeremy who killed Randen, if he's really dead?"

Mucker drew his hand back, to pound the snot out of Vaslov.

"Randen is dead!" cried Malachi, entering the hut. "I saw his remains on a funeral pyre that Jeremy and Weston built, up on the hill!"

"Funeral pyre?" questioned Lorenzo.

"Go outside and see for yourself, Father," said Malachi. "In the foothills below Mount Auric, where Jeremy and Weston are."

The room got deathly quiet as Nikolai dashed outside, to see smoke bellowing up from the clearing. Jeremy had just ignited the brush pile holding the bodies of Randen, and a mess of dead abarbeauses.

"Jeremy and Weston?" McClusky asked Malachi.

Malachi nodded YES.

"Well, there's your answer, Lorenzo!" said McClusky.

"Explain, McClusky," requested Lorenzo.

"Malachi and Mucker oppose our agreement with the Kuschans," said McClusky. "So does Leader Rey and Weston. Weston for obvious reasons. He's a lowdown Embrian diplomat. Jeremy is Rey's stepson, and Weston's cousin!"

"Weston might be a lowdown Embrian, but Jeremy sure ain't!" said Mucker, getting madder by the minute. "He's Branellian. By the way he thinks and acts, might as well say he's from Infernus."

"Jeremy's a young fool in a loincloth," dismissed Lorenzo. "And he's got a thing for Errol's daughter Ericha, and she's as much a fool as he is!"

"If I was half my age, I'd have a 'thing' for Ericha too!" hollered Mucker. "What's that gotta do with Randen's killin'?"

"This is getting us nowhere," sighed Antonov.

"You shut up, Kuschan," said Mucker. "Ain't no one says you got any say here."

"Commander Antonov's got every right to speak his mind here!" exploded Lorenzo. "More right than you do, Mucker. You keep a civil tongue in my home, or you and my . . ." Lorenzo paused, as he looked at Malachi. "My oldest son can leave and never come back, for all I care!"

Malachi lowered his head in shame.

"The Kuschan government has made an agreement with Chief Lorenzo," said Antonov. "We shall honor that agreement in good faith . . ."

"Damn straight," agreed McClusky.

"And we prove no threat to that agreement," added Antonov. "If Lorenzo wishes to make a separate agreement with Weston . . . well, that's his business."

"You're insubordinate, Commander Antonov!" shouted Vaslov. "Our trade agreement's exclusive. You haven't the right to state otherwise. Why are you so compelled to mince words with that ne'er-do-well?" Vaslov pointed at Mucker. "Why, he's as much a fool as that Jeremy fellow!"

"Sir, this is not our country," said Antonov. "It belongs to the winged men, and I'm not about to dictate policy to them. Frankly, I'm excited to be here, and totally fascinated by this unique culture."

"So yer excited to be here?" asked Mucker, suspiciously. "Enough to try and take over?"

"I didn't say that!" hollered Antonov.

"Then what are you sayin'?" demanded Mucker.

"I've never been anywhere like Infernus," said Antonov. "This place fascinates me, how two vastly different species manage to get along, work together, create a functional society. Truly sir, I am fascinated!"

"Don't get too fascinated," said Mucker. "Y'aint gonna be around here long enough to . . ."

"These men are my guests!" yelled Lorenzo. "They're my guests, and I'll treat them as such! And so will you, in my house. Treat them with respect, or go!"

"Does that rule apply to me, too?" asked Malachi, sadly.

Lorenzo and Nikolai was nearly floored by Malachi's tone. The two Kuschans and McClusky felt awkward and out-of-place. Ricardo and Ugo just snickered.

"I feel terrible about Randen," sighed Lorenzo, wanting to make an amends with Malachi. "Believe me when I say that. My stewardship of Persis calls me to meet with his folks, offer my condolences, and get to the bottom of his death . . ."

"I was told that Randen's final words was that he got attacked by some 'angry Kuschan'," said Mucker, as an accusation. "Or so that's what Jeremy and Weston said . . ."

"Enough of that, Mucker!" said Lorenzo, pointedly.

"If a Kuschan was involved," said Antonov, "it wasn't a member of the Matyushenko."

"And I'm not interested in the words of an Embrian diplomat, or a snot-nosed kid in a loincloth," said Vaslov. "And I'm not about to stand here defending an agreement which has already been signed, sealed, and will be delivered upon our return to St. Alexandrov." Vaslov looked at Lorenzo and Nikolai. "If you'll excuse us . . ."

Lorenzo and Nikolai bowed, and accepted the Kuschans' departure. The two Brown Winged Men then gave Mucker the eye. Malachi attempted to hold his ground. Even then, he couldn't help but to blink.

"Ain't no use hagglin' over the trade agreement," McClusky said to Mucker. "It's a done deal. If yer smart, you'll play along, and we'll all win in the end. You gonna throw in with us and ante up, or act like a spoiled brat with yer bottom lip stuck out?"

"I ain't dealin' with no Kuschans," said Mucker. "I ain't dealin' with them, so I ain't dealin' with you or them green-hided freaks you got with ya."

"That tears it!" hollered McClusky. "So you ain't dealin' with me, no more? Fine. I'm better off without ya, then. All this time I thought we was friends. Guess I was wrong. You ain't no kinda friend, ain't never gonna be a friend. You never have been, Muck, and you never will be." McClusky smiled real big. "So what if I deal with 'green-hided freaks'? You just go right on back to that old soak you live with. I get farther dealin' with Kuschans and Green Winged Men, than you ever will with a drunken bum like Seely . . ."

* * * * *

The people and winged men of Persis was in shock and mourning. Randen was a very thoughtful, caring, handsome young winged boy, who never meant no one no harm. He was a devout member of the Brotherhood Church, who'd do just about anything for Leader Rey, and usually did.

Wails of sadness was overheard throughout the huts and homes of Persis. Slowly but surely, a good number of people and winged men headed upon the hill, where Jeremy and Weston kept the cremation fire from burning out of control.

Weston went out of his way to be nice and friendly to them who went to see Randen get a good send-out. On the other hand, Jeremy saw these folks as a bother, which kept him from doing a good job. All them onlookers done was violate a dead winged kid's privacy.

Poor Randen didn't ask to die. Nor did Jeremy ask to watch him die. The last thing Jeremy wanted was to have everybody poking their noses where two men worked, in a place where the poor winged kid met a lousy end. It riled Jeremy when people and winged men kept asking him a bunch of questions, mainly about WHAT HAPPENED?

What them nosey people and winged men didn't know they started making up, until stories got so turned around and wild-assed hairy that nobody for sure knew WHAT HAPPENED? Nobody, except for Weston and Jeremy. Jeremy wasn't up to talking about it. Weston never said much, neither.

As news spread about the event, so did rumors, until nobody for sure knew WHAT HAPPENED? Nobody, that is, except for Weston and Jeremy.

As Persis threw a fit over the death of a young winged kid, life in New Merieko went on as normal. Buildings and houses went up at a quick pace. When not busy, workers had meals with their families, or sat in the shade of trees and told lies while getting slightly drunk. All-in-all, it was a good day.

Jung-su never headed back to Persis, after spending part of his morning with the scaredy-cat Fernandez, and the scaredy-cat's folks. He got too interested in the construction of New Merieko's new Brotherhood Church. His interest turned to volunteering. At first, he put in his time as a gofer, hauling boards and nails. Pretty soon, he up and fetched a hammer himself and went to work nailing boards into this new house of worship. Thanks to men like Leader Rey, Errol, and even the ruffians at The Black Eye, Jung-su never had a lazy bone in his body. He went at it with an enthusiasm and drive to rival even the best workers out there. In no time, the short, little Oriental kid in the Brotherhood school uniform was one of the boys, except for them who didn't like Oriental kids, Brotherhood members, or people in general.

Everything went real good until Ericha showed up to give Jung-su the bad news about Randen.

Pastor Yevgeny sat on a tree stump outside of his hut, reading a chapter or two from The Book of Zachary. His eyes was diverted to the young redheaded girl walking by, wearing only a loincloth and a sleeveless shirt made out of critter hides.

Thoughts of lust conflicted with the convictions of faith and devotion to the Kuen. Yevgeny had saw that same girl the afternoon before, accompanied by a towheaded boy also clad in a loincloth and rags. The boy was the stepson of Leader Rey, a point which wasn't lost on Yevgeny. Why would a servant of God permit his charges to run around in such clothing? Yevgeny frowned. The redheaded girl only re-enforced his attitudes concerning the lack of morality found on Infernus . . .

. . . Along with the savage beasts which certain people treated as equals.

The girl looked sad and distressed as she wandered through New Merieko. Clearly, she never knew her way around.

Yevgeny's heart skipped a beat. That filthy creature he assaulted might have made it home to Persis, despite the wounds inflicted upon it. What if the creature was still alive, and told of Yevgeny's attack upon it?

Yevgeny thought of retreating into his hut. Yet, he wasn't one to run from trouble or a conflict. He reminded himself once more of his youth in the war-ravaged town of Anumun, where he and his dagger delivered justice to the invading Embrian Army.

Yevgeny smiled as he left the stump, placed his book under one arm, and approached the redheaded girl. "Good afternoon," he greeted. "Welcome to New Merieko. I'm Yevgeny, a Kuschan pastor and newcomer to this paradise of Infernus."

"Ericha," the girl said, fighting temptations to weep. "I'm looking for my friend Jung-su. He arrived here, earlier. I have to give him an urgent message."

"A young Kokashima boy, about my height?"asked Yevgeny. "The boy in a school uniform?"

Ericha wiped a teardrop or two from her eyes. "Yes, sir."

"Why, isn't that him over there?" Yevgeny pointed across New Merieko's main thoroughfare, where a group of hearty men sat in the shade, sharing a canteen and a few laughs.

"Yes sir, that's him," said Ericha. "Thank you, Pastor. Thank you very much."

"You're upset, Ericha," said Yevgeny, feigning concern. "Please? . . . What's troubling you?"

"A . . . a dear friend of mine," stuttered Ericha, as she tried but failed to control her emotions. "Randen . . . a winged man who was with Jung-su earlier . . . he's . . ." Ericha sobbed.

Yevgeny was the cause of Ericha's sadness, and knew it.

On the other hand, the stupid, pitiful redheaded girl had allied herself to an enemy. Yevgeny did only what he knew was right. Still, he was moved and deeply touched by Ericha's sorrow, and gave her an innocent little hug. "I'm sorry," he said, Ericha's body warm and comforting against his. "So very sorry, girl. If there's anything I can possibly do to . . ."

"Thank you, Pastor," whimpered Ericha. "I . . . I have to go tell Jung-su . . ."

"Please take care," said Yevgeny.

"I will." Ericha pasted on a strained smile as she made her way to Jung-su.

Yevgeny quietly watched as Ericha went to speak to the Kokashima boy, dressed in a pitiful, pathetic Brotherhood school uniform, the same foolish attire which that coward Fernandez always wore.

Ericha dragged Jung-su away from the other carpenters. The two teens began walking the long, narrow length of the beach.

Seconds later, Jung-su collapsed to his bare knees, covered his face under both hands, and wept.

Ericha knelt next to Jung-su, as they shared a big cry.

Yevgeny couldn't hear what was being said, though his mind's eye imagined it. A winged man . . . a filthy, stinking winged man was dead, and Persis was in an uproar.

Death was no stranger to Pastor Yevgeny. Not only did he constantly see it in the northern Kuschan town of Anumun, he even orchestrated it. He could sort of sympathize with Ericha and Jung-su . . . to a point. Eventually, the two teens would have to lift themselves up, venture onward, and get tough about it.

Tears were of no avail. Yevgeny shed an ocean of tears as a boy. He witnessed his own family getting massacred by the vile Embrian invaders. His sisters were both raped by sweaty pigs disguised under human faces and skins. Entire communities were burned by the Embrians. Yevgeny watched helplessly as members of the Kuschan Underground were beheaded, one-by-one.

Tears never stopped such injustices. And tears wouldn't stop the bloodthirsty plans Yevgeny had studied upon, involving primitive winged savages.

That big, dumb Embrian oaf Greenleaf stepped from a scaffolding, and walked over to Yevgeny. "What's with them?" he asked, looking on as Ericha and Jung-su cried their little eyes out.

"A winged man is dead," said Yevgeny, flatly.

"Dead?" gasped Greenleaf.

"An accident . . . perhaps."

Paolo ventured out from the safety of his tiny hut and headed toward Greenleaf and Yevgeny. He wondered what ailed Jung-su. Paolo was impressed by the understanding and kindness that Jung-su had shown Fernandez. He was alarmed to see that same youth leader kneeling on the beach, overwhelmed with grief.

Paolo motioned at Jung-su and Ericha. "Is he? . . . Are they all right?"

"That's up to them," mumbled Yevgeny, tapping his upper lip.

"A friend of theirs is dead," said Greenleaf. "A winged man, I hear tell . . ."

Paolo's jaw dropped.

"I'd stop working for a spell, but I've got to get cracking on this job," said Greenleaf. He took an authoritative stand over New Merieko, as usual. "Might not hurt to send a group yonder to Persis . . . Show our respects. What do you say, Paolo? . . . Yevgeny?"

"My family and I will go," agreed Paolo. "Maybe several of us should give our support. What about you, Pastor Yevgeny?"

Yevgeny's blank stare altered to that of an angry glare, aimed at Greenleaf and Paolo. His reluctance to walk into Persis was apparent. His thoughts returned to Ericha and Jung-su. Briefly, he revealed disgust and revulsion of two weaklings, who lacked the courage and backbone to face adversity.

However, Yevgeny was a man of the spirit and, like it or not, he had a responsibility to those in the next town . . .

Didn't he?

Yevgeny cleared his throat, tugged on his robe, and said, "You're right, Paolo. I'll tell a few of my fellow Kuschans where I'm going, then get ready to leave."

"That's very generous of you, Pastor Yevgeny," complimented Greenleaf.

"No generosity about it," answered Yevgeny, with an air of resentment and contempt. "It's the least I can do, and I can't afford to falter in my heavenly duties . . . "

* * * * *

By afternoon, the clearing where Jeremy and Weston was filled up with people and winged men. The fire was now mostly red-hot coals, ashes, and smoldering tree limbs scattered around the edges. There weren't no signs that the fire held the body of a young winged kid or a bunch of stinking, smelly critters.

Yet, the memory of Randen lived on, as everybody shared stories about him. A few women and youngsters sang hymns of faith and redemption. While some folks were teary-eyed and mournful, a few loudmouths and braggarts vowed revenge against them who did in poor Randen.

Jeremy and Weston kept the fire under control. Jeremy was dressed only in his loincloth. Sweat mixed with smoke, soot, and ashes. A mild wind from the northwest blew smoke upon him. His face, chest, arms, and legs was blackened from the dust and heat. Jeremy stood by the fire, using a pitchfork lend to him by a local farmer.

Ericha was among the last to get to the clearing. Throughout the day, she held thoughts of sadness, loss, confusion, anger, and numbness. Her and Randen had been the best of buddies since they first met in church, more than a decade back. While she wasn't as close to him as she was with Jeremy, Ericha was still fond of Randen. The young winged kid was good at keeping secrets, and always thoughtful and understanding about everything.

Ericha wandered up the hill toward the clearing. She swore that she could see Randen's pure-white body, hear his soft, kindred voice, and feel his presence. How could he possibly be dead! It couldn't be real . . . could it? Ericha often stopped to cry, as she marched upward and onward through the dark, narrow path to the clearing.

Ericha was devastated by what happened, but not near as bad as Jung-su.

Since Ericha first told him WHAT HAPPENED, Jung-su turned into a mess, and had to be practically dragged back to Persis. He cried like a little bitty baby, blaming himself for Randen, and wishing he would've left New Merieko with the dead winged kid. He was prone to blaming himself for a change in the wind, or a cloudy day. He thought he had to take care of everybody, whether it was his place to do so or not. All the way into Persis, he fretted and carried on about leaving Randen all alone, and not being there to make sure he got home safely.

Once he got to Persis, Jung-su went into Rey's office where he sobbed all over the floor, desk, and even on Rey's long, black robe.

Ericha got to the clearing, where she watched Jeremy and Weston work at the fire. Her eyes gazed upon the thin, masculine figure in the loincloth, his body covered with dirt, smoke, and dust. Jeremy seemed the picture of confidence and courage, even with the angry, cranky look on his face. Ericha was oddly attracted and aroused by him. She knew that Jeremy was upset, though he never showed it.

For the moment, Jeremy kept busy. His fears and anxieties would show themselves later, once him and Ericha was alone, where he'd express himself openly.

Jeremy had no clue that Ericha was around . . . until she squeezed through the crowd and approached him.

Ericha was a huge part of Jeremy's life, as much as the rugged landscape, climate, and lifestyles of Infernus. He no more wanted to part with Ericha anymore than he wanted to leave the island. The sight of Ericha nearing him was a painful reminder of what he stood to lose, should he accept the big money and the big land in Branell.

After Randen's death, Weston stayed clear from talking about the inheritance. For the time being, him and Jeremy wasn't adversaries, but rather cousins and friends, with a common goal in doing right by Randen.

Jeremy and Ericha quietly stared at each other.

Then Ericha slowly reached out and lightly touched Jeremy's shoulder, a gesture he didn't object to nor refuse. Her fingers softly glided along the length of his arm. Finally, the two teens clasped hands. Jeremy's guarded expression changed to that of a sad, depressed kid. His eyes clouded with tears.

"Sorry about Randen," whispered Ericha.

Jeremy lowered his head, nodded YES, and turned away from Ericha. This wasn't the time for whining. Jeremy and Weston had a job to do!

But the fire was dying down, and soon the day would end.

An older winged man grabbed the pitchfork from Jeremy. "I'll take over," he said, leaving Jeremy to be alone with Ericha.

Jeremy fetched his shirt from under a nearby tree, and put it on. Him and Ericha walked away from the crowd, then sat together at a log, overlooking Persis.

Weston couldn't hear what was said between Jeremy and Ericha. Their backs was turned, and they was too far away. Anyway, it was best for Weston to mind his own business, as he minded the fire.

Jeremy and Ericha stared down at the valley, below. The waterfall was as plain as day. Red streaks of the late-afternoon sunset gleamed across an endless cascade of water. Already, a few folks lit up their homes with candles, lanterns, and lamps. It was autumn now, and day would soon surrender to night.

Moments passed, and Jeremy and Ericha still didn't say nothing. Love and friendship spoke volumes. The two teens was united as one, first as buddies and, later on . . . who knew?

Silently, they pondered the life and senseless killing of Randen. Neither Jeremy nor Ericha were strangers to death. Death was just a part of living on Infernus, as birth, being a kid, getting married, raising crops, day-to-day chores, and getting old.

But why did Randen have to die? Of all God's creatures, why him?

Finally, Ericha dared to ask, "Jeremy . . . are you going away?"

The question hit Jeremy like a ton of bricks. He wouldn't talk about Randen. Nor did he care to discuss Branell. But he had to . . . Right? Thoughts of leaving Infernus was beyond reason, acceptance, belief, or possibility.

And yet, leaving might end up being a harsh, painful reality!

"Jeremy!" cried Ericha, examining the boy's tattered shirt. "How? . . . What happened?"

"When Randen . . ." Jeremy smirked. "One of them critters tried to get me, but I got him first."

Ericha looked at Jeremy, as if to say I WANT TO HEAR MORE.

Jeremy smiled proudly as he pointed at his sword.

Jeremy and Ericha wore shirts that were blessed by Brown Winged Men elders and medicine men, including Nikolai. The shirts, made from thick abarbeaus hide, supposedly protected them from all dangers. However, an abarbeaus come within an inch of tearing into Jeremy's ribcage. No matter. The shirt was a barrier from the critter's sharp claws, which never even broke skin.

"I'm okay," said Jeremy. "Soon as we get into town, I'll have Evelyn patch it up . . ."

Before Jeremy finished his sentence, Errol and the Little Oinker, Prince Ari, headed his way.

Ericha blushed and pulled her hand away from Jeremy. Hastily, she scooted away from him on the log. Jeremy smiled in embarrassment and humor, thinking of his misdeed against Ari the night before.

"Sorry to hear about Randen," said Errol, as Ari kept his distance from Jeremy.

Jeremy had said a few unkind words to Errol, and needed to apologize for them. Pride and shame were the worst road blocks! But if Jeremy wished to stay on Ericha's good graces, he had to made peace with Errol.

Prince Ari? That was another story.

"Ericha," said Errol, sternly. "I'm gonna be up here for a spell, and I want you to take your brother home. I'll be there, directly."

Ericha frowned. "But, Father . . ."

"Take Ari home," demanded Errol. "I'll be there, directly."

See ya, Jeremy," groaned Ericha, then left the clearing with Ari.

"See ya," whispered Jeremy, knowing Errol had some awful mean words with him.

Without asking to do so, Errol sat next to Jeremy on the log. "Warm today," he said, awkwardly.

"Yes, sir," said Jeremy, unable to look Errol straight in the eye.

"Cut a cord of firewood today," yawned Errol. "See about doing the same tomorrow . . ."

"I'm sorry about the way I acted last night," interrupted Jeremy, nervously.

Errol leaned toward Jeremy. "Say again?"

Jeremy's heart sank as he repeated himself. "Sorry for the way I acted last night."

"I heard you right the first time." Errol snickered. "Just wanted to make sure you meant it."

Jeremy sighed.

"I don't mind so much for what you done to me," said Errol. "That business of you rubbing supper into my boy's face . . ."

"I'm real sorry for that, too."

"I know Ari's hard to take. But he is my boy, and I can't abide anyone treating family that way. Not even you."

"Sorry," said Jeremy, on the verge of laughing. "I was real bummed out last night and . . . well, Ari just got me kind of mad, and . . ."

"Bummed out?"

"Yes, sir."

"What for?"

Jeremy pointed at his cousin. "Mr. Weston . . . Weston wants me to leave Infernus, and move to Branell for a whole bunch of land and a whole lotta money."

Errol smiled. "Sounds like a mighty fair deal to me."

Jeremy shrugged.

"I'd take it in a heartbeat," said Errol. "You're stupid if ya don't."

"I reckon," mumbled Jeremy, sadly.

"By the time you're my age, you'll understand. Plenty."

"I ain't sure if I'll like Branell all that much."

"I'm fifty-years-old," said Errol. "Wonder how I lived that long. When I was a kid, I never gave it much thought. If someone offered me that much land and money, I wouldn't pass on it. I talked to Rey, and he told me all about it. He seems to think it's a pretty fair deal, too."

Jeremy shook his head and sighed.

"Not trying to get rid of you, if that's what you think," chuckled Errol. "You might not know this. I dunno if Ericha ever said something about it or not. My wife and I come right close to adopting you, right after your mom died."

"Ericha never told me that!" shouted Jeremy, wild-eyed. "I had no clue!"

"Well, Rey beat me to ya!" snickered Errol. "Anyway, it wasn't that long before I took Jung-su in. I had my hands full, plenty, especially after my wife died."

"How is Jung-su? I mean, about? . . ." Jeremy frowned. "Does he know about Randen?"

"He knows." Errol paused. "Taking it pretty hard. Think we all are. It's been a hard day, Jeremy. Real hard day."

"Yes, sir."

"It's not easy for me to say this, but . . ." Errol smiled. "Well, boy, I love you. I'll never understand you, or if anyone does, but . . . I love you."

Jeremy was both touched and embarrassed.

Errol slapped Jeremy's knee. "For what it's worth, I'm glad you're Ericha's friend."

"She's my best friend, sir."

"I know that. . . But something tells me there's more between you two than just being friends."

"I . . . I don't know what you're talking about," stuttered Jeremy, with a stupid grin as he blushed.

"Don't play me for a fool," said Errol, uneasily. "If you want to court my daughter, you got my permission. Only thing is, I want you two to start wearing something better than them rags you call clothes!"

Jeremy laughed at his own expense.

"And one more thing," said Errol, pointedly. "You treat Ericha like a lady."

"Do you think I'll treat her any different?" asked Jeremy. "I rate your daughter real high, and . . ."

"And while we're at it," interrupted Errol. "While you're with my daughter, whatever thoughts you're thinking about her, you make sure they go no further than just thoughts."

Jeremy's anger flared up. Too bad, though. Errol had Jeremy over a barrel, and both men knew it. There were few things more important to Jeremy than Ericha. Jeremy had to deal with Errol and, regrettably, Prince Ari. "What thoughts are you talking about?" he questioned, defensively.

"You know what I'm talking about. Ericha's the only daughter I got. She might not always dress like a lady, but I'm going to make damned sure that's what she'll grow up to be. I want to make sure the fellow she chooses to spend her life with is a gentleman." Errol grinned. "And while we're at it . . ."

"Don't worry," sighed Jeremy. "I ain't gonna rub no more grub in Ari's face."

"He's the only son I'll ever have." Errol put his hand on Jeremy's shoulder. "I can't help but to think that you was almost my son. But Rey beat me to ya."

"Thank you," whispered Jeremy.

"I can't abide the way you acted last night," said Errol. "You're a better man than that. Otherwise, we wouldn't be talking."

With that, Errol got up to follow Ericha and Ari into town.

Weston then wandered over to the log, stretched his aching back, and sat down next to Jeremy. He was smeared in dust, smoke, soot, and sweat. Weston's smile resembled a performer's in a black-face, minstrel show. "Well?" he asked, curiously. "How'd it go?"

"How'd what go?" asked Jeremy, evasively.

"Between you and Ericha . . . and Errol?"

Jeremy shrugged. "Ericha's the only daughter Errol's ever gonna have. So is Ari."

Weston laughed. "So . . . did you mention your birthright in Branell?"

"Ericha's one thing. Errol's another."

"Well, like I was saying, Ericha can't stay young forever. And Errol can't keep her under his thumb, even if he wanted to."

"All I wanna do is fetch a bite of supper, then hit the sack," said Jeremy. "Unless Rey decides to kick me out. After what happened today . . . how can I sleep with that? I mean, after what happened to Randen."

"Remember Randen as the friend he was," suggested Weston. "Not for the way he died."

"How?"

"Just keep telling yourself the same old fairy tale my grandmother told with me when I was a lad."

"What's that?" asked Jeremy.

"Don't fret over Randen," said Weston, pointing at the fire which had been rendered to nothing more than smoldering ash, coals, smoke, and heat. "He's in a better place, now . . ."

* * * * *

Since he first got to Infernus, several years back, Leader Rey never had such a long, stressful, agonizing day . . . until this one.

Rey was busy with his usual ritual of messing with paperwork when word came of Randen's death. Reports was bungled at first, turned all around, sideways, ass-backwards, and sketchy. No one knew exactly WHAT HAPPENED, and yet everyone and their dog had a version as well as an opinion of WHAT HAPPENED.

Rey first heard that either Weston or Jeremy had gotten ate by an abarbeaus. His reaction was shock, panic, and sadness. A few moments later, it was supposedly Jung-su who got ate up.

Rumors spread like wildfire through the town, until Malachi finally set Rey straight, including adding a bit of fiery rhetoric involving 'an angry Kuschan'.

Rey was fond of Randen. He battled his own grief and mourning, while maintaining order in town. Chief Lorenzo was still meeting with the Kuschans, or getting bawled out by Mucker, and never took control of the situation. Meanwhile, Errol and Ari was up cutting firewood, leaving Rey to organize a prayer vigil and uphold calm and sanity.

Rey gave Ericha the task of running over to New Merieko to tell Jung-su of WHAT HAPPENED. Ericha was pretty upset but agreed to go fetch Jung-su.

Jung-su was a wreck by the time him and Ericha got back to Persis. All he could do was cry like a little bitty baby, while blaming himself for Randen's killing.

Rey called Jung-su into his office, where the two sat down privately and talked. Jung-su got worse upset, until all he did was carried on and whimpered. He sat on a bench in one corner of the office, as Rey kept one arm around him.

With his small frame and school uniform, Jung-su resembled a boy of around eleven or twelve, not someone on the cusp of adulthood. Tears streamed like a river down his round, innocent face.

When it came to holding a job or other grown-up responsibilities, Jung-su was much older than his years. That same conscientious spirit proved to be his undoing. Rey didn't know what to do or say, to get Jung-su through this self-indictment and torture. Every trick Rey knew or acquired to counsel had failed him.

Or had Jung-su failed himself?

After nearly an hour or so, Jung-su was in worse shape at this meeting's end, than before it even started. He kept repeating, "Everything was okay when Randen left Fernandez's house," then break into the loudest, high-pitched bawling Rey ever heard. Mostly it was unintelligible babbling, as his words ran on and on and collided with each other.

Rey was exhausted. He had to cope with his own loss and anguish. His occupation and role in the community forced him to place Jung-su and others above his own interests. It was apparent that Jung-su was unwilling and unable to help himself.

Rey and Jung-su knelt to the floor and recited a few verses from the good book. Rey then walked Jung-su to the door and, after wishing the boy well, embraced him. "Go home," he said, his voice soft and soothing. "Go home, get some rest. Take the day off from The Black Eye, and try not to worry yourself."

"Leader Rey," moped Jung-su, with red, dewy eyes. "I'm so sorry I didn't leave New Merieko with Randen . . ."

"Jung-su," said Rey, tiredly. "I'm the one who sent you boys to New Merieko, this morning. It's my fault, not yours."

Jung-su sniffled. "But had I not stayed there with Fernandez . . ."

"There's nothing we can do about it, now. It's too late for anyone of us to change what we may have done differently."

"But . . ."

"Randen is dead," sighed Rey. "I don't like it any better than you do. But the sooner we accept it, the better off we'll all be."

Jung-su leaned against Rey. Once again, tears fell from his eyes, over his face, and onto Rey's black robe.

"Now, Jung-su," said Rey. "You told me earlier that you're an adult. Well, now you must learn to face a painful truth, not as a child, but as a man . . . as an adult. Which is to accept the things we don't want to with courage and the love of the Heavenly Father to guide us through the darkest of days. It's in God's hands now, and not our own."

Jung-su didn't say nothing more. He merely nodded YES, stepped out of the office, and headed to his lonely shed back behind The Black Eye.

As the door clicked shut, Rey nearly collapsed. It had been an awful hard day. And it wasn't over, yet! Rey still had to talk to Randen's folks about conducting a fitting service for their son. Despite his words to Jung-su, Rey needed to find his own separate peace. He had known Randen since the young winged kid was a toddler, and watched him grow into a teenager.

Randen was always involved in mentoring kid members of the congregation. Having him around was a blessing and a comfort to Rey. Randen was a promise that the Brotherhood would thrive and survive on the island of Infernus.

And now Randen was gone.

Also weighing heavily on Rey was thoughts of Jeremy's inheritance in Branell.

Rey wanted Jeremy to do good in life. Well, now Jeremy had that chance, by gaining vast lands and wealth . . .

Far, far away, in Branell . . .

Far, far away . . .

Rey loved Jeremy quite dearly! Life would never be the same without his stepson nearby. Yet, it was to Jeremy's advantage to leave Infernus.

If Jeremy did move away, would Rey ever see him again?

Maybe not . . .

But that's life . . . isn't it?

Rey stared at the log walls of his office. He had never got married and, other than one night in a Sykes' brothel, had never messed around. He had no biological kids. Once in a while, he thought about giving up the Leadership to run a store someplace, or become a farmer. He hoped he was still young enough to get hitched and be a dad for real! He was torn between a devotion to God, and his desires to be nothing more or nothing less than a man.

Rey spent his whole entire life in the Brotherhood, and had a duty and an obligation to his many followers, along with the Master of All Life in the Universe. At the given moment, he was split between his love of God, and one he grew to think of as his own kin.

Jeremy had to accept that inheritance! It wasn't just a question of comfort or security, but common sense and a brighter future for himself. It also meant that Jeremy's departure meant saying GOODBYE forever, until Death reunited all believers in the Promised Land.

Due to the Border War between Embrey and Branell, mail to and from Infernus was slow and spotty. Letters to the island was usually channeled through a dried goods store in Sykes known as Erickson's Imports.

Well, crap! Jeremy wasn't one to write letters, anyway! Even if Rey did send letters to Jeremy, there wasn't no guarantee they'd get to him.

So, when and if Jeremy left Infernus for a better life, it meant saying GOODBYE forever. Was the boy willing to make such a sacrifice, and did Rey really want him to?

Rey was tired and hungry. He hadn't ate since morning. He got up from his desk and began to leave the room when he got a surprise visit. "Pastor Yevgeny," he said, forcing a grin on his face. "It's a pleasure to see you."

"I just got here from New Merieko," said Yevgeny, feigning sadness and concern. "A small group and I came right away, once we got word of a child's passing."

"Thank you," said Rey. The last thing he wanted or needed was to chat with a man he barely knew, and wasn't sure he liked or trusted. "I've had . . . better days. We all have."

"I'm sure you appreciate our fears of the many dangers here on Infernus, especially to newcomers like myself."

"Reports are debatable as to this . . . tragedy, other than Randen was killed by an abarbeaus. The same type of animal that likely took the Kuschan boy, yesterday."

"So, what are you doing about it?" asked Yevgeny, pointedly.

"What do you mean?"

"About the animals who took the young winged man?"

"My son Jeremy and Weston got rid of them."

"And about the creature who killed the Kuschan boy?"

Rey snickered. "Honestly, we have no idea if it was an abarbeaus, or even which one. They're pack hunters, and several were probably involved."

"So, what is Persis planning to do about these . . . abarbeaus?"

"What can we do, Pastor Yevgeny?"

"More and more Farlanders are emigrating to Infernus," said Yevgeny.

"I know that."

"Aren't you afraid of further attacks?"

Rey shrugged. "Of course. All the time."

"As a precaution, has anyone proposed bringing in hunters to exterminate those things?"

"Good luck," laughed Rey. "There are thousands, maybe even millions of abarbeaus on Infernus."

Yevgeny's eyes widened.

"We suggest that no one venture out alone, especially children, and most especially after dark," said Rey. "It's usually best to travel in groups. But, if they can get someone out alone . . . well, that's all she wrote."

"That young winged man wasn't alone!" cried Yevgeny. "You said that he was with your son and Weston."

"I can't verify it, but I heard that Randen was injured prior to meeting up with Jeremy and Weston, and was bleeding profusely when the attack occurred."

"Injured?" Yevgeny swallowed, nervously. "How?"

"Not sure. But abarbeaus are attracted to blood. They're also nocturnal, and very dangerous at night. If I may, you and your group are well-advised to go home, before nightfall."

"Even if we have numbers?"

"Even in numbers," said Rey. "They rarely enter Persis, unless they spot a lone child. You should be reasonably safe in New Merieko. But not necessarily youngsters, especially if they're by themselves. You may want to place doors at the entrances, and board up windows when it's dark."

Yevgeny pondered this matter.

"I strongly urge you and your group to go home, as soon as possible," said Rey. "No one can assure your safety, even during the day. Once you're out in those woods, you're on your own."

Yevgeny grinned, an expression Rey didn't know how to read, nor to trust.

"Thank you for your kindness, Pastor Yevgeny," said Rey. He preferred seeing Yevgeny go away, but wouldn't forget his manners. "Forgive me. I was just on my way to the kitchen, for supper. May I interest you in a meal, before? . . ."

"No, thank you," said Yevgeny. "I'll heed your warning, and we'll leave right away."

"Very well, then." Rey cleared his throat. "Thank you for your visit."

"You've been most kind, and informative," said Yevgeny. "And you're right, Leader Rey. It's best for us to run on home." Smiling, he added, "Surely, we wouldn't care to meet the same terrible fate as your friend, Randen . . ."

Pavel-Ivanovich's life and background wasn't enough to keep him from being the critters' first meal that night.

In thirty years of living, Pavel-Ivanovich had been a gymnast, a ballet dancer, a martial artist, a choirboy, and a captain in the Kuschan Army. He went all over the Farlands, staging spectacular shows with other former military men. The performers of the Cirque St. Alexandrov were known for their wild, death-defying stunts, acrobatics, and high-wire acts. They was somehow seemingly ability to fly! They entertained folks from Agron to southern Actin, and even went to the far-eastern nation of Kokashima.

In the wintertime, Pavel-Ivanovich taught ballet at one of the more prestigious schools in St. Alexandrov, where he was a tough, yet caring instructor.

Thanks to Pavel-Ivanovich's fame and reputation, he was offered a seat in the Kuschan House of Lords, at the age of twenty-five!

Pavel-Ivanovich's stunning career ended, while showing off to a group of schoolboys. He had performed that exact same stunt countless times in the past, and always landed safely on his feet. But not on a late-Tuesday afternoon in southern Embrey, when a dive from a platform resulted in a concussion, a dislocated shoulder, a shattered femur, and a blown pelvis.

Pavel-Ivanovich now suffered from a weakened right arm, severe memory problems, and a limp which only got worse with time. He was still given a seat in the Kuschan Parliament, though it no longer mattered. He fell into a deep, dark depression which lasted for months. He ran off to his parents' farm, where he spent long hours hiding in an upstairs bedroom. He rarely ate, slept, or changed his clothes. He thought about hitching a rope to a beam above his bed, placing his head through the noose, and leaping from a three-legged stool.

Then word came from a friend named Yevgeny of a planned emigration to Infernus.

Pavel-Ivanovich had always heard stories of a mysterious island, somewhere in the North Agron Ocean. Here was the chance to reclaim an adventurous lifestyle he feared was lost forever, and start over in a new land!

During the voyage, Pavel-Ivanovich volunteered as a member of the ship's crew. Despite his injuries, he excelled in many strenuous tasks onboard the frigate, and was granted his previous status as a national hero and celebrity. He dined at the captain's table, rubbed shoulders with the sailors, and felt like his old self again. Once he got to Infernus, he went right to work building homes and businesses in New Merieko. He never felt so good in his life!

Pavel-Ivanovich heard that a young winged kid was killed in the hills overlooking Persis. He was among those to give comfort, assistance, and aide to the mourners. It didn't bother him to spend the day with them of a different culture, nationality, or species. He treated everybody as equals, including the Brown Winged Men.

Pavel-Ivanovich might have been a "giant" among the Kuschan people. His size was another story. His height barely reached five feet. He made up for it with a sturdy, sinewy frame. His long, black hair reached to the shoulders, and concealed a plain, ruddy appearance. He was kindhearted and charming.

Most folks overlooked a lifestyle which others viewed as an abomination.

Pavel-Ivanovich was in love with a former student and protege named Gyorgy-Andreovich, to whom he shared a small hut in New Merieko.

While heading home with other colonists to New Merieko, Pavel-Ivanovich met an untimely end. He was drawn to some exotic, bright-red flowers along the narrow trail. He eagerly went about picking a bouquet of these flowers to give to his boyfriend, when the attack started.

Pavel bent down to collect some flowers, as two abarbeaus jumped out of the trees and landed on his back. Pavel fell to the ground, with the wind knocked out of him. He laughed, thinking another colonist had pulled a prank on him.

Then an abarbeaus chomped into Pavel-Ivanovich's neck, and severed the jugular vein.

The once-tranquil setting turned into a nightmare. Pavel-Ivanovich shrieked in terror as the pretty red flowers were splattered in blood. He realized what was going on and tried to fight back. As one of the critters went to the throat, the second went for the belly. Pavel-Ivanovich was soon ripped to shreds.

This event took place moments after the sun sank in the west, at a period often referred to as Magic Hour.

Among them witnessing this killing was Pastor Yevgeny, an Agronian couple named Paolo and Frida, and their sensitive, fifteen-year-old son Fernandez.

Pavel-Ivanovich's body was splattered across the field as a third critter, then a fourth, joined in the feast. Onlookers fled in all directions. A peaceful jaunt through the woods became a spree of violence and bloodshed.

Leader Rey had warned Yevgeny of the abarbeaus . . . didn't he? What difference did that make, now? A small group from New Merieko was under siege from critters few had ever laid eyes upon, until now.

About a half-dozen people ran screaming from the mayhem, only to be swept up in it. The critters were attracted to the high-pitched shrieks echoing through the deep, dark woods. Those attempting to escape the bloodbath became statistics to it, as they too were overtaken by beasts who ruled the forest.

In less than a minute, the small group from New Merieko was decimated from a number of twelve people to that of four; Pastor Yevgeny, an Agronian couple named Paolo and Yevgeny, and their sensitive, fifteen-year-old son Fernandez.

Yevgeny's mind sprinted from that of extreme fear, to a desire to fight back. In the past, he answered the Embrians' atrocities with atrocities of his own, by utilizing his trusted dagger. He learned to remain calm in the worst situations. Such techniques worked well, when dealing with a human foe. But now, he wasn't dealing with a human foe! These was wild critters! Still, he was determined not to die like that poor little Kuschan boy, or a stupid young winged kid. There was only one person Yevgeny could depend upon. Himself.

Paolo and his family was petrified by the horrific sights and sounds surrounding them. Frida prayed for a swift, painless death, as Fernandez crouched next to her and wept.

Yevgeny despised the soft touch that Paolo and Frida gave Fernandez. Their son was almost grown up, and yet the couple treated him like a little kid. Frida even had the childish habit of calling him Nandy.

Well, Nandy had to become a man!

"Stop your whining!" hollered Yevgeny. "Stop it! You want to draw those things to us?"

Paolo just stared at Yevgeny with a blank expression. Frida went right on praying as Fernandez nestled against her and whimpered.

"Stop it!" repeated Yevgeny, slapping Fernandez' face. "Stop it!"

Yevgeny was distracted by the sounds of footsteps behind him. He turned to see a small kid abarbeaus heading his way. The critter looked the four people over, in anticipation of a meal.

Yevgeny pointed his dagger at the critter, took a defensive position, and squinted. He bared his teeth and released a low, threatening snarl. This wasn't to provoke the critter, but to scare it off.

Paolo and Frida wasn't of no use, at all. Paolo never objected to the rough way Yevgeny manhandled Fernandez, earlier. Where most fathers would've tried to kick Yevgeny's butt, Paolo just stood there with that same, idiotic stare! And Yevgeny already knew better than to rely on Frida! That damned woman was content to die, with a foolish prayer spewing from her mouth.

Yevgeny grabbed Fernandez by the collar and pulled him forward. He retrieved a second dagger from his own jacket and slapped it into Fernandez's hand. As Fernandez eyed the dagger like it was a serpent, Yevgeny turned to the oncoming abarbeaus, less than six yards away.

The screams of another victim echoed through the dark forest. The abarbeaus looked toward the high-pitched shrieks.

This was when Yevgeny picked up a rock and threw it at the abarbeaus. The rock struck the abarbeaus' face with tremendous force.

The abarbeaus rolled backwards, across the trail. Yevgeny threw himself into the abarbeaus, and shoved his dagger into its mangy throat. "Fernandez!" he hollered. "Help me!"

Hesitantly, Fernandez ran help Yevgeny. In confusion and fear, he watched as Yevgeny knifed the beast, over and over and over again, with his dagger.

"Nandy!" squalled Frida. "Get away from . . ."

"Stab it!" Yevgeny ordered Fernandez, having trouble controlling the wounded abarbeaus.

Fernandez ran his dagger into the abarbeaus' guts. Green and red gunk exploded from the gaping hole, which spilled onto his sleeves, torso, bare legs, and sandals.

"Good man!" cheered Yevgeny, proudly.

Fernandez gave Yevgeny a nervous smile.

Yevgeny and Fernandez then saw a grown up male abarbeaus step toward them. This critter was huge, making the one earlier look right puny. Paolo and Frida kicked at the male abarbeaus, which only provoked it. The abarbeaus stared at the two Agronians and snarled.

Paolo and Frida extended their arms out, in a lame defensive move. The abarbeaus swatted and clawed at the couple, like a cat toying with a mouse.

Fernandez screamed.

"Stop that!" shouted Yevgeny, both frustrated and mortified by the mess he was in. His mind wandered from a need to fight, give up and accept death, or save himself by running. Well, running was the worst thing to do. Yevgeny never ran from the Embrians occupying his country. He had convinced himself that Soraq created those Embrian soldiers, making them worthy of death. There wasn't no question in his mind who created those foul winged men, since Soraq did so in His own image.

Clearly, Soraq was responsible for those ape-like demons, which also needed killing!

And, should Yevgeny die that evening on the island of Infernus, then truly it would be the will of the Kuen! Slaying many foes, prior to meeting death, was pleasing to the Master!

"Do something, Fernandez!" roared Yevgeny. "Don't just stand there screaming like a little girl!"

Fernandez threw the dagger Yevgeny gave him at the abarbeaus. The dagger's blunt end struck the abarbeaus' forehead, an inch or two above the eyes. To Fernandez' horror, the dagger landed next to his folks.

The abarbeaus forgot all about the frightened couple, and turned his sights on Yevgeny and Fernandez.

Yevgeny held his dagger to his front. He looked the abarbeaus straight in the eyes, bared his own teeth, and growled. He crawled on all fours toward the abarbeaus, which was now less than ten feet away. Consciously, he mimicked the abarbeaus' movements, voice, and manners.

Paolo and Frida left their present position, seeking to make a mad dash toward New Merieko.

The abarbeaus pounced at Yevgeny.

Fernandez hurled a large rock at the abarbeaus, and nailed it squarely in the mouth.

The abarbeaus let out with a hair-raising shriek, then rolled around in the trail with a bad case of the flip-flops. Shards of busted teeth and blood spilled from its mouth.

Yevgeny sprinted over and slit the abarbeaus' throat. Blood gushed all over the place.

"Look out!" warned Paolo.

Yevgeny turned and frowned at Paolo, when . . .

A baby abarbeaus hopped onto Yevgeny's shoulder, nearly knocking him over.

The baby dug its claws into Yevgeny's shoulder and snapped repeatedly at his throat. Yevgeny hollered in protest and fear. He swung his body wildly in all directions, to rid himself of the baby. "Get it off of me!" he screeched, aggravation and anxiety revealing themselves in his frantic tone. His eyes met Fernandez', in a mute plea.

Fernandez latched onto the baby's maned neck and tried pulling it off of Yevgeny. That never did no good. The baby only dug deeper into Yevgeny's shoulder, and drew blood. Yevgeny's screams echoed throughout the woods.

Just then, the baby chomped into Fernandez' hand.

Yevgeny and Fernandez were now caught in the grips of the baby abarbeaus. Paolo and Frida stood back, as Yevgeny and Fernandez battled something surreal, primitive, and mean as hell. Fernandez let out a shrill cry for his folks' intervention, as Yevgeny squeezed the baby's throat with one hand.

The baby forgot all about Fernandez and once again snapped at Yevgeny's neck.

Fright and anger had gotten the best of Yevgeny, as he struggled to break free. "The dagger!" he yelled, pointing toward the weapon at his feet. "The dagger!"

Fernandez retrieved the dagger, drove it through the baby abarbeaus, and impaled it. The dagger's tip slightly cut the skin of Yevgeny's right shoulder.

The baby hopped off of Yevgeny, the dagger still sticking through it. It bounced all around the trees, then landed where Pavel-Ivanovich died.

After a funny looking case of the flip-flops, the baby abarbeaus died in a pool of its own blood.

Yevgeny unleashed a tirade of dirty words in Kuschan, then pulled the dagger from the baby abarbeaus' body. He looked all around, at the grisly reminder of what just took place. Yards away, several critters fed on the dismembered corpse of Pavel-Ivanovich.

Yevgeny held back tears. Pavel-Ivanovich was a dear friend, as well as a symbol of Kuschan pride and unity. His contributions to society, culture, and the arts helped Kusch get back on its feet, after years of war against Embrey.

Yevgeny regained his composure, then returned to the trail where his remaining companions were. Paolo never said nothing as he wore that same blank, idiotic stare. Frida and Fernandez knelt down, examining the boy's swollen, bloody hand. Frida openly fretted over her "poor little Nandy" as Fernandez maintained a brave face.

Yevgeny shook his head in disgust as he pulled Fernandez away from Frida's affection and care. "Get on your feet!" he ordered, with growing respect disguised as disdain. "On your feet! Stand up like the man you are, not the helpless babe they treat you as!"

Fernandez gasped. "But? . . . Why?"

"You may not know this, Nandy," said Yevgeny, sarcastically. "But you're already more of a man than your father ever will be!"

A few moments later, Admiral Vaslov and Commander Antonov arrived with about a dozen Kuschan Marines and sailors. Vaslov kept a stiff upper lip, acting like it never bothered him to see folks getting ate by critters. Antonov got all worked up the horrors he gazed upon.

"Where were you when we needed you?" asked Yevgeny, angrily.

"I want a report of what happened here," demanded Vaslov, with an air of dry humor.

"We're the only survivors," said Yevgeny. "As for the casualties . . . That's what's left of Pavel-Ivanovich."

"Pavel-Ivanovich?" gulped Antonov. "He's dead?"

"What did I just get done telling you?" barked Yevgeny. "Yes, Pavel's dead! Pavel, and all the others from our group."

"What happened to Pavel?" asked Antonov.

"He went to pick flowers," said Fernandez, absently.

Vaslov smirked. "Flowers?"

"Yes," said Fernandez. "For Gyorgy-Andreovich . . ."

"So, which of us will be given the honors of telling Gyorgy-Andreovich that his boyfriend ended up on a monkey's dinner table?" laughed Vaslov.

"Shut your filthy mouth!" screamed Yevgeny. "Pavel was a great man. Far better than an over-decorated, pompous windbag like you!"

"What did you say, holy man?" questioned Vaslov, through clenched teeth.

"Pavel has to be buried," said Yevgeny. "He was important to the Kuschan people, and deserves a state funeral and memorial befitting his status."

"What's left of him," groaned Antonov, sickly.

"You're injured," Vaslov said to Yevgeny and Fernandez. "Do you require medical care?"

"I'm all right," stated Yevgeny, his anger battling sadness and anger.

"The boy may need help," said Antonov. "Corpsman, I want you to examine Nandy and Pastor Yevgeny . . ."

"His name's Fernandez, not 'Nandy'!" shouted Yevgeny. "And he's got to get tough about his new scars, as he gets tough about this bloodletting! You want to check on anyone, why not his parents? One's chicken-hearted, and the other's gutless as hell! And while you're at it, remove Pavel's body from those things!"

"Commander Antonov," said Vaslov, sarcastically. "You and two other men retrieve fragments of our Kuschan savior. I'll collect the survivors' accounts."

"Yes, sir," said Antonov. "Vladimir, Andropov . . . Come with me to . . . retrieve Pavel-Ivanovich . . ."

Two young enlisted men, both in their late-teens, looked at each other nervously.

"You have your orders," said Antonov, tiredly. "No use thinking about it. Fetch a body bag, and let's get to it."

"But . . . but, sir," moaned Andropov, a tow-headed lad with acne scars all over. "Don't look like there's much to retrieve . . ."

"I gave you an order!" shouted Antonov. "I don't recall asking your opinion. Get to it, so we can leave this wicked place. The sooner, the better."

Vladimir and Andropov reluctantly entered the clearing and approached Pavel-Ivanovich's body.

Vaslov fetched a small notepad and pencil from his jacket, then requested that Paolo and Frida give their stories of the slaughter.

Paolo stared at Vaslov in confusion. He acted like somebody who not only lacked answers, but the means of giving them.

"Well?" Vaslov asked Frida, in frustration and contempt. "What do you have to say about? . . ."

Frida responded by backhanding Vaslov's face, as hard as she could.

Antonov, Vladimir, and Andropov slowly, cautiously crossed the bloody clearing, where a number of critters feasted on Pavel-Ivanovich. The three men carefully unsheathed their swords.

By now, the critters had devoured most of Pavel's face and innards. They ignored the three Kuschans heading their way. It was only when the Kuschans were within a few yards, did the critters take notice. One of the critters lifted its head up from the kill, bared its teeth, and growled.

"Get back!" yelled Antonov. He was scared but tried not to show it. "Get back!"

One of the critters snarled. Both eyes widened, as its furry mane bristled in a warning.

Antonov waved his sword and the body bag at the critters. "Get back!" he repeated, louder than before. "Go on . . . Get out of here!"

One of the critters charged at the three Kuschans. Andropov screamed as he pushed Antonov out of harm's way.

A split-second later, the critter tackled Andropov.

Andropov shrieked to the top of his lungs. The critter bit into Andropov's neck, as blood gushed everywhere. Much of it sprayed onto Antonov, who remained sprawled overtop the pretty red flowers.

As the critter dragged Andropov away, his dead eyes stared at the other two sailors.

A second abarbeaus dropped from a nearby tree, landing on Vladimir. His life also ended quickly, as he was also hauled into the woods by a ferocious animal.

Antonov hollered in shock, denial, and defiance. Hopping to his feet, he decapitated one of the critters swarming around Andropov.

One of the remaining critters pounced at Antonov. The frightened officer backed away, tripped, and landed into a cluster of the pretty red flowers. He cried out for help, just as the abarbeaus leaped on him.

A trio of Kuschan archers killed the abarbeaus, with a volley arrows.

Antonov pushed the dead abarbeaus away from him, then got to his feet. He was shaken, sweaty, exhausted, and hurt. He'd been given orders which resulted in the foolish, horrible deaths of two sailors.

Antonov grabbed his sword and the body bag from the ground, then limped back to the trail. His eyes seethed with hatred and revulsion, as he glared at Vaslov and Yevgeny.

For several seconds, no one traded words, or sought answers for Vladimir and Andropov's demise.

"You're so keen on the idea of salvaging Pavel-Ivanovich," mumbled Antonov, throwing the body bag in Yevgeny's face. "Fine. Take care of it, yourself."

Jeremy Kentworth got back into Persis not long before sundown. He stripped off his shoes, shirt, and loincloth, then took a long, refreshing shower in the waterfall.

The water felt icy and frigid, compared to the earlier heat of that autumn day. Once Jeremy got done, he put his loincloth back on, dried himself in the late-afternoon sun, then soaked his shirt in the river.

The shirt was smeared in sweat, smoke, dirt, dust, gunk, and soot. Worse yet, it was ripped to shreds where an abarbeaus swung its claws at Jeremy's chest. Too bad. The shirt had a beautiful embroidery of a bird in flight, which Evelyn fixed up real good. Hopefully, it could be fixed.

Jeremy sat in the empty field between the church and waterfall. His hair and body was still damp. A breeze swept through a narrow canyon, into the valley. Jeremy hadn't ate nothing all day. He needed a drink, a chew, and a smoke. And sleep. His thin, masculine frame was pocked with goosebumps, and his teeth chattered. He suffered the groggy, dizzying effects of a slight fever and chill.

Life used to be so free and easy. Aside from his various chores for Rey, Jeremy done whatever we pleased. He used his leisure time to hunt, fish, and play. He provided for the town the best way he knew how, with a bow, his arrows, a fishing pole, a knife, and his sword. He was a fair marksman. He was often criticized for taking stupid chances, when hunting. He sort of respected the abarbeaus, but got where he no longer feared them.

Jeremy's respect for the abarbeaus had turned into hatred, after they killed a friend.

Jeremy sat alone, haunted by recurring images of Randen getting ate. Was it murder? No, just dumb critter instinct. Randen got badly injured, before meeting up with Jeremy and Weston, and was an easy target. Even then, Jeremy would never forget Randen's loud screeches for help as he got ate.

So, how did Randen get injured? And what exactly was that business about 'an angry Kuschan', if that's what Jeremy and Weston had heard?

What difference did it make, now? Randen was dead!

Jeremy was cold, tired, hungry, and depressed. He was tempted to let down his guard and cry. He wept, not only for Randen, but in thoughts of losing his childhood, his freedom, his lifestyle, and his home on Infernus.

And maybe even losing Ericha . . .

For the first time in his life, Jeremy harbored unknown, maybe unspeakable thoughts involving Ericha. Jeremy and Ericha had always bathed naked at the waterfall. It was handled in a natural, innocent way. But now, Jeremy not only wanted to bathe with Ericha. He wanted to take their relationship further . . . much further.

He imagined himself pressing his nude body against her, as their lips met in the act of lovemaking. He yearned for the warmth of her soft, soothing skin, as the water cleansed and nourished them. He wished to rub his hands and fingers across her body, as she also explored his. It'd be a moment that the two teens would cherish forever. No one would know, or have to know, about this. Only Almighty God would play witness to this experience, as two young people vowed to spend the rest of their lives together.

From now, till the end of time . . .

"Rey wants you to put this on," said Weston, handing a long-sleeved, woolen shirt to Jeremy. "He also wants you to come in for supper. You must be starving, kiddo. And freezing! It's getting cold out here!"

"Thanks," sighed Jeremy putting the shirt on. "Winter comes earlier every year, I reckon."

"The older you get, the earlier it comes, and the longer it stays." Weston sat next to Jeremy on the ground. "What are you doing up here, all alone?"

"Nothing," said Jeremy, staring vacantly in the distance.

"It's not good to be alone. A man has an easy enough time thinking himself to an ulcer. If he's not careful, he'll think himself to an early grave."

"Like thinking about moving to Branell?"

"Or refusing to," said Weston.

"That land I'm s'posed to inherit," said Jeremy, anxiously. "You ever been there? What's it like?"

"I'm an Embrian diplomat, not a spy. If I even dreamed of entering Branell without authorization, they'll hang me."

"Then how will I know if I like it? What if I go all there, and it stinks?"

"I've been told that it's quite breathtaking," said Weston. "It's in a rural part of the country, far from any city. The only people you're liable to see are those who also live on the property."

"You mean to tell me that I'm a landlord?" asked Jeremy, frowning.

"It doesn't mean you have to be a bad one," said Weston. "The parcel is covered with acres of flatlands, orchards, and timber. The main crops are apples, wheat, grapes, beets, and potatoes. You also own a lumberyard. You can hunt and fish year 'round."

Jeremy smiled. "What sorta critters?"

"Deer, elk, rabbits, chukars, quail, grouse, bears . . ."

"Bears?" asked Jeremy, eagerly.

"The land rests at the base of the Northern Branellian Mountains. Granite peaks, stretching as far as the eye can see . . . or so I've heard. More lakes and streams than you can shake a stick at."

"What if I don't want to shake sticks at lakes and streams?" giggled Jeremy.

"Very funny," groaned Weston. "The house is a stone mansion, sitting upon a rocky hillside."

"Yeah, kinda like God perched upon his throne, peeing and pooping on his subjects, which he keeps an eye on to make sure they ain't up to something."

"That's up to you, kiddo."

"I don't mind the hunting and fishing part. As far as being some sort of landlord . . . sheesh! Ain't sure I'm wanting that."

"Why not?"

"I don't like the idea of people owing me something, or me owing them anything."

"Those folks got to live somewhere."

"On my land?" asked Jeremy. "I mean . . . if I decide to take it."

"Where else are they going to live? You own most everything in that area, not to mention creating most of the jobs. You own the land they work, the homes they live in, maybe even the pub they go to at the end of the day, to blow the froth off a cold one."

Jeremy snickered.

"Even the church they go to that next Sunday, seeking forgiveness for all the trouble they got into the night before," added Weston. "You're responsible for most of the midwives, and all of the babies born there. Those tenants are beholden to you, Jeremy. And if not to you, then to the King of Branell. Something tells me you'd give them a better deal than what they're going to get from royalty."

Jeremy had lots to consider and contemplate.

"Then again," said Weston, "If you wish to spend the rest of your life wearing a loincloth, being nothing more or nothing less than just plain old Jeremy, well, that's your choice too."

"Dunno if I'm wanting it, or not wanting it," moped Jeremy. "The whole thing stinks, Weston."

"Well, one thing that doesn't stink is supper," said Weston, slapping Jeremy's leg. "We'd better get inside before you die of starvation, or the food gets cold."

Jeremy smiled.

"By the way, we've got guests tonight," informed Weston.

"Not Errol or the Little Oinker . . ."

"Not tonight," laughed Weston.

"Then who?"

"You'll see . . ."

Jeremy and Weston went through the back door into the church's living quarters. From the cafeteria they heard Rey's low, baritone voice, answered by a comforting, feminine voice.

Jeremy's heart skipped a beat. It was Ericha!

Jeremy tugged on the bottom of his shirt, sucked in a deep breath, and entered the dining room.

Sure enough, at the far end of the table sat Ericha, dolled-up in her nicest, long-sleeved buckskin shirt and skimpiest loincloth. Next to her was the little tattooed boy Paransky, who Mucker and Seely had taken a liking to. Paransky was dressed in a thin, silk white shirt, knickers, black knee-socks, and spit-shine brogans.

Had it not been for them tattoos scrawled all over him, Paransky might have been a right handsome boy. His scruffy, unruly hair and soft, sad eyes made for a sympathetic figure. Them tattoos was mostly of an erotic or obscene nature, and looked kind of awful.

"Sit down, Jeremy," greeted Rey. "I'll bet you're starving."

"Yes, sir," said Jeremy.

"Evelyn cooked a splendid meal tonight," said Rey. "Steak, green beans, cornbread, fried potatoes . . ."

Jeremy sat at a chair between Rey and Weston, and gave Ericha a toothy grin.

"The town's planning a doings in Randen's honor," said Rey. "Lorenzo's going to say a few words, then me, then maybe Malachi, if he gets over being mad at Lorenzo and Nik."

"What's up with Malachi?" asked Jeremy.

"Lorenzo just signed a trade agreement with Kusch," said Rey.

Jeremy rolled his eyes back. "Oh, hell . . ."

"Watch your tongue," warned Rey.

"That's the last thing Mucker wants!" hollered Jeremy. "Bet he's mad as hell right now!"

"So am I," said Weston. "The trade agreement makes my coming here a bit pointless now . . . for the exception of meeting my cousin Jeremy."

"Mucker says he's fixing to kill the first damned Kuschan he sees!" giggled Paransky, mischievously.

"Paransky," warned Rey, impatiently. "I don't approve of foul language at supper."

"Yeah," said Jeremy. "Well, maybe Mucker's right! Lorenzo don't know what he's getting into! Maybe the best thing is to kick every heathen, vodka-swelling Kuschan off the island, then sink their ship before it leaves the harbor!"

"Jeremy . . ." whispered Rey, tiredly.

"I'm not allowed to say such things," said Weston. "At least not in public. After all, Embrey signed a peace agreement with Kusch, not long ago. I don't like the Kuschans, nor can I trust them. However, the last thing we need is for the war to start all over again, this time within the shores of Infernus."

"And the last thing I want is a political discussion at suppertime," said Rey. "I don't like politicians, nor do I trust them."

Weston snickered.

It's been a long day," said Rey. "One I'd just as soon forget. I'm tired, Jeremy's hungry, and the food's getting cold. As soon as I've had supper, I'm going to bed."

"I can't sleep," moped Jeremy.

"You've got to be exhausted," Weston said to Jeremy. "The way you worked that fire."

"What is it, son?" asked Rey. "Upset about Randen?"

"Kind of," said Jeremy. "But not only because of . . . . But . . . . other stuff."

"Branell?" asked Ericha, nervously.

Jeremy never said nothing. His sad eyes answered for him.

The room got kind of quiet, as everyone pondered the weight pressing down upon Jeremy.

Ericha," said Rey, breaking the silence. "Will you say grace, tonight?"

"Yes, Leader Rey," agreed Ericha, reaching out to clasp hands with Paransky and Weston.

"Weston?" asked Jeremy, urgently. "Uh . . . You wanna change places with me?"

"What for?" asked Weston.

"My . . . my back's killing me," claimed Jeremy. "And . . . this chair's making it worse!"

Rey, Weston, and Paransky snickered, knowing that Jeremy wanted to sit next to Ericha.

"Sure," agreed Weston, changing places with Jeremy.

Jeremy plopped down in his new chair, took Ericha's soft, warm hand, and squeezed it gently.

"Ericha?" whispered Rey. "Grace?"

Ericha lowered his head and closed her eyes. "Oh, Heavenly Father," she began. "For that which we are about to receive, we thank you.

"We give thanks for the bountiful meal before us. We give thanks for our lives, and for our health. We humbly ask that You bless us with safety and peace in the coming days, weeks, and months.

"We ask that You accept our friend Randen into the Kingdom of Heaven . . ."

Ericha's voice cracked. Jeremy was also overwhelmed with grief, as he clenched Ericha's hand that much tighter.

Ericha continued. "We give thanks for our family and friends, here on Insula Infernus, as give thanks for our church family. We give thanks for Your humble servant and our guiding hand in the Brotherhood of Faith, Leader Rey.

"In Your name and Your honor, we pray!

"Amen!"

"Amen," everybody else whispered, in unison.

"Thank you, Ericha," said Rey. "And thank you for your kind words. It means a great deal to me."

Ericha smiled, pleasantly. "Thank you, Leader Rey."

"Very well." Rey cleared his throat. "I wanted to chat with Jeremy about this, before making a decision. I believe this affects him, as much as the youngster in question."

"What's up?" asked Jeremy, fetching a steak from a long platter with his bare hands.

"It didn't take long for me to come up with this proposal, and I know it's in his best interests," said Rey. "I appreciate Mucker and Seely's willingness to take the boy in, raise him to be a hard worker and . . ." Rey paused. "Steady hand in the village. However, for the boy's spiritual well-being, overall health and safety, and moral standing in the church and community, I wonder if our friend here . . ." Rey placed his hand on Paransky's shoulder. "Isn't better off living here at the church, with us."

Weston and Ericha smiled in approval, while Jeremy acted all shocked and offended. Paransky never said nothing, as his tattooed face blushed.

"I want to raise Paransky as my adopted son," said Rey. "And that we accept him as a member of our congregation."

"Congratulations!" cheered Weston.

 Ericha gave Paransky a hug and a kiss on the cheek.

"Let me guess," mumbled Jeremy, in betrayal. "He's taking my place . . ."

"No one can take your place, Jeremy," answered Rey, sarcastically. "Believe me . . . No one . . ."

"Think I better fetch me a drink and a smoke," said Jeremy, pushing himself away from the table.

"You stay right there!" shouted Rey. "Don't you dare leave this table."

"But I need me a drink and a smoke!" cried Jeremy.

"You need food more than liquor or tobacco," said Rey, impatiently. "You haven't eaten all day, and I should think you've inhaled enough smoke for one day."

"Think I'm gonna get sick," groaned Jeremy, his eyes damp and dewy.

"Don't worry," assured Rey. "I'm not kicking you out."

"It sure feels that way," whined Jeremy.

"I'll bet this isn't the first time he's thought about it," commented Ericha.

"This island owes John Mucker a lot," said Rey, ignoring Ericha's remark as he wisely changed the subject. "But he's not the right man to raise a child."

"I agree," said Weston.

"What makes you say that?" argued Jeremy, for no reason than to start a fight. "He did okay by me . . ."

"I was about to raise that very issue," said Rey, giving Jeremy the stink eye. "Seely's likable enough, though I've never known him to do an honest day's work in his life. I meant what I said about Mucker. Persis owes him a debt of gratitude. I can't say I approve of his business practices, if you can call them that. If we need someone to fight for our needs and interests, I can't think of a better man than John Mucker. But what sort of life can Paransky expect, when Mucker leaves on one of his ships to deal in illicit trade? And what happens if Mucker is captured by another nation's navy, or by rival smugglers? Every man onboard will hang, and Heaven knows what they'll do with Paransky."

"Mucker will fight to the death before he's hung!" snapped Jeremy.

"Paransky, too?" debated Weston.

"Better to die by the sword, than to dance in the air with a rope around your neck!" commented Jeremy, boastfully.

"That may sound romantic and heroic in adventure stories around the campfire," said Weston. "But the reality of it all . . . Oh, brother . . ."

"What do you know about it?" challenged Jeremy. "You're nothing but a Farlander, Mister Weston! A lazy, no-nothing, easy-living Farlander!"

"Jeremy . . ." scolded Rey.

"And what do you know about it?" Weston hollered at Jeremy, barely controlling his anger. "Wish I had a shilling for every war zone I've been to, or every hot spot I've traveled to where men tried killing me, simply because I'm an Embrian. I can't count the number of bodies I've buried . . . and some of them weren't soldiers, either. Most were civilians who were unlucky and got in the way, or just a poor, misfortunate schmuck who died to support a wicked man's greed and cussedness."

Jeremy glared at Weston, but never said nothing.

"I don't mean to get mad at you, Jeremiah," said Weston. "Sure, you may know your way around Infernus, I'll give you that. And yes, it was dumb of me to go out alone in the woods this morning! But let me tell you this . . . You know very little of this world outside of this tiny island, and you ain't seen nothing yet!"

Jeremy hopped up from his chair, ready to box Weston's ears for talking back.

Weston kept a close watch on Jeremy. Whether he was scared or not, he refused to show it. He was more afraid of Jeremy getting so mad at him, that they'd no longer be on speaking terms. Neither Jeremy nor Weston said nothing. They just gave each other the eye.

"Sit down, Jeremy!" ordered Rey.

"I don't have to sit down if I don't want to!" hollered Jeremy, madder than he's ever been since watching Randen get ate. "I don't gotta sit here and take that crap!"

"You leave this table, you leave this house," declared Rey. "Weston is our guest, and you'll treat him as such. Treat him with respect, or get out."

For several seconds, one could hear a pin drop. Jeremy, Rey, and Weston engaged in a mean-looking staring contest.

The silence ended, when Paransky responded with annoying, high-pitched giggling.

Jeremy forgot all about boxing Weston's ears. Now, the had a sudden urge to slap all them tattoos off of little Paransky. One, for taking Jeremy's place in the house, two for laughing, and third, just because.

"Let it go," begged Ericha, softly caressing Jeremy's hand. "Don't fight. Please, Jeremy? Just let it go . . ."

Jeremy released a deep breath and slouched. He got where he wasn't no longer mad at Weston or Paransky. He got where he was mad at himself. He didn't have a sassy comeback against Weston, nor did he care to get on Rey and Ericha's bad side. He didn't like having Paransky laugh at him, but what was the use? What good would it do to pound the snot and tattoos out of Paransky? In the end, it'd just make things worse.

What choice did Jeremy have now but to sit down, eat the nice grub that Evelyn fixed up real good and admit this once, just this once, that he was wrong?

* * * * *

After a very quiet, tasty, and sullen supper, Jeremy and Ericha left the church.

There was a bright full moon, shining over the loud, swift rapids of the Persis River. Some residents of town was already in bed. Others sat outside on their stoops or porches, drinking local rotgut, smoking pipes, and enjoying a cool autumn evening.

Most everybody was angry and upset over Randen's death. A silent, depressed mood dominated the community. Some voiced it openly. Others hid it behind warm smiles and greetings. Jeremy and Ericha answered in kind. Seemed that everyone made it their business to know exactly WHAT HAPPENED.

Jeremy never said much, but just sort of mentioned that Randen got attacked and partly ate, but not much more. He wasn't up to talking in the first place and he sure wasn't in no mood to talk about WHAT HAPPENED. More than anything, he just needed silence and solitude, in the company of the one he loved and cared for, more than anybody else on the face of the Earth.

The teens didn't go onto Ericha's house, a modest little shack that she shared with Errol and Prince Ari. Instead, they circled the town, crossed a narrow path around stony embankments and adjoining the deep, dark forest.

Finally, they got to their favoritest spot on the entire island, the empty field at the base of the waterfall. They sat down together and pondered the long, hard day, along with the uncertain days to come.

Minutes passed, and neither Jeremy nor Ericha said nothing. The only racket came from the rushing, unending stream of water pouring from the water-fall, and the pleasant chirps of a cricket, not too far off.

After the longest time, Jeremy got up the nerve to ask, "Ericha, will you come to Branell with me?"

Ericha gasped. "What?"

"Will you come to Branell with me?" repeated Jeremy, more raspy and desperate than before. Tears welled in his eyes, as he placed one hand around Ericha's shoulder. "I ain't going over there alone, and I damn sure ain't going without you!"

Ericha never said nothing. Even then, Jeremy got her attention.

"I ain't going over there without you!" cried Jeremy. "I can't live without you, and I don't care to even think about it! Please, Ericha? . . . Will you come to Branell with me?"

Ericha's smile brightened the gloom and darkness of night. Without so much as a single thought, she threw her arms around Jeremy and kissed him on the cheek.

"You . . . You're my best friend!" sobbed Jeremy. "You're my best friend, and . . . and . . ." He stopped, too scared to reveal his deepest thoughts for the girl he held in his arms.

Ericha embraced Jeremy. She ran her fingers through his hair, showered his face with kisses, and dreamed of a life and a future they'd share, just the two of them. Ericha was so happy that she also began to cry. "I love you, Jeremy!" she bawled. "I love you so much, and never want to let you go! I want to spend the rest of my life with you!"

"I love you, too," said Jeremy, the words muffled as his face pressed against hers. "Will you come to Branell with me? All that land and all that money don't mean nothing to me if I can't have them with you . . . If I can't have you with me! Please? . . . Will you come to Branell with me?"

Ericha answered, not with words, but by planting a firm kiss to Jeremy's lips.

Neither Jeremy nor Ericha returned to their homes, that evening. They retreated to an old, abandoned hut at the edge of Persis, where they'd be warm and comfortable.

Where they'd be alone.

With no one there to evaluate or judge them, Jeremy and Ericha rested in one corner of the lonely, little hut. They cuddled, arm-in-arm, and wrapped their bare legs tightly together. The two celebrated their childhood, while imagining the adult lives they hoped to share.

When Ericha and Jeremy weren't discussing their future plans they kissed, and constantly held on to each other. They vowed never to separate from that moment onward, and promised to remain united as one . . .

. . . Forever . . .

. . . Until death . . .

* * * * *

Damn it to Hell . . .

Weston had trouble sleeping that night. Too many things was on his mind. Fears and frustrations tore at his deep-rooted values and beliefs.

Weston had been a diplomat for King Marco of Embrey for nearly ten years. The job had its share of adventures, let-downs, disappointments, and scares. Few Embrians knew of the countries that Weston had visited. He was given opportunities that most people could never dream of. He considered himself lucky, but wondered if it was due to being Marco's cousin.

Cousin or not, Weston worked hard at his profession, and had the wins to show for it.

He also had too many "defeats" where his efforts failed to pan out.

Weston went to Infernus for two reasons. One was to establish diplomacy and trade with the island. The second was not only to meet a family member named Jeremiah Kentworth, but also to bring him good news concerning a fortune in northern Branell. Well, Infernus had already established diplomatic and trade ties to the rival nation of Kusch, while Jeremy wasn't interested in his property, or his good fortune.

Not only that, but Weston and Jeremy never quite hit it off, and wasn't on the best of speaking terms.

Might be they wasn't on speaking terms at all, now.

Weston came to Infernus with the best of intentions. The best of intentions weren't enough to win over with diplomacy, or Jeremy Kentworth.

Chalk Infernus up as a loss . . .

Damn it to Hell . . .

Weston tossed and turned. Sometimes he lied on his left side, sometimes on his right, and even on his back to try and sleep. Never did no good.

He thought Infernus was the trip of a lifetime. Now, he was anxious and eager to get home.

The light of the full moon shined through the window of the cramped quarters of the Brotherhood Church. Weston stared up at the rough-cut ceiling boards above him, thinking himself a failure as a diplomat and as a cousin.

Weston had a good working relationship with King Marco, and often brought him good results. If the news wasn't so great, there was always a reasonable excuse. Marco gave Weston greater leeway than most in the diplomatic corps. He never once threatened to relieve Weston of his head.

On the other hand, Weston saw no call in pushing it.

Weston sat up. No point in sleeping! It was best to get up, fetch a candle, and head into the cafeteria.

Rey had a small library of scrolls and books he got from the Farlands. There might be a volume or two to entertain Weston, 'til sunrise. Might also be a deck of cards hidden someplace, for a game of Solitaire. Beings this was a house of worship, it seemed unlikely.

Weston stretched his tired, aching back, and yawned. The nights could be long and torturous! Weston scratched his face, then fetched a shirt and pants. He wanted to mend fences with Jeremy. But Jeremy up and left with Ericha, and never come back. Where this gave Rey cause for alarm, Weston marked it up as just a young person being young. He could only imagine what Jeremy and Ericha was up to at that hour but thought it best to mark that up as young people being young, too.

Weston left his quarters, just as someone knocked on the cafeteria door. It was almost midnight, and he wondered who it could be at that hour. He thought it was Jeremy, who got done doing what he was doing with Ericha and needed in.

Weston snickered as he sneaked past the cafeteria tables and chairs, to the door.

It wasn't Jeremy.

It was Jung-su, with a black eye he got at The Black Eye.

Jung-su's face looked like it was beaten on, real bad. His right eye and cheek was swollen, he had a few knots on his head, and blood trickled from his mouth.

Jung-su was working at The Black Eye when a few patrons got to harassing him, first for his race, then for his religion, and finally for WHAT HAPPENED to Randen. He was already worked up on account of WHAT HAPPENED, and the last thing he needed was getting harassed over it.

Badly outnumbered, Jung-su threw off his apron and was leaving The Black Eye when the punishment started. About a half-dozen brutes cornered then pounded him, for no good reason other than because they thought it was fun, and because they could. The management of The Black Eye didn't take part in this beating, nor did they stop it.

Finally, an off-duty cook and bartender jumped in and freed Jung-su from the thrashing.

By now, the damage had been done, and Jung-su had enough. He run off to his tiny little shed back behind The Black Eye, cleared out his stuff, and called it quits.

Tears covered Jung-su's beat-up face. Snot mixed with blood, which ran from his nostrils. The boy had a tote bag slung over one shoulder. Wherever he was going, it sure wasn't back to The Black Eye.

All Weston could see was a darkened silhouette against a moonlit sky. It wasn't until the person stepped forward when he recognized it as Jung-su. "Come in, come in!" requested Weston, scared of the shape Jung-su was in.

"I can't stay," whimpered Jung-su, his voice hoarse and raspy.

"You can't stay?" questioned Weston. "What do you mean, you can't stay? Where are you going to? . . ."

"I'm leaving at first light," said Jung-su, wiping blood, snot, and tears from his face.

"'Leaving'? 'Leaving'? Where to?"

"With 'No-Teeth'. He's taking a few passengers to the Farlands with him in the morning, and I'm . . ." Jung-su sobbed. "I'm going with him."

"You can't do that! Why? . . . I'll be leaving in a few days on a respectable frigate. Come with me, Jung-su. I'll even go so far as to pay for your fare."

"I can't stay here any longer, I won't!" Jung-su took a deep breath, then let it out slowly. "I owe a debt of gratitude to everybody here . . ."

"All right . . ."

"And I'll miss them more than anything!" wept Jung-su. "But I've just got to get off this lousy, stupid little rock! I never once thought that I belonged here, even when I was a little kid. I never belonged here, Mister Weston! All I want now is go somewhere else and start over!"

"I wouldn't start over on the Edith-Marie," advised Weston. "'No-Teeth' Murnau has a terrible reputation, even in the Farlands. I beg you . . . Don't even think about leaving with him, unless you want to die!"

"I can't stay . . ." Jung-su bit his bottom lip. "I just wanted to stop by, and . . . Will you give Leader Rey and Jer a message for me?"

"Why don't you stay, and tell them yourself?"

"I can't!" breathed Jung-su. "I've got to be at the dock, help 'No-Teeth' prepare the ship, and assist the other passengers."

"In the middle of the night?" shouted Weston, his voice echoing throughout the cafeteria.

I've just got to go," mumbled Jung-su. "I can't stay, not a minute longer. Will you please tell everyone? . . . Leader Rey, Jer, Ericha and Errol and everyone else when you see them, that I said . . ." A whimper spilled from Jung-su's mouth, as tears spilled from his eyes. "Tell them . . . thanks, and that . . . that . . . I . . ."

Jung-su lowered his head, unable to say more.

"Why don't you stay, and tell them yourself?" repeated Weston, unsure of what to do, or what to say, or even what to do or how to say it.

Jung-su gave Weston a strained smile. He gave the diplomat a quick hug, turned around, and walked away.

"Wait!" called Weston, stepping outside to catch up with Jung-su. "Wait! We need to talk! Please . . . Wait up, why don'tcha?"

It never did no good. Jung-su wouldn't respond to Weston, nor did he even acknowledge him. He just kept right on going.

Weston stopped just a few feet from the church. Quietly, he watched Jung-su slowly fade away into the darkness.

Never to set foot on the remote island of Infernus. Never again.

Weston frowned. He had failed to secure a diplomatic and trade agreement with Infernus. He failed to make a good impression on Jeremiah Kentworth. Finally, he failed to persuade Jung-su not to board a floating morgue known as the Edith-Marie. Great! Absolutely great! Where else would Weston screw up, before his time on Infernus was up?

Weston shook his head, frowned, and went back inside. There, he hoped to find a damned fine deck of cards someplace, for a long, lonely night of Solitaire.

Damn it to Hell . . .

* * * * *

"Where were you last night?"

In the wee hours of the morning, Ericha woke up next to Jeremy in the abandoned old hut. Despite a chill of the night air, she slept good in the warm embrace of one she regarded as her husband.

Jeremy and Ericha spent much of the evening locking lips, while caressing and comforting each other. It went no further than hugging and kissing. Jeremy and Ericha had a strict, unspoken rule. They'd wait until their wedding night before messing around. Once the time came, they'd do it in the confines of a bedroom, away from eyes, ears, and the suspicions of others.

Ericha got up just as the sun peeked over the horizon. It was cool and dewy outside. Jeremy was still asleep and let Ericha use his shoulder as a pillow.

It was daylight now, and Ericha had to get home before Errol got out of bed.

Too late. Ericha went into the house to find Errol and Prince Ari sitting at a small dining table. They was in the middle of chowing down on scrambled chicken eggs, crispy bacon, and apple cider.

As Ericha stepped inside, neither Errol nor Ari never said nothing. Errol's face revealed anger, worry, and frustration. Meanwhile, Ari looked forward to seeing Ericha get hollered at.

Ericha knew she was in trouble. She had spent the whole night with Jeremy. They didn't do nothing to be ashamed of. Jeremy and Ericha was still virgins.

Did Ericha have to convince Errol of that?

Ericha blushed as she stood silently at the kitchen doorway. Her nervous eyes refused contact with Errol's.

"Where were you last night?" asked Errol, in a harsh tone.

"Nowhere, Papa," sighed Ericha, more anxious than she should've been.

"Nowhere?" growled Errol. "You had to be somewhere!"

Ericha leaned against the kitchen door, wondering how to stand up to Errol.

"Ari," said Errol. "Hurry up. Finish your breakfast, then run along."

"But, Papa!" whined Ari, wanting to stay behind and watch Ericha get a shellacking.

"Finish your breakfast, and go!" hollered Errol.

Ari took his last few bites of his grub, then headed outside.

The silence was unbearable. Ericha couldn't look Errol straight in the eye. Instead, she stared through an open window at neighbors harvesting corn from their garden.

"Might as well sit down," said Errol. "Imagine you're hungry. I'll fix you an egg or two, then you can tell me . . ."

"I was with Jeremy," explained Ericha, standing her ground while trying not to break Errol's heart. Errol raised her and Ari on his own, and her love for the man was unbreakable. She sought his approval for her relationship with Jeremy, and to accept him as a member of the family. "I was with Jeremy," she repeated. "Jeremy Kentworth . . ."

"I know who he is," mumbled Errol. "For all I know, he's the only 'Jeremy' on the island. I want to know what you and Jeremy were up to."

"Nothing."

"Nothing?"

"It's not what you think," stated Ericha, defensively.

"Then what is it?"

Ericha never said nothing.

"Might as well sit down and tell me," sighed Errol. "If it's not what I think, then you got nothing to hide. If you're not going to say anything, then what am I to believe?"

Ericha slowly sat in a chair next to Errol. She placed her hand in his, and held on tightly. She finally got up the courage to make eye contact with him.

Errol already guessed what Ericha might say, and knew it was coming. In time, some boy would win Ericha's heart. Errol even surmised that the boy in question was Jeremy Kentworth.

"I was with Jeremy all night," said Ericha. "But we didn't do anything wrong."

"Anything?"

"Nothing," said Ericha. "I was the perfect lady, and he the perfect gentleman."

"Even with them . . . rags you got on?" Errol frowned. "Ericha . . . when are you gonna start wearing dresses, like 'the perfect lady' I know you are? And when's Jeremy gonna wear pants, like 'the perfect gentleman' he is?"

"Papa . . ."

"I mean it!" shouted Errol. "You got any idea how stupid you look, or how revealing those rags are? You're a very beautiful young woman, but . . ."

"But what?"

"You look so . . . cheap!"

Ericha giggled.

"Well, just look at yourself, sweetheart!" sighed Errol. "How many ladies do you know who show off their legs like that? It embarrasses me to have my daughter roaming around town in such . . . skimpy rags! It was our ancestor who first settled this country. Not only is it embarrassing, it's humiliating!"

Ericha smiled. "Papa . . ."

"You ought to hear what some of these young guys say about you and Jeremy, when your backs are turned!"

"What do they say?" asked Ericha, her anger flaring.

"I don't care to tell," mumbled Errol. "So, what if Jeremy does go to Branell? Will he keep on wearing those same blasted animal hides, while overseeing acres and acres of fine farmland?"

Ericha swallowed, nervously. "Jeremy wants me to go with him. And I . . . I want to go, too."

Although Errol somehow expected it, this news still hit him like a ton of bricks. Sadness mixed with betrayal, confusion, defeat, then the painful resignation of acceptance. He was caught between hugging Ericha, slapping the stuffing out of her, or knocking Jeremy's teeth in.

He kind of understood why Ericha wanted to be with Jeremy. At the same time, he couldn't imagine life without his oldest child under his roof. No matter. Ericha's departure was an inevitable part of life . . . and of growing up.

If Jeremy wished to make something of himself, he had to leave Infernus. Otherwise, he'd end up doing nothing more than cutting trees for lumber, becoming a pirate, or working for one of the local bars or bordellos. Worse-case scenarios meant becoming a man like Seely. So many of the island's young adults moved away. Some returned for occasional visits, a few return to stay.

Some was never seen nor heard from, again.

Assuming Ericha did leave with Jeremy, would she ever come home for visits? If Jeremy did make a go of it in Branell, Ericha would have it made. She'd never know a lean nor hungry day. Nor would their kids. Therefore, Errol should've welcomed this arrangement.

Right?

Errol regarded Jeremy as something of a 'son.' Would he now view him as a 'son-in-law'?

What if Ericha did leave Infernus? Would Errol ever get to know his own grandchildren? He sure wasn't young anymore, and feared he'd never live to see Ari reach adulthood.

Ericha . . . his "little girl Ericha", wasn't no little girl . . . No more.

Errol was speechless. He wanted to bless and support a union between Jeremy and Ericha. Eyeballing a few of the island's other lads, Jeremy might have been the pick of the crop. Some of them boys only wanted Ericha for one thing, and one thing only! Jeremy and Ericha had always been friends.

And yet, Errol suspected that the two had taken it a lot farther, by venturing into the tantalizing, forbidden world of sex.

Was that also inevitable? And would Errol learn to live with it? Or would he now assert his role as a father, and teach Jeremy a lesson?

What if Jeremy taught him a lesson?

Errol gave Ericha the eye. "You sure nothing happened between you and Jeremy, that I ought to know about?"

"Papa," scolded Ericha. "Have I ever kept secrets from you?"

"Have you?" asked Errol, sick-unto-death for not trusting Ericha.

"I love Jeremy," said Ericha. "And he loves me, too. Oh, Papa! If you saw the look on his face when he said he loved me, I . . ."

"If Jeremy loves you so much, why ain't he here to talk to me? I'm your father. Don't matter if you and Jeremy live on the moon! I'm your father. I'll always be your father. From now, 'til the day you die!"

"But, Papa . . ."

"Who took care of you, since Ma died?" interrupted Errol. "I always want to take care of you! How can I do that, if you're not here for me to do my duties as a parent?"

"Maybe I need to take care of myself!" cried Ericha.

"And what's Jeremy gonna be doing, while you're busy taking care of yourself? Letting you take care of him, too?"

"You know Jeremy better than that!"

"Then why ain't he here to talk to me?" sighed Errol. "I talked to him yesterday, said it was fine for him to court you. Seems only fitting that the both of you ought to be here . . ."

"I left him to sleep in that empty old hut by the river."

"That old hut?" snapped Errol. The old abandoned hut had a reputation for being the hiding place for youthful wrongdoing. Many a lad had tasted his first drink of heavy liquor, as well as losing his innocence, in that flimsy, ramshackle mess! "You two slept together in that old hut?"

"Yes, Papa, we slept together! Slept! Slept, and nothing else! I told you, I was the proper lady, and Jeremy the proper gentleman. If you can't trust me, then what's the point of me talking to you?"

Thinking he'd lose Ericha forever, Errol threw his arms around her. "I do trust you, honey! And I want to trust Jeremy. I . . . I just ain't sure I'm ready to let you go . . ."

Ericha kissed Errol on the cheek. She couldn't hold back the tears, and instead allowed them to flow, freely. She realized that leaving Infernus also meant leaving Errol . . . along with Prince Ari. Was she prepared for a reality, where'd she never see Errol or Ari again? The very thought ripped at her aching heart.

"Guess there's no stopping you, if that's what you wanna do," said Errol, sadly. "But don't you go leaving without saying 'goodbye', or before I give you a send-off, worthy of our family . . ."

"I love you, Papa!" sobbed Ericha. "I . . . I always have, and I always will! More than words can tell!"

"I love you too, sweetheart," whispered Errol, at odds with his own fragile emotions. He took a deep breath, then released it in a tired sigh. "Tell Jeremy I want to see him. Figure there's an awful lot we need to talk about . . ."

Since his ill-fated meeting with Mucker and McClusky, McCoy hadn't once been sober.

McCoy laid on a hammock in the sleeping quarters of the Roderick Dundee, doing nothing but drink and think. The more he drank, the more he thought. The more he thought, the more he drank. And the more he drank and the more he thought, the madder he got. Anger mixed with fear, sadness, and regret. Regrets of the death of six men, and fear of what his boss would do once he got word of this blunder.

The Roderick Dundee was one of many ships owned by Stossee, a notorious freebooter. Stossee dominated much of the illegal trade in the Agron Ocean. His men were the most bloodthirsty pirates in the trades. It never paid to encounter vessels in Stossee's fleet. Them unlucky enough usually lost their ships, which were destroyed or taken by force.

Them unfortunate enough usually lost their heads.

McCoy didn't find his way into Stossee's "navy" through his fighting skills. He was a petty thief living in the shanties lining the riverfront of Merieko. He was a small-time hood, and never taken seriously. Due to his shrimpy size and weasely appearance, he was regarded as a joke.

Until a few months back.

In a flea-bitten bordello of Merieko, McCoy entered a card game with four gamblers and cardsharks. On a sultry Wednesday night, the cardsharks made mincemeat of McCoy. It was bad enough for McCoy to see what little money he had go into the other players' pockets. It added insult to injury when the cardsharks humiliated McCoy in front of a sweet little call girl. By dawn the next day, McCoy was broke, and bad deep in debt . . . against men who demanded their winnings from the little pipsqueak.

McCoy was left at the card table with nothing but the shirt on his back, and a hangdog expression on his face. He wanted to get even against the cardsharks who busted him and hurt his pride.

Getting even came later that day. The cardsharks all headed upstairs, in the company of prostitutes, to sleep it off. Three of these men never lived long enough to wake up.

The fourth cardshark's final thoughts were of McCoy, slitting his throat.

After killing the cardsharks in their beds, McCoy scrounged through their pockets to retrieve his money. The law almost caught up with him. As the Merieko constable and his stooges went to apprehend him, McCoy fled, with the help of the sweet little call girl. He spent days hiding in alleys, narrow avenues, and riverside shanties.

One of Stossee's lieutenants was in the bordello when McCoy killed the cardsharks. Such grisly efforts was just the thing to win Stossee's attention and favor. As a result, McCoy got recruited into Stossee's band.

It never paid to screw up with Stossee. . . and McCoy screwed up. Bad. He screwed up with the assistance of two competitors, named Mucker and McClusky.

Then to learn that those bloody damned winged men had signed a diplomatic and trade agreement with Kusch! That deal gave the Kuschan Navy a right to attack unauthorized ships around Infernus, and put the Roderick Dundee in danger.

The Roderick Dundee moored in areas where the Kuschans rarely patrolled. Occasionally, the pirate ship sailed far away from the island, where they were harder to find.

The Roderick Dundee sailed to Infernus in search of booty. It looked like it might leave, empty-handed. It was McCoy's idea to take the ship to Infernus, on Stossee's subsidy and support. Failure to carry out necessary goals meant death.

And the last thing McCoy wanted was to disappoint Stossee.

The Roderick Dundee's Captain Slane also knew the price of failure.

It was two days after McCoy left Infernus' shores, leaving six dead men and some hostages, including an Embrian diplomat. The situation was dire, and Slane had to remedy it.

Slane never set foot on Infernus. He didn't want to. Nor had he met up with any of the weird critters living there. He didn't want to do that, neither. In his mind, Infernus was Hell on Earth. The sooner he left it, the better.

Slane was a tall, lanky fella, age forty. His black hair was tied in a ponytail, and dangled clear to the middle of his back. His thin, tanned face was high-lighted by a creased forehead, deep-set eyes, and a thick mustache. He was one of the more reliable men under Stossee, and didn't want that status to change.

Infernus was scary. The Kuschan Navy's presence made it much more so. McCoy talked Stossee into bankrolling this journey to Infernus. And now McCoy was down below, drunk as a lord and feeling sorry for himself. The little cutthroat was of no use to Stossee, Slane, the ship's crew, or anybody else!

Slane was tempted to throw McCoy over the side, return to Agron, and beg Stossee's forgiveness and mercy for this disastrous campaign.

McCoy took another swig from the bourbon he lathered himself in. He never left his hammock other than to pee or to crap. He hadn't bathed since encountering Mucker and McClusky. His clothes and hammock was soaked in sweat, and he smelled worse than a Campensian shithouse. He couldn't get back at Mucker or McClusky. Therefore, he took his anger and aggression out on them unlucky enough to get near him. Morale was low, thanks to the killing of six men on the Infernus beach. McCoy's stinkwater attitude and stinkwater odor only made things worse.

McCoy drank to ease the pain . . .

Sometime in the morning, he got distracted by a scrawny, fifteen-year-old kid with blond hair, a thin shirt, cut-off pants, bare feet, and tanned, birdlike legs. "Mr. McCoy, sir," the kid said. "Sir, we be needing you to wake up. Up an' at 'em, sir!"

"Bloody hell!" cursed McCoy. "Can't you see? I don't want to be bothered, damn it . . ."

"But, Mr. McCoy sir," the kid said, apologetically. "A Kuschan holy man come aboard. Claims he wants to see you."

"Kuschan holy man? Why in bloody hell does he want to see me?"

"Better come, sir. He's a spooky-looking one, he is! Better come! Claims he wants to see you, and he means business!"

McCoy shook his head, slowly crawled out of his hammock and, with bottle in hand, staggered topside to see the Kuschan holy man.

The hot morning sun blinded McCoy as he blinked his bloodshot, watery eyes. He shielded his face from the harsh light. The severe heat, along with a mind-crunching headache, nearly toppled him over. He come awful close to barfing. Reality and pain made for an exhausting, scalding, unyielding combination.

On the ship's starboard side awaited a young Kuschan pastor.

Neither McCoy nor Slane knew what to make of the Kuschan pastor. What did he want with pirates? Knowing the Kuschan Navy was patrolling the waters around Infernus, as free as you please, was the pastor there to set the Roderick Dundee up?

The pastor and McCoy traded caustic glances. It was as if they stared in a mirror, unable or unwilling to see images of themselves. Both were roughly the same height, short trees amongst a tall forest. Both had violent backgrounds and histories. Neither man was to be challenged in any way.

And yet, that's exactly what McCoy aimed to do with the pastor.

"Who allowed him to board this ship?" barked McCoy. "Someone throw him in the harbor, and let him float back to . . ."

"You so much as think about throwing me over, you and your captain will join me!" the pastor threatened. "Alive or dead . . . it's your choice."

"I don't like Kuschans," said McCoy. "Alive or dead."

"And I don't like Agronians," the pastor responded, smiling. "Alive or dead."

"So, what are you doing on an Agronian vessel?"

"I don't like Embrians, Branellians, winged men, or ape-like creatures that kill innocent people. Do we have certain things in common?"

McCoy snickered. "Your name, Pastor?"

"Yevgeny, of Anumun."

"McCoy, of Merieko. You have my attention, Pastor Yevgeny of Anumun. What have you in mind?"

"To solve certain problems," said Yevgeny.

"You're from New Merieko?" asked Slane.

Yevgeny nodded YES.

"I took a few . . . guests with me from New Merieko, two days ago," said McCoy, struggling to conceal his apprehension. "To enjoy the company of my associates, aboard the Roderick Dundee."

"Children?" asked Yevgeny, staring menacingly at Slane and McCoy.

Slane took a couple of steps back.

"The Embrian diplomat was no child," said McCoy. "It appears that New Merieko took exception to my hospitality. Is? . . . Is that why you're here?"

"We'll discuss your hospitality later," said Yevgeny, evasively. "The enemy of my enemy is my friend . . . for now. Those same enemies we have in common."

"Those enemies who can fly?" assumed McCoy.

Yevgeny nodded YES.

McCoy snickered. "Care for a drink, or to share a pipe?"

"I don't suppose you have any Kuschan vodka?" asked Yevgeny.

"Sorry," mumbled Slane, nervously.

"It's not popular with Agronian seamen," explained McCoy, with a sly grin.

"Pity," commented Yevgeny, sarcastically.

"Campens Rose'?" offered McCoy.

"Thank you," said Yevgeny.

The scrawny fifteen-year-old kid ran to fetch a bottle.

"We have similar interests on Infernus," said Yevgeny. "Me, to make a home for myself, and my congregation. You, to get rich. We have similar enemies who stand in the way of our interests."

"Men who can fly?" asked McCoy.

"Men who can fly," agreed Yevgeny.

Slane rolled his eyes back, took a deep breath, and hastily walked away.

"Too many enemies," said McCoy.

"Yes," said Yevgeny. "We share similar interests to rid ourselves of those enemies. We may even have the same means to rid ourselves of them. Agreed?"

"Agreed!" laughed McCoy, running his finger along his pencil-thin mustache. "Exactly . . . What did you have in mind, Pastor Yevgeny?"

* * * * *

"So, it's like this, Mister Mucker," Leader Rey told his grumpy old guest, in the church dining room. "I'd like to adopt Paransky . . ."

Rey woke up early, just to hear of Jung-su's departure. Urgently, he sent a young winged man to the docks, to see if Jung-su was still there. Minutes later, the winged man returned with news that the Edith-Marie, along with No-Teeth, Jung-su, and everybody else dumb enough to throw in was long gone.

Rey sat alone in his office. His mind was filled with questions, but with very few answers. Jung-su was a personal favorite of his, a good lad who done what he was told when a lot of boys, Jeremy among them, wouldn't do nothing they was told.

Rey knew that Jung-su was eager to paddle his own canoe in the Farlands. Jung-su got all worked up about WHAT HAPPENED to Randen. Then Rey found out WHAT HAPPENED to Jung-su at The Black Eye.

Under the circumstances, he couldn't entirely blame Jung-su for taking off. He expected it all along. But did Jung-su really have to take off in the Edith-Marie, with 'No-Teeth' Murnau?

Rey thought about sending out groups of athletic young winged men to fly out over the ocean, to catch up with the Edith-Marie and fetch Jung-su back. It was useless. Sending winged men out on a job like that might just endanger them, too.

Rey was angry, sad, perplexed, and frustrated. He never dreamed that Jung-su was dumb enough to head to the Farlands with 'No-Teeth'! What point was it to fret over it, now? Jung-su done headed east, the deal was done, and it was spilled milk. The only thing left to do was accept WHAT HAPPENED, take it as a lesson learned, and push on.

Rey uttered a silent prayer on behalf of them traveling on the Edith-Marie, left it in God's hands, and got on with his day.

Rey sent another winged kid out to fetch Mucker. He had Evelyn fix up a nice breakfast of sausage and eggs for him and the old pirate. Rey even filled a couple of shot glasses with Agronian whiskey.

It was way too early in the day for spirits. On the other hand, Mucker's veins was already filled with the foulest rotgut imaginable! Rey had drank two glasses of the brew, one to deal with Jung-su's departure, the other to cope with Mucker.

Rey sat alone in the church dining room, battling anxiety and nerves. He had a proposition for Mucker, involving the life and future of a sad-eyed kid who was covered all up by tattoos.

Rey had a grudging respect for Mucker. There was no question of the pirate's care, concern, and loyalty to the Brown Winged Men. However, Rey couldn't abide Mucker's affliction with smokes, chew, or the bottle. Nor could he fathom Mucker's violent tendencies, or visits to a local brothel.

Rey took a sip of hooch to calm himself, as Mucker entered the church dining room through a back door. Mucker was always suspicious of phonies and hypocrites, and didn't want nobody seeing him entering the church through a front door. He had nothing against Rey in particular, but had everything against "dumb, foolish superstition, and them believin' in an invisible, big man up in the sky."

Even if there was a god, Mucker figured He must've hated people real bad. People was no damned good anyway, and was their own worst enemies. Mucker had the scars to prove it.

A man gets born. He's got no choice but to live his life, the best he can. If he breaks the law, so what? He can hang for it, but dies only once. After that, a man don't know nothing nomore. His body and bones rot forever in the big sleep, the long goodbye, the dirt nap. He can't never wake up from death. Nor is he tormented in Hell, for all his screw-ups on Earth.

Anyway, there weren't no god nowhere! Mucker never saw no sign of a god out there. There wasn't one. Just wasn't. So there.

"Good morning," greeted Rey, welcoming Mucker to the table where a plateful of grub and a shot of whiskey awaited him. "Please, have a seat."

Mucker grunted. He was still mad at Lorenzo for selling out to them heathen Kuschans. He got drunk with Seely the night before, and still suffered from it. Nor was he happy when Rey up and invited Paransky over for supper. Paransky spent the whole night at the church, and Mucker wanted him back. Mucker didn't want no "churchy" influences fowling Paransky up.

"Have a seat," requested Rey, hesitantly. "I'm about to have breakfast, and I thought we'd have a bite together."

Mucker looked at the grub. Though it whetted his appetite, he wouldn't say so. Mucker usually just cut off slabs of dried meat he kept hanging from the rafters of his shack. He threw them on the wood stove, chowed it down, and called it good.

Rarely did Mucker eat "civilized cookin'." He sometimes wondered if he shoulda found himself a wife . . . if only she'd tolerate his bad manner and even worst smells.

Mucker fought off the urge to smile as he sat down. He didn't wait for Rey to say "grace" before digging in. He already knew that Rey had some scheme brewing. Yet, the grub's taste and smell made his visit a bit more agreeable.

Mucker downed his shot of whiskey in one swallow, and felt more at ease.

Rey took his last bite of bacon, then finished off his whiskey. He refilled his glass, then gave some more to Mucker. "I . . . I wanted to talk to you . . . about Paransky," he stuttered.

Mucker never said nothing. His eyes just sort of drilled holes through Rey. He started to say something, but instead clamped his jaw shut, and gritted his rotting teeth.

"So, it's like this, Mister Mucker," said Rey. "I'd like to adopt Paransky . . ."

"Knowed this had to be about him," mumbled Mucker. "A'ready knowed you didn't get me over here, fix me a meal fit for a friar, just to gripe about the weather!" Mucker thought awful strong about walloping Rey right to the chin. He never swung on a padre before, but wanted to several times. If it wasn't for Jeremy, he'd have gladly sent Rey into the middle of next week.

It wasn't because he was afraid of Jeremy, not at all. In a knock-down, drag-out brawl, Mucker knew he could whip Jeremy. Maybe. Be a helluva fight, all right. Mucker just didn't want to lose Jeremy's favor. Nor did he want to take a chance of losing a fight against the loinclothed little numskull.

Bad enough having some stupid Embrian diplomat trying to coax Jeremy off of the island. Then there was a mess of Kuschans poking around, making deals with dumb winged men.

And now this!

"Before you walk out of here, I want you to hear what I've got to say," said Rey.

"I don't give a hang what you gotta say!" yelled Mucker. "And don't you go tellin' me what to do! I don't give a hoot nor holler what you gotta say about nothin'! I come here to fetch the boy, and I ain't goin' 'til you hand 'em over!"

"I hoped to talk reason with you, Mister Mucker."

"Who says I ain't bein' reasonable? And what's with all that 'mister' crap? Name's Mucker. John Mucker. Ain't no 'mister' to it."

"Very well," agreed Rey. "John Mucker."

"Now what I wanna know is where you got Paransky hid in this voodoo-shop," said Mucker. "Know you got 'em hid somewheres, fillin' his head with a mess o' hooey. I ain't goin' 'til you hand 'em over. I don't care if I gotta tear this place down to find 'em. Where is he?"

"Paransky's asleep in Jeremy's room," said Rey. "And I won't wake him."

"You sure about that? Roust 'em out! If he ain't up yet, he'd best learn to get up before the sun. Go fetch 'em, and I'll be on my way."

"Now wait just a minute!" shouted Rey, slamming the palm of his hand against the table. He took a deep breath, and let it out in a sigh. "Wait . . . Just wait until you hear what I have to say. Please take a moment to hear me out . . ."

Mucker almost answered with a snide comment, but was shocked at Rey's anger and intensity. "I'm listenin'," he said, the hairs on the back of his neck bristling. "What is it you gotta say?"

"I've got nothing against you or Seely," said Rey.

"Sure about that?"

"Look, I know you care about Paransky. I know you've got his best interests at heart, the way you've been a . . .good role model for Jeremy."

Mucker eyed Rey, suspiciously.

"However, I know you're gone quite often," said Rey, "hauling goods to and from the Farlands."

"Not if Lorenzo or them Kuschans get their way. That damned trade agreement might just do me in. Gives them Kuschans the right to attack my boats. Don't matter if what we're doin' is right or wrong!"

"I also disagree with that treaty," said Rey. "So does Errol, and Malachi . . . and Jeremy for that matter! For the exception of Lorenzo and Nikolai, I don't know anyone who supports it."

"And then ya got the Roderick Dundee, with its filthy Stossee bunch, hangin' around these parts."

"You're getting to my point, Mucker. I won't debate the wisdom or morality of your work."

"A'right," grunted Mucker.

"But what will you do with Paransky while you're away?" asked Rey.

"Take 'em with me."

"You can't be serious!"

"Why the hell not?"asked Mucker.

"You can't take care of a small boy on the open seas!" argued Rey.

Mucker pointed a finger at Rey. "I spent my boyhood earnin' a man's sweat, while doin' a man's work on them vessels. Wasn't much older'n Paransky when I started."

Rey shook his head. "I can't condone taking children on smuggling ships. What happens if you get caught by other pirates? . . . I mean, by rival traders, or God-forbid by some country's navy?"

"So I'm a pirate, a smuggler, a profiteer, a freebooter, a bootlegger!" Mucker grinned, maliciously. "If you ain't forgotten, most o' them preachy books you got in this here church was brung in on my boats. Never heard you harp over that."

"But is a . . . trading vessel the right place for a small boy?"

"Never hurt me none."

"We're talking about the life of a youngster," said Rey. "That same youngster we love and care about."

"Whadda you got in mind, preacher man?"

"I want to keep Paransky here, with me," said Rey. "I'll provide him with an education . . ."

"Churchy sermons," commented Mucker. "Hellfire and brimstone. Savin' peoples' fat from the fire."

"Reading, writing, and arithmetic! And yes, he will learn the word of God!"

"How long you figger it's gonna be before them do-gooders and hypocrites take a good look at Paransky, write 'em off as a good-for-nothin' heathen, and judge 'em for no good reason other than them tattoos he's got?"

"And what happens if you get stopped by a rival trader or naval warship?" questioned Rey.

"Fight 'em to the death," claimed Mucker, "before they get the chance to string us."

"Does that include Paransky?" asked Rey, nearly coming unglued. "You want him to fight to the death, too? What happens if he's captured by those who'll enslave him, or worse, based on his appearance?"

"Gotta make a man outa him," said Mucker. "Let 'em do a man's job, and earn a man's wage, through a man's sweat. I can't see the boy getting all dolled up in sissy clothes, makin' 'em serve tea and pastries to fat old women after Sunday meetin's, while you preach a mess o' hooey about God an' angels an' life after death, makin' a gentleman and a swell outa him."

"So, how long before he kills or gets killed on one of your smuggling ships, John Mucker? The life you lead is a violent one, and I can't support intro-ducing anyone to that baseless existence!"

"Better to learn the truths of a hard life on a smugglin' ship, than hear tall-tales an' lies under the roof of a church buildin'!"

"Do you refer to a criminal's life as truth?" asked Rey. "Yes, you did bring me several editions of the Word, and I thank you for it. If memory serves, you were well-compensated for that." Rey leaned over the table. "But say you don't fight to the death. Let's say you're captured. Are you prepared to see Paransky die in the gallows, next to you? Are you willing to take that risk, by making him earn a 'man's wage' hauling illegal cargo?"

"You think tellin' lies to hypocrites and cowards is any more honest than what I do for a livin'?"

"Enough of that!" shouted Rey. "I know you don't believe in God, but I do! Maybe Paransky will choose not to follow God when he gets older. It's his choice. I only want him to grow up in a stable environment, where he can learn his letters and numbers, while learning an honorable, useful trade. Surely, you want him to do better than you . . . better than the both of us! I hope he grows up to be a fine, upstanding man. And let's be honest . . . Your friend Seely may be likable, but does anyone respect or trust him? I'd like to see Paransky do more than just occupy a barstool in his old age. I mean, what if we teach him to be a merchant? Isn't that preferable to fighting and dying aboard a ship, or living in poverty while serving the Lord?"

"What sorta merchant you figger he'll be, with all them tattoos?"

Before Rey had a chance to answer, Commander Antonov entered the dining room.

Mucker hopped to his feet and headed toward Antonov. "Get outa here,

Kuschan dog!" he shouted. "Now that you made a pact with Soraq, you figger it gives you the right to go anywhere you damned well please?"

"I didn't come here for a fight," said Antonov, standing his ground.

"Well, you got a fight comin', unless you leave here an' never come back!" spoke Mucker. "No one gave you the right t' come around here!"

"It's all right," said Rey, stepping between Antonov and Mucker. "What can I do for you, Commander?"

"I'm looking for Weston," said Antonov. "Is he here?"

"Weston's with my son Jeremy," said Rey. "I'm not sure if they're in town, or out exploring the foothills."

"Thank you," said Antonov, leaving the room.

Rey and Mucker got into a mean-looking staring contest, but never said nothing for several seconds.

"We won't settle this matter, today," said Rey, finally. "But, sooner or later, we have to decide what to do with Paransky."

"Got my mind made up a'ready," said Mucker. "Soon as he gets up, send 'em over to me. A'ready got my mind made up, and it's done settled."

"Are you sure about that?" asked Rey, sternly.

"Better to die standin' up in a man's fight than to live in constant fear of some damned, invisible god who, even if He does exist, don't give a hoot nor holler about us, anyway." Mucker grinned, as he shook his fist at Rey. "Got anything more to say about it, preacher man? Do I gotta take use of my right hand to send you flyin' into the infernal regions, where you damn well belong?"

At the south end of town, Jeremy and Weston stood on a narrow wooden foot bridge, spanning the Persis River. They leaned against a splintery handrail, staring silently at the endless stream of water below them.

Weston was homesick. As a diplomat, he constantly went from one country to the next, representing the Embrian nation with cordial greetings and kind offerings. He had spent his entire childhood around Sykes. After graduating from that city's university, he went to work for King Marco, and was fluent in many languages. His first mission was to head to the Far-Eastern land of Kokashima. He spent several months there developing friendly relations with Emperor Ko, a man of brutal reputation who sought ties to the west.

Weston had chances to see people and places few Embrians knew about. It was still nice to head home, to the lush green fields of Embrey. He lived in the house of his maternal grandparents, who raised beets, cucumbers, and corn on a spread near Sykes. It was fun to get his hands dirty, cultivating the soil as he gained an appreciation of hard work and toil. He longed for the hot days and cool evenings of an Embrian autumn. By now, crops were ready for harvesting, before the snow flew and nights grew long and bitterly cold.

During the winter, Weston caught up on reading, while relaxing in a favorite chair by the fireplace.

Eventually, his services would again he needed by king and country. Once more, he'd sail away to new lands, new adventures, new challenges, and new opportunities.

Weston's grandparents were now dead and gone, and the land was willed to him. Weston's younger brother Courtney stayed on the property, where he was a farmer.

Courtney was a married man with two young sons and a daughter. Weston remained a bachelor who talked about marriage, but never committed to it.

As Courtney's children grew up, Weston grew old.

Weston was in his mid-thirties. He thought of settling down and leave others to do the globe-trotting. Was he ready to get hitched? Maybe it would've been best to give the land to Courtney, who was more of a farmer than Weston ever hoped to be.

That same envy Weston had for Courtney, he also felt toward Jeremy.

If all went as planned, Jeremy would soon be a married man of great wealth, prosperity, and property. He had no idea how truly blessed he was.

Try telling that to Jeremy!

Jeremy didn't look very blessed. He looked scared. The night before, he planned on moving to Branell, where he'd claim his big money and his big land, and start over with Ericha. By morning, he still wanted Ericha as his wife, but was uncertain of Branell. He woke an hour ago, to learn that Ericha had left to see Errol. He also learned that Jung-su had left, period.

Well, Jeremy had to pay Errol a visit, and seek the man's daughter in marriage. He also fretted over Jung-su, and figured he'd never see the stupid kid again.

Jeremy was only sixteen, and not quite grown-up. He was now forced to make grown-up decisions, and head straight into grown-up responsibilities. His childhood was fading away. Life on Infernus slipped out from under him, like the swift currents of water flowing through the Persis River, into the Agron Ocean. That same water streaming beneath his feet might never find its way back to Infernus. It may help carry him across the sea, to the Farlands.

Like the water streaming beneath his feet, Jeremy might become nothing more than a fading memory, on the lonely isle of Infernus.

"What's on your mind, kiddo?" asked Weston.

Jeremy shrugged. "I was about to ask you the same question."

"Aw . . . Guess I just miss my old stomping grounds in Embrey."

"I already miss Infernus," snickered Jeremy, "And I ain't even left yet!"

An overwhelming sense of panic spread over Jeremy like wildfire. "Oh, Weston!" he cried. "I'm scared, and I dunno what to do!"

"Calm down," urged Weston. "Just calm down . . ."

"But I'm scared!"

"I know. But just calm down, and let's talk. What are you afraid of?"

"My life . . . Me getting married to . . . um . . . you know . . ."

Weston grinned. "Yeah, kiddo. I know . . ."

"And, then . . . About having to move away. Mainly, I'm worried about Jung-su."

"Jung-su chose his own path. There's nothing either of us can do about it. You'll get nowhere dumping these thoughts on yourself, all at once. Get your head together, and decide what you're going to do . . ."

"That's just it!" whined Jeremy. "I dunno what to do!"

"About Ericha? Your property in Branell?"

"Everything!"

"I don't understand you at all!" laughed Weston.

"What do you mean?"

"Yesterday, after . . ." Weston took a breath. "Well, after what happened to Randen, you took on all those abarbeaus, without so much as blinking an eye, or showing a bit of fear. I thought we were goners! Good thing you kept a level head."

"So?"

"If you can stand up to those predators, why are you so frightened now?" asked Weston.

"My life is changing!"

"It does when we grow up. Who knows? It may change for the better."

"What if it changes for the worst?" moped Jeremy.

"I don't know whether to call you 'just plain old Jeremy' or 'just plain scared Jeremy'." Weston grinned. "Take it one step at a time, one day at a time. It's normal to be little frightened by the unknown."

"A little?"

"I've been from here to there in this old world. The morning I prepare to board a ship to who-knows-where, I always get butterflies in my stomach. Even if I'm going somewhere I've already been to and know intimately."

"What do you think of Infernus?" asked Jeremy.

"There's no where else like it!" stated Weston. "You're lucky to have spent your childhood here. If I live to be a hundred, I'll never forget it."

"If you're looking for a good time you won't forget, I'll give you one," interrupted a scantily-dressed woman, stepping from one of the few two-story houses in Persis. The woman, was in her fifties, tried to look like she was twenty or thirty years younger. She was dolled in dyed, red hair and enough make-up and lipstick on to choke a horse. She had black, crooked teeth, and was over-weight. Not really all that fat, but far from skinny!

Above one of the busier pubs was an unnamed establishment. It featured a number of people women and at least a couple of Brown Winged Women, in the world's oldest profession.

Weston gawked at the woman with awe and dry humor. Figures. Where there's people, there's vice.

Weston hadn't had a female since he left Sykes, on his way to Infernus. It wasn't smart to mess with ladies in foreign countries. At any rate, Weston didn't want to spend his morning, or is money, on that woman, who was as pretty as a mud fence.

"What about it, honey?" the woman asked Weston.

"What about what?" asked Weston, with a silly grin.

"It!" the woman laughed, slapping Weston's rump.

"Sorry," snickered Weston. "I haven't got the time."

"You'll always make time for me, baby!" the woman giggled, running her long, painted fingernails through Weston's beard. "After I'm done with you, I'll make a man out of Jeremy!"

The woman's name was Gila, and she'd been trying to get Jeremy in the sack since he was twelve. Jeremy wanted his first time with Ericha, not with a cheap strumpet. "The answer was 'no' yesterday," he said, tiredly. "The answer is 'no' today, and it'll be 'no' tomorrow!"

"You'll change your tune," said Gila, as she slithered away. "When you get tired of using your hand, Jungle Boy, come up and see me sometime."

"Sex sells, alright," said Weston. "She's sure not much of a sales lady."

"Think I'll head over to Mucker's for a whiskey and a smoke," yawned Jeremy. "I need it. Bad."

"What you need is a nice shirt, and a pair of pants. Then you need to sit down to have a man-to-man talk with Errol."

Jeremy smiled, nervously. "Wanna go with me?"

"No!" laughed Weston. "You'd better handle that on your own. If you're man enough to fight off a horde of abarbeaus, then you're man enough to ask Ericha's hand in marriage."

"Think I better have that shot of whiskey!"

"Oh, no you don't! It doesn't pay to speak to your future father-in-law with liquor on your breath. You'll never find courage in a bottle. If you love Ericha that much, and I know you do, it won't take courage to chat with Errol, but a willingness to chat honestly with him." Weston put his hand on Jeremy's shoulder. "You can do it, kiddo. I know you can! First, you have to prove it to yourself."

Jeremy nodded YES. He did love Ericha, more than anything! Was he ready to sit down with Errol, and explain it to him? No matter. He was marrying into that family . . . right?

Well, Ericha might have been a part of that brood, but she was nothing like them!

Jeremy gazed through a narrow maze of shacks and huts, to the tiny house where Ericha lived with Errol and Prince Ari. He had to be on the level with Errol, then convince him that he was the right guy for Ericha.

"I've got some nice duds in my tote bag at the church," said Weston. "That is, if you want to borrow them. I've never heard of anyone making a marriage proposal in a loincloth. Surely not a wealthy land owner and . . . proper Branellian gent."

"Don't worry," assured Jeremy. "I'll put on a good show for Errol."

Jeremy and Weston headed for the church. By now, it was warm outside, as a mild breeze swept through town. Weston felt more accustomed and at-ease in Persis. He said "hi" to the more familiar faces, people and winged people alike. Infernus was not home to him. Yet, he imagined resigning from his job as a diplomat, signing his property over to Courtney, and settling down on the island.

Still, Weston had not spent a whole year on Infernus. Was the winters real mean and nasty? Was it rainy and damp in the spring? What about the summers? Not knowing the answers to these questions, Weston was hesitant about relocating there.

Even if Weston did move to Infernus, he's always be nothing more than a Farlander!

Moments later, Jeremy and Weston ran into Commander Antonov.

"Pleased to see you again, Mister Weston," greeted Antonov, reaching out to shake hands. "Good morning to you, Mr. Kentworth . . ."

Jeremy and Weston was kind of offended by seeing Antonov in town, especially after Lorenzo signed that stupid agreement. "Good morning," said Weston, reluctantly shaking Antonov's hand.

Jeremy had more pressing concerns than to be nice to heathen Kuschans. "See ya later," he told Weston, then walked away.

Weston and Antonov engaged in a spooky-eyed staring contest for several seconds. Years of warfare between their two nations didn't do nothing but stir up suspicion, mistrust, deep-seated resentments, and spooky-eyed staring contests. Even Antonov, who sought a meeting with Weston, was slow going at speaking his mind.

"Commander Antonov," mumbled Weston, concealing his animosities behind a smile. "Lovely morning, would you say?"

"I know you're not happy to see me," said Antonov. "I can't say I blame you."

"Very well," chuckled Weston, in a confrontational tone. "What have I to gain by speaking to you? In light of our nations' histories, along with Kusch's newfound friendship with Persis, I see little or no benefit to me. Indeed, if King Marco got wind of us saying much of anything, it'd mean my job, and my life."

"I have nothing against Embrians," claimed Antonov. "And I've got nothing against the winged men. You have to trust me on this."

"I don't have to trust you on anything. Trust must be earned."

Antonov frowned. "Don't you think I know that?"

"I'm sure you and your country have a great deal to win by my speaking to you," said Weston, thrilled to see Antonov squirm. "What have I to win from it?"

"Neither of us will win anything, if you refuse to listen to me! I know you're unhappy with the trade agreement . . . obviously."

"I don't think anyone is happy with it."

"Lorenzo is," said Antonov, defensively. "So is his son, Nikolai."

"Malachi isn't. Neither is Errol, or Leader Rey. Neither is John Mucker."

"I don't care what Mucker has to say!" snapped Antonov.

"But many on this island do," argued Weston.

"There's no point in even mentioning Mucker in this discussion," Antonov sighed. "As for Leader Rey . . . I think he's a good man. But his business is faith, not diplomacy."

"His business is the happiness and well-being of everyone in his congregation. And many of them aren't happy with that agreement, either."

"We're spinning our wheels, Mr. Weston," said Antonov. "I came to you in hopes of making you a deal, so all of us may come out as winners, including Embrians and the winged men. The war between our two countries is over. Isn't it to our mutual benefit to just sit down and talk?"

"What does Admiral Vaslov have to say about you seeing me?"

"Vaslov doesn't know. Anyway, he's not here. Neither is King Leonid. Neither is King Marco."

"Good point," laughed Weston. Despite his ill-feeling toward Kuschans, he kind of liked Antonov.

"And yes, the trade agreement isn't popular," admitted Antonov. "I'm worried about it."

"Is Admiral Vaslov also worried?"

"What do you think?"

Weston shook his head. "No . . . Probably not."

"I'm a stranger on Infernus, and so are you," said Antonov. "We came here for the same purpose, to open up trade and diplomacy with the island. See here. . . I don't care if Lorenzo wishes to deal also with Embrey. I'm a sailor, not a politician. I only want to make sure that our agreement with Lorenzo is beneficial. I also want to change some minds about the presence of the Kuschan Navy on this island."

"The winning of hearts and minds," said Weston, with a grin. "So Vaslov doesn't know you came to see me."

"No. I left Lieutenant Arkoff to take my watch."

"I see."

"Anyway, Vaslov won't like it, but he doesn't like Infernus," said Antonov. "He only wants more medals on his chest, and a seat on the Kuschan Parliament. I'm a man of war seeking peace in the middle of the Agron Ocean. I hoped you'd be the one to make that possible . . . for everyone's sake."

"King Marco wants to normalize relations with Kusch," said Weston. "However, Kusch has yet to place an ambassador in Sykes. Just like we have yet to do the same in St. Alexandrov. In order to sustain the peace, both sides must make concessions, for the mutual benefit of all."

"Now you sound like a diplomat. And a politician."

"You don't think I got this job, simply by being King Marco's cousin. Did you?"

"Actually, I did," laughed Antonov.

"So, what do you have in mind, Commander Antonov?" asked Weston.

"Have you the confidence and the clout to set up a meeting with the various groups on the island? You, Admiral Vaslov, myself, that McClusky fellow who lives with the Green Winged Men, Chief Lorenzo? . . ."

"Well, I can try," said Weston. "Whether anyone shows up is anybody's guess. You see . . . Embrian diplomats aren't very popular around here, either."

"Wasn't it an Embrian King who first came here, centuries ago?"

"Oh, certainly. But from what I've been told, there's still a few Brown and Green Winged Men who have no interest in dealing with humans. It matters nothing to them why we're here, or even if we were born on Infernus. In their minds, we're all Farlanders, and unwanted. Errol and his two children were born on Infernus, and descendants of that Embrian King you mentioned, Auric IV."

"All right."

"In the minds of those particular winged men, we're invaders," explained Weston. "They'd be happy to see all humans leave. It'll never happen, not without a bloodbath."

"No chance of getting a delegation from that group in our meeting, then?"

"They don't live in Persis, nor will they learn to speak Embrian. They won't even take the time to speak to men like Mucker or McClusky, and both have advocated for them, on occasion. Or so that's what Leader Rey tells me."

"Any chance of getting Mucker into our meeting?" asked Antonov. "I don't like him, and I'm sure his being there will only foul things up."

"I'm with you on that one," agreed Weston. "The last thing Mucker wants is to make peace with Embrians or Kuschans. We threaten his illicit enterprise. Frankly, he'd be all-too-happy to see the Matyushenko sink to the bottom of the sea . . . With his help, of course."

"Hmmm . . ." mulled Antonov. "Our meeting may not have a chance in succeeding."

"McClusky will show up. It's to his advantage." Weston pointed a finger at Antonov. "Which leads to my earlier question. What does Embrey have to gain by our meeting?"

"Peace?" suggested Antonov. "A lasting peace, between Kusch and Embrey. Isn't that enough?"

"No economic gain for Embrey? You're right. It may bridge our two nations. Peace is one thing, Commander Antonov. Money speaks volumes. I don't suppose Kusch is willing to share their trade agreement with Kusch, do you?"

"I'd go along with it," said Antonov. "But Vaslov won't. Neither will King Leonid."

"Well, there you go." Weston shrugged. "Stalemate. I do want to help you, but King Marco won't tolerate me setting up meetings that can only help Kusch. Therefore, I ask again . . . What does Embrey have to gain by *your* meeting?"

Jeremy headed to the church. He ran into a bunch of friends and acquaintances, but never said nothing. He was too scared to talk!

Jeremy wondered if he should take a shower at the waterfall, before putting on the "Sunday" clothes from Weston's tote bag. He didn't know nothing about fancy duds, and hated getting all dolled-up.

Wasn't it best just to be himself, just plain old Jeremy, and face Errol honestly?

Jeremy spent most of his time in buckskins and loincloths. Even if he did move to Branell, he aimed on traipsing around the place wearing the same clothes he wore in Persis! He didn't care if some hoity-toity type looked down on him or not. His new neighbors had to take him for what he was . . . or not take him at all!

Jeremy approached the church's back door, and heard a wild commotion coming from the dining hall. A familiar voice spewed the worst language he'd heard in a long time. Mucker. From the sounds of things, Mucker was mixed up in a big-time brawl. But with who?

Jeremy sprinted into the dining hall to see Rey and Mucker in a game of fisticuffs. Both men had bloody faces. Chairs was overturned. Broken glass, pottery, and dishes was scattered all over the place. Paransky stood at the doorway of Jeremy's room, watching the fight with a combination of fear, awe, and a wicked grin.

Rey had been a bare-knuckled boxer when he was a kid, and even won a few matches before becoming a Leader. He taught Jeremy a few pointers in self-defense, which the boy used to control loudmouths, troublemakers, and malcontents. Jeremy knew of Rey's skills in the ring. He never expected Rey to be getting the best of Mucker. Indeed, Rey had Mucker cornered, and beat on him real bad with a series of shots to the face and gut.

Mucker blocked one of Rey's upper-cuts, and reached for a knife hanging from his belt. Paransky released a funny little giggle. Mucker freed the knife from its sheath, then took a wild swipe at Rey's throat. Rey hopped backwards, and found himself pinned against a long, oak table.

Mucker lunged at Rey with the knife.

A split-second later, Jeremy kicked the weapon out of Mucker's hand. The knife struck a nearby wall, and landed on the floor. This gave Rey the chance to send a right into Mucker's jaw.

Mucker slammed into the wall and reached clumsily for a heavy dining chair.

"Stop it!" cried Jeremy. "Stop!"

Rey and Mucker turned their attention on Jeremy. The only sounds came from the waterfall outside, and Paransky's annoying, high-pitched giggling.

"Hell am I s'posed to do?" growled Mucker, blood dripping from his mouth. "Let 'em beat the hell outa me?"

"What's the matter with you?" Jeremy hollered at Mucker. "Ain't you got sense enough not to pick fights with a Leader?"

"Yellin' at me for?" Mucker hollered back, wanting to throw a chair at Jeremy just because. "Wasn't me who started it!"

"Then who?" questioned Jeremy.

"I . . . I did," admitted Rey, nervously.

Jeremy's jaw dropped. "You?"

"Yeah," sighed Rey. "Me."

Jeremy felt the wind knocked out of him, like he'd been punched in the belly. His whole life had changed right in front of him, and there wasn't nothing he could do to stop it! He didn't ask for none of these changes, nor did he want them. His life spiraled all out of control. He had no choice but to spiral with it.

Jeremy sat down at the table, and thought real hard about what he just saw. He never imagined Rey, a decent, kindhearted man, picking fights with anybody! And yet that's exactly what Rey up and done! He fought with the meanest, orneriest cuss on Infernus . . .

And it looked as if Mucker was losing!

Jeremy's whole wide world was going nuts around him, and home was no longer home.

Where was home, now?

Both Rey and Mucker was like fathers to Jeremy. No way could he have survived without them. After watching the two men use each other's faces for punching bags, he was afraid to pick sides. How could he?

"I . . . I'm sorry, Mister Mucker," apologized Rey, offering his opponent a handshake. "I don't think I'll ever live to forgive myself . . ."

"Aw, to hell with yer handshake and yer callin' me 'mister'!" hollered Mucker. "I don't give a damn if you live to forgive yourself, or if you even live! Only reason I didn't whip you is 'cause I didn't expect that sorta thing from you." Mucker's smile bared his bloody, decaying teeth. "What's yer high and mighty congregation gonna say about ya, now? I don't give a hoot in hell who forgives you! Maybe Hell's where yer headin', an' that's just fine by me. You was wrong in sayin' I oughta just hand the boy over, like you was the Almighty yerself!"

"I'm far from being the Almighty," said Rey, shamefully.

"Hand me over the boy, and I'm on my way," ordered Mucker, staggering from the table. "I liked the grub you fixed for me, but I coulda lived without the fist sandwich that come with it. Next time you get some big idea of kidnappin' some kid, better think twice. You got the best of me, this time. Next time, you'll be picking yerself up off the floor."

Rey glanced over at Jeremy, feeling real bad for whomping on Mucker.

"Let's get outa here," grunted Mucker, motioning at Paransky as he headed to the door. He ended up walking sideways, partly for being slightly drunk, and partly for the beating he took. "Done had my fill o' that hypocrite."

"I . . . I ain't going with you," stuttered Paransky, nervously.

"Whadda you mean, you ain't goin'?" argued Mucker. "Grab yer stuff if ya brung anything, and let's get the hell outa here."

"But I don't wanna go," whined Paransky. "Mister Rey's gonna adopt me."

"And I say he won't," argued Mucker. "Hell's wrong with you? A'ready had yer fill of me an' Seely?"

"You guys snore too loud," said Paransky. "Anyhow, they fix better grub here, the best I ever ate. I never slept so good and warm and sound as I did last night, in Mister Jeremy's room."

Unintentionally, Jeremy laughed at the title Paransky gave him.

Mucker glared at Paransky, then turned to face Rey and Jeremy. He reached for his missing knife.

Jeremy picked the knife up off the floor, and cautiously handed it to Mucker. "I'll give it back," he said, "if your promise not to stick anybody with it."

"Ain't gonna stick nobody with it," growled Mucker. "Ain't nobody 'round here worth the stringin' I'd get for it."

"Look, you may be right, Mister Mucker," said Rey, hesitantly. "Maybe .

. . just maybe. . . . Paransky's better off with you."

"Told you never to call me 'mister'!" yelled Mucker. "There ain't no 'mister' to it."

"I guess not," sighed Rey. "All I know is that I'm truly sorry for . . . for striking you, sir."

"I'll bet you are," said Mucker, sarcastically. He looked at Paransky. "Well, you comin', or ain'tcha?"

"Go with him, young man," urged Rey, painfully. "I'm through fighting about it. Go with Mister . . . Look, just go with Mucker . . ."

"But I thought you was gonna adopt me!" cried Paransky, in betrayal. "You said last night you was gonna adopt me!"

One could hear a pin drop.

"It's up to you, Paransky," said Jeremy. "I'm outa here soon enough, so . . . If you want to stay here . . . If you really want to stay, you can have my room. Looks like I won't be needing it much longer . . ."

"You fixin' to run off with that damn, troublemakin' diplomat?" questioned Mucker.

"I dunno." Jeremy shrugged his shoulders. "Guess that depends on what Ericha wants . . ."

"Ericha?" cackled Mucker. The tone of his voice was laced with superiority, loathing, and disgust. "Hell business does a woman gotta do with it? You lettin' a woman wear the pants? Ain't no kinda man if you let a woman tell ya what to do . . ."

"Shut your mouth!" screamed Jeremy. "If you can't keep a civil tongue about me, or Rey, or Ericha, or anybody else, then get out! Get out! Get the hell out!"

Mucker stepped back, shocked at Jeremy's sudden anger.

"And if Paransky wants to move in here and stay, he's welcome to it!" added Jeremy, his face redder than a beet.

Mucker clenched his fist and took a step toward Jeremy.

Jeremy held his ground. In the back of his mind, he feared standing up to a man like Mucker. Yet, it was too late to take back what he said.

For the longest time, nobody said nothing to nobody. They all just kind of stood around, gawking at each other, waiting for somebody to say something.

"All right," sighed Jeremy, nervously. "I'll be over after a while, for a drink and a smoke. You can whip me then, if you want to. Deal?"

"Don't want you comin' over for nothin'," said Mucker, mad at Jeremy for hollering at him. He hid emotions of loss and sadness behind a gruff exterior.

"Don't want nothin' to do with you, no more. If yer fixin' to leave Infernus, then get to it. Get out, before I stain my knife with yer blood, or that of some damned Embrian diplomat." Mucker eyed Paransky. "You comin' or not, boy?"

Paransky ran over and gave Mucker a hug around the waist. In turn, Mucker smiled at Rey and Jeremy, as if to say I told ya so.

But before Mucker had the chance to savor the taste of victory, Paransky ran over to embrace Rey. Affectionately, he took Rey's hand, and cuddled against him. "I wanna stay here," he said, his voice cracking.

Mucker just stood there with a dumb look. Shaking his head, he stomped outside and slammed the door behind him.

Jeremy sat down at the table, covered his face with both hands, and wept.

"Son," whispered Rey, putting his hand on Jeremy's shoulder. "Jeremy . . . my boy . . . You have no idea how truly sorry I am for . . ."

"What's happening to us?" sniffled Jeremy. "I swear! A few days ago, I didn't have a worry in the world! And then what? Weston shows up to take me back to the Farlands with him. Yesterday, I stood back and watched Randen get torn to shreds! And then to hear that Jung-su up and left with 'No-Teeth'! And . . . and then . . . And then, to find out that I'm in love with . . ." Jeremy motioned toward Ericha's house. "And now I'm getting replaced by a weird little tattooed boy!"

"I'm not replacing you with anyone," said Rey. "How can I ever replace you? No one will ever replace you, not in my heart or mind. You're like flesh and blood to me!"

"Sure feels like I'm getting replaced!" sobbed Jeremy, pulling away from Rey. "You got into a fight with the meanest man I'll ever know, over Paransky. Were you ever willing to fight like that for me?"

"If you don't already know the answer to that, then you never will," said Rey.

"I'm not wanting to replace you, Mister Jeremy!" claimed Paransky, feeling bad over the whole thing. "I'm just wanting to go someplace where I'm wanted!"

"You see, son?" whispered Rey. "Paransky doesn't pose a threat to you. He only wants to be loved, that's all."

Jeremy wiped his eyes. "But I just don't think . . . I just don't understand anything, anymore! I never thought I'd live to see you lay an angry hand on any-one! And what do I see when I get here? You and Mucker . . ." Jeremy glanced at Rey, his vision clouded by tears. "What kind of a man are you? You sure ain't the man I took you for! I never dreamed you'd start a fight with anyone! And now you're stomping mudholes into someone who taught me how to hunt and fish . . . and . . . and what it means to be a man!"

"Haven't I taught you any important lessons?" sighed Rey. "God knows I tried! I only wanted to do what was right, and I'm always willing to fight for that. Just like I'm willing to fight for what I know is right for Paransky! I'll take a broken nose or a knife in the heart for him, and I'm willing to die over you! I love you more than anything, and I know we'll come to love Paransky like a member of our family!"

"Are we still family?" asked Jeremy, sadly.

"You already know the answer to that," said Rey. "If you don't know it by now, then I guess you never will."

"It just seems like you're eager to get rid of me, that's all," moped Jeremy. "You insist that I gotta leave here, and move over to Branell!"

"I don't want to get rid of you," said Rey. "I do think it's in your best interests to claim your inheritance. You and Ericha, both. There's not much of a future for either of you, on Infernus."

Jeremy stared Rey, straight in the eye. "But what if I go away . . . and never see you again? . . ."

Rey had no answer . . .

* * * * *

Pastor Yevgeny got back to New Merieko from the Roderick Dundee. Noon time was fast approaching, and the heat was nearly unbearable. Kids played on the beach or engaged in an improvised game of rugby in the village. Some went swimming, as their doting moms warned them never to go too far out into the water, or near the woods for fear of critters.

Because of last night's deaths in the forest, there was a quiet, yet noticeable sense of anger, outrage, sadness, and loss in New Merieko. Most of the villagers were newcomers to Infernus, and were unaware of the dangers, hidden somewhere OUT THERE. Infernus wasn't yet home to them, though they tried to make it such. Lofty goals were achieved over time, but not without the price of blood.

Yevgeny strolled along the narrow rows of huts and stopped at one of the smaller houses to peek inside. There, he found the lone, solitary figure of Gyorgy-Andreovich, sitting in the darkness of the hut.

Gyorgy was Pavel-Ivanovich's lover and companion. He was a fragile, effeminate young man of nineteen, in overwhelming shock and grief over Pavel-

Ivanovich getting ate. Well-wishers dropped by to offer Gyorgy words of comfort and condolences, along with bouquets of flowers and dishes of food. Most of the Kuschans in New Merieko had asked Gyorgy to move in with them, until he was ready to get on with life.

The food was left uneaten, as Gyorgy refused sunlight and friendship. There were concerns of Gyorgy trying to starve himself, while allowing sadness to beat him. Gyorgy was a child of wealth and privilege, and never worked a day in his life. He wouldn't know what to do with a hammer and nails, had they been handed to him!

Yevgeny stepped into the hut and approached Gyorgy. Softly, he rubbed his hand on Gyorgy's thin shoulders. "Do you need anything?" he asked with a smile.

Gyorgy smiled back, though it failed to hide unbearable pain. He took Yevgeny's hand in his, acknowledging the level of love and support afforded him. Even then, he wouldn't leave the safety and solitude of the hut. "No," mouthed Gyorgy. "Thank you . . . No . . ."

Yevgeny didn't know whether to give Gyorgy a kindhearted embrace or slap the snot out of him. Gyorgy made for a sympathetic character, all right, but also a pathetic one. Yevgeny couldn't abide it. Other men faced worse tragedies and hardships, and handled them courageously. Yevgeny despised self-pity. Eventually, Gyorgy would have to carry on bravely, or die a weakling and a coward.

Yevgeny gave Gyorgy's hand a gentle squeeze, offered a word or two of encouragement, then left him in a quagmire of despair and hopelessness.

Yevgeny went outside, into the blinding sunlight and oppressive heat and humidity. As families sat down to eat, a neighbor played a violin, as his wife sang a traditional folk song. Everybody tried to make New Merieko home. Somehow, it never felt like it.

Kusch wasn't home to bloodthirsty apes or winged demons . . .

Yevgeny headed toward his own house when he ran into a young man who, up until yesterday, he had little or no use for.

Yevgeny grinned. A mouse had finally stood up to became a man!

"Fernandez!" called Yevgeny, stepping toward the gangly teen in the skullcap and skimpy school uniform of the Brotherhood of Faith Church.

Fernandez rarely left the protection of his folks, despite showing a dose of courage against savage critters, the night before. While Yevgeny and "Nandy" fought the beasts off, Paolo and Frida didn't do nothing but huddle together like scared rabbits.

Fernandez was still a sissy and a momma's boy, though he held his own against the abarbeaus. Therefore, he earned Yevgeny's respect and admiration. Maybe it was the parents who sought the protection of their sensitive, fifteen-year-old son!

Fernandez sat on a stump and smiled happily as he saw Yevgeny. "Good afternoon," he greeted. "How are you today, Pastor?"

"Very well," said Yevgeny, examining Fernandez' injured hand. "How are your valiant war wounds?"

"Better," laughed Fernandez. "And yours?"

Yevgeny removed his shirt to reveal the scarred and still raw shoulders, where the baby abarbeaus nearly made mincemeat of him.

Fernandez' mouth gaped open as he stared at the fresh wounds that Yevgeny got from the abarbeaus, along with older ones he received in Anumun. "How? . . . What happened to you?" asked Fernandez.

"Life," answered Yevgeny, vaguely. "You'll have more scars than those you got yesterday . . . if you live long enough."

Fernandez's eyes widened, in astonishment and awe.

"I hope our little episode last night hasn't changed your mind about emigrating here," said Yevgeny, a bit smugly. "Surely this is preferable to what you left in Agron."

"Father was an indentured servant," explained Fernandez. "Grandpa left us deep in debt, to a landowner in Merieko. Father had to work like a dog! He got home every night, real tired . . . I mean, every night, even on Sundays!"

Yevgeny nodded YES.

"When that was over, we had no home, no land, nothing," said Fernandez. "It was Father's idea to come here, maybe get some free land and start over."

"There's no such thing as free land, if you work it," said Yevgeny. "More importantly, if you have to fight for it. I take it that you and your mother are unhappy here."

"Very unhappy," sighed Fernandez. "Especially after . . . last night."

"And what does your father say about it?"

"I don't know. Him and Mom got into an argument, soon as we got home. I don't think they got a wink of sleep, last night!"

"How well did you sleep?" asked Yevgeny.

"Not very good," whined Fernandez. "I couldn't stop thinking about what happened to Pavel-Ivanovich, and everyone else with us."

"It was a sad day."

"Yes sir, Pastor Yevgeny," agreed Fernandez. "It sure was. A very sad day.

I don't like it here. I want to go home, to Agron."

"Home . . . to Agron?"

"Yes, sir."

"What don't you like about Infernus?" asked Yevgeny.

"Everything!"

"Everything?"

Fernandez shrugged. "Just about."

"Infernus is beautiful, though . . ." Yevgeny smiled. "Isn't it?"

"Not when people are getting killed around you!"

"It's the abarbeaus. I'd like to wipe each and every one of them off this island!"

"Yeah," sighed Fernandez.

"And what do you think of the winged men?" asked Yevgeny, pointedly.

"They're scary! I'm afraid of them . . . Even the kid ones!"

"They're not of this world, Fernandez. They're abominations, and nothing like us. It means nothing to me if some of them do attend Leader Rey's church. They'll never make it to Heaven, Paradise, or the Promised Land. They hold no favor in God's eyes, and surely not to the Kuen's! How can such a hideous being belong to God? They belong to Soraq."

Fernandez's eyes widened, this time in fear.

"Will your opinion of Infernus change," asked Yevgeny, "if there were no abarbeaus or winged men?"

"If," said Fernandez, in resignation and defeat. "I don't know what anyone can do about that. I only wish we didn't come here. I wish none of us were here! I wish I was back home, in Agron . . ."

"Wishing will get you nowhere!" hollered Yevgeny, loud enough that his words echoed throughout the narrow streets and walkways of New Merieko.

Fernandez gasped. Yevgeny's harsh, hostile tone intimidated him. Fernandez wanted to retreat indoors, to the safe, secure company of his loving parents.

"You wish we weren't attacked by those animals yesterday," said Yevgeny, not quite as heavy-handed as before. "But it happened. And I'll bet you wished we didn't have to fight our way out of it. It wasn't wishing that saved us, any more than it was the Kuschan Navy showing up when we no longer needed them. You and I had to take a stand . . . just like we have to take a stand, now."

"I . . . I don't understand," stuttered Fernandez.

"You may wish you were home, in Agron. But you're not. You're here. I'm here. A lot of good people came here to make a home for themselves. You said there was nothing left for your father in Agron, and that he had no choice but to move here, to Infernus."

Fernandez hated getting bawled out by Yevgeny. It was a pouncing he didn't expect, didn't need, didn't want, and surely didn't deserve. Why was Yevgeny being so mean? What did Fernandez do or say to merit such lousy treatment?

"My faith tells of a winged demon who is the cause of all evil in the Universe," explained Yevgeny. "Your faith speaks of demons who can take over the minds and thoughts of all other beings, including people. What if I were to say that the animals who attacked us yesterday did so, not of their own spirit or free will?"

"Father told me that it was in their nature to attack us, for food and survival," mumbled Fernandez, feeling inferior around Yevgeny.

"And what if I told you that even the hearts and minds of dumb beasts can be manipulated by the forces of evil?" said Yevgeny. "What if the abarbeaus attacked us, because they were ordered to by those advocating evil, living on this island?"

"By what?" whined Fernandez, panic sweeping over him. "What? . . . What about that winged man who was killed in the mountains, yesterday?"

"He was a friend of Leader Rey, and the young Kokashima boy sent over here to visit you." Yevgeny snickered, knowing he was getting the better of Fernandez. "That winged man had turned his back on Soraq, and paid dearly for surrendering his allegiance to the lord of darkness."

Since his arrival to the island, just days before, Fernandez had been in a constant state of doubt and confusion. He felt isolated, vulnerable, and alone. Agron was so very, very far away. Fernandez now saw himself stranded in a land of horrors. Despite the events from the night before, he wanted to believe that he and his family would create a new life on Infernus.

Hell . . .

Infernus is Hell . . .

Fernandez's lips quivered. Hands shuttered, the heart beat rapidly, body heat increased. Breathing grew shallow. Confidence was replaced by thoughts of dying horribly in a world of mystery and shadow.

Fernandez glanced at his family's hut. He had the overwhelming urge to dash into this parents' arms and seek shelter in a sanctuary that provided only temporary safety, in a place where decency never resided, and good could never overcome cruelty and depravity. "Mother . . ." he whispered. "Father . . . I want to go home . . ."

"None of that!" snapped Yevgeny, shaking Fernandez. "None of that! Get a grip on yourself, and act like a man!"

Fernandez's wild eyes darted all around. "What? . . . What if the winged men send those monsters in here, to finish the job? What if we're slaughtered in our beds?"

"What if we take action to prevent that from happening?"

"But what can we do against? . . ."

"Take action!" shouted Yevgeny. "Take action against evil!"

Fernandez shook like a leaf, as he threw his arms around Yevgeny's shoulder. He found no solace there, as Yevgeny callously pushed him away.

"You proved to me yesterday that you're capable of being a man," said Yevgeny, lacking sentimentality. "Are you going to stand up, and handle this like a man? Are you willing to make tough decisions, like a man?"

"I don't know what to do!" cried Fernandez.

"Well, we'd better do something! We can't just wait around helplessly. Can I expect your help? Or do you bury your head in the sand, and do nothing?"

Fernandez shrugged his shoulders.

"You stood up and fought alongside me, yesterday," said Yevgeny, sternly. "Will you stand up and fight alongside me, once more?"

"But I . . ." Fernandez gulped. "I don't know what to do!"

"You let me worry about that. Can I expect your help?"

Speech failed Fernandez.

"So?" demanded Yevgeny. "I need an answer!"

"What?. . ." asked Fernandez, indecisively. "What are we going to do? . . ."

Jeremy helped Rey clean the dining room all up. Broken glass and dishes was thrown out, while busted chairs were sent to a woodwright for repairs. Rey fixed a nice breakfast for Paransky, then treated his own wounds from his "disagreement" with Mucker.

As Paransky chowed down on a meal of chicken eggs and pork sausage, Rey went to his office to re-think his fight with Mucker. He sought forgiveness from God and find for a way to make an amends. The shame he suffered for taking the first swing hurt far worse than the black eye, fat lip, and bloody nose. He even thought about resigning his post as a Leader. Maybe he'd move to Branell with Jeremy and Ericha, if they decided to go there. Rey was torn between his devotion to the Almighty, and his love for a stepson.

Few within the Brotherhood Church hierarchy knew of Rey's congregation on Infernus. And only a very few in the highest chambers of the Brotherhood were aware of it. Fewer still were privy to the weird winged critters within Rey's "flock." This was a secret which Rey hoped was never compromised or violated. The last thing he needed was busy-bodies and troublemakers heading into Infernus, to get a firsthand glimpse of the winged men. Infernus was already filling up with people who took exception to such critters . . . a matter which concerned Rey.

Rey liked Weston, but could he trust the diplomat to remain quiet about his visit to Infernus? Hopefully so! Surely, Weston kept secrets involving important heads of state, along with their underlings and cronies.

What about Pastor Yevgeny?

Rey studied a few passages of the Word. His conscious gnawed at him. More and more, Rey knew he had to go apologize to Mucker. He still believed that Paransky was in better hands at the church. But there was no denying Mucker's love for the tattooed boy. Maybe Rey would do right by letting Mucker take Paransky off hunting and fishing, sometime.

However, Paransky would know the love of God, with or without Mucker's support and consent!

Rey sat the book on the desk and stared at an oil painting of Mount Patten in late-winter. The painting was Rey's attempt at a career in the arts, and not a very good one. Prior to becoming a Leader, Rey tried his hand at painting. He spent several days standing in the cold and snow, with a paintbrush and canvas, looking out across a wintry landscape of Embrey's highest point. Though Rey admitted it wasn't no masterpiece, he kept it as a reminder of "what might have been."

Jeremy and Weston entered the room. Rey smiled and, for a moment, forgot all about his own problems. Jeremy looked downright handsome in a black jacket, bow tie, white silk shirt, tights, and shiny boots. His hair was neatly combed back, revealing a widow's peak. The fingernails was trimmed, cleaned, and filed. He even washed behind the ears . . . a first for Jeremy Kentworth!

Rey stood and gave his son a paternal kiss on the forehead. "Jeremy!" he shouted, excitedly. "It is you . . . isn't it?"

"I hardly recognize him, myself," said Weston, grinning.

Jeremy didn't say nothing. His blush said everything!

"Well, I declare," said Rey, clasping Jeremy's hand. "Errol should be thrilled to offer his daughter to you. Is it better to wear these fancies, rather than that silly loincloth?"

"These tights scratch my legs!" griped Jeremy. "And this thing around my neck's choking me!"

"You'll get used to it," said Weston. "A fine country gent must look the part, don't you think?"

"Nope," answered Jeremy. "Me and Ericha are gonna traipse around the Branellian countryside in our loincloths . . . or bare naked."

"Indecent exposure is illegal in Branell, as it is in most parts of the world," laughed Weston. "However, there are parts of southern Actin where clothes are viewed as objects of pride and vanity. Those wearing them are punished severely at public floggings."

Jeremy grinned, mischievously. "Did you go naked when you were there, Weston?"

"Yeah . . . Yeah, I did," admitted Weston. "Got my butt sunburned for it, too."

Rey and Jeremy snickered.

"Well, you no longer look like 'just plain old Jeremy' to me, kiddo," said Weston. "You look more like a man of great wealth and distinction."

"Says who?" asked Jeremy. "I think it makes me look like a swell."

"I'd be careful the next time I saw Ericha," advised Weston, a twinkle in his eye. "She'll get so excited by how nice you look, she'll tear those clothes right off and . . ."

"Weston," warned Rey.

Jeremy giggled.

"Ah, get out of here, and go see Errol!" ordered Rey, concealing a smile. "And son, the next time you see Mucker, tell him how truly sorry I am."

"Mucker won't like that at all," chuckled Jeremy. "He'll have lots to say about that, which you don't want to hear. Why, I can hear him already, hollering about pious old hypocrites, sorry for what they up and done." Jeremy tried to impersonate Mucker. "Says he's sorry, goddamnit? Not near as sorry as he's gonna be, when I get my hands on that phony, churchy sumbitch . . ."

"Jeremy!" hollered Rey. "Run along. Go talk to Errol, before I get the urge to slap your face off. You won't look so handsome with your face slapped off. Ericha will change her mind once she gets her first glimpse of you, minus a face! Run along, before I ground you until you're thirty-five!"

* * * * *

Jeremy left the church, self-conscious of the "Sundays" he had on. He figured that everybody in town was staring at him, and a lot of them were! Lots of people didn't even recognize him at first, and stopped to look at 'the new kid in town.' A few even thought he was Prince Ari, which only made things worse.

Jeremy was pleased by the kind remarks given to him. On the other hand, he wanted to mash in the faces of the men who made effeminate remarks about his appearance.

Jeremy stopped at the flimsy old shack Mucker shared with Seely. His heart skipped a beat. Like Rey, he too had to apologize to Mucker. The nice duds he had on were of little use. Mucker hated men in frilly shirts and tights.

But did Jeremy really owe Mucker an apology? It was Mucker who made the foul remarks about Ericha wearing the pants, and having to make all the decisions. Jeremy felt like saying "to hell with Mucker! To hell with Mucker, and his stinkwater attitudes about everything!"

Even then, Jeremy owed Mucker a good deal, besides the smokes, the chews, and the shots of whiskey. Mucker took Jeremy hunting and fishing, taught him how to cure hides, and gave him lessons in archery and swordsmanship. Jeremy's love of the outdoors was all Mucker's doing. In a way, Jeremy did have to mend fences, and needed to get it done before heading to Branell.

If he headed to Branell . . .

Jeremy looked all around, at the place he called home. Was he willing to give it all up, just to get rich?

Jeremy peeked into Mucker's shack, to find Seely alone. As usual, Seely was real bad drunk. The man's clothes was wrinkled and soiled, his face was unshaven, the eyes droopy and bloodshot. The foul stench of bourbon hung from Seely's pale, skinny frame. He was slowly turning a sickening yellow color, from hooching it up.

Seely was usually a happy-go-lucky guy with nothing bad to say about nobody. Not today. The man sat at the rickety old table, with a hang-dog look. Mucker had already told him about the brawl with Rey over Paransky. Seely was right fond of the little tattooed boy, and now suffered the stings of rejection and abandonment. A more pitiful sight Jeremy rarely saw than that of Seely, drowning his sorrows in rum.

"Seely?" greeted Jeremy, sitting at the table.

When Seely first laid eyes on Jeremy, he thought it was a stranger. Only after his vision had focused, did he recognize this newcomer as Jeremy. "Good God Almighty, in Heaven!" laughed Seely. "What the? . . . Why you all gussied up for?"

"I . . ." Jeremy had to think for a second or two. "I'm going to see Errol."

"Does a man gotta get all gussied up for that?" asked Seely. "I see Errol darn-neared every day. I ain't that gussied up when I do. Why, I never once gussied up like that, before! You neither, I reckon."

"I reckon."

"Want me to pour you a cold one?"

"I can't," sighed Jeremy. "I . . . I asked Ericha to marry me."

"Marry you?" shouted Seely.

"Yeah. So now I gotta get Errol's permission."

Seely's eyes brightened, to reveal a bit of happiness. Then they quickly dimmed. "Well," moaned Seely, taking a drag from his smoke. "The more things change, the more things change."

"Where's Muck?" asked Jeremy, nervously.

"He come in for a spell, bloodied and beaten on account of the good Leader Rey. Says he'll cut the padre to ribbons, one o' these days."

Jeremy swallowed.

"Is it true?" asked Seely, mournfully. "Is the good Leader Rey taking the boy from us?"

Jeremy couldn't explain, without hurting Seely's feelings. Then again, how could anybody explain anything to Seely? The man was never sober.

"Is it true that yer runnin' off to the Farlands?" asked Seely, all teary-eyed and sad.

"I . . . I'm thinking awful strong about it," said Jeremy, dang-neared ashamed to admit it.

Seely didn't say nothing. The look on his face spoke of heartache, pain, and loneliness.

"If me and Ericha get over there and it stinks, we're heading right back," added Jeremy, with a strained smile. "You can be darned sure about it."

"Well, the more things change, the more things change," mumbled Seely, absently.

Jeremy frowned, knowing he had hurt Seely. There was nothing he could do about it!

"I'm hopin' you'll see it in yer heart to have a snort or two with ol' Seely, before you go runnin' off." Seely grinned, struggling to accept news of Jeremy's departure.

Jeremy laughed, though he was overtaken by melancholy. Fear of the unknown almost paralyzed him. Somehow, he kept it all together, and painted on a brave face.

The more things change, the more things change . . .

"I gotta get going," said Jeremy, hesitantly.

Seely never said nothing. He turned his head away, to conceal tears streaming down his face.

"Don't worry, Seely," said Jeremy. "You and me are gonna have us a great time, before I even think about leaving this island!"

Seely looked at Jeremy, and forced a smile on his weathered face. Unable to speak, he took Jeremy's hand and caressed it. Then suddenly he pulled away, to drown his countless memories, disappointments, and sorrows in the bottle.

"Be seeing you, Seely," whispered Jeremy, then slowly left.

The last few steps to Errol's house were among the most difficult and crucial in Jeremy's life. He was torn between facing the challenges head on or running off like a spooked buck. Partly, Jeremy felt like laughing at his predicament. The other part felt like a whipped pup, crawling to a beating he couldn't avoid. The one driving force was a commitment to Ericha, a girl he wanted to spend the rest of his life with.

Jeremy got to the door, with a silly grin on his face. He couldn't hold back the laughter of self-deprecating humor, which was replaced by doubt and fear. Jeremy sucked in a deep breath, let it out gradually, and knocked at the door.

"Come in, if your nose is clean," said Errol.

Jeremy wiped away the smile, opened the door, and found the family sitting down to an early lunch of venison, corn on the cob, and boiled potatoes. A bottle of wine had been opened, and everybody's glasses were filled.

Ericha was still in her buckskin shirt and loincloth. Meanwhile, Errol wore his typical scowl, as the Little Oinker thought he was the Center of the Universe.

"May I come in?" asked Jeremy, his voice jittery and high-pitched.

Ericha gasped in astonishment, to see Jeremy in such fine duds. Errol smiled in grudging admiration, as Ari laughed in a self-satisfactory cackle.

"Stand up!" ordered Errol, removing the napkin from his lap to greet Jeremy. "We have a guest. Stand up and show the man some respect."

"Him?" argued Ari, in contempt.

"Him!" said Errol. "Stand up, Ari, and show our guest the proper courtesy."

"Why?" questioned Ari. "It's like putting a tuxedo on a monkey!"

"Ari!" scolded Ericha, leaving the table to embrace Jeremy.

Jeremy threw his arms around Ericha, and squeezed her as hard as he could.

"Ooh!" commented Ari, sickened to see Ericha smooch on someone as lowly as Jeremy Kentworth.

"You know better than to act like that," said Errol, humiliated by Ari. "Get to your room, Ericha. Put something on more fitting for our guest, then come back and finish your meal."

"But, Papa!" moped Ericha. "Why can't I keep these same clothes on?"

"That's no way to dress when we got company," said Errol.

"It's okay," said Jeremy. "She looks fine by me . . ."

"What?" growled Errol.

"I . . . I meant . . . He's right, Ericha," stuttered Jeremy. "Maybe you oughta get something . . ." Jeremy stared at Ericha's slender, tanned legs. He resented that she'd have to change into a dress. ". . . Nicer to wear."

Ericha gave Jeremy a kiss on the cheek, then hurried to her room.

"You too, Ari," said Errol, sternly. "Get some better clothes on, and come back . . ."

Ari's attire not only matched Jeremy's, but was even fancier. As the male heir to the Infernus "monarchy" he was obligated to dress in a manner befitting his status. "But, Father . . ."

"Now!" barked Errol.

Ari groaned, then did as he was told.

Jeremy slouched. Errol wanted to talk to him, alone. Was he ready for this interrogation?

Jeremy sat at the table, trying to look, act, and sound the part of a gentleman. He smiled graciously, although he was a bundle of nerves. Jeremy knew Errol his whole life. At that moment, it was like the two were strangers. It was best not to trade dirty jokes or enjoy a cold drink just for the fun of it. He couldn't afford to be 'just plain old Jeremy' now. He had to rise above that.

"Eaten yet, Jeremy?" asked Errol, fetching a ceramic plate next to a wash tub.

"No, sir . . . I mean, yes sir!" stuttered Jeremy. "I ate."

"Still hungry? If you'd like, I'll fill you a glass."

"That's good . . . I . . . I'm good."

Errol frowned. "I'd be offended if you don't at least sit down to eat . . ."

"Okay," agreed Jeremy, eager to try some of the wine on Errol's table. It was imported from the nation of Campens, a noted wine-growing country, and illegally shipped into Infernus on one of Mucker's ships. Jeremy looked forward to sampling the elixir . . . as long as he didn't get drunk!

After Errol filled his glass, Jeremy took a small sip.

"We picked the corn yesterday," said Errol, scooping some grub into Jeremy's plate. "And the spuds this morning."

Jeremy was tempted to run away, then forget all about Ericha, forget all about Branell, and go back to being 'just plain old Jeremy.' Later, he'd get falling down drunk with Mucker and Seely . . . assuming he was still on speaking terms with them!

What would Rey and Weston have to say about that?

Blast!

Jeremy's path was set. He had to be with Ericha. Errol was the only obstacle in his way.

Jeremy's mouth was dry, and his hands were soaked in sweat. There was no turning back. Sure, he knew Errol his whole life. Yet, there was a great divide separating the two men. Jeremy was subservient to Errol, a truth he absolutely despised. Thoughts of kissing Errol's butt was unspeakable. In the end, Jeremy might win. For the time being, he wouldn't and he couldn't.

"I know why you're here," said Errol, flatly. "Let's get it out in the open."

"I've known Ericha as far back as I can remember," said Jeremy, trying to act all assertive and tough. He came off more as a frightened kid, begging to have his say.

"How well do you know her, now?" asked Errol, suspiciously.

"I love Ericha," answered Jeremy, holding his anger. "I . . . I'm still a virgin, if that's what you're getting at. And so is she . . . So is Ericha . . ."

Errol found Jeremy's straight-forward attitude to be equally admirable and offensive. He was split in taking Jeremy at his word, or pressing a delicate matter and force the kid to fess up to something he might have never done. Errol wanted to trust Jeremy. But could he? Could he afford to give his daughter over to the boy? Could he trust Jeremy to make smart, mature decisions, and be a man when being a man was crucial?

"I love Ericha, too," said Errol. "And I want to make sure she's doing the right thing."

"I want to do the right thing for Ericha," said Jeremy.

"You say you want to. But will you?"

"I want to be with your daughter," said Jeremy. "I want her with me in Branell . . . if I go to Branell."

"Why?"

"I can't live without her! She's my best friend . . . sir."

"Your best friend?" questioned Errol, in a demeaning way. "You want to marry your best friend?"

Jeremy shook his head and sighed. This entire charade of getting all dolled up and acting like a swell was just a crock, a waste of time, a joke! Nothing but a joke! Well, if Jeremy couldn't have Ericha, then he'd refuse to take Branell! To hell with kissing Errol's butt! To hell with wearing "Sundays"! To hell with Weston, Branell, the big money and the big land and the big boat trip over there!

Might as well tear those damned "Sundays" right off my stinking back, right in front of Errol! I'll go back to my loincloth, and be nothing more or nothing less than just plain old Jeremy!

What I wouldn't do right now for a snort of good Agronian rotgut!

"Ericha's my daughter!" hollered Errol. "She's the only daughter I'll ever have. Just like Ari's the only son I'll ever have! I can't just hand her over to anyone, and think that it's gonna be all right."

"I'm not just anyone!" snapped Jeremy, looking Errol straight in the eye. "I've known you since I was a little kid, and I ain't just some 'johnny-come-lately' who just stepped off a boat, looking for a piece of tail. I love her! I love her as a friend, and I love her as . . ." Jeremy took a deep breath. "I'm still a virgin, and so is she! I ain't lying about that. If I was a liar, do you honestly think I'd be here right now, trying to? . . ."

"'Trying to' what?"

Jeremy rolled his eyes back, as both fists clenched.

"You think I like seeing you and Ericha prance around everywhere, in skimpy rags and animal hides?" asked Errol. "I never liked it, and I'm getting where I won't have it! Ericha's a beautiful young lady, and not a little girl anymore! And that business of you two bathing together, buck-naked! Don't tell me you've never thought about taking advantage of Ericha. I wasn't born yesterday."

"It's innocent!" shrieked Jeremy.

"'Innocent'?" laughed Errol. "You expect me to buy that? Just how 'innocent' were you when you humiliated Ari at the dinner table, the other night?"

"Ari's got a big mouth! I was only paying him back for pissing . . . for insulting me!"

Errol took the time to calm down. "Ericha's my daughter," he said, finally. "She's only daughter I'll ever have. How am I going to feel, sending her away with you, thinking I'll never see her again?"

Jeremy bit his bottom lip. "I have thought about that, sir. I won't move away to Branell, if Ericha can't come with me . . . or if she won't. If the only way I can stay with Ericha is for me to stay here, then I'd rather have your daughter, and your daughter's love, then all the riches in the world."

"I can see where a fella might think that way," said Errol. "I just want you to know that I love Ericha, very much. For what it's worth . . . I love you too."

"If you love me, then why can't you trust me? Ain't I just as good as some of the other guys who got their eyes on her?"

"You're better than they are," breathed Errol. "But sometimes you make me wonder. I only want what's best for the both of you. I dunno. Maybe taking that property way back east is for the best. I just don't know if I'm ready to let go of Ericha . . . or of you . . ."

Jeremy again reminded himself that moving to Branell meant possibly saying goodbye to Infernus, forever. Once more, he wondered if it wasn't best to forget about the big money and the big land. Maybe he'd do right to build a modest home someplace on the island, maintain close ties to everyone living there, and expect nothing more out of life than to be what he was, and what he figured he's always be.

Just plain old Jeremy . . .

"I agree with Rey and Weston," said Errol, his voice revealing loss and agony. "You're better off claiming your inheritance. Trust me . . . you are, Jeremy. Ain't much here for a young man. Ain't no good way to make your fortune here."

"Why's everybody so fired up to see me go?" whined Jeremy. "It's like everybody wants me to move away, like I ain't welcome here anymore! Like nobody cares about me!"

"It ain't that. Don'tcha wanna leave Infernus? Don'tcha wanna know what lies beyond these shores, to seek your fortune and adventures someplace else?"

"I was born in Branell," said Jeremy. "I can't remember a whole heck of a lot about it. The longer I'm here on Infernus, the more I think of it as home. I ain't sure I'm wanting that piece of land way yonder, even if it's where I come from. Did you ever leave the island?"

"Sure, I been to the Farlands," said Errol. "Before Ericha and Ari was born, I went to Agron, then spent a bit of time in Embrey. That's where I met my wife."

Jeremy smiled.

"I was making it as a drover for some rancher east of Sykes," explained Errol. "Only thing I got out of the deal was my wife. She worked there as a cook and maid. Never liked Embrey, much. Soon as I tied the knot, we worked our way to Merieko, where I clerked a spell in a dried goods store. Don't say anything, but that's where I first met John Mucker."

Jeremy's eyes widened.

"Mucker took us back to Infernus," said Errol, "in exchange for my blisters and sweat on one of his freighters. Ain't been back to the Farlands since. Ericha and Ari ain't been there, at all."

Jeremy rather enjoyed Errol's story, and felt he got to know a bit more about his future father-in-law.

"I had a taste of wanderlust when I was your age," said Errol. "I understand it when a boy gets the hankering to stray out of the comfort and safety of his old stomping grounds, to see the world. Whether he comes back or not . . . or if he's even able to come back or not."

Jeremy nodded YES.

"Ari says he's gonna live here forever," said Errol. "I think Ari thinks he's gonna live forever. He also thinks this island's gonna be his, since he still believes that business of me being 'king' amounts to anything. I guess the day's gonna come when Ari's gotta learn what lies beyond Infernus." Errol sighed. "I hate to say it, but I guess the same can be said of Ericha."

For several seconds nobody said nothing.

"I don't think I'll ever understand you, Jeremy," said Errol. "I can't see how anyone can understand anybody who runs around in rags and animal hides."

"I wish I had a shilling for every time Rey said that same thing to me!" laughed Jeremy.

"Well," said Errol, quietly. "I can't think of a better man to take my daughter's hand in marriage than you . . . with a few concessions."

"Such as?"

"You need to rethink your way of living."

"In what way?" asked Jeremy, defensively.

"For one thing, that business of you and Ericha wearing loincloths."

Jeremy scowled. "What do you got against loincloths?"

"What do you think I got against them?" snapped Errol. "Ericha's a beautiful girl, too beautiful in them . . . things. Bad enough when half the guys around here see her dressed that way. It's scary when even I begin to take notice!"

Jeremy blushed.

"If you really wanna marry my daughter, then hear me out," said Errol. "I won't yet say 'yes' and I can't yet say 'no', as to your marrying Ericha. Not today, anyway."

"Okay," whispered Jeremy, nervously.

"Starting tomorrow, come by every night at suppertime. You do that for a week, and I'll give it some thought."

"A week?" gasped Jeremy. "Why? . . . Why do I gotta? . . ."

"You agree or not?" Errol knew he had Jeremy over a barrel. "Come by every night at suppertime, have a real sit-down meal with us. Court my daughter like the gentleman I know you are, and I'll give it some thought."

Jeremy sighed. "Then what?"

"What do you mean, 'then what?'" Errol laughed. "Show up at suppertime, get a good home-cooked meal with the family. Whether you know it or not, I'm liable to be a father to you, of sorts. And Ari's gonna be your brother."

Jeremy frowned. "My brother?"

"You marry my daughter, you'll be a member of the family. Better you start acting like it. Meaning, you come around here thinking like a man, and acting like a man." Errol leaned across the table. "You also come here, dressed like a man. Savvy?"

Jeremy sighed.

"Savvy?" repeated Errol, forcefully.

"Yes, sir," said Jeremy, realizing he had to abide Errol. "Savvy . . ."

"Go on, finish your drink," said Errol, gulping his own down in one swallow. "I'll see ya tomorrow night."

Jeremy quickly finished his drink. He got up, staggered slightly, headed to the door, and left.

Less than a minute later, Ericha and Ari reappeared, wearing different clothes. Ericha went out of her way to find the nicest duds in her closet, a formal red dress designed and fitted by some nice church ladies.

Both Ericha and Ari were shocked to see Errol sitting alone at the table. They could hear Errol and Jeremy hollering back and forth. Neither fully heard what was said. Ari wasn't upset to see Jeremy go, but Ericha sure was. "Where is he?" the girl asked, painfully. "Where's Jeremy?"

"He couldn't stay," said Errol, evasively. "He had to help Rey out at a prayer service."

"Prayer service?" shouted Ericha and Ari, in unison.

"You gotta be kidding!" hollered Ari. "A prayer service?"

Ericha leaned against the wall, trying hard not to cry.

"Sit down," said Errol, on the verge of laughing. "Finish your meal."

"I'm not hungry," whined Ericha, wanting to run off and hide in her room.

"What's ailing you?" asked Errol.

"What did you say to Jeremy?" questioned Ericha, angrily.

"That's between me and Jeremy," said Errol, vaguely, as Ari giggled.

"What did you say to him?" demanded Ericha.

"Aw, just man-to-man talk," said Errol. "A father-son kind of thing. I doubt either you'd understand. Now, sit down and finish . . ."

"'Father-son'?" asked Ericha, in confusion.

"You got nothing to fret over," said Errol. "He'll be back tomorrow night, for supper. And the night after that. And the night after that."

"Jeremy's having supper with us?" griped Ari, as Ericha's mood suddenly brightened.

"Ain't that what I just got done saying?" asked Errol, grinning real big.

"He might come over," said Ari. "It doesn't mean I have to be here!"

"Oh yes you are!" ordered Errol. "We're gonna sit down like a family. That means Jeremy, and it means you."

"Why?" cried Ari. "I . . . I don't even like him, and he don't like me! I refuse to be here, if he's going . . ."

"Is that any way to treat a brother?" argued Errol.

"Brother?" shrieked Ari.

"We'll all sit down together, have supper, and get to know each other a bit better," said Errol. "Don't worry, son. If your brother-in-law gets too rough with you, I'll skin his head."

Ericha returned to the table, reached over, and took her father by the hand. As Errol's eyes met hers, Ericha leaned forward and kissed him on the cheek.

* * * * *

Jeremy strolled to the Brotherhood Church, asking himself over and over what he was getting himself into. He never imagined that, by taking Ericha's hand in marriage, he also had to accept the girl's smartass little brother as his brother.

Crap!

Jeremy figured he already had one foot in the door. He began to understand the gravity of the situation. Was he willing to pay such a heavy price, for the girl of his dreams?

Did he have any choice?

Even then, Jeremy did feel better than before. He had an odd sense of elation, along with growing responsibilities and fears. Jeremy openly laughed on his way home, as everybody looked at him strangely. Why was he so dolled up so good, while also having a chuckle at his own expense?

Jeremy passed by the small, rickety old shack. Mucker had got back, mad as a hornet. Jeremy hesitated, torn between apologizing to the old coot, or head back to change into something more comfortable . . . like a loincloth!

Jeremy entered the back door of the church to find Weston waiting for him at the bedroom. He didn't know what to make of the huge grin on Weston's face.

"So . . ." mulled Jeremy. "Why are you in my room, acting like you just got done poking the cat?"

"How did it go?" asked Weston, eagerly.

"What did what go?"

Weston smirked.

"Okay," said Jeremy, smiling. "Thanks for the fancies. Errol likes them more than he likes me!"

"And?" asked Weston.

Jeremy sighed. "Errol wants me to have supper with the whole bunch of them."

"Great!"

"Every night, for a week," mumbled Jeremy. "I might be needing more of your fancies. Hope you don't mind."

"Not at all, kiddo."

Jeremy stripped in front of Weston. Carefully, he laid the "Sundays" on the bed, trying not to mess them up. In no time, he returned to his buckskin shirt and loincloth.

Jeremy sat next to Weston on a deacon's bench, letting the cool breeze sooth his tired, bare legs. "Weston?" he said, anxiously. "How much longer before you gotta head back east?"

"In the next two weeks. My work here is finished . . . if I had any work here, at all. I'm afraid the Kuschan Navy has made my mission a tad pointless."

"And if I decide to head back east, am I s'posed to go with you?"

"That's the idea. The Branellian king will give you time to claim your inheritance, but not for long. If you're a no-show, the deal's off, and he'll take it for himself. Please don't give him the satisfaction. If my mission here has any meaning, I'd like to think it was to meet my cousin Jeremiah . . ." Weston grinned. "And to inform him of his grand fortune."

"Weston," said Jeremy, hesitantly. "Is it right for me to take Ericha with me, away from her dad and snotnosed brother? I mean . . . am I being selfish, by asking her to leave the island with me?"

"Hell, no! You're not being selfish. It's your life, and you're the only one who can live it. You and Ericha, both. Don't let others live your life for you."

"Not even you?"

"Not even me. It's your life, and if you want to share it with Ericha, I envy you. She's a nice girl, and will bear you a slew of lovely, redheaded children!"

"I hate to say it," said Jeremy, "but I kinda feel sorry for Errol."

"And not Ari?" laughed Weston.

"Errol ain't no young man, no more."

"Are you saying that Errol's old?"

"He looks old to me!" exclaimed Jeremy.

"Everyone's old when you're a kid. Just how old do I look to you?"

"Ancient!" giggled Jeremy.

Weston frowned at Jeremy's comment. "Anyway, I'd take the inheritance if I were you. Imagine it! You'll have more land than most men can cross in a day's walk. You're set for life, kiddo."

Jeremy's lips quivered. "But what about Errol? And what about Rey, Malachi, Evelyn? . . . Or even Mucker and Seely?"

"They can take care of themselves. You have to take care of yourself. The best way to do that is by claiming that which is rightfully yours. You're rich! If you don't enjoy it, then you're a bigger fool than you know."

"What about you, Weston?" asked Jeremy.

"I'll take care of myself. Soon as I get home, I'll stay with my brother Courtney until the snow flies. Soon, Marco will send me off to some god-forsaken rat hole, just so I can win a few hearts and minds, spreading love and good cheer in the name of Embrey."

"You ever get scared while you're on them trips?"

"If a guy's not just a little afraid, he's got no business being a diplomat," laughed Weston. "Some people just don't like Embrians. If a man's not careful, he'll lose his head in a hurry. But it's exciting, too! It's fun seeing new places, meeting you people. Branell will be an adventure for you, if only you give yourself a chance to see it that way."

"Do you like Infernus?"

Weston grinned. "Absolutely! I'll sure miss it when I'm gone, and doubt if I'll ever make it this way, again. As it is, I'm sworn to secrecy, and can never speak of Infernus, except to those on a need-to-know basis. Most Embrians know nothing of Infernus. If I have a say in the matter, that will never change . . ."

It was in the early hours of the next day. The sun peeked over the horizon. Bright hues of red, yellow, and orange reflected across the Agron Ocean. The cool, damp, dewy chill of morning would soon give way to the searing heat of midday. All was quiet.

Two twelve-foot launches from the Roderick Dundee rowed from the tiny village of New Merieko toward the deep, dark woods of Infernus' northeastern peninsula, where few vessels dared approach.

It wasn't unusual for boats to disappear without a trace, in these waters. Ships once manned by huge crews were found empty, desolate, lifeless. There were often signs of a struggle, spots of blood, severed arms, heads, and legs. Those stepping aboard those ghost ships usually found a scene mired in violent, gruesome, horrific death.

It never paid to enter Infernus' northeastern peninsula. Winged critters were known to attack sailing ships, not for the wealth of material goods or equipment . . .

But for human flesh.

The two launches neared the peninsula. This wasn't a social call. It didn't involve exploration, diplomacy, or study. It was to remove a threat, a curse, a menace.

Among those in this "mission" was a man of nefarious character named McCoy, a Kuschan holy man named Yevgeny, a couple of dozen men from the Roderick Dundee . . . and a fifteen-year-old kid named Fernandez.

It was nearly impossible to get Fernandez away from his folks. And yet, he snuck away from Frida and Paolo's protection, to join in this hazardous undertaking.

In the dreary, hazy hours of dawn, two launches from the Roderick Dundee picked up Yevgeny, Fernandez, and a couple of other guys named Boutwell and Justice, then headed to the dark, mysterious peninsula. Their goal was to hunt and kill abarbeaus . . . along with green, winged monstrosities.

Forget that the "winged monstrosities" was on Infernus, long before people got there. In the mind of Yevgeny, this mission was of great importance. No one involved in this task quite knew the dangers awaiting them. Most of these men had never saw an abarbeaus or a winged man. Still, they felt endangered by critters who bore more than a passing resemblance to Soraq.

Some of these men, hardened by years of brutality and piracy on the open seas, thought this day's work would be fun. They laughed and carried on like they'd enjoy wiping out the abominations. Not only would they take body parts to keep as souvenirs, but brag and boast of their misdeeds over gallons of ale in some low-life, flea-bitten dive in the port cities of Merieko, Sykes, or St. Alexandrov.

Fernandez didn't know whether to be more scared of the winged demons, or of McCoy. Days before, McCoy kidnapped children from New Merieko, including Fernandez, the tattooed boy Paransky, and a Kuschan lad who, after running into the woods, was never seen nor heard from again.

Fernandez was a scaredy-cat, a momma's boy, and a sissy. He hoped that, by joining Yevgeny in this act of war against winged demons and abarbeaus, he'd prove his courage and manhood.

So, why did Yevgeny trust a filthy little cutthroat like McCoy, who was no friend to New Merieko? Why fall in line with pirates and kidnappers?

When Fernandez put this question to Yevgeny, the pastor simply smiled, toyed with his trusty dagger, and said, "The enemy of my enemy is my friend . . . for now."

Minutes after sunrise, the two launches made a slow, sneaky trip to the shores of the northeastern peninsula. The nearer they got to the beach, the more scared Fernandez got. He had already saw a few of the Green Winged Men with McClusky. No matter how creepy the Browns was, them Greens was downright sinister and demonic!

Fernandez' heart raced, as panic swept over him. He wished he would've stayed in New Merieko or, better yet, in Agron!

If Yevgeny was scared, he never showed it. Rather, he smiled in anticipation of reaching the peninsula, where the winged demons lived. His eyes revealed an excitement and eagerness to do what he believed was right.

Where Fernandez once felt good about Yevgeny, he now felt intimidated by him. Yevgeny rarely spoke of his sadness for Pavel-Ivanovich. He regarded such sentiments as weak and unmanly. He wanted to answer Pavel's death, not with tears or fond memories, but with the spilling of blood.

Fernandez's hands clutched onto the edges of the launch. He tightened his grip, as the knuckles turned white and boney. The last thing he wanted to do was to get off the launch and engage an enemy so heinous and unspeakable as to chill the blood. He should've stayed in New Merieko with his folks! His stomach had been tied in knots since he first set foot on the island. He thought he was going to vomit, but was even too scared to do that!

The night before, Frida had prepared a delicious pie from the fruit trees around New Merieko. The family savored that treat, in celebration of surviving the abarbeaus attack. Occasionally, Frida's eyes met her little Nandy's. Her smile spoke of endless love and devotion to the boy. Later, mother and son shared a quiet moment at the small cot where Fernandez slept. As Nandy rested his head against Frida, she affectionately caressed his thin frame, and long brown hair. She smothered him with kisses, as the two enjoyed the gentle breeze of Infernus at sundown.

Once Nandy crawled into bed, Frida tucked him in, then gave him a goodnight smooch. She blew out the candle, and left her "sweet little Nandy" alone in the dark . . .

. . . in the worst place on Earth . . .

. . . Infernus . . .

Fernandez never slept a wink that night. In the wee hours of dawn, Yevgeny would arrive to collect him. Every sound kept him awake, whether it was leaves rustling in the wind, somebody walking past the hut, or a critter snooping around. He wondered what kind of a mess he was getting into by joining Yevgeny in killing winged men. The small cot was no sanctuary, but a torture chamber where the mind became its own worst enemy.

There was no point in sleeping. Every time Fernandez closed his eyes, his imagination ran wild. He suffered terrible visions of getting captured, killed, and ate by critters or winged demons. He lied there in the dark, unable to sleep. He dreaded the night, but loathed what the day brung.

Before sunrise, Fernandez caught sight of Yevgeny's silhouette standing in the open doorway of the hut. Fernandez quietly slipped out of the sack, as to not disturb his parents. His hands shook mercilessly, and made getting dressed nearly impossible.

Fernandez went outside, just to get bawled out by Yevgeny for wearing a school uniform of the Brotherhood Church, which lacked pants or tights to protect the legs from thick foliage and harsh elements.

"These are the only clothes I got!" moped Fernandez.

"You and your folks came all this way, and they didn't have the good sense to give you better clothes than that?" whispered Yevgeny, angrily.

Fernandez shrugged. There was no point in explaining. Words would only bring on a worse brow-beating from Yevgeny.

Yevgeny sighed, in disdain. Still, he asked for and got Fernandez' help. He patted the boy's back, then headed toward the beach where they were joined by two newcomers to the island, Boutwell and Justice.

Boutwell and Justice had spent ten years working as accountants for a wealthy Agronian merchant. The two men were cooped up in a tight, musty, claustrophobic office, adding up the merchant's growing wealth and good fortune.

The more money the merchant made, the more frustrated and annoyed Boutwell and Justice got, cooped up in a tight, claustrophobic office, away from clean air and sunshine. And people. And adventure. And from a life the two men spoke of, but never lived.

That was, until they quit their jobs, got on the first boat leaving Merieko, and found themselves on the faraway island of Infernus.

Both men were bachelors, in their early thirties. Justice was a squat, heavyset man with lousy eyesight and a thick, black beard, graying at the chin. Boutwell was tall and thin, with muscular arms despite spending long hours hunched over a desk. The two men yearned for a new life in a new land, and thought they found it in New Merieko.

Now, they were on their way to fight for their new land, against a foe they were totally oblivious of. Both men figured that the day would add up to nothing more or nothing less than a good laugh.

Fernandez wondered if he was the only one on the launch who was scared. The other men showed no fear, whatsoever. They casually laughed and joked amongst themselves. A few thought this mission carried honor and virtue. Some wanted to get even for what happened to their fellow crewmates, who made the mistake of messing with Mucker and McClusky. Everybody heard how the Green Winged Men hauled the crewmens' bodies off . . . then ate them.

Anything that disgusting, horrid, and bloodthirsty had to die!

Kill 'em! Kill 'em all! Kill all them filthy monsters!

And when we cleared out them green-hided freaks, we'll go after the brown ones in Persis!

Fernandez sat quietly in the launch, surrounded by the roughest, toughest, orneriest bunch of swashbucklers and buccaneers he'd ever seen. It wasn't yet sunrise, and already them fellas drank rum, beer, and brandy. They were sweaty, unkempt men with unshaven faces and bad teeth.

Fernandez felt like a fool around these scallywags, dressed in a silly school uniform with its skullcap and tunic which bared his scrawny, hairless legs, pocked by goosebumps from the cool, damp morning air. He wanted to think that he was doing the right thing. Not only would he prove his manhood and courage, he'd save the lives of his friends and neighbors in New Merieko. This, for his dear mother and father, who sacrificed so much for him! If he really was a man, shouldn't he demonstrate his love to Paolo and Frida, by eliminating that which brought evil and misery to the island?

What about all those people in Persis who got along with the Brown Winged Men? They had learned to live and work together, without conflict!

Men like Leader Rey . . .

But what if Rey was in league with Soraq, because he either knew no better, or because he fell under a demonic spell? Fernandez kind of liked Rey, and looked forward to Sunday service with him. But not with the winged men! The fact that winged men attended the Brotherhood Church in Persis only meant that Fernandez should not, could not, would not worship under that same roof!

What if Rey was evil, and his followers in Persis were under a spell of evil? What if there was so much evil on Infernus that it couldn't possibly be stamped out, without a bloodbath?

Infernus is evil . . .

Infernus is Hell . . .

Fernandez viewed this mission, not as an act of heroism or altruism, but rather a doomed enterprise where everyone would die. He stared at Yevgeny, in a silent plea to turn the launches around and rush home to New Merieko.

Yevgeny recognized fear in Fernandez. He'd seen it in the cowardly members of the Kuschan Underground, fighting against Embrians in Anumun. Yevgeny never tolerated cowardice in his Kuschan brethren and refused to take it from Fernandez. This was war! In war, there was no room for weak nerves, indecisive minds, or chicken hearts! Fernandez displayed his true self against the abarbeaus. Now, he had to fight the agents of Soraq . . . or die valiantly in the attempt!

"Yeh . . . Yeh . . . Yevgeny," stuttered Fernandez. "I wanna . . . I wanna . . . I wanna go home . . ."

"There's no turning back, damn you!" cursed Yevgeny. "Can I count on your help in this crucial hour? Or must I slit your throat, then dump you overboard?"

Fernandez shook his head. "But . . ."

"Are you with me, or are you going to hide behind your mother's skirt?" questioned Yevgeny. "Answer me! Are you with me . . . or not?"

Those witnessing this exchange reacted with hearty laughter, or sympathized with Fernandez but never said so.

"Cheer up, lad!" snickered Justice, wearing an annoying grin which exposed his crooked, black teeth. "We're here to save you!"

The other men laughed.

"What's your answer?" demanded Yevgeny. "Are you a man, or a mouse? Can I count on your help . . . or must I cut you out of the equation?"

Humiliation battled against fear. Fernandez couldn't win. His only choice was to face adversity, bravely. No longer could he handle the sting of being a scaredy-cat, a momma's boy, a sissy! He had to prove his worth, his courage, his manhood . . . not only to Yevgeny and those on the launch, but to himself!

It might very well be the last thing he'd ever do . . .

Once the launches reached the shoreline, the men collected their weapons and provisions. Some rushed inland to meet up with the critters they never once saw before, then kill them. Fernandez studied these men. They wasn't afraid of nothing, as far as he could tell. Instead, they made jokes of the strange critters they were going to encounter, before killing them. What did they have to fear from hairy apes, Green Winged Men, or Vic McClusky?

"Don't go too far ahead," said McCoy, fetching a sword from the launch. "Wait for the rest of us!"

No one obeyed McCoy. Instead, they armed themselves with bows, arrows, pikes, and swords. Grinning, they voiced their bravado and mean-spirited humor at their buddies. Lacking hesitation or forethought, they eagerly entered the deep, dark woods.

"Bloody fools," groaned McCoy. The little cutthroat threw in with Yevgeny, to redeem himself with Stossee. The last thing he wanted was to have Captain Slane report his blunders to the notorious pirate king. It was McCoy's idea heading to Infernus, on Stossee's support and subsidy. Therefore, he had to make good that day. He had a lot riding on this endeavor, which mirrored the distressed look on his face.

Fernandez reluctantly got off the launch. A breeze swept in from the ocean, as a flock of birds squawked overhead.

"I know you're afraid," Yevgeny whispered to Fernandez. "But fear not! If we are to die, it is the will of the Kuen and not us to decide such matters!"

Fernandez didn't say nothing. Yevgeny's confidence failed to ease his mind.

"Remember that what we do here benefits us all," added Yevgeny, giving Fernandez a dagger. "This is a noble quest, pleasing to God and the Kuen!"

Fernandez took the dagger and gulped. The weapon would do him no good. He was venturing into Hell, and was as good as dead.

Yevgeny grabbed onto Fernandez's arm, and led him forward into the darkness. "Earn your keep," he ordered. "Don't you dare run out on me."

Fernandez wasn't the only one scared. McCoy was also leery of what lay ahead. Despite his tough talk, posturing, and idle threats, he was more scared than Fernandez. It wasn't his behavior to reveal this, but rather his nervous eyes.

Once McCoy realized that Fernandez was staring at him, he got all weird and paranoid. "What the hell are you looking at, you filthy wretch?" he cursed, high-pitched and jittery. "I'll cut your guts out, the next time you give me those sad eyes!"

"You even think about hurting Fernandez," Yevgeny warned McCoy, "I'll hurt you, instead."

McCoy swallowed.

Yevgeny marched onward, into the deep, dark, murky woods. Hesitantly, McCoy and Fernandez took the rear.

McCoy hid his fear behind loud, blustery ramblings and threats of violence. He made no effort in keeping his voice down, or to keep his eyes peeled for trouble. It was no secret how Fernandez felt. As the three men entered a narrow pathway, he questioned if anyone would live for much longer.

Few of the pirates ahead refused to stay quiet. As a whole, they remained jovial. Who among them took this mission seriously? They were confident in their abilities to easily wipe out any and all opposition, and looked forward in returning to the Roderick Dundee, where they'd feast on fish and rotgut whiskey.

McCoy evaluated the character of Pastor Yevgeny. He had never met anyone more determined and fanatical to enter a fight against an unknown foe. McCoy had a fierce reputation, by slicing mens' throats in their sleep. He figured that Yevgeny might very well have been the most bloodthirsty person in this small contingency. Who could say how many men had fallen under Yevgeny's blade, when he was a child fighting Embrians in northern Kusch?

These weren't Embrians that Yevgeny was after now, but something far more hideous, cruel, and savage than anything found on God's Good Earth! Embrians never carried poison darts and blowguns! Embrians can't fly!

And Embrians don't eat people!

The first fatalities occurred less than a quarter of a mile from shore, when frantic shouting, hollering, and screaming sounded from the woods ahead.

Fernandez tried to sprint back to the launches. Angrily, Yevgeny pushed him onward . . .

. . . Until they reached the scene of a nightmare.

Boutwell made the error of standing too close to a tree, as he sipped from a rusty flask and boasted of his good fortune. Grinning from ear-to-ear, he handed the liquor to a hunchbacked carpenter from the Roderick Dundee.

That very moment, a kid abarbeaus landed on Boutwell's shoulder. Boutwell fell to his knees. Moments later, his steaming intestines scattered across the narrow, winding trail. A second abarbeaus, just weaned off of its mother tit, tore into Boutwell's face.

As Fernandez, Yevgeny, and McCoy arrived, they could see Boutwell's rotting teeth through a gaping hole in his cheek. The louder Boutwell shrieked, the meaner and nastier the abarbeaus got.

Boutwell's cries were forever silenced, as he was quickly torn to bits.

Justice had no intentions of saving Boutwell. He only wished to save himself.

As Justice watched Boutwell getting ate, his screeches more than matched his dying partner's. Wild-eyed, he never bothered asking for an invitation to high-tail it out of there.

Justice tackled Fernandez as he ran, screaming, toward the launches. Fernandez landed butt-first into the trail, with the wind knocked out of him. Justice practically ran over him in this escape.

Justice soon joined Boutwell in the Hereafter, as a grown-up abarbeaus pounced on him. Before Justice could fight back or protest in high-pitched howls, the abarbeaus chomped into his jugular vein.

Justice performed a bizarre, dance-like routine, as blood sprayed in all directions. A second abarbeaus jumped right in the middle of him. Justice flew backwards, squalling to the top of his lungs.

Those same lungs were fought over by the two ferocious abarbeaus.

The other men stood back. They were split between helping the two accountants, watching in horror, or fleeing. A young man from the Roderick Dundee broke out in cackling, hysterical laughter . . . then cried like a baby.

A few men turned to McCoy and Yevgeny, seeking answers. Meanwhile, Fernandez lay motionless on the ground, gasping for air.

A third man, then a fourth, were attacked. Within seconds, they too were rendered to piles of flesh, bones, and innards, spread all over the place.

That did it. Whatever brave, noble, foolhardy, or stupid notions these men had about facing critters were now replaced by calls of self-preservation. Facades of courage gave way to terror, as everyone dashed to the launches.

During this mad rush to the beach, three more men became meals for the fierce, ape-like critters.

McCoy got to the beach, in time to see a half-dozen men rowing away from the shore, on their way to the Roderick Dundee. "Bloody cowards!" he cursed. It came out more like a whine, than an insult. "I'll kill you wretched whore-mongers! I swear, I'll kill you!"

A brown-skinned archer from the high-mountain steppes of Vladistan began firing arrows at those chicken-hearted pirates, heading toward the ship.

One of the pirates who rowed away got nailed with two of the Vladistani's arrows. As he lay dying, he dropped both oars which floated away, from the launch. This left his two buddies drifting helplessly, without a paddle. With no other choice, they staged a desperate battle with the Vladistani archer.

A volley of arrows soon zipped back and forth, across the water.

A stray arrow from the launch missed McCoy's pencil-thin mustache by mere inches . . . yet struck the guy next to him in the throat.

This short-lived conflict ended abruptly, as a loud, flapping noise echoed from up above.

Green Winged Men.

For the exception of Fernandez, Yevgeny, or McCoy, none of these men had laid eyes upon a winged man . . . until now.

Those on the launches made more urgent attempts to get away. Lacking protection or cover, they were open targets for the winged men's darts. Those lacking paddles were especially vulnerable, as they turned their arrows toward this new enemy. These were scatter-brained efforts at best, as their arrows missed the oncoming foe.

The winged men, their numbers exceeding twenty, rained darts upon the men in the launches. Within seconds, all had been hit, and died slowly from the venom speeding through their bloodstream.

One man leaped into the water, and swam for shore.

He soon got swallowed up by a humongous, otter-like sea mammal . . .

The winged men lifted these new victims from the launches in their taloned feet, and rushed them to their caves. More winged men then arrived to pursue those pirates remaining on shore.

"Mother of God!" screamed McCoy, as everyone scattered like terrified rodents.

Yevgeny refused to surrender, and did not tolerate Fernandez's cries to absent, ineffectual parents. He was determined to save the sensitive, Agronian schoolboy, as well as himself. "Let's go!" he ordered, taking Fernandez by the arm.

Fernandez faced Yevgeny, tears in his eyes.

"Are you a man, or a mouse?" shouted Yevgeny. "Will you stand up and fight, or let them take you?"

Fernandez struggled to speak. It came out as whines and gibberish.

Yevgeny led Fernandez away from the beach, in a mad sprint back into the woods.

Fernandez and Yevgeny heard ear-shattering howls and hollers from up ahead. The pirates were picked off, one-by-one, by the Green Winged Men. Yevgeny had no idea where he was going, through a twisted maze of foliage, decaying logs, and trees. His survival skills and smarts motivated him to head north, toward New Merieko.

"What the bloody hell plan is this?" a voice called out, in the murky darkness.

McCoy staggered blindly through thick brush toward Fernandez and Yevgeny. "Bet you never prepared yourself for this, did you?" he commented, his voice hoarse and raspy. "You were the one who got us into this bloody mess!"

"You're right, I did," said Yevgeny, maintaining poise and confidence. "And I plan to get us out of here, if you keep your mouth shut so we don't get caught . . ."

"What difference does it make?" bawled McCoy. "We're dead . . ."

"Are you dead now?" questioned Yevgeny, defiantly.

No answer.

"Are you dead now?" repeated Yevgeny, more assertive than before.

"N . . . no," stuttered McCoy, sounding more like a confused adolescent, than a cutthroat and a bandit.

"Where there's life, there's hope," said Yevgeny. "Do you follow me and live, or stand around like a crybaby and get eaten?"

McCoy shrugged his shoulders. "I . . . I . . ."

"Shut your mouth!" commanded Yevgeny. "And maybe we'll live!"

Silently, the three men zig-zagged through the woods. They were uncertain of their path, yet made considerable distance. Occasionally, they heard the flap of wings from above. The Green Winged Men searched for them, blowguns at the ready. The three men remained in the more shaded spots of the deep, overgrown forest, to avoid detection.

Nestled against a steep, rocky hillside, were the caves of the Green Winged Men.

In a desolate, swampy area not far from their domains, a number of winged men slaughtered the pirates they had just captured and killed.

This was the most unspeakable, hideous sight that the three remaining men had ever laid eyes upon. Yevgeny and McCoy had witnessed or participated in their share of bloodletting. This scene went far beyond what either experienced in the past.

The pirates hung upside down from ropes and pulleys, treated as farm animals at butchering time. Their skin was literally peeled from their still-warm bodies, as little winged kids looked on in anticipation and delight. A gut pile was stacked in a shaded spot, as winged women removed hearts, livers, and kidneys.

The pirates' severed heads rested upon bloodied pikes, a few yards above the ground. Flies buzzed around these sickening trophies. The smell was excruciating, nauseating, and overbearing in the morning sun.

Near the entrance of one cave, Vic McClusky sipped a bottle of expensive Campens Rose', and shared a laugh or two with his two winged buddies, Ricardo and Ugo.

Fernandez shrieked.

This racket caught the attention and ire of the winged men. Several sprang into action and took flight.

McCoy slugged Fernandez in the nose.

Fernandez flew backwards and slammed into twigs and dirt. Blood trickled from his nostrils, as tears smeared his face like rainwater.

"Bloody damned fool!" cussed McCoy. "You want to get us all killed? . . ."

McCoy's sentence was cut short, as Yevgeny pierced his chest with the trusty dagger.

McCoy staggered sideways, staring at Yevgeny in mute denial. He opened his mouth to protest. Instead, blood gurgled from his mouth.

Yevgeny lifted Fernandez up and ran away. Meanwhile, scores of winged men gathered around McCoy.

In his final seconds, McCoy screamed as the monstrosities added him to their meals.

Yevgeny knew that his efforts to kill the winged demons was a failure. He was far from apologetic about it. Instead, he figured that this event would only further animosities against the winged men. In an odd sort of way, this disaster may be more consequential than anyone ever imagined!

Nearly two-hundred yards from the Greens' caves, Fernandez and Yevgeny huddled together behind a thick, darkened clump of trees.

"Why?" gasped Fernandez, fighting to catch his breath. "Why did you? . . ."

"McCoy?" asked Yevgeny, lacking emotion. "He served his purpose, and I had no more use for him. The enemy of my enemy is my friend." Yevgeny snickered. "He was no longer a friend."

"What?"

"Look at it this way . . . Those freaks have him cooking over their flames, and not us."

Fernandez' eyes widened.

"Oh, stop it!" griped Yevgeny, in annoyance. "Don't tell me that you care."

"What are we doing?" sobbed Fernandez. "Why did we come here?"

"To protect and defend those we love! Our friends and family . . . the men, women, and children of New Merieko. Can't you see? We're fighting for them!"

From overhead came the sounds of flapping wings . . .

Yevgeny and Fernandez looked skyward to see a couple of winged men scouring the landscape. Yevgeny placed his hand over Fernandez's mouth. "Keep still!" he whispered, reaching for a sword slung over one shoulder.

"Yevgeny . . ."

"Shh . . ."

"Yevgeny . . ." repeated Fernandez, frantically.

Yevgeny spotted a bright orange, cat-sized critter coming toward him and Fernandez. The critter had thick, straight hair and two long, saber-shaped teeth sticking from its bottom jaw. It cautiously approached the two men and snarled.

The critter slowly stepped toward Fernandez, and sniffed his bare leg. Yevgeny and Fernandez was probably the first two people it ever saw. It was equally curious and intimidated by them.

The critter licked Fernandez' shin, just below the knee. This bizarre sensation tickled Fernandez' leg. Fernandez wasn't laughing because of it.

Yevgeny tossed a couple of small stones at the critter, to shoo it away.

The critter forgot all about Fernandez, and stared at Yevgeny. It revealed its sharp teeth and fangs, as the hair on its back and neck bristled.

Yevgeny carefully swatted at the critter. In turn, the critter snapped at Yevgeny's hands, in agitation and annoyance.

"Get back!" whispered Yevgeny, urgently. "Go on! . . . Get out of . . ."

The critter took a bite out of Yevgeny's fingers, and clamped down as hard as it could.

Fernandez screamed . . . but not near as loud as Yevgeny.

In pain and defiance, Yevgeny slammed his free hand, over and over, into the critter's furry spine. Still, the critter refused to let go, and was more determined than ever to take Yevgeny's fingers as a prize.

The Green Winged Men heard the two men's shrieks, and were upon them.

"Help get this thing off of me!" cried Yevgeny, as a winged man landed just feet away.

Yevgeny managed to shake the critter loose from his hand, by inadvertently sent it into the winged man's face.

The critter hissed and howled, as it landed on the winged man. Furiously, it tore into the winged man's face.

The unsuspecting winged man dropped his blowgun and staggered backwards. With extreme ferocity, the critter scratched and chomped and bit into his nose, eyes, and cheeks.

The pain in Yevgeny's hand was nothing to compare with thoughts of getting ate. Drawing the sword from its sheath, he let out with a slew of Kuschan swear words, then charged at the winged man who got his face bit and scratched up by the critter. With all his might, he swung the sword with one bold sweep, and decapitated the winged man.

The critter latched onto the winged man's head as it impacted the ground, then ran like greased lightning, someplace off into the woods.

Fernandez followed Yevgeny through a chaotic jumble of evergreen trees and thick brush. Tears clouded his vision. Death awaited him at every turn. No way could he escape it!

Fernandez's thoughts were of his parents, which he'd never see again. By now, Frida and Paolo were worried sick over their Nandy, who left the hut while they were asleep. It was wrong, indeed stupid, to join Yevgeny and the others in this reckless quest!

Anxiety, fatigue, and fear took their toll on Fernandez. Images of getting hung and quartered by the freaks haunted him. No matter. Yevgeny refused to let Fernandez give up, or give in.

That was, until they came to a steep cliff, overlooking a swift-moving river which spanned a distance of more than sixty yards across.

Yevgeny considered on taking his chances by jumping into the river below, and swim to safety. He had no idea how deep the current was, or if he'd break both legs in a shallow, rocky bottom.

Fernandez glanced over at Yevgeny and whimpered.

"If we're to die," commented Yevgeny, "we have the chance to die like men, with our heads up."

"I . . . I don't want to die!" wept Fernandez.

"We all have to die," said Yevgeny, concealing his own dread under an angry facade. "Will you meet your maker bravely, or like a yellow-bellied dog?"

Fernandez' lips quivered. All was lost. Never again would he see his folks. Nor would he gaze upon the bright moonlight of a summer's evening, or experience the pains and pleasures of his first crush. Never again would he spend a Sunday afternoon window shopping with his beloved mother on the narrow, cobblestone streets of Merieko.

Unable to speak, Fernandez tried to face the end courageously, but knew he'd do so like a coward.

Fernandez and Yevgeny spotted a pale white winged man, flying alone above the river. Fernandez recognized him as Malachi, the oldest son of the Brown Winged Man's head honcho, Chief Lorenzo.

Although he was almost as scared of the Browns as he was of the Greens, Fernandez knew he had to trust Malachi. "Here!" he shouted, waving his arms above his head. "Here! Over here!"

Yevgeny resented Fernandez for seeking safety and shelter from another member of an evil race. He even thought of killing Malachi, once the young winged man arrived.

That was, until he hatched an idea in order to grant Fernandez a longer life.

Habitually. Malachi scoured the northeastern peninsula. He went out of his way to spy on the Greens, and make sure they weren't up to something. Although the Greens disliked this constant intrusion, they got used to it and no longer viewed it as a threat.

Malachi landed a few feet from Fernandez and Yevgeny, at the cliff's edge. He was shocked to see the two men in the peninsula.

"What are you doing here?" he asked, keeping a close, careful eye on Yevgeny.

"I haven't the time nor the inclination to explain myself to the likes of you," said Yevgeny, pointing his dagger at Malachi. "Get Fernandez out of here, and I'll spare you. If you don't, I'll kill you right where you stand."

Malachi looked at Yevgeny, in confusion.

"Get Fernandez out of here!" repeated Yevgeny, with growing urgency.

"What about you?" asked Malachi, as scores of Green Winged Men flew toward him and the two men.

"Too late," said Yevgeny, knowing what his decision meant. His voice jittery and shrill, he added, "Get the boy to Persis, before I cut your stinking gizzard out!"

Malachi lifted Fernandez in his arms, and hastily took flight.

Fernandez was scared, but understood that leaving with Malachi was his only option. He took one last look at Yevgeny, who stood alone at the cliff.

Malachi spread his wings out and made a speedy trip toward Persis.

Yevgeny forced a grin on his face, as the Green Winged Men neared him. He held his trusty dagger firmly in his right hand, determined to use it one last time. He fought off thoughts of being torn to shreds, his head resting upon a pike as a sickening gift to germ-infested flies.

What point was there in worrying, now? Yevgeny would soon take a cherished place in Paradise, his reward for service and devotion to the Kuen.

Yevgeny soon found himself surrounded by a large number of the mangy, green freaks. He thought about denying their pleasure of eating him, by leaping into the river below. But, before dying, he wished to express his true feelings toward them. He might even take a few with him, as he traveled the unknown path to Death. He knew he did right, by picking a fight with them in the first place!

As the freaks eagerly neared him, Yevgeny laughed in anticipation of carving them up with the trusty dagger. Was he afraid? Naturally. Would fear defeat him, as the Greens robbed him of his earthly life?

Hell, no!

Among the freaks was two of Vic McClusky's favorites, Ricardo and Ugo. Both sneered real mean and ugly at Yevgeny, as only Green Winged Men could sneer.

Yevgeny grinned. "It may interest you to know that I do this in the name and honor of New Merieko," he said, calmly.

Then, drawing back his trusty dagger, he drove it straight into Ugo's scaly chest.

The other Greens responded by firing dozens of poison darts into Yevgeny's torso . . .

Yevgeny staggered like a drunk, as his entire body grew numb. His thoughts turned chaotic, disoriented, and silly. He awkwardly removed the dagger from Ugo's now dead shell, stepped toward Ricardo, and fell to the ground.

Yevgeny chuckled as Ricardo retrieved the trusty dagger from his hand.

He then felt the sharpened steel of his own weapon, as it entered his right lung. He struggled to spit into Ricardo's face. It shot out in a geyser of blood from his mouth.

As everything grew dark around him, Yevgeny laughed at his own peril.

Seconds later, he screamed as his beating heart was literally ripped out of his chest . . .

* * * * *

The Kuschan warship Matyushenko patrolled the waters off the northeastern peninsula of Infernus. Commander Antonov stood watch on deck. Even with a brisk wind sweeping in from Mount Auric, it was a warm, humid day.

Antonov removed his cap to wipe the sweat pouring from his forehead. He kept his eyes peeled for unauthorized vessels in the vicinity. He was uneasy and tense, but never understood why. He had trouble sleeping the night before, and had real bad dreams. Fatigue got the best of him.

Antonov peeked through a spyglass and caught sight of another ship, far in the distance. Excitement engulfed him. This beat the slow, painfully dull monotony of the day . . . even if it potentially involved a fight.

With his heart beating rapidly, Antonov ordered the navigator to change course. His mouth grew dry as he nearly dropped the spyglass onto the hardwood surface of the deck.

The Roderick Dundee . . .

"Lieutenant Arkoff!" shouted Antonov, with a sly half-grin.

"Sir!" Arkoff called out, joining Antonov on the quarterdeck.

Arkoff was a short, baby-faced young man with coal-black hair and small, squinty eyes. He wasn't yet twenty, but already commanded the Matyushenko's Naval Infantry. He was a novice when it came to warfare, and had conflicting emotions of anticipation and apprehension. Antonov doubted if Arkoff had ever shaven in his entire life.

"Is that what I think it is?" Antonov pointed at the second ship, handing Arkoff the spyglass.

"Sir . . . it's the Roderick Dundee," reported Arkoff. His appearance resembled that of an adolescent, and not a grown man, as he peeked through the spyglass.

"Are you sure?" asked Antonov, slugging the palm of one hand.

"Sure, I'm sure!" chuckled Arkoff. A toothy grin highlighted his boyish face. "There it is, sir . . . the Roderick Dundee. I'm guessing four, five leagues off the starboard bow."

"Excellent job, Lieutenant Arkoff," commented Antonov. "Are you and your men ready for a brawl?"

"Sir, my men have never been readier for a brawl than they are now!" claimed Arkoff.

"Well, they better be ready for a brawl, because that's what they're going to get!"

"Are we going after the Roderick Dundee, sir?"

"Why not? Its crew aren't men at all, but animals. They pose a threat to every honest sailor between here and the continent, and it's our duty to put a halt to it. Do you agree, Lieutenant Arkoff?"

Arkoff smiled. "I do indeed, sir!"

"Very well. Form a boarding party, and we'll take the Roderick Dundee a prize. What do you have to say about that, Lieutenant Arkoff?"

"I'd say let's get it done, sir!"

Then get it done!" ordered Antonov. "Get the men together, make sure they're armed to the teeth!"

"Aye-aye, sir!" shouted Arkoff, eagerly following his orders.

Antonov bit his bottom lip. More than personal favor or a feather in his cap, he wanted to put an end to the Roderick Dundee's criminal activities. With luck, the Dundee would remain fully intact, and be won over with little sacrifice and blood.

Drummers onboard the Matyushenko rallied Kuschan Marines and infantrymen to do battle against a gang of scurvy buccaneers. Flags from the Matyushenko signaled the Roderick Dundee to throw down their arms and surrender.

Once again, Antonov peeked through the spyglass, and expected to see movement. He saw nothing. Nothing at all. No sign of life . . . as if the Roderick Dundee was abandoned.

"Enemy vessel on the starboard side," Antonov informed Admiral Vaslov, who joined him on deck. "Sir, it's the Roderick Dundee."

Vaslov grinned, excitedly. "Roderick Dundee?"

"Yes, sir," said Antonov. "I see no one onboard. Strange. Very strange."

"It's a trap," surmised Vaslov, taking the spyglass from Antonov to look for himself. He slowly examined the enemy ship from one end to the other. "They're lulling us into a false sense of security."

"Yes, sir."

"We've got a few tricks up our sleeves," said Vaslov, smugly. "They'll soon get a taste of Kuschan steel. Show no mercy, Commander Antonov. I see no cause in taking prisoners."

"Understood."

"Destroy those who won't be taken alive," ordered Vaslov. "Hang those who do. No one will miss that lowlife scum. Why feed or house them on our way home? They're not prisoners of war, but thieves, cutthroats, and brigands."

Antonov frowned. Vaslov made it sound easy . . . too easy. Yet, the admiral was right. Who on the Roderick Dundee deserved to live?

A man was more willing to fight dirty when death was at stake.

It wasn't a question in Antonov's mind of who'd win this upcoming skirmish. The Roderick Dundee had more men, the Matyushenko better ones. Those pirates were a callow, careless, arrogant lot, brutes who cared more about drinking and whoring than defending their own honor or countrymen. Those serving onboard the Matyushenko were well-trained and disciplined, and unafraid to die for king and country.

Or so Antonov wanted to think. He never got used to ideas of his crewmen dying at the hands of rabble, or having to say words over those who had fallen in war. Antonov gazed out at the faces of those about to challenge a worthy opponent. He knew that some would be slain. Briefly, he eyed young Lieutenant Arkoff, barking commands to older, experienced men, many twice his age. Arkoff was a fine officer, and thoughts of seeing him perish were unbearable.

No matter. Antonov wanted the Roderick Dundee with Kuschan colors waving over it. There would be blood, to help secure that goal. There'd always be blood.

"Understood, Admiral Vaslov," spoke Antonov, upholding a fearless demeanor on the eve of adversity.

"The Roderick Dundee sails under no nation's flag," said Vaslov. "We ruffle no diplomatic feathers by attacking them. Our work today supports not only us, but our new allies and trading partners in Persis."

Antonov snickered. "The winning of hearts and minds."

"Give them hell, Commander Antonov," said Vaslov, thrilled of the prospects of adding a new member to the Kuschan fleet. "Leave no one alive."

As the Matyushenko neared the Roderick Dundee, the silence was unnerving. There was little sound, other than waves crashing into the sides of the ship, seagulls calling overhead, and the wind. Antonov marveled at the Roderick Dundee's incredible size, with its four towering masts and length exceeding that of the Matyushenko. He was intimidated of swinging onboard that mighty vessel, and what he'd find once he got there. Still, he relished thoughts of such a large craft ultimately serving Kusch, and how proud she'd be doing so. She'd be christened with a new name, given a thorough going-over, and be refitted to suit Kuschan fighting men!

The one concerning thought running through Antonov's mind was the lack of movement and activity onboard the Roderick Dundee . . . and what it all meant.

"Roderick Dundee!" summoned Antonov, through a bullhorn. "Lower your sails, and surrender! We come to take your ship! Give up, and no one will be hurt!"

"They think," whispered Vaslov.

"They don't answer, sir."

"They'll answer soon enough. You and Lieutenant Arkoff will see to that, Commander Antonov."

"Aye, sir!" agreed Antonov, bravely.

"I know we haven't always seen eye-to-eye," said Vaslov, apologetically. "But I know you're a very capable officer, and an outstanding Kuschan. I promote you to captain, upon your victory over the Roderick Dundee. Good luck, Antonov!"

"Thank you, sir!" said Antonov, shaking Vaslov's hand. "No worries, Admiral! We'll make the Roderick Dundee sorry she came here!"

As the Matyushenko drew steadily closer to the Roderick Dundee, Antonov once more ordered the enemy to surrender. No reply. No refusals, no insults, no foul language stemmed from the opponent's deck. Only the sounds of wind beating against the red, canvas sails stated that the Roderick Dundee remained a living, viable ship, fraught with danger and menace. Silence was scarier than threats of death.

Antonov coped with overwhelming anticipation of a fight, along with realizations that some of his men would die. There was no getting past that. He wasn't afraid for his own well-being and safety. He'd been in worse scrapes against the Embrians! He thought only of each and every member of the Matyushenko. Still, he had men to lead! This was a fight to the death, and Antonov knew it wouldn't be grand or glorious!

It might very well be justified . . .

Well, to hell with it . . .

And to hell with the trash awaiting him onboard the Roderick Dundee!

Antonov ordered his boys to throw grappling hooks to the Roderick Dundee, swing across, and make swift work of the pirates. He whipped out his sword, waved it over his head, and joined his crewmates in this effort.

The men released loud, thunderous cheers, and did what they were told.

True to his devotion to the Matyushenko, Antonov was the first to swing out over the explosive waves below, onto a hostile deck. Arkoff was next to follow.

Both cried for their men to follow them.

The deck of the Roderick Dundee now swarmed with hearty Kuschan sailors, Marines, and naval infantrymen, eager to spill pirate blood!

Nothing.

No one one the Roderick Dundee was there to pick a fight, or deny commands to give up. As more and more Kuschans transferred from one ship to the other, they sprinted across the empty decks, their swords gleaming in the hot midday sun.

No enemy warrior was found topside of the desolate ship. There were, however, signs of blood trails and deep scratch marks, where someone dragged their fingernails against the hard wooden deck. Weapons of every imaginable sort were scattered here and there . . . . . including a blowgun.

A few feet from the open door of a stairway, leading to the ship's belly, was a severed arm . . .

"Everyone search downstairs," ordered Antonov. He eyed the missing body part, which crawled with flies, maggots, and other bugs. Though it made for a disgusting sight, Antonov had seen worse before. Not Lieutenant Arkoff, who threw up on the spit-shine of his black leather boots.

As the men cautiously entered the lower decks of the Roderick Dundee, Antonov grinned as he placed one hand upon Arkoff's back. "Are you going to be all right, Lieutenant?" he asked, struggling not to laugh.

Arkoff wiped bile from his lips, nodded YES, and gave Antonov two watery, embarrassed eyes.

"Carry on," said Antonov, pointing his sword to the doorway. "And do be careful. I know not what we may find . . ."

"Yes, sir," mumbled Arkoff, escorting Antonov into the Roderick Dundee's interior, where the other Kuschan officers and men dared to tread.

The mystery of the pirate ship's fate was solved down below, in a discovery which chilled the blood of those unfortunate enough to encounter it.

Spread all throughout the galley, mess hall, and sleeping quarters, were the grisly, disfigured, and dismembered heads of the Roderick Dundee's crew . . .

* * * * *

"So, young man," Rey said to Fernandez, in a tense voice. "What were you and Pastor Yevgeny doing in the peninsula?"

Malachi had just got back to Persis with Fernandez, who was still terrified from his morning with the abarbeaus and Green Winged Men. What began as a "grand adventure" and a calling of arms turned into a mess, where Fernandez alone survived.

Rey led Fernandez to the church's dining hall, where the Agronian schoolboy had a lunch of chicken noodle soup and goats' milk. Fernandez shook like a leaf, as he struggled to lift the spoon. His wide eyes and slurred, jittery speech told of unimaginable horrors.

Malachi told Rey what little he knew about finding Fernandez and Yevgeny on the cliff, overlooking a river. He also mentioned Yevgeny's nasty attitude and, in hushed tones, the pastor's death at the hands of the Green Winged Men.

People and Brown Winged folks used the church as a place to catch up with the latest gossip. That day, everybody's attention was on Fernandez, in his dirty, tattered school uniform. As everyone took quick glances at Fernandez, they whispered quietly among themselves.

Rey was equally concerned and frustrated. Concerned for Fernandez, and frustrated of the various stories and versions of an event, which no one fully knew, nor understood. As Fernandez finished the soup, Rey thought it best to get the boy alone, away from suspicious eyes and ears. More than anything, he wanted the truth.

Rey took Fernandez to his office at the end of a dark, narrow hallway. He calmly sat Fernandez in a chair, and looked him straight in the eye. "So, young man," he said. "What were you and Pastor Yevgeny doing in the peninsula?"

Fernandez gave Rey a perplexed, befuddled expression. Unable to speak, he merely shrugged his shoulders.

"What happened?" questioned Rey, forcefully.

Fernandez opened his mouth, but only a whimper came out. He shook uncontrollably, as tears dripped freely from the eyes.

"Don't give me that!" hollered Rey. He took a step toward Fernandez, then stopped. "Forgive me," he apologized. "But I want some answers, and I want them now. What were you and Yevgeny doing?"

Fernandez wouldn't say.

"What business did you have with the Green Winged Men?" pressed Rey. "I'm sure that's what you were doing, making contact with that tribe . . . or causing them trouble. Just what were you doing?"

"I told him I wouldn't say anything!" bawled Fernandez.

"Him? Yevgeny?"

Fernandez's darting eyes betrayed him.

"If you meant to bring harm upon the Green Winged Men, it may bring harm to us all," said Rey. "The Greens don't like anyone poking around their homes, and their reaction may cause more trouble than you can imagine. Who else was involved in this? Don't tell me you two walked all that way on foot. I'm sure you weren't there simply to wish the Greens well."

Fernandez shrugged.

"Don't lie to me," said Rey, slamming his fist to the desk. "You didn't go into the peninsula, just for the fun of it. What were you doing?"

Jeremy suddenly popped into the office with Paransky, the little tattooed boy.

Rey was already aggravated and stressed out. He lost plenty of sleep over Jeremy's inheritance, the boy's proposed marriage to Ericha, Randen's horrible death, and Jung-su's departure with 'No-Teeth' Murnau.

It pleased Rey when Jeremy wore nice clothes to meet with Errol, the day before. Now, his stepson was back to wearing that damned loincloth. Worse yet, Paransky was also dressed in a buckskin shirt and loincloth.

To Rey's animosity, Paransky's feet and legs were also "decorated" with tattoos!

"Look what me and Ericha did for Paransky!" laughed Jeremy. "What do you think?"

"You don't want to know what I think," mumbled Rey, leaning against the desk. The look on his face was scary.

Jeremy slowly backed out of the office. "Uh . . . I'll come back . . ." he mumbled, nervously. "Later?"

"Thanks, son," said Rey, tiredly. "Do come back, later. Much later."

"Later," said Jeremy. Closing the door behind him, he added, "Love you, Dad . . ."

"What did Pastor Yevgeny say to get you to follow him out there?" Rey sighed to Fernandez.

"He . . . he told me never to tell," stuttered Fernandez.

"I don't care what Yevgeny told you! He's not here, and for all we know he's dead!"

Fernandez sobbed.

"I don't mean to get angry with you," said Rey, impatiently. "But you must understand that Yevgeny and you violated an unmarked border, separating us from the Green Winged Men, so . . . Well, perhaps you're unaware of the severity in this matter, but let me tell you that everyone on this island, and I mean everyone, will feel the consequences of . . ."

"He said that the winged men were followers of Soraq," confessed Fernandez.

"That doesn't surprise me," said Rey, sitting behind the desk. "What else did he tell you?"

Fernandez shrugged.

"Come on!" snapped Rey, tiredly. "This is important. What else did Yevgeny tell you?"

"He . . . he said that the winged men can talk to animals, and that it was them who told the ape-things to attack us the other night . . ."

"And you believed him?"

Fernandez shrugged.

"All right," said Rey, angrily. "I want the truth, and I want it now. What were you and Yevgeny doing in the peninsula? If I find out you're lying to me, I'll . . . I'll . . . I'll bring my son in here to slap your face off, if I don't go right on ahead and do it myself!" Rey felt a bit embarrassed and humiliated by his idle threat against Fernandez. "What were you and Yevgeny doing in the peninsula?"

Fernandez refused to answer.

"Jeremy!" shouted Rey, his voice echoing throughout the church.

"Yevgeny wanted to start a war with the Green Winged Men!" cried Fernandez.

"A war?" gasped Rey. "Just the two of you?"

"No!"

"Who else was involved?"

"A couple of guys from New Merieko, and . . ." Fernandez clammed up.

"And?"

"And . . . and a bunch of guys from that pirate ship . . . the Roderick Dundee . . ." said Fernandez.

Rey sucked in a breath, and repeatedly counted to ten. If only he could contact Vic McClusky, before the more radical elements of the Greens' society decided to strike.

If it wasn't too late!

"What happened to those other men?" asked Rey, struggling to remain calm.

"Dead," mouthed Fernandez.

"What?"

"Dead," repeated Fernandez, his voice raspy and hoarse. "They're all dead."

"Any Green Winged Men killed in this exchange?"

Fernandez lowered his head.

"So you took it upon yourselves to start a war with the Green Winged

Men?" questioned Rey. "On the word of a fanatic? You started a war, all right! Who else is going to die, before it's all over?"

"You call for me?" asked Jeremy, wearing a silly grin as he entered the office.

"Jeremy," sighed Rey. "Go find Malachi, your cousin Weston . . . Errol, I suppose . . ." Rey bit his bottom lip. "And I guess you'd better fetch Mucker, too."

Jeremy smirked.

"Don't laugh, son," said Rey, pacing the floor. "This is no laughing manner. You might as well know that it also involves you and Ericha."

"What's going on?" asked Jeremy, nervously.

"That fool Yevgeny and a few other knotheads sneaked into the peninsula this morning," whispered Rey.

"What?" gasped Jeremy.

"Shh! All I know is that they started a fight with the Greens! The only one who got out alive is him." Rey pointed at Fernandez.

Jeremy's heart skipped a beat.

"Let's put our heads together and find a way to smooth things over with McClusky and the Green Winged Men," said Rey. "Do what I tell you. Go fetch Malachi, Weston . . . yes, and Errol, I suppose . . ."

"Mucker, too?"

"Yeah, Mucker, too. Get them over here." Rey patted Jeremy's shoulder. "No matter what, stay calm. If we're lucky, nothing will come of this. If were not . . . well, son, then it's the Devil to pay . . ."

* * * * *

It was a festive celebration at the Green Winged Mens camp, as they ate the bodies of the pirates they won over, from their sneak attack on the Roderick Dundee.

As the Greens fried meat over open fires or on spits, their victims' severed heads rested upon pikes . . . gruesome trophies to Yevgeny's hatred of a violent species.

The Greens lived in dark, damp, desolate caves and cool, shaded areas, often next to swamps. Their grub usually consisted of small critters, birds, bugs, and fish. They also ate plants and berries.

By far, their favorite food was people meat.

McClusky had allied himself to the Green Winged Men, not long after he first got to Infernus. He admired the Greens for their refusal to put up with crap.

In his mind, the Greens were the most perfect, well-suited critter on the whole entire island.

Life on Infernus was harsh, brutal, unpredictable, and savage. Such a description fit the Greens, right down to the teeth! Based on what happened that morning, the Greens proved they were at the top of Infernus' food chain. Farlanders thought they were in charge, and yet were no match to a critter who showed no hesitation nor conscience when it came to survival. Where a person might think twice when it came to killing, Greens went right on ahead to end the life of another critter . . . especially when self-preservation was at stake.

Abarbeaus never held back when it came to killing. They were just dumb beasts, and didn't know no better. All abarbeauses knew how to do was eat, sleep, poop, and make baby abarbeauses. That's as far as an abarbeaus went.

The Greens . . . they was thinking critters. They was aware of their own existences. They understood living and dying, and still placed their own living above that of other critters. They didn't give a hang if that other critter walked on two legs, wore clothes, or come from some other place than Infernus. Food was food, living was living, and survival was survival.

And when it come to living or dying, the Greens placed themselves and their own kind before anybody or anything else on Infernus.

At least the Greens shared their bounty equally among the other members of the tribe. Humans was known for their own greed, and ability to stick it to the other guy to get ahead. With that in mind, the Greens still put themselves at the top, when it come to all critters.

When Farlanders first got to Infernus, centuries ago, the Browns also had their wild, savage side to them. Years of living alongside Farlanders made them act more like people, than something belonging to the island. Humans was the worst thing that happened to the Brown Winged Men! After years and years of getting civilized, the Browns lost their equality with the Greens, and their advantage when it come to living and dying. Unfortunately, their allegiances to people made the Browns so weak, so trusting, so willing to tolerate breeches and insults! No wonder Mucker and Seely was at home with that bunch! Mucker's orneriness and mean-spirited nature put him in a position to bully-rag the Browns, and secure selfish motives. The Browns had lowered themselves to something not quite as low as an abarbeaus, but never as good as a person.

After years of dealing with Farlanders' crap, the Browns got tame . . .

They got docile . . .

They got stupid . . .

McClusky was an advisor, an ambassador, and a trusted advocate to the

Green Winged Men. He had argued for their rights, against the often hostile advances of Farlanders. He had just started a profitable diplomatic and trade agreement with Kusch. For this, the Greens happily accepted McClusky as one of their own. Never once had they even considered placing him on their dinner trays . . . As far as he knew . . .

As the Greens shared their kills within the tribe, McClusky had a meal of fried spuds and venison. He wasn't a cannibal, and never ever took a bite of people meat. He believed that the Greens' victims was deserving of their fate.

When he first joined up with the Greens, McClusky was sickened by the depravity and debauchery of watching people get cooked and ate in front of him. In time, he regarded people carcasses as he did any other dead critter.

In most ways, people was the lowest of the low.

McClusky envied the winged men. He dreamed of having the ability to take flight and explore the island, if only he could. How splendid it'd be to spread your wings, and examine uncharted regions of the island!

Based upon recommendations of winged men, along with accounts of the more daring human explorers, there were sections of Infernus few men entered. Still, McClusky remained curious of undiscovered country, down south.

His wishes to check out the mysterious regions were only that . . .

Wishes . . .

A number of Green Winged Men returned to the tribe, carrying the remains of McCoy and Yevgeny . . . along with the bodies of Ugo, and another winged man who was minus a head.

While a few Greens were thrilled to see more grub for their bountiful feast, others were upset that it came at a terrible price. McClusky regarded Ugo as among his favorites, and one of the few Greens who talked good Embrian.

Ricardo made mention of Yevgeny's words that his attack on the Greens was on behalf of New Merieko. Therefore, he proposed to attack the small village.

"No, Ricardo," said McClusky, keeping his cool despite the growing anger within the Green tribe. "Whatever you do, don't attack New Merieko . . ."

"Why not?" growled Ricardo, his crazed eyes seething with rage.

"There are Kuschans living in New Merieko," explained McClusky. "You start trouble there, it'll undo our agreements with Admiral Vaslov and Commander Antonov . . ."

"Forget your agreements!" snapped Ricardo, baring his long, jagged teeth. "Two of our brothers are dead, 'in the name and honor of New Merieko'. I say that, in our name and honor, we kill every man, woman, and child in New Merieko!"

"And I say no!" hollered McClusky. "Look, I know you're upset about Ugo. So am I." McClusky pointed a finger at Ricardo's face. "But this is no time for rash thoughts or decisions!"

Ricardo pointed Yevgeny's trusty dagger at McClusky's face.

McClusky backed away, shocked and offended by Ricardo's actions against him. He thought about whomping on Ricardo's nose. Not once had a winged man threatened him, and he wouldn't put up with it. Yet, the expression on Ricardo's face gave McClusky reason to pause.

For several seconds, no words were exchanged between McClusky and Ricardo. However, McClusky wondered if Ricardo not only sought to turn against the agreement with Kusch, but range against him, as well.

For the first time in many moons, McClusky felt endangered by the Green Winged Men. What if his efforts to support them amounted to little or nothing? What if he was about to join the crew of the Roderick Dundee, and become part of the Greens' dinner? What if his head joined those other grotesque, hideous displays, and rest upon a grisly pike? McClusky was torn between arguing against Ricardo's planned invasion on New Merieko, or wisely keeping his damned mouth shut.

Ricardo gave McClusky a menacing grin, waved the dagger in the man's face, the turned to rally his brothers in his bloodthirsty cause.

McClusky took a deep breath. He had to sit down on a nearby stump, before he fell down. He almost passed out, from anxiety and alarm.

As Ricardo chattered loudly in that crazy winged man lingo of theirs, his fellow critters responded with enthusiastic support and fervor, bordering on the obsessive. While McClusky couldn't understand what was said, he knew full well what they was chattering about. The Green Winged Men were going to invade New Merieko, and there wasn't a thing he could do to stop them.

Panic swept through McClusky. The influence he once held over the Green Winged Men was eroding. They were now following Ricardo's cries, as well as their very instinct, to satisfy a craving for human flesh.

McClusky wanted to warn New Merieko, but realized it'd do no good. The Greens were going to do what they damned well pleased, and he was helpless in preventing a catastrophe.

McClusky was overwhelmed with shame, guilt, and sadness. Perhaps he was wrong all along, when it came to the Green Winged Men. While they remained at the top of Infernus' food chain, they were no better than the Brown Winged Men, or even the abarbeaus.

The Greens were nothing but a mess of uncouth, disgusting animals!

Malachi quietly hid in a nearby tree, eavesdropping on the Greens' conversation. Unnerved by what was about to take place, he swiftly took flight and made a beeline straight toward Persis.

* * * * *

"Whadda ya got brewin' now, you old hypocrite?" hollered Mucker, as he entered Rey's office. "You got yer hands on Paransky . . . Who ya gonna kidnap now? Seely?"

It was a tense afternoon as Jeremy summoned Weston and Mucker to the church. The boy had no trouble finding Weston, who sat down to a lunch of boiled chicken and parched corn in the church's dining hall. Jeremy motioned him to a quiet corner, where he told what he knew about the mess Yevgeny had stirred up. Weston quickly headed to the office, leaving his meal only half-eaten.

Jeremy also had no trouble finding Mucker. The crusty old pirate sat in his small shed, drinking a cold one with Seely. His jaw was still swoll up real bad, and both eyes black and blue from his "disagreement" with Rey.

Jeremy knew that Mucker was mad at him. Mucker was always mad at somebody. But this was the first time he was mad at Jeremy. There were a few guys on Infernus that Jeremy would never tangle with, and Mucker was one of them.

Still, Jeremy was told to fetch Mucker, and that's what he aimed to do. He was also kind of mad at Mucker, for saying mean things about him and Ericha. Mucker was probably still mad at Jeremy, for wanting to run off to the Farlands with Ericha. So, any way you looked at it, Jeremy was in a no-win situation, when it come to Mucker. This wasn't lost on Jeremy, as he cautiously approached the small, rickety shed, where Mucker and Seely was in the middle of a midday drunk-fest.

Jeremy wasn't all that scared of abarbeaus. He had every reason to be scared of Mucker. And the closer he got to the shed, the more scared he got. He was also scared of Rey, who somehow put Mucker in his place. He was also scared about the possibility of war with the Green Winged Men. Added to thoughts of getting hitched to Ericha, then moving off to Branell, Jeremy was scared of something.

The only person who was more scared than Jeremy was Fernandez, who was always scared of something.

The closer Jeremy got to the shed, the more he figured he comer closer to getting his throat cut, his ass kicked, or his head propped up on a Green Winged

Man's pole.

Jeremy pasted on a grin as he peeked his head through the shed door and said, "Hey, how's it going?"

He learned how it was going, when a booze bottle nearly struck him.

Mucker then dragged Jeremy into the shed, and had him pinned up against a wall. The foul, fiery smell of booze and smoked venison getting blown into his face wasn't the worse of it all.

Mucker had a long-bladed knife pressed right up against Jeremy's loin-cloth.

"Hell ya pokin' around here, for?" growled Mucker. "Why don't you and that redheaded girl get yer butts to the Farlands, and leave the rest of us alone?"

Jeremy was no longer scared. He was mad. He knew that Mucker wouldn't really cut him, hopefully not in the area where the knife was pointed. Mucker was a lot of loud, blustery talk and threats . . . but did he really want to slice Jeremy? Even if Mucker and Jeremy wasn't on the best of terms, the two men had been too close for too long to let it forever break the bonds that tied them. Mucker had to get a bluff in, that's all.

No matter. There was still a lingering fear that Mucker might liberate Jeremy of his manhood, out of pure cussedness . . .

Seely sat quietly in one corner, wearing a lazy, crooked smile, oblivious to everything around him . . .

"Hell ya doin' around here?" cussed Mucker, his hand clenching the collar of Jeremy's buckskin shirt. "I oughta cut you from nuts to nose . . ."

"Wait just a minute!" cried Jeremy. "Wait!"

"Don't tell me what to do!"

"Listen to me!" screeched Jeremy. "Just listen!"

"I'm listenin'," grunted Mucker, his tone somewhere between a whisper and a rumble. "What is it ya gotta say?"

Jeremy sucked in a deep breath, and straightened up his buckskin shirt. "I just heard that a few morons from New Merieko and the Roderick Dundee picked a fight with the Green Winged Men."

Mucker never said nothing. He wanted to know more.

"From what Rey told me, there was only one person who got out of it alive," continued Jeremy.

"Who?"

"That dumb Agronian kid you pounded on the other day."

"Hell was they thinkin', goin' at it with green-hided freaks?" growled Mucker.

Jeremy shrugged his shoulders and sighed. He stared at the dirt floor of the shed, in worry and concern.

"Man's gotta have more sense than to go tearin' around a place like that!" hollered Mucker. "Ever'one get ate, except that dumbass kid?"

"That's what Malachi told Rey, and what Rey told me." Jeremy pointed at the church. "Rey wants to get everybody together for a meeting, and asked me to fetch you."

"Me?" argued Mucker. "Hell does he wanna see me for, after that . . . after the thrashing I give him yesterday?"

"All I know is what he told me! He told me to go get you, so here I am."

Mucker slipped the knife back in its sheath, then turned to look at Seely. The lush hadn't heard a word that was spoken, which was just as well. Mucker went outside and headed through the narrow streets to go see Rey.

Meanwhile, Jeremy went looking for Malachi and Errol.

Once Mucker got to the office, Rey and Weston was trying to figure out how to stop a war with the Green Winged Men. Mucker was rarely in a good mood, and the last thing he wanted was to be nice to an Embrian busy-body, or holier-than-thou padre. He had no use whatsoever for Weston, and damned little use for Rey, after the fight they got into over Paransky, the little tattooed boy.

Ericha was also at the office, putting her two-shillings worth into it. Just like a woman!

Mucker felt badly outnumbered in that group, but had to put his two shillings worth as he stomped through the door. "Whadda ya got brewing now, you old hypocrite? You got yer hands on Paransky . . . Who ya gonna kidnap, now? Seely?"

Jeremy couldn't find Malachi or Errol no place. Errol was off cutting firewood with some neighbors, and took Prince Ari with him. No one knew where Malachi was. After saving Fernandez, the young winged man took off on a second flight, and hadn't been seen since.

Jeremy got back to the church office to find Ericha there. The future Mrs. Kentworth sat on Rey's desk, dressed in a tight-fitting, long-sleeved shirt and loincloth, and never said nothing. She couldn't get a word in, thanks to the hollering, screaming, and cussing between Rey, Weston and Mucker. Rey and Weston argued for a peaceful, diplomatic way to solve the problem, by trying to talk with McClusky. Mucker figured there wasn't no talking with McClusky, or any of the green freaks. The truce between the Brown and Green Winged Men was always fragile. It looked now as if the truce was as good as broke, thanks to the growing colony of New Merieko, a "damned fool agreement with Kuschan heathens," and a "damned fool attempt" to fight with the Greens.

Mucker figured that war was inevitable between the Browns and the Greens. No one wanted it. In Mucker's mind, "a helluva lotta people and Browns are gonna get theirs before it was all over." But blood had been spilled.

Blood spilled from either New Merieko or the Roderick Dundee . . . Who cared?

Blood spilled from Persis . . . Well, that just couldn't be tolerated!

And, according to Mucker, if the Greens attacked Persis, "then Hell awaited them."

"Naturally I don't want to see us get attacked," agreed Rey. "But don't you think we should help those in New Merieko? And while we're at it, warn the sailors on the Matyushenko?"

"The hell you say!" hollered Mucker, nearly coming unglued. "If them green freaks want more meat for their cook-out, Kuschan meat's just as good as anything!" Mucker glared at Weston. "Might as well throw in a big-shot Embrian appetizer, while we're at it . . ."

"Why not that of an Agronian loudmouth?" questioned Weston. He smiled and avoided temptations of taking a swing at Mucker. He didn't like Mucker, and was indeed offended by him. He smiled to show that he wasn't easily angered, in hopes of rattling Mucker. If he couldn't whip Mucker in fisticuffs, he'd beat him in a game of wits.

Rey turned his attention on Jeremy and Ericha, who never said nothing in this verbal exchange. The two teens held hands, united now as they'd remain united, forevermore.

Before Mucker answered Weston, Malachi entered the office. He was real tired, and needed a long rest.

"Where ya been hidin' yerself?" grunted Mucker. "All hell's breaking loose, and here you been out lolligagging . . ."

"I've been spying on the Greens!" answered Malachi, frantically.

"Spying on the Greens?" gasped Rey.

Malachi nodded YES.

"What did you learn?" asked Weston.

"Pastor Yevgeny is dead," said Malachi. "So is McCoy . . . and everyone else from the Roderick Dundee."

Nobody said nothing, though their attention was on Malachi.

"I overheard a discussion between Ricardo and McClusky," said Malachi. "A group of hunters went after the Roderick Dundee. There were no survivors, once they got finished with it."

Mucker snickered.

"Now they've set their sights on New Merieko," added Malachi.

"We've got to get over there!" shouted Weston. He hadn't been that afraid, since almost losing his life during a meeting between members of the Brotherhood of Faith Church and the United Westerland Brethren, in East Corapal. "Not only do we have to notify the colonists, but talk the Greens out of attacking . . ."

"You can't talk the Greens outa nothin'!" roared Mucker. "You can't even talk them outa fighting over who they'll eat first. You, me, or the girl over there." Mucker pointed at Ericha. "By the time they're done with us, ain't no way o' tellin' who's who, once we're roastin' on the grill . . ."

"Enough of that!" yelled Rey. "There's no point in that kind of talk!"

"It will be enough, if we get caught up in the freak's feedin' frenzy," said

Mucker. "Them critters get the blood-lust, bad, where they'll kill everything that lives and breaths. Kinda like a bunch of locusts. They'll kill you, soon as look at ya. And they don't give a hoot in hell about peace, except a piece of yer arms, yer legs, yer head sittin' on a sharp stick, as pretty as ya please . . ."

"This is getting us nowhere," sighed Rey. "I don't know about the rest of you, but I must stand by my fellow man in New Merieko and guarantee that . . ."

"Guarantee what?" interrupted Mucker. "Guarantee that you and everyone else in this here room's gonna be part of the critter's cook-out, tonight?"

"I know Vic McClusky," said Rey. "But you know him better than the rest of us, Mister John Mucker. Don't you think it's best to try and stop a war?"

"I agree with Leader Rey," said Weston. "He's a man of God, and I'm a man of peace. We have a responsibility to . . ."

"The hell!" snapped Mucker, staring at Weston. "You got a responsibility to get on the first boat to Embrey, and mind yer own damn business!"

"I didn't ask you over here for that!" Rey yelled at Mucker. "We've got a crisis on our hands, and it's liable to blow up unless we do something. I need your help and advice, Mucker . . . not another fight."

Mucker gave Rey the eye.

"You can count on my help," assured Weston. "My visit here hasn't amounted to much, other than to meet my cousin Jeremy. If I can prevent a war, then I'll throw my hat into the ring."

"Me, too," said Jeremy. "If my cousin and father are sticking their necks out, guess I'd better stick mine out, too."

"Well, if you're sticking your neck out," said Ericha, "then I'm not going to stay here, waiting for your return . . . I'm going, too!"

"But you can't!" cried Jeremy.

"Why not?" argued Ericha.

"'Cause you're a girl!" said Jeremy. "My girl!"

"He's right," said Rey. "The best thing is for you to stay here."

"If my boyfriend and my best friend's willing to stick his neck out, then who am I to be left behind?" questioned Ericha.

Rey sighed. "But, Ericha . . ."

"And if my spiritual leader's about to walk through the Valley of the Shadow of Death, then what sort of parishioner am I, if I refuse to walk with him?" commented Ericha.

Jeremy and Rey shook their heads, in dismay.

"Looks to me like she's going," laughed Weston.

"Very well, Ericha," agreed Rey, hesitantly. "You're going. I just pray we don't live to regret it."

"If I am to take my place as the future Chief of the Brown Winged Men, I too must join in," said Malachi. "Should I refuse to take part in this, how can I face myself as a winged man, or a member of the Brotherhood of Faith?"

Rey smiled. "I knew you'd never let me down, Brother Malachi."

"Well, if you damned fools are fixin' to get yerselves cooked for stickin' yer necks out," said Mucker, reluctantly. "Reckon you need a mean-as-hell fightin' man to get cooked, right next to ya."

Jeremy giggled. "Does that mean? . . ."

"Yeah," said Mucker, already figuring he was as good as dead. Everybody in Persis might be dead before this was all over . . . so what the hell? The more he thought about it, the more he figured Persis was worth fighting and dying for! "Reckon I oughta throw in, too . . ."

* * * * *

Malachi headed outside. Life in Persis went on as normal. Few in the village, people and winged men alike, were aware of the crisis, other than rumors floating around. Malachi wondered if everyone should be notified.

Malachi fought overwhelming fear. As Infernus 'royalty,' he had to act calm. In time, everybody would know about Fernandez and Yevgeny's blunder against the Green Winged Men. He prayed no one else died because of it.

"Malachi?" a familiar voice asked. "What's wrong?"

Malachi turned to see Lorenzo approach him. The older winged man's face was creased with worry.

"Father," mumbled Malachi, coldly.

"What's wrong, son?" asked Lorenzo. "I know there's something on your mind, and I ask that you share it with me."

Malachi frowned.

"What's wrong?" repeated Lorenzo, forcefully.

Reluctantly, Malachi told Lorenzo WHAT HAPPENED. He also explained his role in saving Fernandez. He finished by telling Lorenzo of the Greens' planned invasion of New Merieko.

"Why didn't you tell me sooner?" asked Lorenzo, angrily. "How dare you not inform me?"

"How dare you sign a trade agreement with Kusch, without first gaining a consensus?" responded Malachi.

"Our trade agreement has been finalized!"

"Our trade agreement? Your trade agreement, not mine. I never signed the agreement, and I for one won't endorse it."

"Why must I obtain a consensus?" argued Lorenzo. "This isn't a democracy, and for what it's worth I'm doing the right thing for Infernus, as a whole!"

"While you made agreements with Kusch, some Kuschan lunatic started a war with the Green Winged Men!" shouted Malachi.

"And what are you proposing to do, to stop this war?" questioned Lorenzo. "Soon, you will be chief. I'm asking you to take charge of this situation and make wise decisions. So, what's it going to be, son? What do you propose to do?"

"Leader Rey's sending a group to New Merieko, in hopes of talking the Greens out of violence. I'm on my way there, now."

"I'm going with you," said Lorenzo.

Malachi shook his head. "No disrespect, Father, but . . ."

"But what?"

"I'm faster than you, and will be scanning the skies over New Merieko," said Malachi, apologetically. "Please, Father, try to understand. If you come with me, I'll be worried about you."

"I reign over the Brown Winged Men," said Lorenzo. "Therefore, I have to go with you to New Merieko." Mockingly, he added, "Please try to understand, Malachi. I'll be worried about you, if you go it alone. As your father, I have to be with you."

"You're right," said Malachi, with an embarrassed grin. The anger he once held toward Lorenzo was gone. The two were now reunited, in a common goal. "Please try to understand, Father. I'm still worried about you. I'll always be worried about you! Where's Nikolai?"

"Delivering a baby. He's got his duties, and I've got mine. If we're to save New Merieko, we won't get it done standing here, making shadows. Let's get going!"

Minutes later, the two winged men glided hundreds of feet in the sky, not far from the tiny village of New Merieko. The wind was calm, although a cool breeze swept in from Mount Auric.

Malachi couldn't help but notice that Lorenzo's advancing age had caught up with him. Where Lorenzo could once go miles without tiring, he was now badly winded, and had trouble keeping up. For his father's sake, Malachi flew slower than normal.

Malachi wanted Lorenzo to stay home. This mission was dangerous enough as it was! Why risk two lives, instead of one? Malachi didn't want to think of Lorenzo as a liability. More and more, it seemed that Lorenzo was just that.

Less than a mile from New Merieko, Malachi's concerns got worse, when he saw a half-dozen Green Winged Men sweeping toward him from the southeast.

A dart fired from a blowgun punctured Lorenzo's torso, an inch below the right arm.

Lorenzo gave Malachi a look of shock and horror. He felt the dart's force, as it penetrated into the thin layers of hair and skin. This was replaced by an odd, numbing sensation, spreading throughout the right wing.

With the dart's poison rushing through him, Lorenzo's flight became awkward, erratic, clumsy. In no time, he spiraled downward, toward a thick growth of evergreen trees.

A second dart missed Malachi by mere inches, as the Green Winged Men were upon him. Malachi used all his strength to outrun and outmaneuver the enemy. Flying with the sun at his back, he soon got shy of the oncoming Greens. Once the coast was clear, he headed to where he figured Lorenzo had impacted, someplace in the forest.

Malachi spotted Lorenzo sprawled over the thick, spindly limbs of a fir tree, about fifteen yards above the ground. Lorenzo's body was twisted in a bizarre, contorted manner.

Malachi landed softly in a sturdy limb, next to Lorenzo. "Father!" he shrieked, frightened by the sight of blood splattered across Lorenzo's broken frame. One wing was shattered in several places. Both eyes remained open, as Lorenzo's arms and legs pointed in all directions. The white of a bone from Lorenzo's thigh exposed itself, as it protruded through the hide.

"Father!" screamed Malachi, his cries echoing through the stillness of the forest. He ran his fingers over Lorenzo's face and neck.

Lorenzo didn't respond.

Lorenzo couldn't respond.

Lorenzo was dead.

Malachi was struck with denial, shock, grief, and sadness. The sting of unbelievable truth swept over him. Malachi shook his head, refusing the terrible evidence before him.

This was replaced by a shrill scream, followed by an uncontrollable shedding of tears.

Malachi knew he had to do something . . . but what? There was no bringing back the dead. Pain and confusion mired with indecisiveness. Malachi wasn't sure whether to return to Persis, or surrender to ideas which were more primal, brutal, and ultimately more savage, than anything he ever considered before.

In an unexpected, sick twist of fate, an abarbeaus jumped right in the middle of Lorenzo's lifeless body.

Malachi leaped to a nearby tree.

By now, two more abarbeauses went after Lorenzo. The weight of the beasts upon Lorenzo proved too great a burden, as the body with the three assailants fell from the limbs, and crashed to the ground with tremendous, bone-crunching force.

Malachi turned away from the sight of Lorenzo, who was torn to shreds by the three abarbeaus.

Unable to vent his rage against the beasts consuming Lorenzo's corpse, Malachi had only one solution . . . to get back at those responsible for this tragedy.

* * * * *

After taking down one of the Brown Winged Men, the half-dozen Greens hunted for the second. Unable to locate Malachi anywhere, they grew frustrated by their plans to get rid of him.

Speed and agility weren't the only qualities that Malachi had as a winged man. Stealth and silence were also among his attributes as he snuck up on his opponents and struck, before anyone noticed he was even there.

One of the Greens learned this lesson the hard way, as he caught a brief glimpse of Malachi in one eye . . .

Moments before Malachi split his head open in mid-flight, with a stout tree limb almost thirty inches long.

As the first Green hurled down dead to the trees, Malachi pursued his unsuspecting foes with a determination and ferocity he never felt before. Less than ten seconds after slaying the first Green, Malachi took aim at another one who was unaware that he was about to die.

The second Green fell under the shadow of a vengeful adversary. Looking around, he was surprised to see an image of a pearl-white winged man, coming toward him. As the Green opened his mouth to protest, Malachi let out a scream. The Green turned a sharp left to flee from Malachi's wrath.

Malachi swung the tree limb and smashed the Green's wing, shattering the bones like they were matchsticks. The Green shrieked as he fell, helplessly, to his death.

A minute later, a third Green Winged Man's face was flattened by a severe blow from Malachi's tree limb.

The last three Greens were now aware of Malachi's presence. The mission switched from that of revenge and the seeking of human flesh, to halting Malachi's advance upon them.

One of the Greens fired a dart at Malachi. No good. Malachi flicked the dart away with the tree limb, like it was a gnat. He then led the three Greens to the dark, shadowy woods below.

The three Greens confidently followed Malachi into the trees, thinking they'd make quick work of him. They landed in a small clearing, looking everywhere for him. Not far away, an abarbeaus ate on Lorenzo's remains, giving the Greens scant satisfaction and glee.

The Greens spread out, their blowguns and darts at the ready. Fear didn't play a role, here. The Greens who had fallen under Malachi were careless and foolish, and therefore worthy of their fate. Still, it was shocking to find one of the comrades who, after being killed by Malachi, was slowly devoured by a couple of abarbeaus.

As the three Greens wandered deeper into the woods, they lost track of each other. Occasionally, they made loud, high-pitched calls back and forth, to keep contact. The Greens moved slowly, cautiously, through a thick growth of trees. They experienced a combination of emotions, from anticipation, to eagerness, to mild dread.

Emotions of dread increased when two of the Greens heard a low, dull thud! sounding from one side.

A third Green failed to answer, as the other two called to him. As his name was shouted, over and over and over, the third Green never answered.

The youngest Green Winged Man, an adolescent equal to that of a person of thirteen, went to check up on his silent companion.

To his disbelief and horror, the adolescent found his companion lying on the ground, suffering from a bad case of the flip-flops. The right side of his face had been crushed in. Bones, brains, and blood sprayed everywhere, as the injured Green gave up the ghost and died.

The adolescent then encountered Malachi, who stepped out from behind a tamarack, holding the bloody tree limb in both hands.

The adolescent placed his blowgun to his front, using it more as a shield than as a weapon. Malachi busted the adolescent's blowgun, with one swipe of the tree limb.

The adolescent backed away, tripped over his own feet, and landed next to a red fir. In the chaos of the moment, he saw Malachi coming for him. The adolescent covered his face under both hands, begging to be spared.

Malachi stopped to eye the frightened adolescent, sprawled upon the ground before him. He wanted to get even for what happened to Lorenzo. But was he willing to commit murder on a critter he never learned to respect, nor trust?

Out of sympathy for the adolescent Green, Malachi lowered the tree limb.

He forgot about the one Green Winged Man who was unaccounted for . . . unaccounted for, until a dagger impaled his left wing.

Excruciating pain shot through the injured wing. Malachi didn't want to believe that he'd just been wounded. He spent a lifetime looking down upon the Greens, unable to treat them as equals.

And yet, a Green Winged Man had just gotten the best of him.

Malachi now found himself at the mercy of a critter with a reputation of showing no mercy. He made a weak, awkward, clumsy swing against the Green who had just stabbed him.

A split-second later, Malachi was knifed through the right wing.

Malachi's thoughts ranged from a need to retaliate against the Green Winged Man, to realizations that he might soon die. It was an unimaginable possibility! Malachi had to act, and act swiftly! Ignoring the pain jolting through the damaged wings, Malachi placed his fleeting strength into stopping the Green Winged Man.

With the dagger still impaling his right wing, Malachi swiveled on two weakened, shaky feet. With a howl of defiance, he smacked the Green Winged Man's face with the tree limb.

The Green staggered away, his jaw hanging crooked and slack. Blood drooled from his mouth. The Green tried to speak, but words never come. Before he retreated by taking flight, Malachi once again slammed him with the limb.

The Green dropped to the ground, dead.

Malachi whacked the Green's head repeatedly with the tree limb, until his skull was mashed to an unrecognizable pulp.

This left only the adolescent Green who, one-by-one, watched Malachi wipe out the small contingency sent to attack New Merieko.

Malachi reached over, pulled the knife from his right wing, and threw it somewhere in the brush. He was unable to stand straight, or even walk for long distances. Forget about flying! Both wings were badly damaged, and the blood dripping from them was extreme.

Malachi staggered to a small clearing, where he dropped the tree limb used to destroy five Green Winged Men. He wondered if he was able to ever fly again. Even if they were properly treated, the wings would never fully heal. Malachi was grounded. And, for the time being, he was totally helpless.

Dizzy from pain, fatigue, and the loss of blood, Malachi dropped to his knees.

Malachi detected movement from behind. Perhaps it was an abarbeaus, on its way to finish him off . . . a frightening thought to be sure!

Malachi turned to see the adolescent Green, slowly approach him. He grabbed the tree limb and waved it at the adolescent, who now had the upper hand. If the adolescent wanted to make a fight of it, Malachi refused to die easily.

"Back off," ordered Malachi, in that weird language known only to the winged men. "Go home . . . Go away . . . Get out of here . . ."

The adolescent stopped. He was more afraid of Malachi, than Malachi was of him. The look in his eyes revealed a genuine concern for Malachi, along with grudging admiration and respect. The Greens worshiped those who distinguished themselves in combat, and Malachi had clearly earned the adolescent's favor.

The adolescent stepped closer to Malachi. He offered Malachi a hand, in peace and friendship.

Malachi wanted nothing from the adolescent than to get lost. He would never, could never, trust the Green Winged Men. Why start now? This might have been a ploy, a means to get Malachi to lower his guard, for the adolescent to pull a dirty trick.

Malachi refused the adolescent's kindness and generosity. Still, the adolescent wasn't discouraged, and gave Malachi a warm smile.

Malachi sighed in humility, along with a dose of self-deprecating humor. He frowned at the adolescent. It shamed him to seek assistance from one so lowly, so despicable, as a Green Winged Man.

In the back of his mind, Malachi reminded himself that he now ruled over the Brown Winged Men of Persis, and had to conduct himself as such. Did his title afford him to gain assistance from an enemy? In his present condition, he did require help. But from a kid? And a Green kid, at that?

"Blast it," Malachi cursed, in Embrian. He had no other solution than to accept the adolescent's hand. For all he knew, this might have been the first step toward cooperation and peace, between two adversaries.

Reluctantly, Malachi reached out toward the adolescent.

The adolescent then let out a shriek, resembling the screams of hogs at butchering time. It was a sound Malachi was doomed to remember for the rest of his life.

Looking up, Malachi noticed an arrow impaling the adolescent's chest. A second arrow then punctured the adolescent's back.

Panic-stricken, the adolescent struggled to take flight. He launched himself skyward, about twenty feet above the ground.

A third arrow, then a fourth, struck the adolescent.

Soon, the adolescent spun down and landed on his back, next to Malachi.

The adolescent cried out for Malachi. He flapped both of his wings, to escape a fate he could not avoid. He chattered in his native tongue, begging for Malachi to save him. It was too late.

Malachi wondered who sent those arrows into the adolescent who, less than a minute earlier, wished him no harm.

The answer came when Jeremy, Mucker, and Nikolai arrived.

As Nikolai ran to examine Malachi, Mucker stood over the dying adolescent. The old pirate held a bow and some arrows in his hands. Meanwhile, Jeremy stared at one of the Green Winged Men, who had his head bashed in with the tree limb.

Rey, Weston, and Ericha then showed up, mortified by the carnage surrounding them. By now, scores of abarbeaus ate on the dead winged men.

Malachi leaned his tired body against Nikolai. He tried to keep a brave face, but instead wept.

"That'll teach ya, freak," commented Mucker, smiling at the adolescent. "Messed with the wrong people, boy."

The adolescent insulted Mucker in broken, nearly unintelligible Embrian.

Mucker responded by pressing one foot against the adolescent's throat. Frantically, the adolescent flapped its wings, as it was being killed by Mucker. Rey, Weston, and Ericha watched in disdain, as the adolescent finally stopped breathing.

Mucker snickered as he spit into one of the adolescent's lifeless eyes.

Rey and Weston knelt to the adolescent. As Weston gazed upon the corpse with curiosity and revulsion, Rey caressed its still warm body.

"What do you care, preacher man?" growled Mucker. "He wasn't nothin' but a heathen, according to yer idiot superstitions, and the only good Green Winged Man is a dead one."

"How many were there?" Jeremy asked Malachi, as Ericha watched an abarbeaus drag a dead Green into the brush. "Malachi . . . how many?"

"Too many," answered Malachi, evasively. Staring into space, he allowed Nikolai to nurse the crippling knife wounds in his wings. "But I took care of them. They won't bother us, anymore."

"Where's Father?" asked Nikolai, applying an ointment to Malachi's wings.

Malachi wouldn't answer.

"Where's Father?" repeated Nikolai, anxiously.

Malachi was unable to speak. His lips quivered, as both eyes filled with tears.

Nikolai dropped the clay container holding the ointment, where it spilled onto the ground.

Rey, Weston, Jeremy, and Ericha gathered around the two Brown Winged Men, in their moment of sadness and sorrow.

Malachi and Nikolai tried to face grief as adults, and royal members of their tribe. Lorenzo was dead. And now the two sons were forced to carry on, without his guidance, support, love, and devotion.

Malachi and Nikolai embraced. This, as their human counterparts, minus Mucker, joined hands to recite a silent prayer.

Work progressed at a quick and steady pace, as New Merieko looked more and more like a small town on the eastern shores of Infernus. The mood there was generally upbeat and positive.

Yet, there were worries about the disappearance of Justice, Boutwell, Yevgeny . . . and a scrawny, fifteen-year-old Agronian schoolboy named Fernandez.

Despite efforts to complete work on new buildings, a dark cloud lingered over the village. These was dire matters few talked about, though they never really left their minds. Most of the colonists knew that starting over wouldn't be easy. Few expected just how violent and dangerous it could be.

Once Malachi's wounds were treated and stitched, everybody began their final stretch into New Merieko. The temperature neared a humid eighty degrees.

The group from Persis made an odd-looking sight as they paid a surprise visit to New Merieko. Most everybody recognized Rey, who had made a name for himself in the colony. A few knew Weston, since they sailed on the same boat with him to Infernus. Just about everyone knew of Mucker, along with his fiery reputation.

And who could ignore the two loin-clothed teens, Jeremy and Ericha?

Some in the colony had yet to encounter a winged man, except that one who was with Jung-su the other day . . . and got killed and ate in a suspicious manner. Several colonists still viewed the winged men with fear and disdain. Those critters were to be looked down upon, and not to be treated as anything other than what they were . . . dumb critters.

A small number of boys gazed curiously at the newcomers from Persis. Mainly, their focus was upon Malachi and Nikolai, who didn't fly into town but rather hobbled. Nikolai helped Malachi in a slow stroll. Every step brought Malachi extreme agony and pain. Often, he had to stop and catch his breath.

Paolo and Frida left their tiny hut at the end of town and darted toward Rey and Weston. "Where's Nandy?" cried Frida, her eyes red and moist from crying for her only child.

"He's safe in Persis," said Weston.

"Persis?" asked Paolo, in astonishment.

"It's a long story," sighed Rey. "And I plan to share it with you, in time. But first, you must evacuate New Merieko."

"Is Nandy safe?" whined Frida.

"He's safe," assured Ericha, taking Frida's hand to comfort her.

"I want to see my Nandy!" squalled Frida, pulling away from Ericha. For a moment or two, it looked as if she might take a swing at the redheaded girl.

Ericha returned the angry stare and stood her ground. She refused to be bullied or harassed by Frida. The tension was unbearable, as onlookers wondered if the two women might tangle.

Jeremy led Ericha away, as Paolo put his arm around Frida. "They're not here to bring us any harm," Paolo told his wife. "If they say that Nandy is all right, I'll take their word for it. Thank you for the news, Leader Rey. Thank you very much."

"No need to thank me," said Rey, with humility.

"Has Fernandez been any trouble?" asked Paolo, apologetically.

"No trouble," said Rey. "Not . . . too much. I'll explain it to you, when I can. But first, you must evacuate New Merieko."

"Evacuate?" gasped Paolo.

"The Green Winged Men are coming to attack your village," said Weston. He soon regretted his choice of words, as Paolo and Frida's expressions revealed shock and horror. "We . . . we don't want to start a panic," he added, quietly. "But there's no time to lose. We have to organize everyone in an orderly fashion, then safely escort . . ."

"Green Winged Men?" asked Paolo. His mouth gaped open as he eyed Malachi and Nikolai.

"Goddamn you!" hollered Mucker, impatiently. "Unless you wanna get ate by them green-hided buggers, you best get yer ass in gear, and get packin'!"

Paolo's eyes widened.

"Don't make no difference to me," said Mucker. "If yer just gonna stand around with yer thumbs up yer butts, endin' up on the Green Man's grill, good for you. Don't mean that everyone else wants . . ."

Frida turned a suspicious gaze on the two Brown Winged Men. Where Nikolai was slightly humored by Frida's frightened look, Malachi was troubled by it. Increasingly, he wondered if he truly was a good, upstanding member of Rey's congregation or, as Yevgeny suggested, a disciple of Soraq. This, based upon Lorenzo's death, and his response to it. Malachi wished for Heaven, but figured he was heading straight for Hell. He feared that his race and species had condemned him from birth. No way out of it.

"I don't mean to be overbearing or pushy," said Rey. "Unless you want a bloodbath on your hands, I suggest you get together, and move everyone into Persis."

"I came here to start over," said Greenleaf, stepping out of his own hut. "I'm digging my heels in, Leader Rey. I'm helping to build this community, and damned if I'll get pushed off of it by anyone."

"To hell with ya then," grunted Mucker.

Greenleaf took a step back, shocked by Mucker's tone and profanity.

"I admire your steadfast and courage," said Rey. He chuckled at Mucker's remark, despite being a man of God. "But if you don't want anyone to get killed, I strongly urge you to . . ."

"Only cowards run, Leader Rey," said Greenleaf, with an arrogance leaning toward recklessness. "I spent twenty years as an infantryman in the Embrian Army. I never ran from a fight against Kuschans, Branellians, or Agronian smugglers. I never ran, then. Damned if I'll run, now."

"Have it your own way," said Weston. "I'm an Embrian diplomat, sir. When I'm told to run, I see it as a good idea."

Greenleaf stared at Weston with conceit, but never said nothing.

"See here," spoke Weston. "Years ago, I was in eastern Corapal, when Vladistani radicals breeched a peace accord and crossed the border late one evening. Those of us who fled were spared. Those who didn't were . . ." Weston swallowed. "I won't say what happened to those who stayed, and I'm sure you don't want to hear about it."

Greenleaf puffed his chest out. "I'm staying."

"I'm not going to argue about it," said Rey, gravely. "Whatever you decide to do, I won't stop you. But what about the others? You want to see them die, to appease your ego and vanity?"

Greenleaf gritted his teeth, too mad to talk.

Jeremy and Ericha walked away. They were supposed to have dinner that night. Jeremy took a deep breath. The island was once familiar, comforting and tranquil, like a dear friend or acquaintance. Little by little, tranquility was replaced by doubt, uncertainty, chaos, and fear.

For years, a truce existed between the Brown and Green Winged Men. There were always thoughts that war between the two tribes was imminent. That was just the way things were. It was so common a reality that nobody felt endangered or threatened by it. Until now.

Jeremy took Ericha's hand. The warmth of her touch was the only constant in life, and he was afraid to let go. Without giving it a second thought, Jeremy pressed his lips to Ericha's, for a kiss.

Ericha ran her fingers through Jeremy's long, unruly hair. She couldn't imagine life without him! She locked her arms around his thin, masculine frame, and showered him with kisses.

Jeremy and Ericha had vowed to make a life for themselves, whether it be in Branell, Infernus, or the eternal bliss of the Hereafter.

The two teens let go, once Errol and Prince Ari showed up, joined by Seely and Paransky.

Jeremy rolled his eyes back. Though he didn't always get along with Errol, the man was handy at times like this. Seely was a liability, and Ari was of no use, at all. Paransky's heart was in the right place, but this was no time or place for little tattooed boys, or any boys for that matter.

To his credit, Errol had brung more arrows.

"I ran over here as fast as I could, when I heard what was going on," said Errol, a bit awkward after seeing Ericha smooching all over Jeremy.

"Thanks," said Jeremy, unable to conceal a blush.

As Ari examined the colony of New Merieko with awe and curiosity, Seely was perplexed by it. He looked around the joint, as if it seemingly popped out from nowhere, with no explanation or reason. He licked his lips, hoping a new bar or bordello set up shop.

"I don't know why Seely had to throw in with us," whispered Errol. "That old soak ain't worth a plug shilling when he's sober . . . if he's sober."

"Maybe he just wants to feel needed," said Jeremy, with equal sarcasm and sympathy.

"Well, he sure ain't much use here," said Errol. "Ari ain't either, but I needed his help hauling these arrows."

"Thanks," repeated Jeremy.

Paransky approached Ericha and Jeremy, still dressed in the buckskin shirt and loincloth they had made for him. He grinned eagerly, in anticipation of a fight.

"No one's debating your bravery, son," Errol said to Paransky. "Reckon the best thing for you is to run on home, with Ari and Seely."

Paransky wanted to be with the men, and thought less of himself when they refused his participation.

"Errol's right," said Mucker, his weathered eyes revealing a genuine love for Paransky. "But run on back. They'll need you in town, just in case them green-hided freaks attack there."

"But I thought you liked me!" whined Paransky. "I can kill green-hided freaks just as good as anyone . . . just as good as you, sport! You'll see!"

Mucker snickered. "Well, I know you'll be a right fine green-hided freak killer. But for now, it's best you head back to Persis, and keep your eyes peeled for . . ."

Mucker stopped when, in the corner of one eye, he saw a thin, metallic object puncture the back of Errol's right hand.

At first, Errol thought he'd been bit by a skeeter. Looking to slap a bug away, he soon realized what had just happened.

Just below the knuckles was a dart . . .

"Papa!" cried Ericha, yanking the dart from Errol's hand.

Slowly, Errol's fingers went numb and tingly.

"Ericha," said Errol, fighting back the panic sweeping over him. "Take . . . take care of Ari for me . . ."

"Look out!" cried Jeremy, pushing Ericha and Ari to the ground.

Mucker tackled Paransky, as a rain of darts scattered everywhere.

Errol managed to stay on his feet . . . even as his chest and belly was covered with darts. Staggering like a drunk, he collapsed. His expression altered to a crooked, half-smile, as he blithered in a silly, nonsensical manner.

Less than a minute later, he lied face-down in the street.

The skies above New Merieko filled with scores of Green Winged Men, armed with swords, axes, and blowguns. There were enough of the critters to block out the sun.

Paolo and Frida ran to their hut, which proved to be a lousy hiding place as several Greens followed them inside. High-pitched screeches echoed from the hut, as furniture was overturned and blood splattered against the glass panes of a window.

Seconds passed by.

Finally, the Greens left the now-silent hut, dragging the bodies of Paolo and Frida. Two husky Greens took flight and eagerly carried their kills away, in the sharpened talons of their bare feet.

Ericha and Ari hid in the bushes on the outskirts of New Merieko. Both stared at Errol, who lied motionless just a few feet away. Errol wasn't asleep, to be easily awakened or resurrected once the danger had passed. Moments before, he was living and breathing.

Then, like a flash, Ericha and Ari were orphaned.

Ari screamed like a frightened infant. He grew even more shrill and emotional, as two Green Winged Men landed next to Errol. One of the Greens grinned as he bent over to slit Errol's throat.

He didn't expect to have his own neck sliced, as Ericha ran a knife over his windpipe. The second Green was also taken off-guard, as he looked up to see Jeremy swing his prized sword at him.

The second Green fell next to Errol, his skull split apart.

Ericha knifed her own victim in the gut, over and over and over, to get even for Errol.

Jeremy dragged Ericha away. Darts and arrows impacted the trees and grassy soil, around them. "Ari!" he shouted. "Fetch arrows for me and Ericha!"

Ari gave Jeremy a confused look, as his jaw hung slack.

"Ari!" repeated Jeremy. "Fetch me and Ericha some arrows!"

"Okay," mumbled Ari, weakly.

Jeremy looked out across the besieged village. Residents fled in all directions, just to be cut down by the marauding Greens. Mucker stood behind a woodshed, as Paransky crouched next to him. Paransky grinned mischievously, treating this event as a bizarre, joyous spectacle.

Jeremy couldn't see Rey or Weston, anywhere. Seely hid behind a large tamarack, sipping cheap bourbon to lessen the effects of the horrors he played witness to. While a few colonists joined in the fight, most fled from their shelters, just to be captured or killed by an airborne menace.

To make things worse, the Greens began shooting flaming arrows into the newly-built homes and structures of the tiny village.

Gyorgy-Andreovich was forced from the hut he once shared with Pavel-Ivanovich. He shrieked loudly as he was carried high into the air by a Green Winged Man . . . never to be seen again.

In the smoke-filled skies above, Malachi and Nikolai engaged in a desperate fight against a countless number of Greens. Even with his sore, injured wings, Malachi battled with courage and determination. At ground level, those from New Merieko were decimated by the ferocious Greens, who ended their victims' lives in relentless, bloody fashion.

Paransky cried out as a dart penetrated his left shin.

Mucker hastily removed the dart from the tattooed boy's leg, then waved urgently at Nikolai to come quickly.

"Boy!" shouted Seely, sprinting awkwardly toward Mucker and Paransky.

An arrow struck Seely's chest.

Seely stumbled backward, gurgling as blood flew from his lips.

Before anyone could help him, Seely was hit by three more arrows . . . one in the thigh, one in the shoulder, and one in the backside. Somehow, he remained on his wobbly feet, as he struggled to reach Paransky.

Mucker cradled Paransky in his arms. Poison streamed through the child's veins, which brought on confusion and delirium.

A fourth arrow flew into Seely's mouth, then burst from the back of his neck. Seely was dead before he hit the ground.

A horde of eager Greens were upon the old lush, as they happily chopped him to pieces.

"Nikolai!" hollered Mucker, smoke and dust choking him. "Get down here!"

Nikolai did as he was told. Hastily, he applied a liquidy antidote to Paransky's wounded leg, to halt the poison's toxic effects. "This will do for now," he said.

"He gonna live?" asked Mucker, anxiously.

"He will," said Nikolai, "if only I can get him to the infirmary."

"Get to it," said Mucker, urgently. "And don't get yerself killed."

Nikolai smiled, nervously.

"Hell, we might all get killed, if this keeps up," said Mucker. "Get Paransky and yerself outa here. Least someone might live to tell about it."

Nikolai lifted Paransky into his arms, took flight, and headed straight for Persis.

Mucker spied out across the smoky, blood-soaked field, which once was the colony of New Merieko.

Lying flat on the ground, back behind an outdoor privy, was Rey and Weston. Mucker shook his head in anger and frustration. Figures. The local padre and Embrian busybody acted like scared rabbits. Well, if they aimed to get outa this one alive, they'd best fight their way out!

A flaming arrow flew into the woodshed, where Mucker was. The smell of dry, smoldering wood and pitch gagged the old pirate. In no time, the entire building would be a raging inferno.

Cursing, Mucker dashed outside and ran to the big fat tamarack, where Seely used as a hiding place before he kicked the bucket. An open bottle of bourbon still sat in the damp, dewy shade of the tree. Needing a dose of liquid courage, Mucker took a big drink, then got back into the fight. He stared at Rey and Weston, who were still crouched down behind the crapper. Them damned fools just begged to join Errol and Seely in the winged man's pot! "Whatcha doin' way the hell over there?" hollered Mucker, loudly.

Rey and Weston peeked up to see Mucker giving them the eye.

"Get yer butts over here," ordered Mucker, "and help me kill them green-hided freaks!"

Rey and Weston sprinted to the tamarack, dodging arrows and poison darts.

By now, every man-made structure in New Merieko was burning, as fire shot hundreds of feet into the air. The once promising village was destroyed, as its citizens were picked off by the Green Winged Men.

All hope was fleeting. Dreams of forging a lasting peace between two tribes faded away in ashes, dust, fire and smoke.

And just when things couldn't get much worse, Ericha caught an arrow in the left thigh.

Ericha fell backwards into the deep grass. The initial blow of the arrow into flesh, along with the extreme pain running through her leg, brought on shock, denial, and agony. Blood sprayed everywhere from the wound. Ericha lied on one side, her thoughts trapped between removing the arrow, and her own mortality.

It was tough enough losing Errol, then Seely. For the first time since killing the abarbeaus with Jeremy, Ericha thought she was about to die. She was split between saving herself, of fighting to save Ari and Jeremy. Hopes of marriage, leaving Infernus, and moving to the lush, green fields and rolling hills of Branell were out of reach, an elusive goal never to come true.

Ericha rolled her eyes back, weakened by panic and the loss of blood. Breathing heavily, she wanted to believe that all would turn out in the end. The torture stemming from her wounded leg, the sadness of losing Errol, and the destruction of New Merieko defeated optimism in a bright future.

Prince Ari ran blindly into the forest, toward Persis.

Before Jeremy could stop him, the Little Oinker had disappeared, likely to get ate by something. It was too late for that showy, pompous coward anyways. It wasn't too late for Ericha!

Jeremy turned his full attention to Ericha, the love of his life, and sole reason for being.

Jeremy sat his weapons to the ground, then pulled the arrow from Ericha's thigh. He retrieved a tourniquet from a leather pouch belonging to Nikolai, and tied it above the wound. "We've got to get you back!" he sobbed. Desperately, he threw his arms around Ericha, and gave her a kiss.

Even with the sharp pain in her injured leg, Ericha wanted to be with Jeremy. She shed tears over a truth which couldn't be refused, nor denied. She had just lost her father, the only father she'd ever have, a good man she loved her entire life . . . a man who lived now only in memories.

Ericha's sole comfort and assurance came from the young man she held in her arms, the young man she'd spend the rest of her life with.

Ericha kissed Jeremy's cheek, opened her eyes, and saw a couple of Green Winged Men land next to Errol. Both aimed their blowguns straight at Jeremy's back.

Ericha shrieked as she pushed Jeremy away.

Seconds later, two poison darts punctured her neck, above the windpipe.

Frantically, Ericha clawed and tore to remove the darts, lodged deeply into her throat. Blood, foam, and phlegm trickled down the corners of her mouth. As the poison streamed through her body, she flailed and convulsed uncontrollably. Inadvertently, she reached out and slapped wildly at Jeremy.

Ericha's eyes fluttered, as consciousness slipped away. Delirium took charge, now. Ericha imagined living in a humble cottage, acres and acres of farmland before her, nestled against the rugged, breathtakingly beautiful mountains of Branell.

Ericha's hands clutched tightly against Jeremy's forearm.

Jeremy turned to look deeply into his girl's lifeless eyes, staring blankly at the trees above.

"Ericha?" he screamed, shaking her like a crazy man. "Ericha . . . Ericha . . . ERICHA!" he repeated, over and over and over again.

Jeremy grabbed his treasured sword from the grass and, with an unspeakable vengeance, decapitated one of the Green Winged Men approaching him.

Blood cascaded from the headless Green, and splashed into Jeremy's face, shirt, and bare legs. Blinded by rage, Jeremy went after the second winged man.

The Green placed a dart into his blowgun, then sent it into Jeremy's hip. The dart easily broke skin, as it poured deadly venom through Jeremy's body.

A numbing sensation spread through his crotch and thighs, as Jeremy swung his sword into the Green's belly. The Green stumbled to one side, his innards spilling onto the brush and deep grass.

A third winged man threw a wicked-looking battle ax at Jeremy, which impacted the boy's right knee.

Jeremy's screeching howls echoed through the burning homes and buildings of New Merieko. His strength fleeting away, he lifted the sword over his head, swung it at his oncoming adversary . . .

. . . and slayed yet another Green Winged Man, bent on destroying New Merieko.

Jeremy collapsed next to Ericha. His body grew increasingly numb and tingly. The pain jolting from his shattered knee was crippling, excruciating, unbearable.

Jeremy gritted his teeth and removed the ax, embedded into his knee. Carelessly, he flung the weapon somewhere out in the bushes. He fought to get up. But it was of no use. The paralyzing effects of the poison proved too great.

Jeremy dropped flat to the ground and sighed. Tears filled his eyes, as he looked straight into a smoke-filled sky. Above, Green Winged Men fired darts and arrows at people, below. This was usually followed by high-pitched screams, as the Greens swooped down to claim their prizes.

Jeremy lifted his head, to see Mucker shooting at the enemy. Rey and Weston pressed themselves against the tamarack, scared out of their wits. In the corner of one eye, Jeremy caught the blurred image of Green Winged Men dismembering Seely, as others hauled Errol off to their caves. To his right, he saw Ericha lying next to him, resting in eternal sleep, unaware of the violence and mayhem around her.

Greenleaf fled from his home in New Merieko. He didn't get very far. His hair and clothes were on fire, and flames engulfed him. More than a dozen Greens flew after him.

Jeremy saw an odd, demented humor in the gruesome proceedings. He knew he was dying, though it didn't seem to matter. Like his dearest friends, he too would perish and end up in a winged man's pot.

Mucker, Rey, and Weston would soon join him.

Jeremy glanced at his injured knee. Blood pulsated from the massive gash.

Jeremy wiped sweat, tears, and snot from his face, and smiled wistfully. Sly laughter and black comedy won the day!

A Green Winged so-and-so now stood over Jeremy . . .

Jeremy wondered if the so-and-so was there to finish him off, or let the poison do the job.

The so-and-so whipped out a butcher knife from his belt, then leaned over to slit Jeremy's gullet.

"Having fun, yet?" chuckled Jeremy, at his own detriment.

Before the so-and-so committed a dastardly deed upon Jeremy, he let out a wild screech and fell upon his intended victim. A dagger handle protruded from between his shoulder blades.

Jeremy snickered as Nikolai lifted the so-and-so off of him.

"Are you all right?" asked Nikolai, removing the dart from Jeremy's hip. "Jeremy, are you all right?"

"Never felt better!" giggled Jeremy, unaware of how sick he truly was. "Gotta fetch me a drink, a chew, and a smoke. Gotta have it, Nik . . . Just gotta."

Nikolai pressed a cloth bandage against Jeremy's knee, to halt the bleeding. He then dug through his medical pouch for an antidote to stifle the poison's deadly effects. "Lie still," he urged, working swiftly to save Jeremy's life.

"Nik?" asked Jeremy, oblivious to it all. "Can I? . . . Can I ask you a question?"

"Sure," agreed Nikolai, rubbing ointment to Jeremy's hip. "Ask away."

"I know it's a strange question, and I hope you don't mention it to anyone . . . especially Rey . . ."

"What is it?"

"Is it . . . y' know . . . Is it okay? . . ." Jeremy swallowed. "Is it okay for me to sleep with Ericha, before we get married?"

Nikolai closed Ericha's lifeless eyes. Smiling awkwardly, he whispered, "We'll talk about it later . . ."

Jeremy smirked. "I mean . . . Look, we've a'ready slept together, but what I meant was . . . y' know . . . *Slept* together?"

Nikolai wiped a teardrop or two from his eyes.

"I already know what Rey has to say about it," said Jeremy. "He'd tell me to wait until we're . . ."

Jeremy stopped. The antidote had entered his bloodstream, to halt the mortal venom. Slowly, gradually, common sense and reason were restored. "Nik!" cried Jeremy, fear nearly undoing his fragile mind and body. "Where's Ericha?"

"Jeremy . . ." mumbled Nikolai, sadly.

"Where's Ericha?"

"She . . . she's gone . . ."

"Gone?"

"She's dead . . ."

Jeremy stared at Nikolai, in disbelief.

Nikolai clutched Jeremy's hand. "She's dead . . . and you will be too, if we don't get you home . . ."

Jeremy rolled himself into a ball and wept.

Nikolai wrapped Jeremy's knee in thick bandages. "Jeremy," he said, fully aware of the dangers around him. "I'm going to take you in my arms, then fly back to . . ."

"Leave me," bawled Jeremy.

"What?"

"Leave me. I don't wanna live. I wanna die . . . with Ericha! I wanna be with her in Heaven!"

"Do you want to be part of the Greens' smörgåsbord?" asked Nikolai, sarcastically.

"I love her, Nik! I love her, and wanted her for my wife! Why must I keep on living?"

"My father's dead, too!" cried Nikolai, emotionally. "Why give up? The point to keep on living is to keep on living! And I'd rather live!"

"What about that story you told me about me and Ericha's shirts?" sobbed Jeremy.

"What about them?"

"According to Brown Winged Man lore, if our shirts were blessed they'd protect us!"

Nikolai laughed. "And you believed that?"

"What about Ericha?" whined Jeremy. "We can't just leave her here!"

Nikolai sighed. "If I can, I'll come back for her."

"What about me?" a childlike voice asked, from the woods.

Nikolai looked to see Ari dashing toward him. "Ari!" he snapped. "Or must I call you Prince Ari? Where were you?"

Ari shrugged.

"Never mind," whispered Nikolai. "Just stay out of sight."

Ari knelt beside a tree. In the thick dust and smoke, he was barely able to see Mucker, Rey, and Weston. He then turned to Ericha, lying still upon the ground. "Ericha?" he mumbled, reaching out to touch the girl's cold face. "Ericha? . . . Nik, what's wrong with? . . ."

"The same thing that's gonna be wrong with us," stated Nikolai, "if we don't get out of here!"

Ari bit his bottom lip and cried.

"Take Prince Ari," Jeremy said to Nikolai, flatly. "I'm staying here . . . with Ericha . . ."

"You stay here, there's no point in coming back," said Nikolai. "You've got to get to the infirmary, or you're a goner."

"So, I'm a goner," said Jeremy, grudgingly accepting his fate.

"Ari," said Nikolai, sternly. "I'll be back for you, as soon as I can. For now, I must get Jeremy home."

"What about me?" questioned Ari.

"Stay here with Ericha," ordered Nikolai. "Make sure nothing happens to her. I'll return, as soon as I . . ."

"I can't stay here!" screamed Ari. "I'm afraid!"

Nikolai slugged Ari in the nose.

Jeremy laughed out loud as Ari glared at Nikolai, in anger and betrayal.

"Don't give me that," Nikolai warned Ari. "You're royalty, aren't you? Then act like it! With your father and sister gone, you're now the 'King of Infernus'!"

"King Little Oinker," commented Jeremy, with a silly grin.

"I have to get Jeremy home," said Nikolai. "And you have to keep watch over Ericha. Are you going to earn your esteemed position, King Ari, or behave like the coward you truly are?"

Ari allowed the tears to flow freely.

Nikolai lifted Jeremy in his arms. "Hold tight!" he said, launching himself skyward, high above the trees and raging inferno.

Nikolai held his breath to avoid inhaling fumes and smoke from the burning buildings, below. He straightened his body, expanded his wings, and pointed himself toward the familiar, comforting city of Persis.

Confusion and delirium ruled over Jeremy. One moment, he was on the ground, in the company of a winged man, a spoiled brat, and a dead girl.

The next, he was hundreds of feet into the air.

For the first time in his life, Jeremy got a spectacular, birds-eye view of Infernus. Below was a thick growth of evergreen trees. To one side, he caught sight of the vast Agron Ocean. To his front was the steep, rugged, snow-covered peak of Mount Auric.

Jeremy's mind and body suffered the ill-effects of the poison, while his knee was in the worst pain imaginable. Logic gave way to severe memory loss. Looking all around, Jeremy wondered how he got so far up off the ground. Briefly, he forgot his own past, and even his own name.

And just what was that weird critter, carrying him off someplace?

Sickened by the toxin and a loss of blood, Jeremy tried breaking free from Nikolai. Fever had gotten the best of him, as existence took on a surreal, dream-like state. Bright sunlight blinded him, while he got chilled by the wind and cold of the high altitudes.

Jeremy opened his mouth, to issue a plea for Nikolai to let him go.

Instead, he vomited on Nikolai, himself, and upon the trees. He gave Nikolai a wicked-looking smile.

He relaxed, closed his eyes . . .

. . . . and passed out.

* * * * *

Prince Ari was left alone at the edge of a clearing, watching the horrific battle. He was torn between running, staying put, or screaming. His thoughts sprinted from the red-hot, fiery destruction of New Merieko, his sister Ericha just feet away from him, and his own self-preservation. Fear and sadness paralyzed him. There was no fleeing this nightmare. Death was in session.

Errol was dead. So was Ericha.

Errol and Ericha were dead!

And Ari didn't want to die.

Two Green Winged Men landed near the edge of the clearing and headed for Ericha's corpse.

Ari knelt behind a thick cluster of grass and brush. His breathing was heavy and erratic. He never felt such terror!

Could he keep from dying? Would he accept death bravely and graciously, and take it like a man? Or would he whine and whimper, seconds before getting killed?

Greens were notorious for torturing their victims . . .

The two Greens stood above Ericha. They chattered between themselves, in a language Ari never understood. Ari had never been this close to any Greens, and was deathly afraid of them. He had reason to be, long before they attacked New Merieko! Not only were the Greens real mean-looking and scary, these ones stunk like hell!

The two Greens whipped out their knives to cut on Ericha.

Ari spotted Jeremy's sword on the ground, within arm's length. He was told to protect Ericha, until Nikolai got back.

But what if Nikolai never got back? And what if he did, and it was too late?

Ari's heart beat like a drum.

One of the Greens split Ericha's shirt open, as the other removed her loincloth and discarded it to one side.

Ari quietly looked on, as the Greens exposed Ericha's bare breasts and vagina . . . a violation in itself. Soon, they'd hack Ericha to bits, a possibility which Ari couldn't imagine or tolerate.

Despite Ari's many differences with Ericha, she remained a sibling, even in death. Errol placed the love of the family unit above all else! Ari was heavily grilled in this rule. It was bad enough to look upon Ericha's nudity. Ari refused to see her torn to shreds.

The two Greens were startled by a shrill, boyish yell. Neither expected to see the tiny, well-dressed child latch onto Jeremy's sword, and leap out from behind a tree.

Before the Greens evaluated or comprehended Ari's arrival, one of them had his left wing severed from the rest of his body.

The injured Green shrieked. Blood splattered against the tree, his buddy, and onto Ari. The Green attempted to fly away . . . to no avail.

Meanwhile, the severed wing twitched, contorted, and flapped on its own.

The second Green then had Jeremy's sword driven into his crotch, and exit through his butt.

As Ari pulled the sword out of him, the second Green fell over, reaching desperately for his emasculated privates.

Killing is a sin. Ari watched the two Green Winged Men die. His mind was divided between justice, revulsion, and glee. He didn't know whether to be sickened by the gory spectacle, or ecstatic and delighted. He crossed a line between that which was moral, righteous, and decent, to that which was hateful, immoral . . . the worst abomination ever! He had just killed two of God's creatures. Murder had went from being unspeakable, to proper and legal. For the moment, killing was downright enjoyable!

Trapped by instincts of blood-lust, and wishing to get even for Errol and Ericha, Ari threw himself into the battle, increasing the butchery and madness of violence.

Ari sprinted into the open. With no hesitation, he disemboweled a third foe.

Rey, Weston, and Mucker looked on with surprise, shock, astonishment, and (in Mucker's case!) mean-spirited humor.

Even then, Prince Ari wasn't dart nor arrow-proof, as several Greens pursued him.

As Ari downed yet another enemy, it appeared as if it might be curtains for him, as a number of Greens surrounded the boy.

Mucker roared with laughter, as Ari wiped out two more Greens. Rey,

Weston, and Mucker bravely left their hiding place.

The three men fetched bows, arrows, and swords from those who had died in battle. Risking their own safety, they cut down the Greens threatening Ari. As one Green turned to face Rey, Weston stabbed him in the back with a jagged-edged, Agronian dagger.

This fight didn't just mark the first time that Ari had taken the lives of others. Rey, too, was a novice to butchery as he destroyed a couple of Greens threatening him.

Rey had spent his adult life sharing the Word of God. Assuming he lived to see that day's end, he'd suffer insurmountable guilt and sleepless nights. What choices did he have, but to fight? Sentiments of love and peace were useless here! Still, Rey feared he'd answer for this debauchery, when it came time to meet his maker.

Rey didn't go to New Merieko with malice. It was the Greens who shed the first blood. One could easily claim that it was the Greens to blame for this! Rey was merely defending himself, from the man-eating marauders.

The Word spoke of upstanding, God-fearing men forced to battle evil, where it essentially became His will. Therefore, was Rey excused for slaying Green Winged Men, in order to uphold his fellow man?

Were the Green Winged Men truly men, at all? Or was Yevgeny right in his assessment of them? Did God truly love the Green Winged Men? Or did they indeed align themselves with one who served only evil? . . .

Such as Soraq?

A good number of Browns joined in the battle, as they warred against the aggressive Greens, high above New Merieko. The two tribes engaged in a spectacular, grisly series of dogfights. Those winning individual duels remained in the contest. Those who lost met death in the flames which, minutes before, had been the colony of New Merieko.

Rey slit a Green's throat, when he turned to see a bunch of them charging toward him. Ari, Mucker, and Weston were also in harm's way. Nearly every colonist had fled, or were killed. Bodies scattered the lanes of the burning village or were taken to the Greens' caves. In his worst dreams, Rey never thought he'd get eaten by a winged man! He only hoped that, if he was soon to die, he'd earn God's everlasting love and support.

More than anything, Rey figured that, in a few short moments, he'd gain a better understanding of what death truly was . . .

Rey cut a Green's chest open with a sword, then got knocked over. He hit the ground with extreme force, as air rushed out of his gaping mouth. His aching head grew dizzy. He reached awkwardly for the sword, which remained lodged within the body of the Green he just killed. Looking up, he saw several Greens looming over him. He let out a cry of mortal terror, closed his eyes, and waited for the end to come.

Rey didn't expect to hear the sounds of horns in the distance.

In a flash every Brown Winged Man scattered from the aerial combat, leaving only the Greens to fight.

"Fire!" a familiar voice shouted, in Kuschan.

Dozens of arrows sprayed overhead, making mincemeat of the Green invaders.

"Fire!" was again ordered.

More arrows streamed across the sky, to slaughter the enemy.

A third, then a fourth, then a fifth volley of arrows soared overhead. More and more of the Greens were shot down, or hastily returned to their homeland. Many suffered severe wounds and scars.

Dead and dying Green Winged Men splattered to the ground or were cremated in the burning homes and structures.

Rey hopped to his feet, then ran for cover.

A squad of Kuschan Marines and Naval Infantrymen, led by Antonov and Arkoff, entered the charred ruins to clean out the Greens left there.

What had been viewed as a Green victory soon turned to a rout. In no time, the surviving Greens hightailed it. A few stragglers surrendered, or met their doom at the end of Kuschan arrows and steel.

Mucker had spent his whole life hating Kuschans. He still had little use for them. Yet, he couldn't demean those who just saved his fat from the fire.

For the most part, Mucker also had little regard for Brotherhood Leaders or Embrian diplomats. Still, Mucker quietly acknowledged that Rey and Weston had done some good, after all.

The bloody work was completed . . . for now. Without another word, Mucker began heading to Persis.

The shed where Mucker lived would now be lonely, without Seely. The two men had traveled to Infernus years ago, with McClusky. Well, now Seely was dead, while Mucker and McClusky were no longer on speaking terms.

Mucker spit when he recalled Seely's death. Damned drunken fool! What the hell stupid idea was it, coming to New Merieko, and bringing Paransky with him? Seely croaked for being an idiot, and Paransky suffered from a dart wound . . . if he wasn't already dead!

Seely paid for being a damned fool. Hopefully, Paransky was okay.

Mucker had high hopes for the little tattooed boy. Wasn't nobody, not green-hided freaks or churchy hypocrites, gonna stop him from spending time with the strange, sad-eyed child.

Mucker walked at a steady pace, keeping his eyes peeled for critters. Not only was he worried about Paransky, but also the well-being and safety of a young man named Jeremy Kentworth.

Weston dropped the sword he used against the Greens, brushed himself off, and approached Prince Ari. Or was it King Ari, now? Did such a title mean anything to the lad, now? Ari wasn't hurt or nothing, at least not physically. Even then, the boy was in distress, as he wandered aimlessly through the ruins of New Merieko. Everything was gone. What reason was there to rebuild it?

Like a godsend, a heavy downpour of rain drenched the eastern coastline of Infernus. Flames which engulfed a once-promising community was extinguished, replaced by steam, smoke, smoldering logs and boards, and ash. This left the foul, dank smell of death, rot, and decay. No matter. The danger had passed, and with it the hopes of revision, re-examination, and recovery. Those left standing were blessed, and cursed, to live another day.

Thank God and the Kuschan Navy, and not themselves, for it . . .

Ari was angry, upset, humiliated, and devastated. Tears were concealed by rainwater, dripping from his face. With a blank, hollow expression, he went to check on his sister Ericha who remained, intact, at the forest's edge. It sickened him to look upon her nude body, resting peacefully in the wet, dewy grass.

Ari covered Ericha in his fancy jacket, then knelt to caress her cheeks and hair. He placed his hand in hers, afraid to let go. "Ericha . . . oh Ericha," he sobbed. He failed to stifle the warm memories, or cruelties of sorrow. He stayed by her side for more than an hour, not knowing and not caring of what happened around him.

Rey joined Ari in this vigil. He sat next to the boy, and whispered a prayer for those lost on that bitter day in New Merieko. He kept at Ari's side. No words were exchanged.

Weston's opinion of Kuschans mirrored that of Mucker's. Still, he grinned as he watched Antonov and Arkoff examine the battlefield.

Antonov was no stranger to the fog and horrors of war. In terms of logistics and casualties, New Merieko was a "minor skirmish" when compared to other scrapes he'd been in. Yet, the numbers of civilian dead was unacceptable. And never once had Antonov saw the remnants of a conflict, where most of the combatants were men with wings.

Weston and Antonov shared a laugh as they shook hands.

"It's a pleasure to see you, Mister Weston," said Antonov.

"The same with you, Commander Antonov," said Weston.

"Captain Antonov," the officer said, proudly. "Captain Antonov, of the Kuschan warship *King Leonid* I."

"Pardon me," said Weston. "I've never heard of the King Leonid I."

"Formerly known as the Roderick Dundee. This morning, we ordered it to surrender. When we got no answer, my men and I boarded it. To our surprise, the Green Winged Men got there before we did, and left none of those outlaws alive."

"I see," sighed Weston. "Well, Captain Antonov, I can't thank you enough for your help. Tell me . . . What motivated you to come to our . . . rescue?"

"We saw smoke bellowing from the distance. We also got a visit from a couple of young Brown Winged Men, notifying us of your situation." Antonov smiled. "The officers and men were all-too-happy in coming to the aide of our new allies."

"Thank you."

"It was the least we could do."

Weston took a deep breath, as he looked all around. "Well, Antonov . . . I'll be damned."

Antonov sought clarity.

Weston snickered. "If I'm not mistaken, this is the first joint Embrian and Kuschan military campaign, in the history of our two nations . . ."

Nikolai left Jeremy at the infirmary at Persis, rushed back to New Merieko, and joined in the fight. Once they heard the Kuschan horns sounding in the distance, the Brown Winged Men dispersed as Antonov and his archers unleashed hell upon the Green adversaries.

It wasn't just fatigue that plagued Malachi at the battle's end, but the injuries he received earlier. Forever would he be haunted by images of Lorenzo's passing, added to his bloodthirsty reaction to it.

Malachi contemplated the aftermath of that day's warfare. Once more, he pondered if he was worthy of the Kingdom of Heaven.

The Holy Father created man in his own image.

Who created the winged men of Infernus?

Malachi was certain that all hope of salvation was fleeting. He pondered if all winged men were products of a sick, celestial mind, belonging to a sick, celestial being.

Malachi stood to the side, watching as Rey and Ari knelt to Ericha. Briefly, he thought back to Randen. No one would come out of this ordeal, unscathed! Weakened by exhaustion and sadness, Malachi wiped his eyes, as the emotions proved too great a burden. Quietly, he evaluated the costs of this pivotal fight for survival, and wondered who else had died.

"Malachi?" someone shouted, through the sounds of a cleansing rain.

Nikolai approached his big brother Malachi, who didn't want anyone to see him weep. What was the point? The two winged men grew up together in the same house, with the same loving parents. Nikolai easily read Malachi's mind. There was no reasons to keep secrets, or deny their feelings at that given moment.

More than anything, Malachi was relieved knowing that Nikolai was okay. The differences which separated them days before were forgiven. Brotherly love eroded the pain of hurt feelings and angry words.

With warm smiles, and even warmer hearts, the two winged men threw their arms around each other and embraced.

* * * * *

The Greens retreated from New Merieko, then headed home to their caves in the northeastern peninsula. They collected most of their kills, even as the Kuschan Navy shot hundreds of arrows at them. Despite the day ending badly, the hunters celebrated as their tribe gathered for a communal feast.

It wasn't just the slaughtering of people that the Greens engaged in. They also "cared" for their wounded. Depending whether an injured Green could fully heal and be a providing member of the tribe, determined whether they lived or died. Those Greens who were permanently disabled, or sustained life-threatening wounds, were put to death and became part of the grub.

A few Greens had serious wounds, caused by Kuschan archers. While the majority of the injured Greens were all right, some were helped back, just to get done in by their own kind.

"What happened?" asked McClusky, all worked up.

"Antonov," said Ricardo, flatly.

"Antonov?"

"Him and those other Kuschan dogs."

McClusky seemingly felt the earth shift from beneath him.

New Merieko wasn't the only thing to go up in smoke. McClusky had advocated for the Green Winged Men, and sought to develop a lasting peace with the Browns. He examined the Greens' blood lust and fanatical cravings for human flesh and wondered if the tribe revealed their true colors. Perhaps they weren't worthy of admiration and respect. Perhaps they'd never be civilized. Perhaps the Greens would remain as they always had . . . Brutes, criminals, and savages.

McClusky's treaty with the Browns and Kuschans was shattered. Based on their aggression against New Merieko, the Greens would never, could never alter their fierce reputations.

"You realize what you've done?" McClusky shouted at Ricardo, who was busy cutting off pieces of a colonist's leg. "You destroyed everything I worked for you! What do ya gotta say about that?"

"What do I care?" snickered Ricardo. "We got what we wanted."

"That tears it!" hollered McClusky, his face red with anger. "I'm done with you . . . all of you! I tried helpin' you out all this time, and you repay me by butchering innocent civilians!"

Ricardo wiped his bloody hand against McClusky's shirt. "That's how much I care . . ."

"I'm done with ya, then," said McClusky, in resignation. "I'm leavin' tonight! If I'm lucky, it might be that the Browns will let me stay in Persis. If not . . . well, guess I gotta tangle with Mucker."

Ricardo shoved a dagger at McClusky's throat . . . the same, trusted dagger that Yevgeny used against Embrians in the Kuschan village of Anumun, the same trusted dagger used against Randen, McCoy, and Ugo. "You ain't going no place!" said Ricardo. "You leave, I'll hunt you down. You even think of going to Persis, I'll kill you! Then I'll kill everyone over there!"

McClusky backed away. His heart beat wildly out of control. He looked all around, at the sight of people getting cooked on open flames.

In the distance, he saw Seely's head get perched upon a pole, right next to McCoy and Yevgeny's.

McClusky staggered away from the Greens' camp, to a large, bald rock overlooking the Agron Ocean. He sat down to watch a pale, full moon rising over the eastern horizon. There, he sought a moment of solitude, and seclusion, on the Infernus shore at sundown.

McClusky had no use for Seely, whatsoever. Seely had always been a lush, even in the days of living in the bars, bordellos, and shanties of Agron. Once he got to Infernus with Mucker and McClusky, Seely's thirst for booze threatened their partnership.

Finally, McClusky got tired of Seely's slobbery mouth, slurred speech, and tired, bloodshot eyes. As Mucker took it upon himself to care for Seely, McClusky forever distanced himself from the old soak.

Recalling their wistful, dreamy days of youth, McClusky was saddened to learn that Seely was dead.

McClusky's relationship with Mucker was forever strained. While Mucker befriended the passive, peaceful Brown Winged Men, McClusky allied himself with the aggressive, warlike Greens.

Thanks to the destruction of New Merieko, Mucker and McClusky would never again trade a kind, civil word between them.

The skies grew dark, as night fell on Infernus. McClusky regarded himself as a lone, alienated, isolated figure on the island. He defended and upheld the Green Winged Men. That day, he got his answer for years of hard work, sweat, toil, and sacrifice.

He had no one to blame, but himself . . .

* * * * *

That following morning, Infernus had its first frost of the season.

The icy dew of the dawn, along with hazy, dull skies and frigid temperatures, dampened an already dreary, downbeat mood in Persis. Everyone was saddened to hear of Lorenzo and Errol's death. They were even more dismayed about Ericha.

Seely's "contributions" to the town merited little, other than to throw money into the coffers of the local taverns and whorehouses. Except for Persis' shadier elements, few gave him much thought.

Ericha was another story. She was Errol's daughter, and very well-liked. She'd be remembered for her fiery red hair, lovely smile, and feminine figure, concealed only by a loincloth and buckskin shirt. She was beloved in the church, and an object of attraction for the young men and boys of Persis.

She was also the best friend and fiancée to Jeremy Kentworth . . .

The night before, Rey held a candle light vigil for the victims of the New Merieko Massacre. The event was punctuated by hugs, kisses, and the shedding of tears. Friends and family found courage, comfort, and the resolve to heal their wounds, and move on.

That morning, Malachi arranged an informal, undistinguished ceremony, commemorating his rise as chief of the Brown Winged Men. He stood on a podium alongside King Ari, as they accepted rulership of the human and winged man population.

Even with smiles and well-wishes for a successful transition of power, the ceremony failed to halt anger, animosities, and sadness. Sentries kept watch in the skies above Persis, making sure the Greens didn't stage an attack during these dark, depressing hours.

After the ceremony, Malachi went straight to work as chief. Meanwhile, King Ari fled to a bedroom he now shared with Paransky, at the Brotherhood of Faith Church.

Malachi was known for a passive, indecisive nature. Yet, his first ruling brought on cheers from the vast majority of folks in Persis. He called Admiral Vaslov and Captain Antonov to his hut, where he canceled the trade agreement between the Brown Winged Men and the Kuschans.

"You can't stop the treaty between our two nations!" protested Vaslov. "The Kuschan Navy offered it in good faith and standing, and this is exactly how we intend to . . ."

"The treaty wasn't just between St. Alexandrov and Persis," interrupted Malachi. He didn't wish to be rude, although he disliked Vaslov. "Vic McClusky and the Green Winged Men were also part of that agreement."

Vaslov frowned. "That is true, but . . ."

"Since the Green tribe took it upon themselves to break the peace, I see no reason to honor our previous commitments," said Malachi. His stomach was tied in knots, even as his actions reflected a strength he never once displayed before. "The Green Winged Men are no longer part of that agreement and, regrettably, neither are we."

"Chief Malachi," said Antonov. "It wasn't the Kuschan Navy to break the ceasefire. And, if I may add, it was the Kuschan Navy to quill the violence inflicted upon New Merieko."

Antonov had a point. Still, Malachi was determined to free himself of the Kuschan Navy, altogether. "I have made my ruling, and my ruling is final," he said, struggling not to show a lack of courage or convictions.

"The treaty also gave us a right and responsibility to defend our new trading partners from all enemies," explained Vaslov, retrieving a document from within his jacket. "Your father's signature is right here. Captain Antonov held onto our end of the bargain. We insist that you uphold yours."

"My father is no longer in charge," said Malachi, his voice cracking. "My father will no longer be in charge. He is dead, and so is the contract. I will not abide by its ruling, and neither will you."

"And who do you propose to take charge of your defenses, as well as handle commerce between Infernus and the Farlands?" asked Vaslov, angrily.

"John Mucker," said Malachi.

"Mucker?" Vaslov and Antonov gasped, in unison.

"Mucker has been a true and loyal friend to the Brown Winged Men," explained Malachi. "He had proven his devotion to us, and I will reward him for his years of service to Infernus . . . and to me."

"You can't do that!" screamed Vaslov, getting madder by the minute.

"I have done that!" responded Malachi. "I have made my ruling. I shall abide by it, and so will you."

Malachi stood, bowed to the two Kuschan officers, and bid them farewell.

Vaslov hopped to his feet and, with a huff, stormed from the hut.

Antonov smiled, removed his cap, and also bowed. "Chief Malachi," he said, cordially. "Thank you for your time, and your consideration."

"Thank you, Captain Antonov," answered Malachi, acknowledging that the young naval officer wasn't a bad guy . . . for a Kuschan.

"As you wish, Kusch will no longer seek further interests on the island of Infernus," said Antonov. "However, I shall never forget my time in this land, as your citizens have been very kind and generous to me."

"I appreciate that," said Malachi.

"While I can't entirely agree with your decision, I do at least understand it," said Antonov. "For what it's worth, I will also obey it. Rest assured . . . Once I return to my homeport in St. Alexandrov, I will never discuss my mission here."

"Thank you."

"I will take my leave of you, Chief Malachi." Antonov placed his cap back onto his head. "You have my respect, my blessings, and my support."

With that, Antonov left the hut.

Now came a meeting that Malachi was NOT looking forward to.

According to laws and customs of the Brown Winged Men, Fernandez was regarded as a criminal for violating the Greens' borders and starting a war with them. Though he wasn't jailed, Fernandez was shunned, and never left the safety or sanctuary of the Brotherhood Church.

A fair number of residents, people and winged men alike, blamed him for WHAT HAPPENED to Errol, Lorenzo, Ericha, and Seely. Louder critics placed a death threat on him. Fernandez remained at the church, under Rey's care and custody, until his hearing with Malachi.

A small entourage of bodyguards, including Weston, accompanied Fernandez to the hut. No one approached Fernandez with violent intent. Still, he was given the stink eye.

Although Weston wasn't happy with Fernandez, he wished to speak on the boy's behalf. The diplomat wore his finest jacket, boots, and breeches, while Fernandez was dressed in a school uniform lent to him by Rey, to replace those destroyed at New Merieko.

Fernandez was a bundle of nerves as he entered the hut. He was devastated knowing that Paolo and Frida were killed during the Greens' siege. He was unaware of the details in their passing, yet knew they met horrible ends.

Malachi's sore wings agonized him, terribly. Exhaustion and fatigue had also gotten the better of him. All he wanted to do was retreat to his quarters and spend the remains of the day in quiet solitude. Fernandez's hearing was the only thing keeping him from needed rest and relaxation.

Originally, Malachi had a speech planned for Fernandez's hearing. The pain in his wings proved too much. Therefore, he made his spiel short, sour, and not at all sweet.

"In the past," opened Malachi, glaring at Fernandez, "I would've had you stoned to death . . ."

Fernandez's mouth gaped open, as both eyes widened in fear. Weston put one arm around the boy's shoulders, to assure and comfort him.

"You are to leave Infernus on the next available ship," said Malachi. "Once you leave this island, you are never, never, to set foot here again. Is that understood?"

Fernandez was too scared to say anything, so Weston answered for him. "He understands, sir."

"Very well," said Malachi, his lips quivering. "You are free to go . . .Now, get out of my sight! . . ."

Fernandez tried to voice his apologies for what he had done. Instead, it came out as sobs, whines, and gibberish.

"Get out!" screamed Malachi.

Weston and the others hastily escorted Fernandez from the hut.

They stepped outside to a bright, yet cool morning. Overhead, the sky threatened rain. Frightened by the shellacking he took from Malachi, Fernandez leaned against a pole and wept.

Weston spotted Antonov getting a final glimpse of this strange, wondrous little town. Soon, the Kuschan officer would return to his duties of refitting a notorious pirate ship known as the Roderick Dundee, into the proud Kuschan warship christened the King Leonid I.

"Captain Antonov," greeted Weston, warmly.

"Mr. Weston," answered Antonov.

"It may seem a bit . . . odd for an Embrian diplomat to ask a favor from a Kuschan sailor. But, may I ask? . . . When do you set sail for the Farlands?"

"Within a week."

"I hoped to stay longer, but I have to get this young man . . ." Weston motioned toward Fernandez. ". . . To Sykes, where he's to attend one of the parochial schools there. Leader Rey's writing a letter on his behalf, to be enrolled in either Lord William's, or Lord Kelly's."

"I see," said Antonov. "Go on."

"There have been threats on Fernandez's life, so I need to get him somewhere he'll be safe," explained Weston, hesitantly. "I hate to inconvenience you, but do you think it's possible for him to hitch a ride with you, at least as far as Agron?"

Antonov glanced at the awkward kid in a silly skullcap, and an even sillier tunic which exposed his bare legs to the weather. He couldn't imagine Fernandez being such a big sissy, yet assumed it wasn't entirely his fault. Paolo and Frida had babied the teenager his entire life. Someone had to step up and undo the damage. "I'll take him straight into Sykes, if you like," accepted Antonov.

"I'd sure appreciate it," said Weston.

"Admiral Vaslov won't approve, but no worries. It won't be on the Matyushenko where Fernandez will be transported, but with me on the King Leonid I." Antonov snickered. "I just hope the Embrian Navy doesn't mistake it for the Roderick Dundee, and blow us to smithereens."

"That would make things a bit . . . inconvenient," agreed Weston.

"I'll put Fernandez to work scrubbing the deck, helping out in KP, and doing a real sailor's job, on a real sailor's ship. Looks to me like he's been given the soft touch for too long. Rest assured, I'll make a man out of him before we reach the continent."

"That's good," said Weston. "Between you and me, it's a man that Fernandez must learn how to be . . ."

Malachi was beat. It wasn't just the injuries he got during his fight with the Greens. The job of being chief was enormous.

When Malachi was a kid, he took Lorenzo for granted. He had no idea of the pressures, weighing heavily upon the elder winged man. Not only was Lorenzo chief, he raised a family, and was a tough, yet loving father.

Malachi wasn't married, and already he felt unbearable strain. Perhaps it was the manner in which he became chief. Lorenzo gained power in a time of peace and stability. Now, Persis remained in high alert.

Malachi stood, sighed, and stretched his sore, aching back. He used to spend mornings on long flights, not only for pleasure, but to deal with stress. He'd been warned not to fly until the wounds healed. Never again was he able to obtain the same speed and agility as before. He faced permanent injuries, in body and in spirit.

He began to realize what it meant to get old.

Malachi went to his quarters, which once was his parents' bedroom. He needed to sleep, but just couldn't get himself to relax in that particular spot. In his heart, the room still belonged to his folks.

Malachi frowned. The master bedroom was passed down from generation to generation, whenever one took on the role of chief. Malachi couldn't enter in there, and make himself entirely at home.

Though it broke with tradition, Malachi chose to slumber in the room he called his own, since he was a child.

Malachi had gotten his second wind. Rather than spending the rest of the day hidden away in the hut, he needed sunlight, along with the assurances of friendship.

Malachi disliked Kuschans, and refused to trust them. His handling of Vaslov and Antonov was harsh. Yet, he needed to send out a message that he didn't want other nations' ships to patrol Infernus' waters.

Malachi was also unhappy with his treatment of Fernandez. The Agronian was just a boy, and coerced by the words of a madman. Not only did Paolo and Frida die in a quagmire, but so did Errol, Ericha, Seely . . . and Lorenzo. Maybe Malachi cut too deep into Fernandez. Yet, the anguish that all Persis now experienced would forever be felt by its people, humans and winged men alike.

Did Fernandez deserve any better?

Malachi saw Weston chatting with Antonov. He avoided eye-contact with them, knowing his decisions weren't popular. He couldn't afford to explain himself, nor to apologize. He was now Chief Malachi of the Brown Winged Men. It wasn't a route to conceit or arrogance, but a harsh, grueling road to accountability. Malachi lived in a world where he had to be decisive, and stick to his values.

It was a lonely path. Malachi still needed the support of a mentor, a spiritual leader, and a role model. More than anything, he sought Rey's help during this crucial transition.

Malachi strolled toward the church. A cool breeze signified the coming of fall and, eventually, winter. Malachi smiled at everyone he met, but said little other than simple greetings. He noticed a number of young adults and children, gathering around the house of worship. Ericha was already buried at a cemetery upon a bald ridge, overlooking Persis. Rey had set up a service for youth, to celebrate her life. Desserts, fruit drinks, and fond memories were dished up.

"Run them damn Kuschans off?" grunted Mucker, stepping out of his shed.

"Yeah, I runned them off," snickered Malachi, trying to impersonate Mucker.

"Well, if you didn't, I woulda. Where you headin', in such a hurry?"

"To the church."

"Got time for a sit-down?" asked Mucker.

Malachi smiled. He looked up to Mucker, since recollection. In a way, he even kind of worshiped the man, and was even kind of scared of him. That morning, Mucker was a little less grouchy than usual. The old coot was missing Seely, and needed someone to jaw with.

Well, Malachi wanted someone to jaw with, too. Since Rey was tied up at the moment, then Mucker was as good a man to jaw with, as anyone. Maybe even better!

It was strange to enter the rickety old shed, and not see Seely hunched over the table, holding off a hangover by creating an even worse one. Reluctantly, Malachi sat at the chair where the old lush called "home." Mucker offered him a shot of rotgut, but Malachi refused.

Malachi opened a conversation by saying, "The Kuschans didn't like it when I said I placed you in charge of the military and shipping."

Mucker grinned. "I don't give a hang if they like it or not. I only want 'em outa here, before I get the mind to kill 'em."

"One more thing," said Malachi, hesitantly. "The Kuschans have laid claim to the Roderick Dundee."

"Huh?"

"The Kuschans have taken the Roderick Dundee a prize," said Malachi. "They renamed it the 'King Leonid I.'"

"Sons of bitches," said Mucker, straight-shooting his drink. "I was gonna claim that junk heap, and name it after me."

"Who cares?" snickered Malachi. "You'll build a fleet of ships to rival that of any navy's."

Mucker only grunted.

"But, just remember this," said Malachi, half-joking. "I'm in charge, now."

"Bullshit."

Pain jolted through Malachi's wings, as Mucker uttered that profanity. Still, the young winged man giggled. What else should he have expected from a cranky, mean old buccaneer?

"It ain't just them damn Kuschans I oughta run off," said Malachi, once again trying to sound like Mucker. "Whadda ya gotta say about that, you ugly old brute?"

"Good luck," said Mucker, pouring himself another drink.

Minutes later, Malachi headed to the church, where a bunch of kids held a memorial for Ericha. Patiently, he stood by the main entrance, not wishing to dampen the festivities with his presence. No longer was he part of the younger crowd. From now on, he had to be a grown-up.

Rey took note of Malachi, excused himself from the church, and went to greet the new chief. He asked Malachi to chat outside at the benches.

As they sat down, Rey asked Malachi to speak freely.

Malachi took a deep breath. "I've got doubts as to my own faith," he admitted painfully.

"What for?" asked Rey, in concern.

Malachi wiped away a tear. "Because of what happened yesterday. I had to kill several Green Winged Men, Leader Rey."

"You weren't the only one," whispered Rey, as to not draw attention.

"But where do I stand with God, now?" asked Malachi. "Does He still love me? Or am I forever cursed?"

"Why are you cursed?"

"For my hatred of the Green Winged Men . . . and because I'm not a man, as you are." Malachi glanced at his two hands. "Look at me . . . just look at me! I'm not human . . . I'll never be human!"

"Give thanks that you're not human, Malachi," commented Rey. "Frankly, it's overrated."

"God created man in his own image, but who created me? Soraq?"

"Malachi . . ."

"It wasn't godly what I did, yesterday!" sobbed Malachi. "After my father was . . . afterwards, I killed those responsible, and I didn't bat an eye over it! Does that make me worthy of God's Kingdom, or does it condemn me to damnation and hellfire?"

"Should I also be condemned to damnation and hellfire, for what I did?" questioned Rey. "Do you think I liked what happened at New Merieko? We both had to kill. Neither of us went there for a fight. We didn't start it, but still we have to answer for it. Not only must we answer for ourselves, but to our fellow man. And yes, we have to answer to God."

"I hate myself for what I done," said Malachi, fighting back tears.

"You think that because I'm a human, and you're a winged man, it makes me better in the eyes of God? We both love God, and wish to serve Him. If I could go back, I'd stop Yevgeny from what he did. But I can't, so now we're stuck answering for his choices. Just like we're stuck, answering for our responses to them. I'm in deeper trouble with God because I'm a Leader. I resorted to violence yesterday too, Malachi. Don't forget that. I didn't want to, but I did! So did Nik . . . So did Weston. So did Ericha, before she died! Jeremy, Mucker, even Ari and Paransky got into it. Maybe we're all condemned . . . who knows? The alternative meant paying with our lives. I'm not sorry for living this day. I am sorry for living with the knowledge that I had to kill, in order to save myself. There's blood on all our hands."

Malachi frowned.

"I suppose I should feel heroic, but I just can't," said Rey. "I'm sick unto death. I doubt if I'll ever be washed clean. All I can do is seek God's forgiveness, and keep working to do His will on Earth."

"Yes, sir," whispered Malachi.

"You probably don't think you're quite ready to be chief of the Brown Winged Men," said Rey. "In my heart, I know you'll do your best. I'll keep doing my best to serve God. That's all anyone can ask for. And I guess the best either of us can expect is to seek God's forgiveness, and work to uphold it for the rest of our lives. What more can we hope to achieve in our insignificant, corrupted, mortal existences?"

* * * * *

Jeremy woke up, after nearly two days of sleep. It was a long slumber, haunted by cruel dreams, surreal images, sadness, and regret. Chills and high fever only made things worse.

It was a few minutes before sunrise. There was light, but no shadow. Dew covered the rolling hills and narrow valley of Persis. It had rained most of the night, then cleared off at dawn. A cold wind swept through the draws and canyons. The air was frigid.

Jeremy opened his eyes to see the rafters lining the ceiling of the infirmary. His stomach was empty, and his throat dry. He was lightheaded and dizzy. There was a dull ache in the center of his forehead. His knee felt like it was on fire, where it had been struck with the ax. Jeremy's blankets were moist with sweat, and the room was as dank as a grave.

Jeremy didn't even know where he was . . . until cloudy, faded memories slowly crept into his head. Slowly, painfully, he recalled those terrible events in New Merieko.

Jeremy was dressed only in a loincloth, and felt like ice. He struggled to sit up in the tiny cot, and nearly threw up. He had a bright, blinding aura in his vision. Everything was out of focus. Each move was a struggle. Jeremy was exhausted, even after long hours of sleep. Most of the blankets were knocked to the floor. Jeremy rolled himself in a ball. The stained, yellow bandages on his knee loosened. Blood and puss leaked from a deep gash, and drained onto the cot.

Jeremy closed his eyes to visualize Ericha lying next to him, in the village of New Merieko. By now, the spirit had left Ericha's beautiful, young body.

Dead.

Ericha was dead.

This wasn't merely a phantasm brought on by fever, but an inescapable reality. Ericha was dead! And now Jeremy had to face life on his own, without the love and comfort of one he chose as his wife.

He was alone.

Jeremy whimpered, as tears seeped from both eyes.

"Jeremy?" asked Nikolai, entering the room. "Are you all right?"

Jeremy shivered.

Nikolai lifted the tangled blankets from the floor, then placed them softly upon Jeremy. "You're freezing!"

"Tell me about it!" cried Jeremy.

"I'll get a fire going," said Nikolai, pressing his hand against Jeremy's head. "The fever's lifted. I'll bet you're starving!"

"Yeah . . ."

"I'll go to the church, and have Evelyn fix you some breakfast. Then I'll build a fire."

"Why's it so cold in here?" complained Jeremy.

"It rained last night, cleared off, and got chilly." Nikolai ran his fingers over Jeremy's unruly hair. "Real icy this morning."

"Icy?"

"Yeah, icy," said Nikolai. "Summer's over."

Jeremy frowned. "Nik . . . Why did you save me?"

"What?" asked Nikolai.

"Why did you save me?"

Nikolai grinned. "Because you're Jeremy."

"Because I'm Jeremy?"

"That was a good enough reason for me," said Nikolai. "You're not sorry I kept you alive, are you? You're not wishing I left you out there to be eaten by the Green Winged Men?"

"I dunno," moped Jeremy.

"You nearly died, even after I got you here. You had me worried! Everyone's worried. We've taken turns staying with you."

"Like who?"

"Me, Leader Rey. Weston spent much of yesterday. He stayed by your side, keeping a close watch on his cousin Jeremiah." Nikolai laughed. "Even Mucker was here for a while. The whole town's asking about you. Your fever finally broke, but I want to keep an eye on your knee, making sure it doesn't turn black. If it does, then I'll have to cut."

"Cut?"

"Don't worry, it's not that bad . . . yet."

"How's . . ." Jeremy scratched his head. "Oh, what's-his-name'?"

"'What's-his-name'?"

"Aw, you know . . . The little tattooed boy?"

"Paransky," said Nikolai.

"Yeah, Paransky! How is he?"

"He'll make it."

Jeremy sighed. "That's good. He'll keep Rey and Mucker company. So . . . Will I make it?"

"That's up to you," answered Nikolai. "If you want to live, you'll make it. If you don't, you'll settle on staying here until you let yourself die. It's up to you."

"Where's Ericha?"

Nikolai turned his head away.

"Look, I already know she's gone!" whined Jeremy. "A'right?"

"They . . . buried her . . . Night before last."

"Buried her?" cried Jeremy. "Night before last? Why didn't you wake me?"

"You were delirious."

"But why didn't you let me attend? . . ."

"You were delirious!" shouted Nikolai, tiredly. "You had a high fever and was as sick as a dog. What point was there getting you out of bed? Then you'd be dead, too."

Jeremy's eyes flooded with tears.

"Had you been there, it would've been your funeral too," said Nikolai.

"What? . . . What good is living?" sobbed Jeremy. "Ericha's gone, and I don't see any reason to go on!"

"Had it been the other way around, would you want Ericha to give up?"

Jeremy couldn't answer. He just lied there in bed, staring at the log walls of the infirmary.

"Now, may I go to the church and get you some breakfast?" asked Nikolai. "You haven't eaten for days, and you must be starving!"

"Yeah, I guess," whispered Jeremy, his thoughts remote and distant.

Nikolai wrapped new bandages around Jeremy's knee, changed the blankets, then went to grab a bite for his young patient. Minutes later, he returned with a meal of scrambled eggs, sliced potatoes, bacon, milk, bread with butter.

Jeremy devoured the food and drank the milk down in one swallow. He still felt dry. Nikolai went to fetch more milk, and a pitcher of water.

Jeremy got his fill of liquids, and said that he wanted to get up.

"Why?" questioned Nikolai. "You're weak. You need to stay here, until your knee's better!"

"If I just lie here, I will die," said Jeremy. Although he felt groggy, he craved fresh air, along with the pleasures of life around him. "I'll think myself to death! You said so, yourself. I can let myself die or let myself live."

"True, but . . ."

"There's nothing in this bed but sadness!" whimpered Jeremy. "Broken dreams and sadness. I can't take much more of it!"

"You'll feel worse, if that knee doesn't improve!" argued Nikolai. "I doubt if you'll be able to walk very far, the shape you're in."

"I want to see everyone. I need me a drink and a smoke with Mucker." Jeremy took a deep breath. "And . . . I really oughta go talk to Rey and Weston."

"What about?"

"I . . . I'm thinking about checking out that parcel of land I got yonder, in Branell."

"Branell?"

"Might give me something new to think about," said Jeremy, his tone sad and mournful. "And give me something new to forget. I gotta get out for a while, until I forget about somebody, or learn to live without her. If I don't, I'll go plum off my rocker!"

"You'd better let that knee get better, before you go on a long sea voyage," warned Nikolai. "Do us both a big favor, and stay in bed . . . at least for the day."

"If I stay in here for much longer, I'll make you wish I didn't."

"Oh? Why is that?"

Jeremy laughed. "Because I'll piss and poop the bed!"

Nikolai rolled his eyes back. "Just plain stupid Jeremy."

"Don't worry, Nik," assured Jeremy. "If I get over to Branell and it stinks, I'll sell the land and get my butt back over here, then live happily ever after . . . or something like that."

"I'll sure miss you while you're gone. We all will! Infernus will never be the same without you!"

Jeremy was overwhelmed by Nikolai's kind words, and grief nearly got the better of him. "Aw hell, Nik," he spoke, with a nervous grin. "You'll see me again. I won't forget you. How could I ever do that?"

Nikolai smiled. "There's no forgetting you, Jeremy. That's for sure."

"Anyway, a sea voyage might give me something new to brag about." Jeremy shrugged. "Kinda like to see what that property's like. Might think different about things, soon as I get home. Might think different about a lotta things! Might even think differently about myself. Anything's better than lying here, freezing . . . and thinking about them we lost . . ."

* * * * *

After two days in a narrow cot, Jeremy was drenched in his own stink and sweat. Nikolai warmed a small tub of water, then gave him a sponge bath.

This was the first time Jeremy had suffered such an "indignity". In truth, he wanted to bathe at the waterfall. The cold weather, along with his injuries, prevented it. By mid-day, the temperature outside remained under fifty degrees, even with the blue skies and sunlight.

The pain in Jeremy's knee flared up. It didn't compare to the pain in his heart. It was like a vital part of him was missing, and he wondered how he'd ever get over it. The reality of death conflicted with denial. Throughout the day, Jeremy half-expected Ericha to walk through the door, wearing a huge smile. It agonized him in realizations that, never again would he see Ericha's smile . . . not in this world, and certainly not in this lifetime.

Jeremy struggled to avoid thinking about it. Life would never, could never be the same. How was he expected to carry on, without that special someone by his side? Soapy water, running from his hair, mixed with tears.

Jeremy sat naked on the cot, as Nikolai rubbed water over his head, chest, neck and back. He stared at the bandaged knee, and finally got up the nerve to ask how long it'd take before he'd be able to hunt and fish.

Nikolai pulled up a chair and sat next to Jeremy. "I knew that, sooner or later, we'd have this talk," he sighed. "I was hoping for later."

Jeremy dreaded the sound of Nikolai's voice.

"Jeremy," said Nikolai, gravely. "That knee will never fully heal, and I . . . I just don't think the pain will entirely go away. Some days it won't be so bad, others it will hurt more than you can stand. Chances are, the joint will always hurt. In time, it'll get a lot worse." Nikolai paused. "Even at your . . . tender age, you may have to walk with a cane, if you even feel like walking at all. But, Jeremy . . . I don't think you'll be climbing too many hills. If you do, they won't be very steep hills. You'll get very tired, very fast."

"Liar!" screamed Jeremy, in anger, betrayal, and sadness. "Anyone who thinks that don't know me very well! Just . . . just you wait and see, Nik! I'll be up and running before you know it!"

"Jeremy," breathed Nikolai. "If only that was the case. That axe did some pretty bad damage. I hate to break it to you, but I just don't think your knee will fully heal . . ."

"Ain't? . . . Ain't there a way you can fix it? Ain't there something you can do to? . . ."

"Well, I can cut the rest of your leg off," said Nikolai, in dark humor. "Then we'll have to get you a wooden peg, a parrot, and an eye-patch to go with it . . ."

"You think it's funny?" wept Jeremy.

"Sorry," apologized Nikolai. "I just thought you needed a laugh."

Jeremy gave Nikolai the eye.

An awkward silence separated Jeremy from Nikolai. The only sounds came from the waterfall, along with the constant drone of conversation from outside. A couple of banty roosters crowed in the distance.

Nikolai got done with the sponge bath, then gave Jeremy a clean shirt, a pair of moccasin shoes, and a loincloth. Jeremy dressed quietly. Due to the sharp pain in the knee, he needed help with the shoes. Nikolai constructed a crutch from a sturdy, y-shaped tree limb, leather straps, and a touch of ingenuity.

With great determination and difficulty, Jeremy hobbled the short distance from one wall of the infirmary, and back again.

Nikolai wished Jeremy well, then reluctantly permitted him to spend a short time outside.

Jeremy left the infirmary, as a cold blast of air swept inside. He was unaccustomed to the harsh wind, and nearly toppled over. The chill inflamed his bad knee.

Then, with unbreakable will-power leaning toward obsession, Jeremy ventured onward, toward the Brotherhood Church.

Nikolai watched Jeremy wander away. Knowingly, he never informed the boy of what to expect in the coming weeks, months, and years.

Few ever recovered from getting shot by the Greens' poison darts. Nikolai had saved Jeremy life, all right, though the venom's effects would forever stay with him. Jeremy would have his good days, and his bad days. He'd be prone to fever and chills. Occasionally, he'd refuse to get out of bed. Sometimes, he wouldn't be able to! The simplest tasks may become a burden.

Finally, the poison would be Jeremy's undoing. Rarely did anyone live more than fifteen to twenty years, upon getting affected.

Jeremy didn't need to hear this. Neither did Paransky, the little tattooed boy. The end would come, soon enough. Why make it worse?

Nikolai sucked in a deep breath, then turned his attention to Mount Auric. Already, the peak had a layer of fresh snow. Winter was on its way!

It seemed to come sooner and sooner, every year.

Nikolai went back inside and closed the door. Silently, he agonized over what Jeremy was liable to face, as time progressed. It was better to stay busy, and Nikolai had enough on his plate, as it was.

So much work, so little time . . .

* * * * *

Jeremy walked at a snail's pace. Every step was torture. Pain shot from his foot, to the injured knee. The cool breeze only made it worse.

Still, Jeremy wouldn't allow himself to stop. More than anything, he wanted to prove Nikolai wrong. Once he got back from Branell, he'd celebrate by killing as many critters as possible, for no good reason than to prove he could. He looked forward to constant improvement and progress on the knee.

Jeremy forged ahead, no matter how bad it hurt, and kept his sights on the church. With a hearty smile, he convinced himself that he was okay.

Jeremy ran into several friends and neighbors along the way. Some gave him the oddest looks, wondering why he was already up and around. Others viewed him with a combination of curiosity and pity. Rumors ran wild concerning New Merieko, and no two stories were quite the same.

Most folks asked Jeremy if he was all right. Jeremy claimed he never felt better. Some people only wished to pry further into exactly WHAT HAPPENED at New Merieko. There was so many conflicting reports from the local gossips, snoops, and busy-bodies. Still, it wasn't right to lean on Jeremy, just yet . . .

However, in a week or two . . .

Jeremy soon tired out. He removed beads of sweat from his forehead, breathing heavily. Already, this had been a workout! Jeremy looked back, realizing he hadn't gone further than a few hundred yards from the infirmary. He still had a fair distance to the church.

Sheer will battled self-doubt. Jeremy refused to give up, no matter what!

Grudgingly, he acknowledged the challenges before him, along with the need to take it easy . . .

For now . . .

Jeremy spotted Paransky playing with a couple of winged kids and people kids. Cheerfully, the little tattooed boy tossed a ball back and forth, seemingly unaffected after taking part in a fight, before getting shot with a dart.

Jeremy laughed. Paransky was a tough little brute. He faced terrible obstacles, and came through just fine.

Well, if little tattooed boys can hack it, so can I!

Jeremy took a breather, straightened his shoulders, and pushed on.

Moments later, Jeremy again stopped to regain his energy and ambition. A walk which took a few minutes would take an hour or more. Jeremy gritted his teeth. He wouldn't surrender to grief, sadness, humility, or defeat! He ignored the extreme pain, even as fatigue and dizziness overtook him.

Keep goin', Jeremy, keep goin' . . .

You ain't done nothin' yet . . .

First thing I'm gonna do, soon as I get to Embrey, is kick Jung-su's ass for running off without even saying 'goodbye'!

Jeremy leaned against the crutch, and held back temptations to cry. The last thing he needed was the haunting image of Ericha, slipping away from him. There was no bringing back the dead! Pleas and prayers couldn't ease terrible memories.

Tears dropped from Jeremy's eyes. He was devastated by the thought of a peace-keeping mission which turned into a catastrophe, leading to the deaths of Lorenzo, Seely, Errol, and . . .

"Ericha!" wept Jeremy. Like the pain stemming from the injured knee, he'd never escape what happened to her.

Death was a constant on Infernus. Jeremy had witnessed it his entire life. Death. Too much death. Jeremy once thought he could deal with it. He never dreamed it'd bother him, so badly.

He never imagined standing back, as Randen was killed before his very eyes!

Jeremy was weary of death. He wanted to run from it . . . and never could. He sought a new life, where he'd put the past behind him.

"Sir?" a soft, feminine voice spoke, from behind. "Sir, are you all right?"

Jeremy slowly regained his composure and broke from a self-induced Hell.

He turned to see a blonde-haired, fair-skinned teenage girl approach him. She was right around the same height and age as he was. She was dressed in a drab, brown woolen dress, which dragged upon the ground.

Jeremy somehow managed a weak, lopsided grin. "I . . . I'm fine," he stuttered, sadness revealing itself in his voice. "Just a bad day . . . I reckon . . ."

"What happened to you?" the girl asked, staring at the bandaged knee. She was drawn to the thin, masculine figure in a buckskin shirt and loincloth.

"What?" begged Jeremy, his tone high-pitched and screechy.

"Your knee?" the girl asked.

"The doc tells me I'm a cripple," chuckled Jeremy, evasively. "He don't know me as well as he thinks! Why, shit . . . *shoot*! . . . I . . . I'm fine . . . just fine.

Just you wait and see!"

"So, what happened?"

Jeremy turned away from the girl. "I got hurt a few days ago . . . in New Merieko . . ."

"Oh, I'm so sorry!" the girl exclaimed. "I was there when they . . . when those things attacked us! My mom and brother and me, we got away . . . My dad, they . . ." The girl lowered her head, unable to say more.

Jeremy slouched. "I'm sorry, too. I guess we all lost somebody. The worst day of my life! What I wouldn't do to . . ." Jeremy bit his bottom lip. "There just ain't no going back . . . is there?"

The girl threw her arms around Jeremy, as the two embraced.

For more than a minute, Jeremy and the girl shared a special moment together. Loneliness was unforgiving. It was just enough to know they didn't have to endure it, alone.

Once Jeremy and the girl separated, they carefully removed tears from each other's faces. Then, inadvertently, they broke out in unexplained laughter.

Perhaps it was divine intervention to bring them to this same exact place

. . .

Who knows?

More than anything, both were in need of a friend . . . which is always a good thing!

"I'm Jeremy," the boy sighed. "Jeremy Kentworth. I was on my way to the church, when . . ."

"Do you need my help?" the girl offered, hoping Jeremy said YES.

"No, that's okay," said Jeremy, blushing. "I . . . I can make it . . . I know I can."

"But you look so tired. I'd love to give you a hand!"

Jeremy laughed at his own expense. "Aw, what the hell? . . . I mean . . . Yeah, sure! I'd love to let you gimme a hand . . . "

The girl carefully placed one hand around Jeremy, then began walking him to the church. "You're Jeremy?" she asked, her eyes glimmering in the faded, autumn sunlight.

"Yeah . . . Jeremy Kentworth."

"That's a beautiful name!"

"Well, it's a name, a'right," snickered Jeremy. "A lot better than Ari . . ."

"Who's Ari?" the girl asked, steering Jeremy through the narrow streets and corridors of Persis.

"A little oinker who thinks he's God . . . and King."

The girl responded with a cute giggle, which Jeremy found attractive . . . indeed alluring. Despite the cold temperatures and brisk wind sweeping from Mount Auric, he felt warm and comforting next to her.

"So, what do I call you?" asked Jeremy, with a shy, awkward grin.

The girl rested her head on Jeremy's shoulder. "Angelica," she answered. "My name's Angelica . . ."

* * * * *

Cody gasped as he dropped the aging scroll upon the floor of KENT-WORTH'S. Pages scattered throughout the cramped store room.

Angelica?

ANGELICA?

That was Mom's name!

Anxiety swept over Cody. Reason gave way to chaos, fear, and panic. Nothing in life made sense, as life was suddenly turned upside down! Cody's heart raced. Fingers tingled, breathing grew erratic and shallow. The walls seemingly closed in on him.

Cody's nervous eyes darted in all directions. The familiar seemed other-worldly, out of place, bizarre. Cody feared going insane. He had the urge to flee the store . . . immediately. This, despite warnings never to walk the city streets at night.

Cody had just closed KENTWORTH'S. The doors were bolted shut, earnings had been collected, counted, and placed in a safe. For now, Cody was not obligated to the store. It was just as well. All that once seemed normal and safe had evolved into a nightmare reality.

A nervous laugh slipped from Cody's lips. He was scared of everything . . . including existence itself.

Cody gripped the counter's edge, thinking he'd soon collapse and perish from uncertainty and fright.

Cody knew very little of his parents' histories and backgrounds. JT, in particular, refused to discuss his own childhood.

Cody now wondered if he knew too much about his father.

JT, or Jeremiah Terence, or Jeremy, or whatever he called himself, grew up on a faraway island, populated by pirates, fierce simians . . .

. . . and winged men.

The scroll couldn't be true . . . could it?

Why would God create such creatures as winged men? Wouldn't the rest of the world know of Infernus, by now?

Cody didn't know who or what to believe! He only knew that, if he didn't get out and go for a walk, he'd go crazy.

Cody staggered to the door. Both hands shook uncontrollably, as he unlocked the bolt and rushed outside.

It was dark. Harsh winds and pouring rain literally slammed Merieko, with excessive force. Only a lunatic would venture out into this weather! Even the most die-hard drunks, lowlifes, and prostitutes knew better than to wander about, in a downpour.

Cody stood in the doorway, drenched as rain blew in and sprayed everywhere. The streets and sidewalks resembled lakes, rivers, and streams.

Cody was trapped in the confines of the store. He was also trapped in a maze of questions, confusion, and no answers. More and more, he pondered the validity of the wrinkled pages of a scroll. Was any of that tale true?

Was there any truth to it, at all?

Or was it all true?

How could he know?

One thing was for certain . . . The story had affected Cody in ways he couldn't imagine!

Cody's mom was named Angelica.

Was his father Jeremiah Terence Kentworth?

Jeremy Kentworth?

Cody had to do something, anything, to handle the doubts and fears overtaking him. Otherwise, he'd be consumed by them! He'd go from being a sixteen-year-old kid, mourning the death of his father, to an inmate at the local asylum!

Cody found a bottle of the foulest booze from the shelf. He uncorked the bottle, lifted it to his mouth, and took a swig.

And then another . . .

And then another . . .

And then another . . .

In less than an hour, Cody stumbled to one corner of the store room, collapsed, and hit the deck with a loud, explosive THUD!

Then, after slurring the words of an obscure, lusty Agronian drinking ballad, Cody closed his eyes and blacked out . . .

* * * * *

"Cody?" someone asked, in the haze, murkiness, headache, and fog of intoxication.

Cody opened his tired eyes. The once warm store room, with a fire snapping and popping from the sounds of burning wood, was extinguished. KENTWORTH'S was left chilly and damp. Cody blinked a number of times, as blinding sunlight beamed through the windows. His head felt as if it might explode. His mouth was dry and cottony. Cody managed to sit up, from where he impacted the hardwood floor.

"Cody?" someone repeated. "What's going on?"

Cody looked up to see the familiar, kindly old face of Leader Rey, kneeling over him. The man smiled, as his eyes revealed care and concern.

"What . . .what going on?" groaned Cody, struggling to get on his shaky feet.

"You tell me," snickered Rey, removing the near-empty bottle from Cody's hand.

Cody leaned against the wall, suffering from a queasy stomach, weakened arms and legs, humility, and embarrassment.

"How'd you get down there?" asked Rey, his voice assuring and comforting.

"I . . . I dunno," whispered Cody.

"Looks like a pretty eventful 'I dunno' to me," said Rey, helping Cody to a chair behind the counter.

Cody sat down and looked deeply into Rey's weathered face. "What time is it?" he asked, weaving back and forth.

"A bit past nine."

"Past nine?" screamed Cody. "The store's supposed to be open by eight!"

"Forget about the store!" shouted Rey, handing Cody a glass of water. "Just forget about it, for a while."

"But . . ."

"But, nothing! Take the day off and give yourself a break."

"Dad wouldn't want me to take a break!"

"Your dad's not here," said Rey. "Not now, not anymore. The store's your responsibility. It's also your burden, and your trouble. You need to take a day off."

"What do I tell the customers?"

"Tell them nothing. It's your life, and your business . . . not theirs."

"But . . ."

"But, nothing!" said Rey. "You need some time away from it. It's driving you to drink."

"So, what am I supposed to do?"

"I'll take you to a local restaurant," offered Rey, in sympathy and support.

"Dad wouldn't want me to . . ."

"Your dad's not here! Not now, not anymore! KENTWORTH'S belongs to you. If you want to skip out a day or two, that's your right, and your privilege."

Cody sipped the water. "When did you get back?"

"A few minutes ago, before I found you decorating the floor," said Rey, kneeling to examine the disorganized pages of the aging scroll. His expression revealed fear and animosity. "Go on ahead, Cody," he urged, collecting the wrinkled pages from the floor. "I'll catch up with you."

"Where are we going?" asked Cody, staggering to the door.

"Starr's Diner." Rey cleared his throat. "Give me a chance to clean up. I'll be there, directly."

Cody stepped outside to a blustery, cool, windy day. He closed the door behind him, leaned against a hand railing, and sighed.

From inside, Rey took the hundreds of pages he found scattered here and there, then threw them into the wood-burning stove. With a lit candle sitting upon the counter, he ignited the pages, shut the creaky stove door, and stepped outside where Cody awaited him.

The two men made a steady pace to a small, yet pleasant and casual corner restaurant in a quiet neighborhood. The streets were wet, cold, and clammy from the rain. The morning sun peeked through thick, black clouds. Neither Rey nor Cody spoke. They merely smiled and waved at the friendlier folks they met along the way. The evening's riff-raff were gone now, leaving a world of respectable businessmen and citizens.

Rey and Cody entered the warm, inviting diner. The smell of fried eggs, bacon, and potatoes whetted their appetite. The two men sat in a private area, next to a mortar wall, and patiently awaited their menus.

Rey made warm conversation about his trip through rural Agron. Meanwhile, Cody searched for a way to "interrogate" him about the material found in the scroll.

The boy had tremendous respect for Rey. However, he couldn't help but to think that both Rey and JT (Jeremy!) had deliberately kept secrets from him. He debated the wisdom of even getting into the subject. Yet, he had spent several hours reading the scroll, and feared that certain issues would drive him insane, unless he got answers.

Rey sipped a glass of apple cider, when Cody finally got up the nerve to ask, "Was Dad's first name 'Jeremy'?"

Rey glared suspiciously at Cody.

"Was Dad's first name 'Jeremy'?" pressed Cody. "I'm sure he wasn't christened 'JT'!"

"Why? . . . Why do you ask?" stuttered Rey.

Don'tcha think I got a right to know?"

"Yes, Cody," breathed Rey, staring at a whiskey drummer who peddled goods to the owner of Starr's Diner. "You do have a right to know. His name was Jeremiah Terence Kentworth . . . Jeremy Kentworth."

"And did he run around with a girl named Ericha?"

"Where did you find that document?" demanded Rey.

"After you left, I went into a closet in Dad's room."

Rey frowned.

"I found a lotta strange things in there," explained Cody. "A loincloth, a shirt made from animal skins, a blowgun . . ."

"Your dad didn't want you near that closet!" snapped Rey.

"Dad's not here." Cody gave Rey a sly grin. "Not now, not anymore. KENTWORTH'S is my responsibility . . . You said so yourself. I'm responsible for everything under my roof, including things in that closet."

"You're right," sighed Rey. "You are . . . Now."

"Did Dad ever wear a loincloth?"

"When he was a kid," groaned Rey, with embarrassment. "He stopped once he got to Branell. I'm glad he got over wearing it. It was always a thorn in my side."

"Why did he dress like that?"

"Because he could. Because he knew it aggravated me. Because he was Jeremy . . . Just plain old Jeremy."

Cody snickered, yet suffered a nagging sense of regret. He had lost somebody, and something, which he'd never get back again. The aching in his heart was more than he could stand, and he wasn't sure how to endure it. "You loved Dad," he mumbled. "Didn't you?"

"More than you'll ever know," answered Rey. "I loved him the same way I love you."

"What about the story I found?"

"What about it?" asked Rey, evasively.

"How much of it is true?"

Rey hesitated. "To be honest, I can't stay . . . I never got into it. Just to let you know, it was a bunch of malarkey. I'm surprised you found any interest in it, at all."

"I'm curious."

"You know what curiosity did to the cat? Do yourself a favor, and don't be the cat."

"Please, Rey?" begged Cody. "Dont'cha think I got a right to know about Dad? He's the only dad I'll ever have, and . . . I'll never see him again."

"Only in the Hereafter." Rey frowned. "What do you want to know?"

"Everything!" shouted Cody, impatiently. "I want to know about the people in that story . . . and the island of Infernus . . ."

"There's no such place," claimed Rey, forcefully. "It doesn't exist, except in old wives' tales and sailor lore. It's mythological, Cody, like mermaids, uni-corns, leprechauns . . ."

"The abarbeaus?"

"What?"

"The abarbeaus!" repeated Cody. "Those man-eating furballs who lived in trees!"

Rey shook his head. "Guess I never got that far into the story."

"Who? . . . Who do you think wrote it?"

"Your dad, I'm thinking." Rey snickered. "He was quite the storyteller . . . and a fibber! I mean, you get him started, he'd spin you a yarn so wild and far-fetched, he'd . . ."

"He never told me any stories," moped Cody. "He never really spoke to me, at all."

"Your dad was a man of deep feelings, closed emotions, and great sad-ness . . . especially after your mom passed away. He did love you, though."

After a moment of silence, Cody asked, "Was there really a guy like Weston?"

"Sure. Your dad's cousin . . . And your cousin, too."

"Was he really an Embrian diplomat?"

Rey nodded YES.

"Where is he, now?" asked Cody.

"I lost touch with him." Rey took a deep breath. "Rumor has it he ended up on the wrong end of a sword, somewhere in Vladistan."

Cody frowned. "What? . . . What about Jung-su?"

"He got pressed into service of the Embrian Navy." Rey smiled, proudly.

"In time, he became a naval chaplain, and is now a Leader at Lord Werner's."

Cody sipped his apple cider.

"I can't say anything more about that story," said Rey. "I never got that far into it. It got too silly and long-haired for me." Ray frowned. "Now, if you don't mind, I'm tired and hungry. Let's cut the chatter, and eat."

"But . . ."

"But, nothing!" shouted Rey. "I'm tired, I'm hungry, and I need to sleep, soon as we return to the store. And that's the end of it."

"Are you going back to Infernus?" asked Cody, persistently. "Or Izwe-Something . . . or Fairy Land?"

"Cody," warned Rey. "I told you . . . there is no such a place. It's a myth, and nothing more. And for your information, I've been offered a position at a school in rural Embrey. I was born there, and I'm not getting any younger. I'm spending my golden years in my native land."

Cody bit his bottom lip. "Can I? . . . Can I come with you?"

"What?"

"Can I come with you?" repeated Cody, desperately. "Rey, I don't wanna run that store, anymore! I hate it! It was Dad's dream, not mine! Not only that, but I've gotten where I hate Merieko! Please? Take me with you! Please?"

"What about your cousin, who lives on the other side of town?"

"Hilary." Cody lowered his head. "She likes me, but Franklin sure don't. Franklin don't like anyone, but Franklin."

Rey looked outside, thinking about the sadness, anger, bitterness and regret which had defeated his stepson in adulthood. Despite being a man of great wealth, Jeremy Kentworth never did acquaint himself to his vast estate, near the base of the Northern Branellian Mountains. He drank heavily, rarely exercised, and put on excessive weight. The chronic pain stemming from a knee injury grew progressively worse. He was overwhelmed by constant melancholy.

After his wife's untimely death, Jeremy vowed to leave Branell and become a Merieko merchant. He never made a single shilling in exchange of his property. Instead, he chose to sign deeds over to the sharecroppers residing on the land, who appreciated it far more than he did.

To his dismay, the Branellian King confiscated that land for himself . . .

As for the grand monetary wealth, Jeremy gave most of it away to charity, to build schools and orphanages throughout rural Branell.

Part of it, however, went to support a growing army, navy, and fleet of freight ships on a tiny island nation, somewhere between Agron and Ko-

kashima . . .

As it was, Jeremy and his son Cody had nothing more than their small store in Merieko. Obviously, Cody would've been glad to separate himself from that, now!

Rey chuckled. "I was hoping you got tired of running KENTWORTH'S. You're too young for that sort of responsibility. It's no place for a boy your age."

"So?" begged Cody. "Can I come with you?"

"We'll put the store up for sale, then get the paperwork going to make you an Embrian citizen. I'll sponsor you, so there shouldn't be any hassles." Rey smiled, warmly. "Yes Cody, you may come with me. It's the least I can do for JT's . . . Excuse me . . . For Jeremy's only son."

For the next few minutes, neither man said a word as they ate breakfast in silence.

Later, they stepped outside to the hustle and bustle of life in the Agronian city of Merieko. By now, the clouds had dissipated, and replaced by blue skies, above. Cody contemplated taking a stroll through town, to get some needed sunshine. He hadn't felt so free, so liberated, since his father's passing. He looked forward to starting over, with a caring father-figure in a new land.

More than anything, he daydreamed of his father . . . the father he never really knew, but could only imagine. Instead of JT Kentworth, a sad, lonely, overburdened man with a bad knee, Cody thought about Jeremy Kentworth, a lively, carefree, spirited young man hunting wild, vicious critters . . .

Hunting wild critters . . . somewhere far to the west, in a mythological land known as Infernus.

A lively, carefree, spirited young man that Cody never really got to know, but only wished he knew . . .

Just plain old Jeremy . . .

As they approached the store, Cody dared to ask Rey one final question, and hoped it didn't get him into trouble. "Are there? . . . Are there any such things as . . . ?"

"As what, Cody?" asked Rey, curiously.

Cody hesitated ". . . Well, you know . . . winged men?"

"Cody," sighed Rey. "I'm tired, and I really need to get some sleep."

"I mean it!" pressed Cody. "Are there any such things as winged men?"

Rey chuckled as he unlocked the door of KENTWORTH'S. Looking away from the boy's intense gaze, he said, "Now Cody . . . Aren't you too old to believe in fairy tales? . . ."

THE END